THE

SCRIBE'S

FAMILY

THE
SCRIBE'S FAMILY

A GOLDEN AGE SAGA
SPANNING FIVE MILLENNIA

A NOVEL BY DON JACOBSON

Hypatia Press **Balboa, California**

The Scribe's Family
Copyright © 1997 by Donald A. Jacobson
Printed and bound in the United States of America.
All rights reserved.

Published by Hypatia Press
P.O. Box 512, Balboa, California 92661

**Publisher's Cataloging-in-Publication
(Provided by Quality Books, Inc.)**

Jacobson, Donald A.
      The Scribe's Family : a golden age saga
spanning five millennia / Don Jacobson. — 1st ed.
      p.   cm.
      ISBN: 0-9657196-1-8

      1. History, Ancient—Fiction. 2. Middle Ages--
History--Fiction. 3. History, Modern--Fiction. I. Title.

PS3560.A36S37 1997   813.54
                                       QBI97-605
                                                    CIP

Cover: The seated figure is Ramses II posing as a scribe. Design by Danny Green.

For Julie . . .

Who is a part of this novel in many ways.

And special thanks . . .

To Curt Herberts for his daring ideas—
To Ron Rothschild and Jim Hague for their valuable
editorial and literary comments—
And to Tim Press, the first to read it, for his steadfast
encouragement.

Foreword

We unfortunately cannot choose when or where we are born. We must play out the story of our lives with what we are given: a time, and a place. Some lives come and go under the worst of circumstances, played out in troubled times, in places of little hope, such as Cromwellian England in the 17th century; or Viking ravaged northern France in the 10th century; or Italy during the dying days of the Roman Empire. Some lives, on the other hand, bask in the embrace of good times, in places of opportunity, security, and freedom, such as Elizabethan London; or Florence, Italy during the Renaissance; or Athens, Greece under Pericles; or Egypt during the Age of the Pyramids.

The latter eras we often call "Golden Ages." They are usually brought about by the efforts of one extraordinary leader—a president, chancellor, premier, king, queen, general, or chief—who we come to call, sometimes even during their lives, "the Great." These are civilization's high points, the Golden and the Great.

They were not utopias. A great many people still suffered. A few lives were inevitably tragic. Some elements of the population would have gladly chosen another era. In Athens, Greece during the height of the Classical Era, the majority of the population were slaves. No one would term as "golden," lives played out in London's slums, in Elizabethan England. Yet, if we had the ability to choose, these and other Golden Ages are the best that civilization can offer.

Suppose we gained the power to alter the circumstances of our lives, the when and where, with a snap of the finger? Suppose we could change everything, to a new time and place, but change not at all who we are: our goals, our personalities, our positions in society?

1

Or suppose the changes came about without our knowing it, for example as an author's prerogative? *The Scribe's Family* is such a saga. It is the story of one family, as told through the eyes of a youngest son, who is a scribe in ancient Mesopotamia, a librarian in Renaissance Florence, and a playwright in Elizabethan England, to name three of the ten Golden Ages of his life.

Shakespeare's plays are occasionally restaged in different settings, different eras, from those originally envisioned by the playwright. Imagine a play in which the setting changes in every act, but the story maintains its continuity. *The Scribe's Family* is a novel in ten parts, ten Golden Ages spanning nearly 5000 years, that does exactly this.

Why do it? one may well ask. Because the culture and customs, the physical, economical and political environment of each era provide new stimuli for the family, new sources of tension and triumph. Conversely, the family's reactions to the culture and customs of each era provide a new means for viewing the changes in civilization throughout the ages.

Finally, it is a means for dramatizing the unchanging character of human nature, despite the radical changes in everything else.

Enjoy!

Don Jacobson

The Golden Ages

I. Uruk, Sumer—3000 BC
The first great city-state

II. Memphis, Egypt—2580 BC
During the age of pyramids

III. Knossos, Crete—1500 BC
Capital of the Minoan empire

IV. Tyre & Jerusalem—925 BC
Two cities in odd alliance

V. Athens, Greece—445 BC
During the age of Pericles

VI. Rome, Italy—AD 175
Under Emperor Marcus Aurelius

VII. Constantinople—AD 1015
Capital of the Byzantine Empire

VIII. Paris, France—AD 1252
During the reign of St. Louis

IX. Florence, Italy—AD 1490
At the height of the Renaissance

X. London, England—AD 1600
Under Queen Elizabeth I

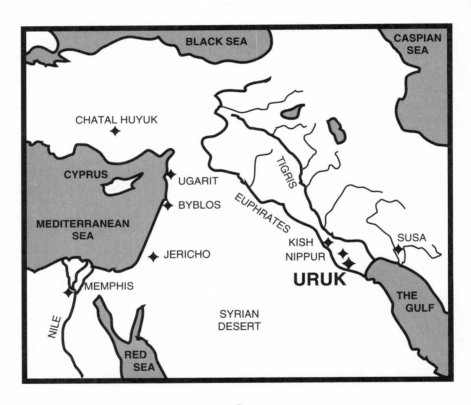

Uruk, Sumer

I. Uruk, Sumer
3000 BC

The ruins of Uruk lie silent and serene in the deserts of southern Iraq, near a former course of the Euphrates river, not far from where the Persian Gulf once reached. Five thousand years ago this Sumerian city-state was quite likely the most highly populated city in the world. It was also one of the first. People had already lived settled lives along the lower Tigris and Euphrates rivers, on land the silt-laden rivers stole from the Persian Gulf, for at least two thousand years.

The Sumerians came later to the valley, perhaps around 3500 BC, probably from the east. They brought with them, or soon invented, new and better ways of doing things: the wheeled cart, a clever counting system based on the number 60, the potter's wheel, and a way to record speech in the form of markings on clay tablets. They invented writing at about the same time the Egyptians incised their first hieroglyphics.

Immigration never ceased, waxing and waning with conditions in the surrounding lands. Throughout the centuries, nomads from the deserts of Syria and Arabia continued to wander into the fertile lands of the Tigris and Euphrates. They sought a better place to live, attracted to a fabled land of promise.

The Temple Priestess

1

I, Abdullah ben Rashad Barakah, a scribe, son of Rashad ben Qadir Barakah, write these words. I record for the generations to follow, the story of my family's coming to Uruk, the greatest Sumerian city. I tell of what we saw and felt, the troubles we met and overcame, our struggle to make Uruk our home for the rest of our lives. I tell of the joys that brightened my family's days, and the troubles that sometimes threatened to tear us apart. Inscribing these words has been a labor of love, and a tale of love.

As I look back from the lofty vantage point of three score years of life's strange turns of fate, I conclude that the extremes of joy and sorrow, the high peaks and deep valleys of life's journey, result in one way or another from the odd dance that man and woman make with each other. We are both a prisoner of this dance and liberated to great achievements by it. The tale I tell, sadly and happily, proves this assertion. We live in order to love.

We were desert people of the Barakah tribe, a noble people—Semites as the Sumerians called us—from a distant land of harsh majestic beauty in the southern Arabian desert. My mother, Makarim, was a chief's daughter. My father, Rashad, was the youngest brother of a chief, and the son and grandson of chiefs. My sister, brothers and I came from the marriage of two royal families. People treated us with respect. We were among the privileged in a land without many privileges. Our future seemed secure.

We lived a nomad's life, an unsettled existence, but the only life we knew. Our possessions were few, but they were all we needed. The land could be cruel, when oases withered, when the sands blew, when tribes fought, but we had always survived. What more could anyone ask?

My father wanted something more. He had listened to the tales of travelers from the east, and believed. He had a vision, and the rest of us followed. His vision had nothing to do with his being a younger brother, who would likely never attain power, his off-spring relegated to a lesser branch of the family. His brothers and sisters could not understand his need. Neither did my mother. An outspoken woman, she frequently made her opinions known, but she obeyed. It was her duty.

My father made a special effort to explain his grand plans to his children. He wanted us to want this as much as he, but of course that was impossible. We could not imagine, as he did, but we could sense the adventure we faced, and that was enough to make us all enthusiasts.

"There's a land called Sumer," Rashad said, "many days travel to the east, where water is always in abundance, where grains grow tall in vast fields, where people live in peace and harmony. In this land are cities, many of them, some large, some small, where people live in permanent houses made from bricks cast out of clay from the soil that can never in a million years be depleted. The greatest of these cities, I'm told, is Uruk. This is where we'll go. This is where we'll live."

Like thousands before us and many thousands after us, we endured the long journey through the Arabian desert, not because we had to, not because enemies drove us from our lands, but because my father sought something more, though he had only the vaguest idea what that was. The journey was arduous, but we were accustomed to such travel, never knowing any fixed home for longer than a season. We only needed to keep on. We only needed determination. My father's vision, though it was naive and false in many respects, provided that.

Now, as a father four times over, as the grandfather of two, as a man growing old who cannot help looking back, a man who has lived the life of a scribe, the most noble of professions, I write of my family's adventures in Uruk. Reliving the years, I laugh and cry, I grow discouraged with an imperfect memory, and relish the sudden emergence of long forgotten adventures. But I keep on. The woman who sits beside me, her deep azure-blue eyes still able to make my heart flutter, demands that I do.

May immortal Anu, father of the gods, bless and preserve these words.

2

I was seven years old, and already known for my love of words over deeds, or so my brother's claimed, when we came to the land called Sumer in the valley of the Tigris and Euphrates rivers. Jamal, my impatient, unlucky brother was nine. Kadar, the steady oak under which I often took shelter, was fourteen. My little sister, Fadilah was barely five, my family's lovable trouble-maker.

I remember my first glimpse of the city called Uruk. What a wrenching disappointment. I wasn't sure what to expect, and probably neither was my father, but I could not stop imagining. At first, when my father tried to describe a city, I had imagined an oasis of huge proportions, with tents scattered as far as the eye could see. When my father later mentioned permanent houses made out of mud bricks formed from the sands of the desert, with even the smallest much larger and higher than any nomad's tent, including that of the chieftain, I imagined something different, and no less inaccurate. I pictured a desert filled with small mountains, a kind of sea of human-sized ant-hills. Reality failed to live up to my imagination, but only at first.

My father, leading the way, halted us with a raised arm. He excitedly clutched my mother's arm and pointed towards the horizon.

"What is it?" Makarim asked.

"It's what they said to look for," Rashad said

I couldn't see anything. I looked at Jamal, who shrugged his shoulders. Kadar, nearly as tall as my father, stood next to him, eyes shielded, nodding his head.

Fadilah jumped up and down beside Kadar, grabbing at his overshirt. "Lift me up. I want to see too."

"You can see it, can't you?" Rashad said. He looked around at Jamal and me, face flushed, his excitement contagious, dangerous.

We shook our heads in unison, looking vaguely off into the distance.

"Not that way," Kadar said, his voice mimicking father's impatience.

"Over here on the horizon. Look, open your eyes," Rashad said. "It's still a long ways away, probably another two days of travel. We haven't even reached the river yet." He lifted Fadilah into his arms.

"I see it. I see it," Fadilah said, pointing in the wrong direction.

Makarim laughed. "She at least has a good imagination."

"You two boys have the glazed eyes of a snake," Rashad said, an edge to his voice.

"I see it," Jamal said, putting me to shame, so that I had to try to see.

"I see it too. There it is," I said.

I wasn't at all sure I had seen anything. It seemed less than a mirage, no more than the vague hint of a hill poking above the horizon, shimmering in the heat. I was disappointed.

"It's nothing but a little hill," I said, unfailingly saying the wrong thing.

My father gave me one of his looks. "You'll soon see what that little hill signifies." He meant for me to hold my tongue until then.

My mother, I am sure, was alarmed, as disquieted as I by the insignificance of the place, but she said nothing.

I had heard the word city many times from my father's lips. I couldn't believe this was it, a place where many thousands of people supposedly lived their lives, and never wandered the land seeking better stands of wild grains or animals to hunt, never searched for a safe site to raise tents, never fled bands of marauders who would kill for the gain of an antelope skin. It seemed so inconsequential from a distance. I could not comprehend it, and consequently I longed to see it, to learn its secrets. I had hundreds of questions. I assumed that my father knew the answers, but I think my mother knew better. She refrained from questioning him, and gave me strong looks when my questions became too insistent.

"We'll find out. We'll learn. We have nothing to fear," Rashad finally said, impatient with his anxious family, tired of trying to answer the unanswerable.

"I'm not afraid," Fadilah said, and we all laughed.

Our pace quickened after this. Uruk beckoned alluringly, a beacon that grew ever larger. The next day we came to the Euphrates river, an astonishing sight for desert people, nothing in our experience to prepare us for the wide expanse of silt-stained water, fringed with a green mantle, slashing a scar across the landscape toward Uruk.

We could smell the river before we could see it, a smell that desert nomads knew well, and yet this was somehow different from the musky smell of a palm-fringed spring oasis. There was a cool freshness about the smell, mingled with the dark aroma of unfamiliar vegetation. We wrinkled our noses, and hurried on. Even Fadilah knew what we approached, that we would soon replace the stagnant liquid in our leather water bags.

"I'm thirsty. I'm thirsty," she called out, running in front of us, her short robe pulled up to reveal spindly legs that would one day take on a form to attract men like bees around honey-suckle flower.

"Be careful. Don't go close to the water," Rashad said, knowing something that the rest of did not, that the river could be a great danger, as well as a source of life.

We approached the river with trepidation. The oddly quiet rustle of the water made me uneasy. I took Fadilah's hand, when she started to march up to the water's edge. She tried to pull it away.

Makarim whispered, as if to keep the Euphrates from hearing. "How will we cross the river?"

"I don't know. We'll find a way," Rashad said.

My father's quiet firm words, as usual, gave us confidence. He had never failed us. We walked along the river's edge for most of the morning, following a well-traveled roadway that showed the unfamiliar signs of wheeled traffic. Wagons, their strange wooden wheels rolling easily over the packed clay, passed us in both directions, pulled by teams of oxen. Jars, bales and sacks filled the wagons, leaving no room for riders. Two men walked alongside, constantly encouraging the animals to keep moving, sometimes singing or chanting. They glanced at us without much interest, sometimes saying things we could not understand, often laughing. Much later we would learn that the wagons held trading goods destined for, or coming from, unimaginably distant places.

In time, through my work as a scribe, I learned everything there was to know about trade, the avaricious Sumerian's most avid obsession. It was a clever system that took advantage of the services, skills and products each region could best offer. Uruk, and the other major Sumerian cities, exported mostly manufactured goods such as pottery, gold jewelry, shell cylinder seals, and textiles. They imported scarce and needed raw materials such as timber, copper, silver, gold and gems. Traders arrived in all seasons, from distant lands many weeks travel away, such as Canaan in the north, the Indus river in the east, and Egypt in the far west. Without trade, Uruk would have been a miserly, poor city.

As we grew nearer to Uruk, we came to vast fields intricately woven with irrigation ditches taking water from the Euphrates. We watched laborers, bent over like palm trees in a wind storm, working nearly naked in the sun. The fields seemed immense. My father nodded in their direction, making us look, as if to say I told you so. Still, we could see no way to reach the other side of the Euphrates, as my father claimed we must to reach Uruk.

"A boat will take us across," he said, which made me even more apprehensive.

By then we had seen boats on the river, some transporting goods down the river, some with fishermen wielding nets. The thought of venturing out on the river in such a craft frightened me. I hadn't yet learned to swim. What use was that skill to a desert nomad?

The miserly hill that had disappointed me before, grew into what looked like a tall mesa with steep walls by the time we reached the ferry. My father pointed the craft out to us from a distance, a low raft edging its way across the Euphrates, crowded with people, making its way by a means that I could not figure out. The raft had landed and let off its travelers by the time we reached it. The rest of us stood high on the embankment as my father went down to the river's edge. We watched as he indicated with a wave of his hand what he wanted. The man in charge laughed and gestured for us to climb on. By then, a number of other people had already waded through the shallows and crowded aboard the flimsy looking raft. There didn't seem enough room left for us. My father shouted for us to come.

Water splashed over the low sides of the raft. "There isn't room. The boat will sink," Jamal said, when we reached the water's edge.

"Take your sandals off and get on. Hurry," Rashad said.

We dutifully obeyed. Everyone seemed to be laughing at us, jabbering away. I couldn't understand a word. One of the raft men pushed the raft away from shore. The raft pitched and swayed, water splashing around our feet. A moment later, I heard a scream and turned in time to see Jamal pitch over backwards into the river shallows. My mother yelled at my father to do something as she knelt down and tried to reach Jamal, who was thrashing about in the water, slowly drifting past the raft. The Sumerians all laughed. One or two extended hands to Jamal, but he could not grab hold.

My father pushed past me, nearly knocking me in too. He jumped into the water, though he could not swim either. He stood up, the water reaching barely to his waist. Seeing this, Jamal stood too, and we all began to laugh. One of the raft men helped them climb back aboard, dripping water. My father looked furious. Jamal looked sheepish, brushing away tears.

Two bare-chested men, who sang as they heaved, pulled us across, the long rope that spanned the brown waters stained black with their sweat. I admit that I was afraid. But so were my two brothers. Only Fadilah seemed impervious to the danger, laughing gaily as water washed over her feet. It did not ease my shameful fright to see Sumerian lads my age, happily naked, play in the river's shallows, and others older, wade out with nets into the calm waters of side pools to cast for fish.

Finally grateful to stand on firm ground, I pretended that it had been nothing. I bravely walked along the river bank, daringly close to the current, toward the Sumerian boys, who halted their play to stare at me. I was probably a familiar sight to them, a nomad, clothed in the rags of a desert dweller. They pointed at me and laughed and started toward me.

I stood my ground, feeling their eyes on me. I heard my father call me, then Kadar. I ignored them. The Sumerian lads stood in a line in front of me, seemingly friendly, laughing and jabbering and pointing at my rough sandals and tattered trousers. None of them wore a stitch of clothes, and seemed not to care.

I heard a giggle and felt Fadilah take my hand next to me. "Look at their little things," she said, pointing at their penises.

"Fadilah," Makarim called.

The Sumerians stared at Fadilah, their laughter vanquished. A kind of standoff took place, until Kadar grabbed up Fadilah in his arms and carried her away.

I laughed, for once pleased with my sister's meddlesome antics. The Sumerians smiled, regained their composure, and, with another flurry of incomprehensible jabbering, turned and ran back to the water. I resolved at that moment to learn their language as quickly as I could, more than ever curious of these city-dwellers who seemed to have not the least shred of modesty.

3

A half-day later we stood outside Uruk's walls. We faced a magnificent masonry mountain, no longer a miserly hill. The walls reminded me of the cliffs that rose up out of the desert near our homeland, but men had built these. We could see nothing of the city except for a few taller buildings that rose two stories high, and one commanding structure that we would later learn was the Great Temple.

"It's so huge. Dare we enter that place?" Makarim said.

"It's only bricks and mortar," Rashad said, though I heard a hint of uncertainty in his voice. "The people, you see, come and go freely. There's nothing to be afraid of." His words did little to quell our anxiety over the unknown future that awaited us in Uruk.

With hearts pounding, we picked up our meager belongings and joined the crowd heading for the gates. We did not gain entrance. A tall thin-faced man who stood next to the gate watching everyone that entered, waved us aside. Bare-chested, he wore a large medallion on a gold chain, which I would later learn gave notice of his official duties. Even without the medallion, his demeanor told us he was someone we must treat with respect, and obey.

"Where are you from?" he asked, speaking the Semitic language he guessed we would understand.

My father half-turned and extended his hand in the direction from which we had come. "From across the river, many days to the south, in the open land." He didn't know any better way to explain.

The official looked us over one by one. He paused at my mother, who met the official's appraising gaze with disdain. She was a black-haired, olive-skinned woman who always attracted stares, her figure strong, almost masculine, her chin high, defiant, eyes dark, unwavering.

"You can't enter the city. There's no place for you in Uruk."

"We'll find a place," Rashad said.

The official shook his head. "There is none. The city is already too crowded."

"But we've come from far away to live in the great city. We're prepared to work. I have three strong sons. We're willing to do anything. We've no where else to go. We can't go back."

I hated to hear the way my father pleaded. I hated worse the official's bored shrug, as if he had heard the same words a hundred times a day. He gestured behind him to a sloping hillside outside the walls, peppered with a crowded sprinkling of tents of all shapes, colors and sizes. We had wondered about this when we came to the gates. Now we knew what it was for.

We lived a half year encamped in the shadow of Uruk's walls, crowded together with hundreds of other desert immigrants. My father, my brothers and I labored in the fields that surrounded the city. Every day a few Semitic families left, as more arrived to take their place. Many gave up and returned to the desert. Others left to try other cities. My father heard of towns to the north that Semites akin to us had founded in a region called Akkad, but he steadfastly held to

Uruk.

Mother and father often argued about what to do. She wanted to leave, and go anywhere, preferably back to the comfortable familiarity of the desert. She said she hated cities, though she had yet set foot in one.

"We should never have come here," Makarim said. "These are not our people. They treat us like slaves."

"Be patient, Makarim. Be like the rock in the desert and let the sands of the Sumerian's indifference drift over you, leave you untouched, except for sharp edges rubbed smooth," Rashad said.

My mother laughed. "I'll preserve a few sharp edges just for you."

Kadar, Jamal and I enjoyed these months, though we worked hard, or at least my brothers did. As it was spring and the river threatened to flood, we spent most of our days repairing dikes, and digging silt from irrigation ditches. For desert people, the sight of the recently planted fields of barley breaking ground amazed us. A vast sea of green began to form, as far as we could see. I admit that as the youngest, half-grown, I only worked with a kind of playful ineptitude. My mother, I suppose, worked the hardest, her labors never finished, though she had Fadilah's mischievous help to ease the long days.

Everything was new and exciting. We used every spare moment to explore our new surroundings, wandering far off to neighboring villages, taking long walks along the river. We liked to run, even after working long hours, racing each other around the perimeter of the city walls. Jamal always won. I came last, inevitably, but didn't mind. I think Kadar let Jamal win. I was too slow to convincingly let win.

Occasionally I found myself alone, and would always head for the Euphrates to look for Sumerian lads to talk to. I quickly picked up the rudiments of the Sumerian language. Some of the Sumerians, when they discovered what I sought, went out of their way to teach me new words. Others seemed to resent my ambitions. I made a few good friends, taking great pains to memorize their names, and the proper way to pronounce them. Only occasionally did I see Sumerian girls, at a distance, and never dared to go near them, except once.

It was weeks before I let the Sumerians talk me into shedding my clothes and joining them in the river. I made sure that none of the Sumerian girls were within sight, and that Jamal or Kadar had not followed me to the river. It was wonderfully refreshing, as I thrashed around, trying ineffectively to copy the skilled ways the Sumerians swam in the shallows. The appearance of my thin body, mockingly white where the sun had seldom touched, naturally brought laughter.

It was all innocent revelry.

After I emerged, glorying in the feel of the sun on my wet body, and had reluctantly donned my ragged clothes, I saw her. A girl, most assuredly Sumerian, judging from the way her finely made dress draped her thin body, stood high on the embankment looking down at me. Her hands rested on her hips. Her head tilted back slightly. She didn't move as I caught sight of her and blushed, wondering if she had seen me earlier, my shameful white body.

The Sumerian boys took no notice of her, though they remained as naked as ever. However, she did not look at them. She stared at me, I knew, with uncanny certainty. I had to walk past her to return home. She didn't move as I approached, and she never took her eyes off me. When I reached the place where I would start down the river, I stopped and turned to face her, perhaps a dozen paces away.

"What're you staring at?" I said.

Of course she didn't understand me. Instead she walked towards me. I nearly ran. When she got near, I saw her eyes, the azure-blue color I would never forget. I must have had an idiotic expression on my face, for she smiled and then laughed. I felt like grabbing her and throwing her down.

"What's so funny?" I said instead, my fists clenched.

She shook her head not understanding. She said something, and I recognized the word for clothes. As she said it she stepped forward and felt the sleeve of my shirt. I felt ashamed of my attire. At the same time I felt angry with myself for being ashamed.

Someone called out from farther up the river. I looked up and saw a woman, the girl's mother I guessed. The girl turned away and started up the embankment, leaving me standing foolishly staring after her. Halfway back, the girl turned and said something more that I didn't understand. Then she ran off to her mother, and soon disappeared down the opposite side of the embankment.

I looked for her on other days, but never saw her again by the river. From that day, I doubled my efforts to learn the Sumerian's language.

In a few months, I was skilled enough to crudely translate whenever my father or mother, or even my brothers, slower to learn, needed to talk to a Sumerian official, or tradesmen, or landowner. Strangely, my father never learned more than a few words of Sumerian. Fadilah was almost as quick as I at picking up the new language. My mother learned enough to get by, but seemed uninterested in more.

4

We had lived outside Uruk for seven months when Ennunadanna, the landowner we worked for, found his way to our tent. Fortunately, I was there to translate, or else we might never have gotten out of that crowded encampment. Father pulled me to his side, holding me painfully by the shoulder, as if I needed to be close to him to translate properly. Mother stood behind. I noticed Ennunadanna frequently glance at her as he spoke.

I had to concentrate, because Ennunadanna liked to talk fast, gesturing grandly, as if making a speech to a large crowd. After he greeted us, he rattled off a long sentence that I only got part of, and I began to feel hot and uncomfortable, and wished my father did not hold me so tightly.

"He said that he thinks we're good workers," I translated, though I knew he had said much more.

Ennunadanna noticed my abbreviated translation, and spoke slower, in shorter sentences.

"You have three strong sons, which is an advantage," he said.

Father nodded in agreement when I translated.

"I therefore have a proposition for you to consider. I also own a beer brewing shop in the city."

I said the word beer in Sumerian because I didn't know what it meant. Ennunadanna realized, and laughed.

"Of course. Where would you have ever tasted beer?" he said.

He paced around a little, as much as was possible in the confined space. "You'll have to come with me, right now. The only way is to show you, all of you."

"He wants us to come with him," I said, mimicking Ennunadanna's excitement, enormously curious about this stuff called beer.

We all went with him, even little Fadilah. The landowner walked ahead of us, away from the tent city, and towards the city gates.

"Where's he going?" father asked me, urgently.

"I don't know. I don't think he said. I think he wants to show us what beer is."

When we reached the gate, Ennunadanna said something to the guard and gestured back at us. Then he waved for us to follow him into Uruk, at last.

What a sight. What smells and sounds. What crowds. People hurried everywhere, seldom walking, swerving around kids playing in the streets, dodging wagons and carts. Houses, many two stories high, loomed precariously over our heads. Shops on the ground floors invited people to enter their cool, dark interiors. Hawkers tried to sell us things, then turned away impatiently when we didn't understand. Three young Sumerian boys trailed after us, curious as ever. We hurried after Ennunadanna, frantic that we might lose him.

We had found our way across hundreds of miles of open desert land, with the flimsiest of landmarks to guide us, but without Ennunadanna, we would have become quickly lost in Uruk's crowded streets. We kept turning onto new streets, left, then right, so that I soon lost track of direction. The number of streets amazed me. I noticed narrow alleys diving off in every direction. Later I would learn that away from the few wide avenues, Uruk was a maze of narrow, winding unpaved alleys, some so constricted that walkers edged sideways to pass each other.

We turned along another wide avenue, with stalls along each side, offering food for sale, all useless to us, for we had accumulated none of the magical Sumerian coins they demanded. Ennunadanna had paid for our labors in food and cloth. The avenue soon opened onto a modest square, a delightful change for desert nomads accustomed to space, even though people crowded about us. Ennunadanna stopped near some tables and chairs and waited for us.

"Sit down," he said, gesturing to emphasize his point.

I didn't need to translate this. Fadilah perched on her mother's lap. Rashad sat next to them. Jamal and Kadar sat on the opposite side grabbing the last two chairs. Ennunadanna pulled two more up for him and me, side by side. I felt enormously important, and smiled teasingly at Jamal and Kadar.

"Now you'll all taste some beer, even your little girl."

Ennunadanna laughed and waved to someone under a dark awning. A moment later, a man brought out a large pottery bowl filled with a frothy liquid. Seven reed straws stuck out of the bowl, like leafless marsh plants.

"Here, I'll show you how," Ennunadanna said, leaning forward to suck some beer up, letting out a satisfying ahhh when he had swallowed it. "Go ahead, try some. If you want to live in Uruk, you must know about beer."

I caught what he said, and grabbed my father's arm. "He said to try some. And he said we're going to live in Uruk."

"Are you sure?"

"Yes. I think so. But we must drink this beer first, otherwise we can't."

17

I was actually not far wrong. As we came to learn, it was doubtful that Sumerians could survive without beer. Not only was it a refreshing, nourishing drink, and a wonderful enduring way to make use of a large barley crop, but the Sumerians used it frequently as a commodity of exchange, many workers paid entirely with portions of beer.

Kadar started to lean forward, but my father waved him aside. He would be the first to try. We all watched, holding our breaths, except Fadilah who could not help laughing. Father nodded his head and smiled toward Ennunadanna after he had taken his drink.

Then my father turned to me, wiping foam from his mouth. "Terrible stuff," he whispered, trying to smile. "Burns the mouth, but don't tell him that. Say that I like it very much. And be sure you don't make a face, any of you, when you try some."

"Who's next?" Ennunadanna said, needing no translation, thoroughly enjoying the show, as did many other patrons of the beer shop.

"I want to go next," Fadilah said, understanding the landowner. Before Rashad could say anything, she had half climbed onto the table from my mother's lap and grabbed the reed between her teeth, biting into it. She couldn't get anything to come out.

The landowner laughed and touched my arm. "Tell her not to bite, just suck."

I leaned forward and showed her instead, sucking in my cheeks, taking a long drink, immediately coughing it half up onto the table when the thick, fiery liquid hit the back of my throat. Father groaned. My brothers laughed. Fadilah clapped her hands, and grabbed another reed. She took a long sip, looked up and smiled, then took another.

"I like it," she said, and everyone laughed.

I didn't, but I wasn't about to say anything. By the time we finished the large bowl, I had gotten used to the taste at least. I also felt a kind of dizzy feeling, sort of light-headed. My stomach felt funny and I worried that I was going to be sick, and spoil everything. Fadilah had been laughing and giggling, entertaining all of us, until she suddenly laid her head down on the table and fell asleep. This was our first experience with the intoxicating levity that beer induced.

Having performed our initiation, Ennunadanna explained his proposition. I had trouble understanding him, probably because the beer had destroyed my ability to concentrate on his words. He had to keep repeating himself, which, after a time, began to try his patience.

"I think he wants us to work in his brewery, making beer like we've been drinking," I said, letting out a belch to punctuate my announcement.

My father furrowed his brow, but there was excitement in his eyes. "We don't know anything about how beer is made. Ask him . . . no better not. Tell him we'll be happy to learn how to make beer."

I translated this, but Ennunadanna had trouble understanding me, and I had to repeat myself three times, making everyone impatient. I begin to sweat.

"We'll teach you all what to do," Ennunadanna said, or at least that was how I translated his answer for my father.

My father nodded his head towards Ennunadanna and smiled broadly to indicate his approval without need for me to intervene. "Ask him where we'll live. No. Tell him we'd like to live in the city. That we'll work hard if we need to."

This took a long time to get across. When I finally got through to Ennunadanna and he got through to me, I smiled broadly and clapped my hands, waking Fadilah up. "He says we'll live in the city. He's already arranged a place for us. He wants to know right now, if we're willing. We are aren't we?"

"Tell him we'll be honored to work in his beer making place," Rashad said, with deep gravity.

5

Two days later we moved into our new home, set on one of the alleys on the lower slopes near the city walls. This was where Uruk's carpenters, brick-layers, metal-smiths, potters, brewers, sculptors, weavers, leather-workers, and lesser scribes lived. The crowded conditions were hard to get used to, especially for desert nomads. In contrast, the houses of landowners, traders, merchants, high-ranking city officials, and the most skilled scribes overlooked the wide, paved avenues. I had lived three years in Uruk before I managed to see inside such a grand two story edifice.

Whatever the social status of Uruk's city-dwellers, their houses had one sensible design. No windows opened onto the street to let in the city's strident sounds and noisome smells. A single door led to a central courtyard, open to the sky, where families cooked and ate meals, played games, exchanged news, entertained guests. In the larger houses, a steep stairway led to rooms above, that opened onto a verandah. Such rooms were for storage, sleeping, bathing, weaving, brewing and other household industries. Owners annually white-washed every wall inside and out to fight the sun's unrelenting heat.

There was one ubiquitous construction material in Uruk, which formed the walls of every structure, including the Great Temple—sundried, mud bricks. Stones suitable for building were non-existent in Sumer. Wood was almost as rare. Carpenters sometimes honed palm tree logs into ceiling beams, eventually covered with palm fronds and dirt, but otherwise, everything stone or wood had originated in a distant land few Sumerians had ever seen. Immigrant workers made sundried bricks, of a uniform size and shape, from a raw material which Sumer had in infinite abundance: a fine silt-like soil that packed tightly into molds when wet, and dried nearly rock-hard after a few hours in the sun.

The drawback was that mud-brick walls seldom endured the weathering of wind and rain more than a dozen or so years. When walls appeared unstable, too far gone to repair, laborers knocked them down, and trampled the rubble flat to make a base for the new house. With each cycle of rebuilding, Uruk grew a few inches taller. When I learned this, I understood why Uruk appeared built on a hill, in a landscape devoid of hills.

Uruk's streets presented hazards we had never experienced. Residents threw trash into the streets for scavengers to pick over, the residue eventually trampled under foot. All too often, human and animal waste waited in ambush for the unwary, despite city regulations that required their disposal outside the city. The smell could overcome the weak or unwary. We newcomers suffered the most, especially in the heat of the summer. It was one price we paid for the privileges, opportunities and security that the city provided.

Another, more deadly price, was the risk of succumbing to the periodic plagues, illnesses rarely experienced in the desert, that swept through the population every few years, bringing misery, and often death. It was impossible to predict when they would hit the city, and the priests were powerless against them. Many people left the city to live apart when their neighbors began to fall ill with raging fevers. We were lucky, at first.

Not all was squalor and crowds and noise and noxious smells in Uruk. My brothers and I soon discovered an oasis in Uruk. Near city center, not far from the Great Temple, an island of spaciousness known officially as Temple Square, diverted neighboring houses and streets aside like a broad sandbar in the Euphrates at its summer ebb. Without this open area, and a few smaller ones, we would have found life in Uruk unbearable. Benches surrounded a sunken brick-paved area, always crowded. Food stalls offered dates, beans, apples, onions, garlic, turnips, dried fish, and of course beer. People came to meet friends or make new friends, sip from a convivial urn of beer and watch Uruk's human tide pass by, at all hours of the day, and into the evening twilight. There was no lack of entertainment. Magicians, acrobats, storytellers, dancers, board games, musicians, and an occasional wrestling match competed for our attention.

People mostly came to watch each other. There was no better place to observe the many faces of Uruk's inhabitants. The city was a complex, ever-changing mix of social and ethnic groups. Desert people mixed with mountain people. Newcomers sat next to peasants of ancient ancestry. Destitute immigrants looked in awe at rich Sumerian traders.

I went there often, sometimes with my brothers, sometimes alone. I loved to watch the people, especially the haughty Sumerians. The men proudly wore their beards long and curly, like a badge of distinction. Except in rare cold weather, they went bare-chested, displaying their slim builds encased only in a kilt-like wrap-around garment. The women too made no attempt to hide their beauty and charm, unlike Semitic wives and daughters. Sumerian women arranged their hair in braids coiled around the head like a hat. They wore gowns skillfully woven of flax and wool, efficiently form-fitting to unabashedly catch the eye of every male they encountered, their right arm and shoulder bared in the current style.

I was eventually to succumb to such charms, but when my brothers and I first went to the oasis I was just eight years old, and the magicians and acrobats held my closest attention. It was a wonderful place to go and escape the brewery.

6

My brothers loved to work in the brewery, Kadar because it got him out of the fields, Jamal because he labored along side his older brother. I was never sure how my father felt about it. He never complained. He had achieved what he sought—life in a city. That was enough.

From the first moment, I hated the brewery. I hated almost everything about it, from the suffocating heat, to the terrible smell, to the drudgery and sameness of the work, from day to day, month to month, seemingly destined to eat up a lifetime. My work showed it. Kadar and Jamal learned the intricacies of making Sumerian beer. I turned my back on it, doing as little as I could get away with.

Only one thing interested me in the brewery. I discovered it soon after we started there. Wandering away from the others during a break, I came across a young Sumerian man seated on a bench next to another older man, a merchant I later found out. The young man had a kind of tray set on his knees, filled with smooth clay. He used a chisel-like tool to make odd wedge-shaped marks in the clay as the merchant spoke of orders and deliveries. I tried to get a look at them. They were sort of drawings, but not quite recognizable. I waited patiently until the older man finished and left.

"What are you doing?" I said.

The young man had put a damp cloth over his clay markings, and set it aside. He looked up at me and frowned impatiently. "I'm writing, of course. What do you think?"

"What is writing?"

"You don't know?"

"I will if you tell me."

He shook his head. "I don't have time for ignorant desert people."

I kept coming to watch him whenever I had a chance. I would creep up quietly beside him, to not disturb him. I didn't want him to tell me to go away, as he once did, ruining my day. If I got too close, he would angrily tell me to move aside, and I would scurry back. But, minutes later I would edge back close again, unable to resist the temptation to examine his rapid, purposeful movements.

When I dared, I asked him questions. "Why did you make that mark? What do you do with these tablets? What are they good for? What is writing?"

The Sumerian sometimes laughed, sometimes gave me a quick answer I seldom understood, but most often raised his hand as if to strike me, effectively silencing me.

My persistence finally beat down his resistance. When I again, for the hundredth time, ventured to ask "What is writing?" he groaned, held his hands to his head as if it were about to burst, and turned around to face me.

"Abdullah, if you promise to never ask me another question, I will tell you."

I promised. The Sumerian stared at me closely to see if I was serious, which of course I wasn't. He took out the tray he had worked on.

"See these marks. Each one, or each of a few together, mean a word.

Like, this here, means barley. And this is a number. The amount of barley the brewery is buying from that merchant."

"I see," I said, but I didn't really.

Thus began, in a stumbling fashion, my education in the mysteries of writing. I continued to seek out this young man, the brewery's scribe, every chance I could get. Despite my promise, I asked him endless questions, but only when he was not busy. My enthusiasm won him over. He let me try out the reed stylus, as he called his writing tool, and I copied two wiggly lines that he said meant river. Then I got it. I wanted to scream and dance. Marks in clay could mean something, could say something, could communicate a message to someone else, who understood, who could read the signs.

My brothers and my father thought I was crazy. Kadar and Jamal made fun of me mercilessly, until mother put a stop to it. She took me seriously. She asked me to tell her what I knew about this writing. I went to her every day when I found out something new, and tried to draw the signs in the dirt floor of our house to show her.

She understood the importance. "You must learn all you can of this," she said. "And I want you to come here, always, when you are able, to teach me. I want to understand this Sumerian magic too."

I needed little encouragement. However, I spent so much time with the scribe that I lost pay for the family. Ennunadanna told my father, while I translated. "Tell him," he said, when I hesitated.

"I'm sorry father. I haven't worked enough, he says."

He knew why, without my saying. My mother had no doubt lectured him on what I was attempting to do, and had tried to explain to him the power of the Sumerian magic. He looked at me long and hard while I held my breath.

"Tell him that I approve of my son learning the ways of the scribe," he finally said.

I smiled my joyful thanks, resisted hugging him and turned to Ennunadanna. "He wants me to become a scribe."

This had just come out, as if the gods had spoken through me. I had never before thought of the possibility. I had only thought to learn what it was all about. After I had said the words, the reality made me as dizzy as drinking a bowl of beer. I would never be happy if I could not be a scribe. Then Ennunadanna slapped aside my joy.

"Only Sumerians can train as scribes." He turned and walked away without another word.

"What did he say?" Rashad said.

I could not bear to tell him the truth. "I must wait a year or so, before learning the craft of the scribe."

He nodded his head in understanding. "Then you must work harder in the brewery."

For a time, I obeyed, miserably, only rarely able to find time to watch my scribe at work. I didn't know what to do. I tried to learn on my own, keeping elaborate records of the symbols I had picked up. I scratched their forms onto spare pieces of clay tiles I had managed to scrounge in the streets, near houses torn down.

Then one day, nearly a year later, after I had turned nine years old, Ennunadanna came to watch the scribe work, or so I thought. By then, I had taken to spreading sand on the floor next to the scribe, carried with me in a little sack, and copied as best I could the marks he made in his clay tablet. When I saw Ennunadanna, I thought he had come to scold me, or drag me back to cleaning the smelly brewery vats.

Instead he surprised me. "You do that well, Abdullah," he said.

I looked up at him and nodded.

"Would you like to learn to be a scribe?"

I wasn't sure I had understood him. "I thought you said only Sumerians can train as scribes."

He nodded. "That's true. But there are always exceptions."

For a moment I was speechless. He clapped me on the shoulder. "Well, would you like that or not?"

"Yes. Yes. More than anything."

"You won't find it easy, since Sumerian is not your language. The trainers will expect you to keep up with the other students. And some of them will resent you."

"I can do it. Thank you, thank you." I couldn't wait to run off and tell my family, especially my mother.

"Once you master the mysteries of writing," Ennunadanna said, "you'll be kept well employed. Not just by me."

I kept nodding my head like a fool, my mouth hanging open.

"Every ambitious father is anxious for his son to enroll and succeed in the scribal schools. Your father should be pleased."

I wasn't so sure, but Rashad turned out to be no exception, once he got over his initial displeasure at the loss of much of my brewery earnings. Of course, I had no idea what I would have to go through to attain the lofty status of scribe.

I attended a temple school nine out of ten days, five hours a day. I faced five years of arduous training, just to become usefully proficient, twice that long to become a sought-after expert. Teachers were cruel and demanding, pain in several devious forms used to induce

24

study. I often went home with bruised hands and an aching neck. But I only had to work in the brewery half the day. And I could more often go to my oasis. Temple Square was a favored place for students with clay tablets in hand to practice their strokes, worn styluses pressed into clay kept damp with an occasional spray of water.

Teachers instructed us in the history of writing, though at the time I found this utterly boring. What did I care that writing had already had two centuries to evolve? I was impatient to learn the next symbol, the next shortcut technique, the next rule of writing. Yet, I found one aspect of the origins of writing fascinating. The first scribes had used simple sketches of the thing identified, such as two wavy horizontal lines for a river, a bowl-shaped outline for a bowl, a half-arc above a curved horizon line for the rising sun. However, with a stylus, a newly favored tool that made wedge-shaped impressions in wet clay, straight lines were easier and faster to make. Pictorial shapes gradually changed to become the more stylized, cuneiform writing, easier to quickly make with a few pressings.

I came to understand that the role of a scribe was as much an inventor of symbols, for new ideas, for new objects, for complex combinations of objects and ideas, as he was a craftsman to record what others prescribed. Writing was a living, growing gift of the gods. And it was destined to be my life's work.

7

A month after moving into the city, I learned the secret to finding my way in Uruk.

"Look for the Great Temple," Kadar said, exasperated, when I had arrived home again late.

The Great Temple commanded the city's highest elevation, where two wide thoroughfares meet. Visible everywhere in the city, the Great Temple served as a beacon to judge direction, a reference to measure distance, and, as a last resort, a haven for the lost. It became far more than that for me.

The Great Temple was dedicated to Inanna, the Sumerian goddess of fertility and love, the divine patroness of Uruk, and consort of Anu, god of heaven, father of the gods. It was the largest man-made structure in the world, at least so the traders, who travel the world, claimed. To reach the temple, supplicants had to climb a hundred stairs to the summit of a flat-topped knoll as expansive as many villages, an island within the city, a place of refuge from the hectic squalor below, a place of tranquillity, a step nearer the gods. I was nine years old when I first got near the Great Temple. I would have to wait longer to get inside. My father took my brothers and me up to the summit, the first time any of us had entered this sacred domain. He did not dare take us inside the temple, with no offerings in hand.

Before, I had only seen the Great Temple from a distance. It had not impressed me greatly. Now it stood frighteningly near, overpowering, an enormous rectangular block, towering overhead. The sinking sun had set the temple on fire. Its plastered sides glowed red and pink, and flames seemed to dance and glitter from points of light I later learned was something called a mosaic.

Months later I saw an artist create a mosaic. He worked with amazing speed. An assistant spread a thick coat of white plaster on a section of the wall, as large an area as the artist could master before the plaster dried. Beside the artist, ready at hand, were baskets of small clay cones, of a size to comfortably fit five or six in the palm of a hand. Rapidly, one by one, without apparent thought, the artist dipped a clay cone's wide end into a jar of colored dye—red, white or black—waved it around in the air for a few seconds, and deftly shoved it into the wet plaster, only a portion of the dyed end left exposed, a tiny colored eye. Magically, these individual points of light worked together to create an image of great beauty. Everything was within their powers of creation, from simple eye-catching rectangular patterns, with mystical meanings, to wild jaguars ready to leap out at those who strayed too close. Mosaics seemed to cover every surface of the Great Temple.

I had to wait five years to see and experience the mysteries of the Great Temple, when I reached the memorable age of fourteen, officially a man, at last. Kadar and Jamal had seen it already. They told me what to expect, well not quite everything.

I stood in awe when my father led me into the Great Temple for the first time. It had the shape of an elongated cross, something I had never noticed before. The building looked much bigger from the inside. The lofty ceiling, high enough to easily engulf a two-story house, accounted for this impression. I felt as if I was in an immense cavern, every sound echoing mysteriously, the goddess Inanna repeating the priests' chants for my benefit.

"See those beams," my father said, pointing above us. "They're from Canaan, brought all the way here, each from a single cedar tree.

Each is nearly forty feet long."

I nodded, not as interested as my father in such technical matters. It was the impression, the feeling of the temple that absorbed me. I noticed a series of arched doorways around the temple's perimeter, evidently leading to private rooms.

"What are those rooms for?"

My father looked at me strangely, a half-smile on his face. "Has Kadar or Jamal been telling you things?"

"Nothing much," I said, feeling increasing apprehensive about the visit.

"They're used by the priests and the priestesses who serve in Inanna's household."

I nodded, though his answer didn't help since I knew nothing of what priests and priestesses might do in their private rooms.

My father led me to the life-size statue of Inanna that stood in the sacred area at the far end of the temple. This, my brothers had not adequately prepared me for. I swallowed nervously, unable to take my eyes from the goddess, a sensuous figure a head taller than me, naked, with arms slightly outstretched. At the foot of the statue on a low brick ledge, my father, with a noticeable degree of reluctance, placed half a kid that he had slaughtered that morning.

I gasped at the magnitude of the gift, but I didn't say anything. The occasion must be more significant than I thought.

My father stepped aside to whisper something to a priest who looked on the offering with obvious approval. It would help feed the priests and priestesses for a day or two. I remained in front of Inanna, transfixed.

"This is my son, Abdullah. He's studying to be a scribe," my father said, taking my arm and drawing me towards the priest. "He has just reached the age of manhood."

The priest looked at me, head tilted, eyes narrowed skeptically. I was short for my age, which annoyed me greatly. My brothers claimed it was because I spent so much time bent over my clay tablets. The priest placed a hand on my shoulder.

"Since he's fourteen, and a man, and since you, his father, have made a gift to Inanna appropriate to the occasion, it is proper that he give himself into her hands."

He said some other things, but I didn't listen. It seemed to me that Inanna had extended her arms toward me, invitingly.

A moment later the priest took me firmly by the arm. "Come with me Abdullah, and we will invest you in the mysteries of Inanna. "

"Where are we going?" I looked in panic at my father, who frowned at my too blatant timidity.

"You will see," the priest said, his voice solemn.

He led me to one of the perimeter rooms. My heart began to beat wildly, uncertain what terrible ordeal I faced. A young priestess awaited us, her mischievous eyes brazenly fixed on me, well aware of the priest's mission. I had to look away. The priestess wore only a short cloth wrapped around her waist, and a gold necklace around her neck. Only once or twice before had I seen a woman's breasts, and then only from a distance. I felt myself grow hard, and my face flamed when the priestess noticed and nodded solemnly.

"He's ready," she said to the priest, who nodded sagely.

"This is his first time. Treat him with care."

"I can tell," she said, smiling quickly. She stepped close to me, and took one of my hands and raised it up. I could hardly breathe.

"He has strong hands. The hands of an artist," she said.

"He's training to be a scribe."

"That's wonderful," she said, dropping my hand. "For then he'll surely come here often."

The priest turned to walk away, and in utter panic, I started after him. The priestess laughed. The priest turned back, holding up his hands.

"No, no, you must remain with her, and allow her to teach you," he said, vigorously shaking his head, and trying to keep from laughing.

I looked around for my father, but he was nowhere in sight. "I don't know what to do."

"She'll show you," the priest said. "Do as she says. She's one of Inanna's most proficient priestesses, and it's her duty."

"I don't understand."

"You will," the priest said, raising his voice, annoyed at my innocent obtuseness.

I heard the young priestess laugh lightly behind me. I slowly turned back to her. "What do you want me to do?"

The priestess held out her hand and I took it, my palm damp. She led me into the cool interior of the side-room and began her sacred duties, her first act to remove the last of her clothes, her second to begin removing mine. I realize now how skillful she was in doing this, for one careless touch of her silky hands and I would have ended my first session with Inanna without having laid a hand on the priestess.

The priests later instructed me to believe that Inanna herself had confirmed my manhood, but the twinkle in that skillful priestess's eyes seemed all too human. It was over rather too quickly I later came to realize. When I looked guiltily away from her nakedness she gently took me by the shoulders and turned me back to face her.

"Now you are a man, in the divine eyes of Inanna," she said. "And in my eyes too," she added, laughing.

I met her gaze and stolidly kept my eyes from straying, still discomfited. She touched my cheek momentarily, as if to anoint me. "When you feel the need, come back and reconfirm your devotion to the goddess."

I never learned her name, though I returned to her embrace on a number of occasions. Perhaps Inanna did direct her limbs, her movements, her clever testing of my manhood, I thought, as I slowly made my way down the hundred steps. There were greater mysteries and miracles.

She was a priestess of the second caste, one of the Sal-Me, I soon learned, for now that I was initiated I wanted to know everything about those magical inhabitants of the Great Temple. They lived in the convent attached to the Great Temple, but they were free to go about the city, and some even engaged in commerce. Their duties in the temple inevitably led them to bear children. Adoptive families raised them. The Sal-Me could marry a man and live with him, but could not officially have children by him, and were required to continue their lifelong temple devotions. The man who would so marry had to be content with one of his wife's slaves, or a concubine, to bring children into the world that he could call his own.

When I left the Great Temple in a daze, I knew none of this. Jamal and Kadar teased me unmercifully when I returned home. They also quickly and thoroughly educated me. I refused to answer Fadilah's questions, though she plagued me with them relentlessly. She was twelve years old and feeling the first dangerous impulses of womanhood.

8

Having reached an age to recognize and crave the unique beauty of Uruk's women, my fondness for the sights in the Temple Square took on a deep passion. I went there often with brother Jamal, two years older, and as interested as I in these uncommon sights. By then, Kadar had married, and kept too busy for such pleasant pastimes.

On such a day, no different it seemed than any other, the gods smiled upon me, diabolically as it turned out. I sat on a brick bench, in the shade of an adjoining building, my practice tablet in hand, when the girl walked by. She pretended, with studied determination, not to notice us, but we noticed her. She was Sumerian, about my age, I thought, or maybe a year younger. I followed her with my eyes, my head slowly swiveling as she walked by, too far away to quite see her expression, or the color of her eyes. Jamal noticed her too. He nudged me in the ribs with his elbow, and made a vulgar remark that oddly infuriated me.

"A typical Sumerian virgin, too good to lose it to such as us," he then added.

I clenched my teeth. We watched her until she passed out of sight, engulfed in a crowd. We sat in silence for several minutes. I kept re-playing in my mind every movement of her brief appearance, as she made her way across the Temple Square.

"I'm going to marry her," I said, matter-of-factly, breaking the silence.

"Who?"

"That Sumerian girl."

Jamal laughed loud enough to bring stares our way.

I meant it, though it astounded me that I had said it, as if Inanna had put words in my mouth.

For a Semite to take a Sumerian woman as his wife was not unheard of, but rare, especially if the Semite was a recent immigrant and the Sumerian woman was of noble birth, as this girl turned out to be. I gave no thought to such obstacles, and it wouldn't have mattered if I had known who she was. I was inordinately proud at this age. I would soon be a scribe, and command the respect of everyone. Every day I would have dealings with Sumerians of all strata of society. And I would live in a two-story house on a wide avenue. Anything was possible, I thought.

I continued to see the Sumerian girl in Temple Square where I sat bent over my clay tablet, busily practicing, but not busy enough to miss her. I was sure she noticed me, but she gave no indication. I thought she was the most beautiful girl I had ever seen. When I gazed on her languid body, I imagined what it would be like to hold her, as I occasionally held the temple priestesses. Her shift, of the finest flax cloth, seemed to flow over her body like a shower of milk, accentuating every curve, every movement, every hidden secret. I dreamed of her, and thought of her when I lay with a priestess. Thankfully, Jamal no longer came with me, bored with my scribal exercises, more interested in a Semitic girl he had met in the brewery.

In time, emboldened, I tried to catch her attention, unsuccessfully. I ached to see the color of her eyes. I was sure she had begun to walk closer to where I sat, and once I thought I saw her look around the square before entering, as if searching for me. But I still didn't know her name.

I was utterly ignorant of marriage. I went to my father and asked him how I could get a Sumerian girl as a wife.

"It isn't possible," Rashad said. "In Sumer, marriages are arranged by family elders and none would allow their daughter to marry an impoverished Semitic immigrant."

This rebuff discouraged me for a month. Then I went to Kadar for enlightenment. Kadar was equally discouraging, but told me what I wanted to know, and much more.

"Sumerian elders arrange marriages, so that's who father must talk to."

"I don't even know her name," I said.

Kadar hurried on, impatient of any interruption. "Once the elders agree on the terms, you must present the bride's father with a gift whose value is equal to the girl's position in society. If you fail to carry through with the marriage—"

"I won't."

"Then the gift is forfeited. If the girl changes her mind, going against her father, you recover your gift two-fold."

"What about the marriage itself?" I said.

"That's the easy part. You're married when you and the girl press your seals into a tablet setting forth your duties to each other. Those of course must all be negotiated before hand, in careful detail."

I groaned. The process seemed full of pitfalls, and I had not yet spoken to the girl I intended to marry.

Kadar went on to explain a Sumerian woman's rights, though this little interested me. "You can't treat her like a slave. Your wife will retain control of your betrothal gift and a dowry her family should provide. You can't use it, without her permission, to pay your debts, but I don't suppose you have any."

"None. That's enough. I don't need to know any more."

Kadar shook his head. "Better to learn these things now, before getting entangled with this girl. You'll have rights that you should not forget." He grabbed my arm to keep me from escaping. "If your wife fails in her conjugal duties, if she refuses you repeatedly, without reason, you can legally drown her."

I didn't believe this, but said nothing. It sounded like one of those customs spoken of, but never followed.

"Under certain conditions—I'm not quite sure what they are—you could sell your wife."

"I would never do that," I said.

Kadar nodded. "You never know. And of course, you'll be free to take a concubine, if you so desire, and can afford one."

"Enough, Kadar. I don't want to hear any more."

I could not so easily silence him. He spoke rapidly, still gripping my arm. "You can also legally turn your wife over to your creditor to serve as a slave for three years in payment of a debt. Remember that you can divorce her on the slightest of grounds. It's fortunately much harder for her to divorce you. Adultery on your wife's part is punishable with death, if you so choose. Of course, you're expected to divorce a barren wife. Alternatively, you can take a second wife, though your first does not thereby lose her position or support. Yet another alternative, your wife can present one of her slaves to serve as your concubine."

"I'm not listening. I don't understand any of that."

Kadar laughed. "There's more, but I see you've had enough. Do you still want to marry this Sumerian girl? One of our own would be much simpler."

"I will marry her."

A short while later I found myself in the Great Temple, not to seek a priestess to quell my despair, but for the quiet peace the place provided.

Then I saw her, my Sumerian girl. She was talking to a priest. I stood transfixed, uncertain what to do, even more inflamed to see her in the Great Temple, with which I associated activities that I could only with difficulty think of as reverent. The statue of Inanna loomed behind her, and seemed to mock the desire that swelled within me. The priest looked my way. He knew me, and beckoned. The confusion of Kadar's words buzzed in my head as I grew closer to the girl, who looked startled when she saw me.

She stood taller than I expected, taller than I. Close to her for the first time, I noticed her eyes. I had never seen eyes their color, a deep azure-blue, like the precious lapis lazuli gem from the Indus, except one time years before, in the eyes of a Sumerian girl beside the river.

Nothing else of the girl from my childhood did I remember, and yet I felt certain that this was she. Her gaze flickered over my face curiously. I wondered if she too remembered. I could not look away. I tried to stand taller.

The priest took my arm. "This is Abdullah, a talented scribal student who I have been watching closely. This is my youngest daughter Sarah. She has come to take her vows, to join Inanna's household."

In one breath I learned her name, and her mine, and then lost her. She was to join the convent of temple priestesses, the Sal-Me, to devote her life to the goddess, the consort of Anu. I could have her in the way I had feverishly dreamed of, or I might marry her, but I could not have her to myself.

I backed away uncertainly, shaking my head.

"What is it? What's the matter?" the priest said.

I saw a tear form in the corner of Sarah's right eye and begin a tortured drift down her cheek. I turned and ran out of the temple.

I stayed away from the Great Temple, unable to face seeing her there. I went almost daily to the Temple Square, but Sarah did not appear, until many days later. When she did, she wore the distinctive garb of a Sal-Me. I sighed and looked down at the pavement. My hopes had been scattered like grains of sand in a desert storm. I looked up, saw her watching me as she slowly walked by, and started to approach her anyway. She kept walking until she reached a less crowded area, where she stopped and turned around. I stopped a few feet away. For a long time we just looked at each other.

"Why did you run away?" Sarah said.

"Isn't that obvious?"

"Then why were you waiting for me here, Abdullah? Why do you look at me that way?"

"Because I can't forget you. I hoped that maybe you would change your mind. But you haven't."

"You know that's not possible. My life is committed to serving Inanna." She hesitated. Twice she started to speak before managing to get the words out. "You can still visit me. Any time, Abdullah. I'll wait for you."

I suddenly stepped forward and clumsily took hold of her hands. She gasped and tried to pull away, but I held on. "I don't want to share you with every man in Uruk. I don't want to share you with anyone."

"Please let go."

"Why can't you leave the temple?"

"My father . . ." She pulled her hands away, and backed up.

"I wanted to marry you," I said, staying close to her. "But now I'm confused."

She covered her mouth with her hands, her eyes growing wide. Then she turned and ran from the square. She didn't come back the next day, or any day thereafter. She had accomplished her purpose, showing me what she had become, and what we had lost.

After two months I could stand it no longer. I went to the Great Temple, fervently hoping that the priest, Sarah's father, would not be there, and that she would be there, unencumbered with some slovenly Sumerian man consorting with Inanna.

Unfortunately, her father was there, waiting, as if he expected me, beside the statue of Inanna. "Abdullah, I haven't seen you for many days. I've wondered about you."

"My studies . . ." I said, trying not to look at Inanna.

"You must be near completion, ready to take on clients, and make your fortune," he said.

"Yes. My father waits anxiously for that day."

He nodded, looking at me closely, I think seeing into my soul. I was within an instant of fleeing again. He remembered. Smiling, he touched my arm. "You ran away last time. I asked Sarah about that, but she acted as strangely as you."

"Is she here?" I blurted out, unable to endure another moment of suspense.

"You want to visit her? To be with Inanna?"

"Yes. I mean, no. I just want to see her, to talk to her."

"Do you understand what she has become? What her vows entail?" the priest said.

I nodded. "Is she happy in what she does?"

"Of course. It's a great honor."

I could feel my heart beating rapidly. "Can I see her?"

"What do you intend to say to her?"

I took a deep breath. "I'm going to ask her to marry me. My brother said it was possible. That she could marry, and still remain with Inanna. Is that true?"

The priest nodded, not surprised. "It requires a great sacrifce on the husband's part. Not many men are able to endure such a life."

"I seem to have no choice."

"You can find someone else. Someone more suitable."

"I can't imagine anyone but Sarah."

"You can still be with her."

I shook my head wildly. "That's not enough. Can't you under-stand?"

"I understand completely. You should know what you're getting into. I've seen a number of such marriages, and few have worked out well, for either party."

"I can't help it."

"You know that when she has a child—"

"I know all that. Is she here now?"

He sighed and nodded his head. "In the third room."

I stood in front of the curtains blocking the door for a half-minute, my heart racing, my forehead damp, before getting nerve enough to push through. Sarah stood waiting, as if she expected me, and I won-dered if the priest had some secret way of getting a message to their priestesses.

She looked so beautiful, her long hazel colored hair cascading over her shoulders to just graze breasts tenderly small. Her eyes returned my gaze, unwavering. I could not speak. She came forward, and took me by the hands and pulled me into the room. Her hands shook a little, and I saw her start to blink rapidly.

"I wondered if you would come," she said, "after what you said in the square."

"I wanted to, long ago. That could never change."

"I'm glad. I've waited for you." She smiled. "Long ago, I remem-ber a small boy beside the river, dressed in rags, who dared to look me in the eye."

"I knew it was you, when I saw you up close."

"But not in the Temple Square, at first?"

I shook my head.

She laughed. "I knew it was you then, instantly. Isn't that strange? Something about the curious, yet restrained way you looked at me, reminded me of the desert boy who dared to shed his clothes and plunge into the Euphrates river, though he could not swim a stroke."

"For months I worried that you had seen me."

Sarah squeezed my hands sending a chill up my spine. "You've greatly improved in appearance since then."

"So have you."

We stared at each other, barely breathing, for a few seconds. "Are you ready?" she said, in a husky voice.

"I don't think I can. Not this way," I said.

"It's all right. It's my duty," she said.

"The others—"

"Don't think about them."

"No. This should be different."

Sarah let go of my hands and backed away. "What are you trying to say, Abdullah?"

"I want you to marry me."

She put her hands over her mouth. Her eyes widened and she took another step back, stumbling slightly. "You know—"

"I understand. I must share you with Anu," I said, feeling that everything would now be all right, since I'd managed to tell her.

"Our children—"

"May not be mine. I understand. I'll adopt any that you have, and treat them as my own, I promise you."

Sarah walked towards me and took my hands again. "Come with me."

"Are you sure?"

"I'm sure. If you want me, I will marry you, Abdullah."

Any thought that I might abstain from going with her until after we were married vanished when she removed her gown and stood naked before me, shaking a little, her azure-blue eyes staring wide. I tried to forget the others who had done the same, and those of the future who would follow in my footsteps, as I took her in my arms, but couldn't quite manage. Then I remembered the times I had come to the Great Temple to lie with other priestesses, and felt that perhaps I only deserved to share Sarah.

Two months later, Sarah and I married. My family objected and tried in every infuriating way to get me to change my mind, all except Fadilah, who loved the idea, and came to love Sarah like a sister. I suffered when Sarah went to the Great Temple to carry out her solemn duties as Anu's consort. I would never get used to it.

Sarah bore two children in the first three years of our marriage, the first a girl, the second a boy. I didn't know whether they were mine, and I dared not claim them, for to do so was to admit a sacrilege. But I treated them from the day they were born as ours.

By then, Fadilah had failed to carry through on three marriage contracts, infuriating her father and mystifying her mother. Fadilah was sixteen, too old to be unmarried, with dangerous temptations. Jamal had married and within a year lost his wife to a plague that swept through Uruk. Kadar kept having children, nine in all, of which seven lived past infancy.

Sarah and I named our first child Leila, for she was born during the night. She had her mother's azure-blue eyes, and would be equally beautiful. The boy we named Lufti, because he was Anu's kindest of gifts, a child unmistakably with my dark brown eyes.

I trudged up the one hundred stairs every day to the Great Temple, to pray and give lavish gifts to Inanna in the hopes of a miracle—to have Sarah all to myself.

Memphis, Egypt

II. Memphis, Egypt
2580 BC

A thousand miles to the west of Uruk, in the Nile Valley, another civilization developed in parallel with that of the Sumerians. Memphis was the capital of the world's first stable, unified, centrally ruled nation. At a time when the city-states of Mesopotamia embroiled themselves in warfare, Egypt enjoyed nearly uninterrupted peace and prosperity. At a time when desert nomads swarmed into the Tigris-Euphrates valley from the west and barbarians launched invasions from the east, the people of the Nile valley, for the most part, lived secure, productive lives.

Geography made the difference. Egypt was a nation tied closely to the Nile valley, a thin oasis cutting through a nearly impassable desert. The Nile provided sustenance, transportation, and the link that tied the nation together.

No nation in history, before or after, has enjoyed so many decades and centuries of peace and unity, only occasionally interrupted by brief periods of chaos and disunity.

By 2580 BC, the Fourth Dynasty (a modern terminology) was firmly in power, and the Age of Pyramids was well underway. The first pyramid, the Step Pyramid, was a century old, its genius architect, Imhotep, already deified. The construction of Pharaoh Khufu's tomb, the Great Pyramid, began with his reign.

The Nubian Dancer

1

My older brothers, Khaldun and Jumoke were alike in many ways, both skilled stone-carvers in the employ of the Pharaoh's architects, both taking after their father in stature and temperament—strong limbed, sturdy of build, methodical in their attitude towards everything. Yet, the gods seemed to find amusement in giving my eldest brother, Khaldun, mostly good fortune, while Jumoke had to often endure the opposite.

Khaldun and his wife Omorose, a woman as sturdy and dependable as her husband, had nine children of which seven, miraculously lived past infancy. Jumoke tragically lost his young wife to a plague that swept through Memphis in their first year of marriage. He never completely got over it. Though only twenty years old, and childless, Jumoke made no effort to find another wife.

In contrast, my eldest brother, Khaldun, had not only his wife, but two young concubines he kept fully employed. I could never afford three women, but he could. Pharaoh Khufu's Vizier paid him well to supervise a small army of stone-carvers at the pyramid site, among them, Jumoke and my father.

Rashidi, nearing forty, proudly claimed to be the oldest pyramid worker who still worked with his hands and not his mouth, meaning he was not a foreman or supervisor. He had no interest in such duties. He had worked with his hands all his life, first in a Delta papyrus factory, before he dragged his family south to Memphis twelve years ago, since then as a stone-carver on the Great Pyramid, as some people now call the magnificent mountain of stones, slowly taking shape across the Nile.

Jumoke did not resent his brother's good fortune. He never complained because Khaldun received rapid and regular promotions, while he lingered far too long at the first master stone-carver level. He seemed content with his lot. As to marriage, he rejected every suggestion I made, every woman I put forward, showing no interest, letting opportunities drift away, like boats descending the Nile.

I should have given up. And Jumoke, with his penchant for disaster, should never have attended Yazid's banquet.

It was my fault that he did. I had come up with another plan, one more ill-advised strategy to find Jumoke a woman. I had to practically beg to get Jumoke invited. Yazid, the tax-collector I served as a scribe, would never think to invite a stone-carver to his lavish, and aristocratic affairs.

"You want me to invite your brother, the stone-carver?" Yazid said, eyebrows raised, the guest list he had been working on, sliding from his lap to the floor.

I picked it up and handed it to him. "As a special favor, Yazid."

"You amaze me, Abubakar. I suspect you have ulterior motives. What is it? What are you planning?"

I shrugged my shoulders in an exaggerated fashion. "He lost his wife a year ago, during the plague. He seems unable or unwilling to find another. I want to give him a little help, a little nudge."

Yazid laughed, showing a wide gap in his teeth where he had just had one pulled, awaiting a false tooth. "You're mad, Abubakar. Never meddle in family affairs. It only means trouble."

"What can go wrong?"

"You shouldn't ask that. The gods have their ways with people who attempt to mastermind other people's destiny."

"I'll make a large sacrifice to Osiris."

Yazid shrugged. "That will at least make the priests happy, and a little richer. Who is Jumoke supposed to meet? I imagine you have another name—a woman's—you want me to add to this list?"

"She's already there, fourth from the bottom, the daughter of a reasonably successful trader."

Yazid retrieved the list from the floor and looked, shaking his head. "That won't do, Abubakar. That trader is a good friend of mine. I've invested money with him."

I looked at Yazid closely, trying to figure out whether he had designs on the daughter himself, someone to add to his growing harem, or whether he really felt protective.

"My brother Jumoke would be a good match for her," I said. "He'll one day be a supervisor. His profession is an honorable one, well-paid, always in demand."

Yazid shook his head. "Jumoke will probably still have granite dust in his hair when he sits down at my table."

"Do it as a favor to me. I'll see that he behaves. Haven't I served you well all these years? Does any tax-collector have a more skilled scribe? Haven't I detected enough evasions on my own to support two of your concubines for half the year?"

"Enough. I get the message. To keep you happy I'll add him to the list. But I'll wager you'll have trouble getting him to come, and if he does, watch out."

Yazid was right. It was a mistake to meddle in family affairs, especially affairs of the heart. Of course, if Jumoke had behaved as he should have, and concentrated his attentions on the trader's daughter, everything might have worked out, and the trouble avoided. Alas, those mischievous gods were at it again. I should have left an offering to Horus too.

As if Jumoke's presence at Yazid's banquet was not concern enough, I had my young sister Femi to worry about. With her it was different. I would have done anything I could to get her name crossed off Yazid's list. But it was too late for that.

Femi came to me on the eve of Yazid's annual banquet, the largest of the year. She said, without warning, in her most defiant tone of voice, "I *will* attend your tax-collector's banquet."

"Thanks for telling me."

"You can't stop me, Abubakar."

I took a deep breath before replying, an attempt to keep the conversation from getting out of control. "Am I trying? What has gotten into you?"

"You're about to try to talk me out of going."

I laughed. "If you want, I'll try. I suppose you'll enjoy the banquet more if you think you're defying your family, especially me."

"I know what you're thinking. I won't let you run my life. And don't you dare mention that little favor you did for me, or I'll never speak to you again."

I kept calm, or appeared to, the only way to deal with my sister. Otherwise, we inevitably ended in a shouting argument.

"I love you dearly, Femi, and would not dream of telling you what to do. Just try not to embarrass me."

Femi, at sixteen, rarely took my advice, though she did readily accept my help in getting her an abortion the year before. No one in the family knew about it. No one even suspected. Her secret was safe with me, but it continually worried her.

I didn't need to ask Femi how she got herself invited. Yazid knew my sister well, too well I sometimes worried. He fanatically adored beautiful women, and Femi most certainly fit that description. Yazid delighted at their presence at his banquets to enliven the affairs. He filled his household with beautiful women, most notably his three wives and a dozen or so female Nubian slaves. Unfortunately, this oversupply of beauty would be my brother Jumoke's undoing.

2

Yazid held his annual banquet, as he did every year, after he successfully completed his seasonal tax collection duties. I was often away from Memphis for a month or more at a time, recording tax-payment information, writing receipts, logging wealth in every form imaginable, and detecting evaders. We most often traveled in the fall and winter during the season of Emergence, when the Nile gave back the land, replenished with a new layer of rich silt. Some years we also ventured forth during the winter-spring season of Drought, when crops were high and harvesting began. Travel during the summer Inundation was useless, the land covered in water.

Yazid's assigned territory extended both north and south of Memphis, from Abusir deep in the Delta to Qarara one-hundred miles south along the Nile. That had been a lucrative year. The tax revenues, paid in kind in the form of produce, livestock, and factory products, greatly exceeded the previous three years. The Pharaoh expressed great pleasure, Yazid said, which meant that the tax-collector also prospered. His reimbursement was a fixed percentage, plus what he could safely hold back. He even passed a few extra morsels my way to keep me happy when I complained about the long periods away from my wife and children.

Yazid sympathized. He knew Sharifa and he knew my worries

about her. But he also delighted in teasing me, every chance he got.

"The Pharaoh probably knows nothing about her," he once told me, as we sat idly sipping beer in a tavern in a small town to the north of Memphis. His tone of voice, as opposed to his words, revealed hidden doubts.

"We're only a few miles from Memphis," I said. "I can hire a boat and be there and back before you're ready to move on."

He laughed. "You worry too much. Be like me. I have three beautiful wives, and it doesn't concern me in the least when I leave them. I trust them to do whatever they want."

"None of your wives are daughters of the Pharaoh."

"You can't be certain," Yazid said, more seriously.

"It is what Sharifa's mother loudly claims, to everyone she talks to." She was formerly one of Pharaoh Khufu's many concubines.

"Such women say anything to get attention. She only grieves because Khufu has had enough of her."

"If word gets back to the Pharaoh that he has a beautiful daughter, such as Sharifa, even if it isn't true, I'll lose her, or at best have to share her."

"Think what you will gain when Khufu adds Sharifa to his harem," Yazid said, his voice thoughtful, as if this idea was something new. "You'll no doubt become a royal scribe and live in luxury the rest of your life. You won't have to follow me around, recording mundane tax records."

"Without Sharifa, it will be no life."

"You're much too attached to this woman. Get another wife, or a concubine, and spread yourself out a little." He laughed and clapped me on the shoulder.

He knew I could not easily afford another wife, and a concubine was barely within my reach. But I had not the remotest desire for either. Sharifa was enough for me, and I knew the risks when I married her. Pharaohs lived by godly rules, encouraged to marry their sisters and daughters to preserve the blood. As gods after their death, and sometimes before, they could do as they wished.

I would have liked nothing better than to become a royal scribe and live in luxury the rest of my life, as Yazid astutely perceived. We were not a noble family, and this was the highest position I dared hope for. Well, not quite. I could conceive that as a royal scribe I might one day attain enough influence to get appointed to Amon's priesthood, in which case I would be set for life. I would be exempt from taxes. But this was useless dreaming. I would remain in the pay, and under the beck and call of Yazid, or some other tax-collector for the rest of my life.

I contented myself with the knowledge that what my fellow scribes and I did mattered to Egypt's prosperity, to its very existence. Pharaoh Khufu could not control the lives of Egypt's hundreds of thousands of people without his bureaucratic army, under his trusted Vizier's direction. And no official could long survive without a scribe at his side to record every meticulous detail of accountability, to create the mountains of papyrus scrolls required to keep Egypt flowing as smoothly as the Nile.

The Pharaoh sat placidly, godly, at the head of a great bureaucratic pyramid, every stone in this edifice dependent on those they rest on, down to the foundation: the artisans, laborers and peasants who bore the entire nation's load on their shoulders. At the pyramid's every level, it was the scribe who ensured that the blocks fit, and communicated their forceful efforts. How else could one man, though said to be a god, control a nation strung out along the Nile river for more than seven-hundred miles? How else could one man command an army of ten-thousand pyramid workers to spend three decades building his tomb?

Each summer when the Nile began to rise four-hundred miles south of Memphis, an official took careful note, a scribe recorded the fact, and in a few days the information reached the Pharaoh's palace in Memphis. When a farmer harvested wheat anywhere in Egypt, a tax-collector measured the quantity, exacted his tax, and a scribe at his elbow recorded it all, to be dutifully read in Memphis a few days later. When a calf was born, when a blight felled a crop, when a quarry-worker met an accident, when a trade caravan arrived from a desert oasis, an official was first at the scene, his scribe ready to scribble entries in Egypt's unique hieroglyphic script, all for the Pharaoh's benefit.

Pharaoh Khufu was the father of Egypt, the nation's soul, its link with Amon and the lesser gods. Yet, all but a tiny fraction of Egypt's population had never laid eyes on him, and most never would. They saw only his administrators, the local officials they had to deal with, and those dealings were sometimes good and sometimes bad, often cooperative and nearly as often filled with acrimony and deception, as all human relationships are.

I told myself repeatedly that I must remain content with my lot as an ordinary scribe, and shrug off the doubts. I also told myself I must learn to enjoy the family I had—my beautiful wife Sharifa, and young Layla and Lateef—without concern for the future. Yet I worried, for it was dangerous to be content. The gods laugh at such smugness and cleverly plan their tricks.

3

Jumoke stared at me in disbelief. "The tax-collector Yazid has invited me to his banquet?"

"That's what I said."

"Why?"

Because I went down on my knees and begged him to. What could I tell him? I shrugged. "Perhaps he has heard of you. Pharaoh Khufu's most famous stone-carver."

He looked at me sideways. I could never keep a secret from him. "What crazy scheme are you planning, Abubakar?"

Braving the dust, noise, and heat, the smell of unwashed bodies, I had gone to the pyramid building site to find Jumoke. We stood beside the limestone block Jumoke continued to work on as we spoke. It reached shoulder height and was wider than the span of his extended arms. The dust and chips flew with each strike of his wooden mallet, driving his copper chisel into the stone. I brushed dust off my blue linen kilt that Jumoke's chips threatened to turn grey. Jumoke wore only a brief loincloth.

"This will be one of the most lavish banquets in Memphis in months. Yazid made a fortune this season, and is in the mood to spend some of it."

"I won't know how to act. I'll look like a fool. You said you hardly enjoy these affairs yourself, and only go because Sharifa insists on it."

There was truth in this. I sometimes think Yazid only invited me because of my wife, another beauty to adorn his house and banquet. I invariably felt uncomfortable, and ill at ease among the notables. I inevitably drank and ate too much. Sharifa was wonderfully adroit at these affairs, her royal concubine mother's careful training, I supposed.

"Someone will be there that I want you to meet," I said, finally admitting what Jumoke had already suspected.

"A woman."

"Right."

"I guessed as much. You never give up."

"Should I? You'll be twenty years old next month. Practically middle-aged."

"Who is she?"

I shook my head firmly. "That's my secret. The last time you acted like a fool. Enjoy yourself, and let nature takes its course."

"You've told the woman about me?"

"Of course."

I should have told him who she was, and perhaps then the accident wouldn't have happened. Who can say?

When not away from Memphis with Yazid, I frequently visited my father and brothers at the pyramid construction site at Giza. Sometimes I brought my mother with me, to see what her sons were up to. Mukarramma still missed the Delta, and still felt that the papyrus industry was more honorable than carving stones for a monstrous tomb. The pyramid's overwhelming majesty usually managed to silence her for a time.

Khufu's pyramid enthralled everyone, except perhaps the ten-thousand peasants who had to drag the huge limestone blocks around. Travelers, many from beyond the Nile valley, journeyed enormous distances to stand in awe before the nearly finished pyramid tomb, to marvel at the incredible efforts Pharaoh Khufu demanded from his subjects.

My brother's team of stone-carvers were a proud bunch, because they viewed their work, correctly, as critical to the pyramid's construction. As Khaldun loved to explain to visitors, stone-carvers had to dress their blocks to exact dimensions, as specified by architects, each stone designated for a particular resting place. They wore out copper chisels at an alarming rate, keeping metalsmiths busy. If they erred by more than a tiny amount, which Khaldun claimed seldom happened, the stone-carver had to climb the pyramid and alter the block's dimension in place, a dangerous task. Even a short fall from one of these shoulder-high blocks could lead to injuries.

The most grueling and dangerous task was dragging the blocks up the long ramp that wound around the pyramid to the level of current construction, increasingly laborious as the pyramid grew taller. If a block escaped, which despite precautions periodically happened, it would slam into following blocks in the procession to launch a chain reaction that set back work for days.

Eventually the pyramid would gain a smooth facing of the finest white limestone. The lower levels had already gotten their facing when Jumoke's troubles began. Jumoke and Khaldun were among those who worked these stones, whose dimensions had to be extremely accurate, tight enough to prevent the inspector's knife from slipping between adjoining blocks.

All day long, from dawn to dusk, the long line of blocks, inched their way up the incline to a final resting place, and a returning line of weary laborers carried their transport sleds back for the next block. Only a small fraction of them were slaves, or conscripted peasants. Khufu's agents paid and fed them well, and most lived near the building site in houses provided for them free of charge. To work on Khufu's pyramid was considered a great honor, a highly lucrative life's work.

4

As the day of the banquet approached, I became increasingly worried. I had nightmares of Jumoke at the banquet table, covered with limestone dust and chips, of my sister Femi arm in arm with the Nubian dancers, equally naked, of the Pharaoh, in disguise, locked in a passionate embrace with Sharifa. Alas, the troubles we dream of are never the troubles that rain down on us, unexpected, unanticipated. Amon sends dreams to mislead us.

I sighed with relief when I saw Jumoke. He had cleaned off the stone dust at least. He wore a white linen kilt, no doubt his finest, reaching mid-calf as the latest styles demanded. His chest was bare, gleaming with the oil he had rubbed in to remove every grain of stone dust. He wore a serpent bracelet on his right upper arm, and another lower down on his left arm. I knew it was the best he could do, and nodded my approval, though I worried about how he would react when he saw the ostentatious opulence of most of the tax-collector's guests.

Jumoke and I had to wait for Sharifa to finish getting ready, a long arduous task for a woman intending to impress at all costs. When Sharifa did enter the room, Jumoke gasped and I let out a lingering groan.

"Do you approve?" Sharifa said, spinning around, arms outstretched.

"Yes, of course. Beautiful as always," I said. I was proud of her, but at the same time, I wished she would restrain herself just a little.

"Jumoke, what about you? Your brother is too worried that the Pharaoh will make an unexpected appearance, to say what he really thinks."

"What can I say, that I haven't said before? You're by far the most beautiful woman in Memphis, and I greatly envy Abubakar his good fortune."

Sharifa gave Jumoke a quick kiss on the lips, and me a flashing frown.

She could have been a little more restrained, I thought, but I didn't dare say anything. That she had bared the smooth olive skin of her upper body to deep below her navel, was not entirely unexpected, certain to bring attention to her, and greatly please Yazid that he had invited her. Her breasts, still amazingly youthful, a shame to hide Yazid would have said, projected a light rose color, accentuated by the magnificent ruby that dangled between, jostling them lovingly as she moved about. The pale blue skirt hung precariously low on her hips, reaching her ankles, exposing gold-colored thong sandals and toes painted a deep red, though most men and few women would never look down to notice. A black wig covered her head, just touching her shoulders. She had powdered her face white, except for a deep blue smudge beneath her eyes.

She would, as usual, mesmerize every man she met. And I, as usual, would suffer terribly, and drink until my eyes glazed over. I hated those banquets.

"I should go to the banquet with you and leave stuffy old Abubakar here with his scrolls," Sharifa said, taking Jumoke's arm as if to leave without me.

I was tempted to let them go. We took cloaks to throw over our shoulders against an expected evening chill, and left for the short walk to Yazid's villa. We didn't wait for Femi. She would meet us there, she said.

"I've never been inside a nobleman's villa," Jumoke said, as we approached the walls of Yazid's compound.

"It's large enough to get lost in," Sharifa said. "Don't go wandering off."

It was too bad Jumoke didn't listen to that advice. Yazid's villa was typical of the residences of Egypt's most affluent citizens, secure, self-sufficient, and sensuously luxurious. High walls enclosed a sprawling two-story main house, separate servant's quarters, a horse stable, a cook-house, several storage sheds, a cattle yard sufficient for an oryx or two, three baking ovens, an elegant private temple, a quarter-acre vegetable farm, and a garden with a formal pool. Yazid claimed that they could feed themselves for three months without anyone stirring outside the compound walls.

We arrived a fashionable half-hour late, and were still among the first to enter. We entered the villa compound through a towered gateway, where a tall, regal gatekeeper met us and unobtrusively checked our identities. He made a mark next to our names on the invitation list. The entrance led to a tree-lined pathway that wound past the family temple to the main house. Torches burned beside the path to light the way. Jumoke looked as nervous as I felt. Sharifa laughed at something a remote acquaintance whispered in her ear. Everything seemed normal.

My brother, the stone-carver, caught my arm when we got near the house, laughing and pointing. "Not a stone in sight."

I nodded. The house was built of sun-dried bricks, Egypt's universal building material for every structure except temples and tombs or the flimsy reed shacks of field workers. Despite its humble construction, the house was extravagantly spacious, a dozen rooms arrayed around a central hall, reached through a magnificent column-supported entrance. Yazid's women, his three wives and a gaggle of nearly adult daughters, gained privacy in a large sitting room, where even he was not welcome. There was a children's nursery, several smaller bedrooms, the master bedroom, two guest rooms, and a bathing room with running water. Outside and above, a wide balcony caught the prevailing breeze, a refuge from the heat. Yazid and his family slept on outside porches when the summer heat made the interior unbearable. Windows opened wide to let in the cooler night air.

We entered the house through an inner courtyard, up a shallow flight of stairs through an open doorway, into the columned vestibule. Murals decorated every wall. Tiles and rugs covered the floors. Yazid had furnished the house with the finest products of Egyptian carpenters, honed and fitted from rare and expensive imported woods. He had neglected no comfort or convenience.

Servants met us there and took our cloaks. A servant placed a scented animal fat cone on top of Sharifa's wig. It would slowly melt during the evening, and mask any hint of body odor, hers or other's. Finally ready, we walked through another columned entrance way to the central hall, where Yazid and his first wife met us. Yazid's greetings were typically effusive.

"Ah, Sharifa. You look lovely beyond comparison, as usual. You're a lucky man, Abubakar, as I've often told you."

Marriage to one of Memphis's most beautiful woman had its dark side. Yazid's careful, lingering scrutiny of Sharifa produced a rare blush, but she did not divert her look.

"I thank you, as usual," she said. "But you shouldn't say that only Abubakar is lucky. We're both lucky, to have each other."

Yazid made a little bow of mock acquiescence. I looked at Sharifa in surprised gratefulness.

"You are as gracious as you are beautiful," Yazid said. "You remember my first wife?"

The formalities continued at the lackadaisical pace typical at such affairs, the language and speech patterns somehow foreign sounding. When Yazid's first wife took Sharifa aside, out of her husband's reach— a practiced move—I finally had a chance to introduce Jumoke, who had stood at my side as silently and stiffly as a granite statue.

Yazid looked him over with interest, while Jumoke mumbled something neither Yazid nor I could understand. "Your brother says that you're one of the Pharaoh's most skilled stone-carvers. I congratulate you, and welcome you to my simple abode."

"There are many more skilled than I, but I do my best," Jumoke said, mumbling with his head averted.

"I hope you find my guests interesting," Yazid said, with a glance at me. "Many, especially the women, will be fascinated to hear all about your occupation. To go out to the building site and watch progress is a favored pastime of many of these pampered women." He laughed, but I sensed that he meant the obliquely disparaging remark.

There were twenty-three guests, besides the tax-collector and his three wives. Femi, I saw, had already arrived, and animatedly conversed with a young man I had never seen before. He couldn't have been more than fourteen. Leave it to her to immediately find the handsomest young unattached youth in the room, I thought.

Preliminaries were brief. Dining, a serious business, began as soon as everyone arrived, and lasted half the evening. The hostess, Yazid's first wife, a darkly beautiful woman dressed in a white linen skirt, breasts firm for her age, the only woman at the affair that could compete with Sharifa, urged everyone to take their assigned seat around a long table.

I had arranged for Jumoke to sit between two young women, both beautiful, either of which could have been the one intended for him. I wanted to keep him guessing. He couldn't tell if they were married, for husbands and wives never sat together. Sharifa seated herself across the table from him. He looked at her imploringly, but she only laughed and turned to talk to an older man.

The banquet began with a first course of bread, figs and dates, washed down with beer and wine, served in painted pottery chalices that seemed never to go empty. The serving girls, one for every three guests, hovered nearby, ready to fulfill any wish. They were all Nubian slaves, naked except for a narrow woven cloth that circled their hips. The guests took no notice of them. They might as well have been invisible.

The guests talked animatedly, increasingly so as they relentlessly consumed beer and wine. Musicians played lightly in the background, the haunting notes of a flute, accompanied by a lightly strummed lyre. They soothed the senses with whimsical melodies of ancient tradition. Femi behaved herself at first, and Jumoke managed a few words with the woman on his left. After an hour I began to relax. Then things began to go inconspicuously wrong, as I would later learn.

The food platters kept appearing, to Jumoke's obvious dismay. Inexperienced, he had consumed too much of the first courses. He tried to talk with his two female companions. But despite Sharifa's not too subtle hints, he soon ran out of things to say. The more he drank, the more quiet he became, in great contrast to everyone else. I began to lose heart. But worse was to come.

5

Not until nearly a month later did I learn the full details of what happened next. While Osiris and Horus and a few lesser gods played with Jumoke's future, like children tormenting a kitten, I kept drinking and eating and pretending that I was having the most enjoyable evening of a lifetime. And while Jumoke stumbled onto true love, Sharifa, sitting at the far end of the table, basked under the revered attentions of every male within reach. And, across from me, annoyingly close by, while Jumoke set out on a course of self-destruction, Femi thoroughly distracted the young lad she had targeted for the evening, with intimate whispers and the clever efforts of her flirtatious hands. For me, the evening's events were all the proof I would ever need that the gods have a ridiculously malicious sense of humor.

Midway through the second hour, Jumoke had to relieve himself, but didn't know where, and was too embarrassed to ask anyone. When I got up and left the room, he surmised my purpose correctly, and followed. He caught up with me as I passed through a curtained door into the back of the house.

"How do you like it so far, Jumoke?" I said, when I noticed him.

"Too much food."

I laughed and lightly punched him on the shoulder. "Is that all you can think of, when two beautiful women sit at your side?"

"Where's the toilet?"

"I thought you looked a little agitated. This way."

I finished first and left Jumoke to go back by himself, a careless error. When Jumoke left he turned the wrong way and suddenly found himself where he knew he shouldn't be—the women's sitting room. Several women quietly gossiped while they adjusted their makeup and clothing. One woman, just inside the door, reapplied colored rouge to her enormous sweaty breasts. Another fitted a new scent cone atop her wig. Three slaves administered to their needs. Jumoke turned quickly, but not in time. He heard the big-breasted woman's deep laughter as he backed toward the door.

"Come back, my sturdy young friend," she called, amidst more laughter, "if you wish to understand our female secrets. We'll share everything with you."

"Sorry, sorry. I lost my way."

Another, younger woman turned to look at him. "He's Abubakar's brother, the stone-carver. I'll wager he has strong hands."

"Don't let him go," another said, and more laughter rained on Jumoke, making his head spin, his face blush.

Jumoke turned and dashed through the door. He swung around the corner and crashed into a slave girl, knocking a full wine goblet out of her hand, wine splashing both of them. He caught her to keep her from falling, and almost fell himself. She cried out softly, and gripped his shoulder. Their eyes met.

In that instant, Jumoke, mildly impervious to women's charms most of his life, fell madly, irrevocably, in love.

I cannot criticize him for this, or make light of it. When he told me, I had to take it seriously, for that is how it was with me when I first saw Sharifa walk across the temple square. But Sharifa was not a slave.

The slave girl started to pull away. Alarmed, she averted her eyes. "Sorry. Stupid of me to get in your way, honorable sir. Oh! I spilled wine on you. If you'll let me, I'll get a cloth, and water. . ."

Her voice, soft, lilting, deeply accented, made Jumoke shudder. He didn't let her go. Their eyes met again, and this time the girl did not avert her gaze. She struggled for a few seconds to get away. "Please. I'm very sorry." She gasped and relaxed, sinking down, as if about to faint, then recovered herself.

"What's your name?" Jumoke said, urgently.

She hesitated. A momentary frown. "I'm only a slave."

"Please. What is your name?"

"Don't report me. He'll beat me, and send me to live with the animals."

Jumoke frowned. "Who beats you?"

"No one. I'm a good slave."

"The overseer?"

"He's a good man. I'm lucky to be here. Please don't say anything."

Jumoke found the courage to move his eyes off her face, and looked her over. She was young, thirteen or fourteen, Jumoke guessed, but old enough. She was Nubian, or part Nubian. Her brown ebony skin gleamed with perspiration, yet she smelled like some mysterious flower, waiting to be explored. Her legs were slim and athletic, her hips narrow, almost boyish, her breasts barely discernible, and only a little hair had grown between her legs below the slim decorative band she wore around her waist.

She noticed his gaze. "Can I serve you? Will you take me into another room, so I can please you? You are a guest. My master will be pleased that I have—"

"No. Not that. I didn't mean to—"

Jumoke suddenly heard laughter at his back. Turning he saw three of the woman standing in the doorway watching, enjoying his discomfort, waiting for developments.

"Take her," one of them said. "Practice with her, and then come back for us." More laughter.

Jumoke, still gripping the slave girl's arm, turned her around and pushed her ahead of him down the hall and into another, blessedly empty, sitting room, laughter driving them along like a biting sand storm.

He let her go. She turned to face him, arms hanging at her side. Tears overflowed her eyes. She wiped them away.

"I'm ready now," she said.

"You've never done this before, have you?" Jumoke said.

"I know what to do. I will please you."

Jumoke shook his head. He ached to the center of his being, to wrap this delicious dark creature in his arms, to enfold his body around her, to savor and enrapture her, but he couldn't, he wouldn't let himself.

"To please me, you only need tell me your name. I'll repeat it to no one. I'll hold it in my heart, like the memory of this precious moment, as a priceless secret treasure."

A veil of puzzled relief flowed down over the girl's agitated face, and she shuddered slightly. "My name is Nefertiti," she finally said, after what seemed like an eternity of silence.

A queenly name, for a slave, thought Jumoke, and fell more irrevocably in love.

"Nefertiti," Jumoke repeated. "Nefertiti. It is I that must apologize, for frightening you so. You've nothing to fear from me."

He didn't want to leave, to let her out of his sight. He could have easily remained where he stood for the rest of the evening, staring at the beautiful figure before him. But he had already remained away from the banquet a long time. He knew I would be wondering about him, and might even be looking for him. And the horrible women in the next room might pursue him and torment him further. He turned reluctantly to leave.

"Will you tell me your name, sir?" Nefertiti said, her voice suddenly more forceful.

Jumoke turned back. Nefertiti walked up closer to him, gazing into his eyes. He found it difficult to breathe, and his voice sounded as if it came from the depths of a well.

"My name is Jumoke Barakah. I'm a stone-carver."

"Thank you Jumoke," Nefertiti said, lightly touching his arm, and then drawing quickly away.

It felt to him as if a butterfly had landed on his arm. She darted around him and disappeared. When Jumoke returned to the table, after so much delay, and two missed courses, I noticed his glazed, wide-eyed expression, and attributed it incorrectly to the wine.

6

The banquet culminated with a delicious roasted goose that experienced diners had assiduously saved room for. Jumoke forced down a few bites, but his mind was clearly elsewhere. Worried, I began to watch him. I saw that my strategy had failed. He ignored both women. His mind floated somewhere in the clouds, I thought, or perhaps he was worrying about the next day's stone-carving assignment. He was hopeless.

Late in the evening, servants removed the table and the entertainment began while the beer and wine continued to flow as steadily as the Nile. A pair of twelve-year-old twins, Cretan contortionists, boy and girl, tied themselves into human knots. A Sumerian magician made two women gag and turn away when he seemed to swallow a foot-long knife, handle and all. Finally, Nubian dancing girls took to the floor, and men fell silent while women whispered and pointed. Nefertiti was one of the dancers, though I had no idea of her name, or significance, at the time. I noticed her, as everyone did, for she was by far the most skilled of the dancers, her limbs like swaying papyrus reeds as she sinuously projected her body into unlikely, gasping positions. She wore ring bracelets on each wrist, a matching choker neck ring, and a thin gold cord around her hips, and nothing more.

Jumoke could not take his eyes off Nefertiti. Her sensuous positions and movements inflamed him. His forehead glistened with sweat as he gulped his wine as if it was water. When she slowly danced her way towards him, her eyes fixed on his, I noticed and wondered. When, only a step away, she whirled around in a new direction, I saw Jumoke let out a great gasp of breath and stagger into a woman behind him. Nefertiti tantalized other men the same way, and wives began to whisper louder. A few moved across the room to grip their husband's arm. I glanced at Sharifa and she gave me a familiar provocative smile that said, "I can do that too, if you enjoy it so much." And she could.

Thank Amon, and every other god that Femi did not decide to leap out onto the dance floor with the others. I thought perhaps that Nefertiti's beauty and skill were too much for her to compete with. Then I caught a glimpse of her, away from the crowd, in a small alcove, with the boy I had seen her talk to earlier. She performed her own private, highly localized dance for him. He was the only man in the room who didn't notice Nefertiti.

After the banquet, as the dawn lightened the sky and we made our way home, Jumoke pulled me aside. "I'm going to marry that dancer," he said.

"Sure. Good idea," I said. I thought he was joking, although I knew whom he was talking about.

"I'm serious."

"I believe you."

"Her name is Nefertiti."

"An unusual name for a slave. How did you learn that?"

He didn't reply.

I forgot this brief conversation in the days following the banquet. I decided to give no more thought to finding a wife for my brother. He would have to do it himself. I had more pressing worries.

Femi dragged my mother and father to see me exactly one month after the banquet. Mukarramma and Rashidi looked worried as usual, and I knew it must have something to do with my sister.

"Femi thinks she has found a husband," my father said, before we had even sat down.

"We've found each other," Femi said. "You make it sound as if I have trapped him."

"Let your father speak," my mother said.

"He wouldn't be that young man at the banquet, Femi?" I said.

She nodded defiantly, and watched me closely to see how I would react. I knew better. I nodded back, sagely.

"You are serious this time?" I said.

"She sends him love poems. Repeatedly," Mukarramma said.

"She begs him to have her, like a street woman," Rashidi said.

I raised my eyebrows to please my parents, though I didn't think Femi's behavior was so unusual. In Memphis, upper society women pursued men with rare freedom. What was wrong with that?

Femi ignored her parents and turned to me. "I have always been serious, Abubakar. The other times I found out things, as you well know."

"She wants you to negotiate a marriage contract," Rashidi said.

I expected that. Femi didn't trust her father to do that, and would no longer speak to Khaldun, and Jumoke was out of the question. I sighed. "Who is he? What's his name? Tell me about him." We all sat down, and it began again. I had been through this once before, and my father twice before that.

"His name is Chafulumisa," she began. I leaned back, closed my eyes, and listened to Femi's familiar words of adoration.

Unfortunately, the boy's parents lived in the Delta, at a seaport, as inconvenient as possible.

"Please, Abubakar," Femi said. "You must go and talk to them."

"Why can't they come here, or send an agent. It's the duty of the boy's father to present a marriage proposal."

"They're old and cannot easily travel. For you it is nothing," Femi said.

"It is not nothing. I have business to attend to, duties to Yazid the tax-collector. And I have only just gotten back from a trip. I want to spend time with my family."

"Please, Abubakar."

"You ask too much."

"Please. He's the one. We love each other."

I looked at my father. He would never go, that I saw. My mother looked at me imploringly, but didn't say anything.

"This better be the last time," I said.

"Thank you, dear faithful brother," and she gave me a warm hug before dashing out the door on some mysterious mission.

Two days later, still unaware of Jumoke's discovery, and mental turmoil, I left Memphis on my errand of the heart. I wanted to complete the journey quickly, so I hired six oarsmen and a boat. I paid them well. I had no time to allow the Nile's slow current to carry me into the Delta.

In a few hours, I fell into the Delta's familiar clutches, a labyrinth of snaking river channels, often alarmingly narrow, fringed by lagoons and sand dunes. I enjoyed the Delta, perhaps because I had lived there for the first seven years of my life. Since becoming a scribe, I had traveled through the region numerous times. It was a mystical topography, never the same, the Nile its architect, in a never-ending battle with the sea. In high flood years, the Nile rescued new lands from the sea, then reluctantly returned them during low flood years.

Crocodiles outnumbered humans in many parts of the Delta, a danger to fishermen, a good way to lose a careless child. But many people considered it a portent of good fortune to spot a hippopotamus wallowing in the shallows. A century ago, the Nile was home to herds of hippos, but hunters had taken their toll. They were now hard to find. Lions were rarer, virtually hunted to extinction.

The tall, sharp-leafed, reed-like plant, seen everywhere along the channel banks, was papyrus, Egypt's most famous and unique resource. The pith from its thick triangular stems, after processing, made an excellent writing material, the lifeblood of my profession. The Delta harbored hundreds of miles of channels lined with these remarkable reeds, seemingly an unlimited supply. Many of the Delta villages clustered around a papyrus factory, which I usually found time to visit, to renew old acquaintances and buy supplies.

I liked to watch the young deft hands of the girls making paper. The papermaking process was surprisingly straightforward, but had to be carried out with great skill to produce the finest product. In one part of the factory, workers sliced the reed's cellular, triangular shaped pith into strips and placed them in vats of water for soaking. After three to five hours, workers brought the strips to the pressing room, where they aligned the limp slices carefully in two crossed layers between smooth wooden plates. Other, less skilled workers, moved these to a stacking area and weighed them down with stones requiring two strong men to lift.

In another room I watched my favorite part—when the dried papyrus emerged from the press, ready for finishing. Girls with more patience than I could ever muster, then polished and rubbed the papyrus surface smooth with an ivory scraper. The longer they rubbed, the whiter the surface, and the costlier the paper. In the final step, in yet another room in the factory, workers meticulously glued together individual sheets to produce papyrus rolls ten to thirty feet long.

I remained longer than I intended, and bought a six month supply of papyrus. The trip would not be a total waste of time, even if the negotiations went bad, or Femi—as I feared she would—later backed out.

I managed to reach the seaport and return in fifteen days, a record for me. The trip was a success, I thought. I returned to Memphis with a fair marriage proposal, the contract ready for Femi and Chafulumisa to sign. Alas, by the time I got back, they had split up. I could have strangled Femi. Then I found out about Jumoke and Nefertiti, and Femi escaped my fury.

7

I thought Jumoke was a fool, and told him so. He needed a wife, not an enchanting Nubian dancer, who probably could not even speak Egyptian.

"I can't live without her," Jumoke said, in a frenzy, unable to stand still. "After I buy her, I'll free her, and then marry her."

"Have you said anything to her?"

That's when he told me of his adventures in Yazid's house, how he came to fall under Nefertiti's spell.

I could not think what to say. I could barely keep from laughing. I could just imagine Jumoke in the back hall, lost, this delectable nude dancer standing before him, wide-eyed, offering herself to him, the sex-starved matriarchs behind him, laughing, urging him on. I would have given a lot to have seen it myself.

Jumoke sensed my mood, and scowled at me. I put on a serious expression. "What are you waiting for? Buy her if you must."

"I've talked to Yazid. He wants too much for her."

"If she's so wonderful, I'm not surprised. A superb dancer, as I recall. And she's probably Yazid's favorite concubine besides."

I thought Jumoke would hit me. "She's not anyone's concubine. She's a virgin. I'm certain."

I felt instantly sorry for him. How could a man his age be so naive? "What do you expect me to do?"

"I asked Khaldun for help. A loan. He refused," Jumoke said. "He said it was too much for just a bed-mate, and a marriage to a Nubian would not be proper."

This didn't surprise me. Khaldun was annoyingly conservative.

"Can you lend me the price Yazid asks?" Jumoke said, in a challenging voice.

"How much?"

Jumoke hesitated. "It's a high price, Abubakar, but I'm desperate."

"You're crazy. How much?"

"Six head of cattle and forty-five bushels of wheat."

"Dear Amon. She must do more than dance for Yazid. I'm sorry. I didn't mean that." I had to shake my head. "Such a sum is impossible. Forget her."

"Talk to the tax-collector for me. You work for him. Maybe he'll listen to you and make an adjustment, or give me time to pay him."

I told him it would be pointless to hope, but he argued with me until I gave in and agreed to talk to Yazid. In part I agreed because I wanted to get a look at Nefertiti, and see why she was worth a small fortune, an enormous sum for a thirteen-year-old Nubian slave girl. Jumoke could have picked one up at the slave market for a fraction of what Yazid demanded.

I came upon Nefertiti in the garden, while I waited for Yazid to get free to talk to me. She was working with a hoe to keep back the weeds. She took my breath away. In the afternoon's suffocating heat, she wore practically nothing, her firm pointed breasts agleam with sweat, hips swaying as only a Nubian girl's can. I remembered those movements when she danced at the banquet. If by some miracle she was still a virgin, she would not be for long. Perhaps Yazid was just waiting for the right moment, when the bloom was fully ripe, but still tightly budded. For him, she was no doubt worth the price, I decided, and I knew Yazid would never come down. I wouldn't have. Although Sharifa satisfied my every need, Nefertiti sorely tempted me, though I could not afford her any more than Jumoke.

Yazid laughed when I told him this. "She's no virgin. What nonsense. Do you think I would leave such a flower of desire, unused, wasted?"

"It did seem unlikely."

"Your brother has a good eye, but most certainly dreams far beyond his means. Perhaps I'll be generous, and give her to him for a night."

"I think he wants more."

Yazid laughed. He stepped closer and lowered his voice. He began to explain in great detail how skilled Nefertiti was in bed, the techniques he had taught her, the amazing positions she could open into. I begged him to stop. The images made my flesh tingle and my heart race. I asked him, half jokingly, half seriously if he would loan her to me for just one night.

He laughed. "I will, gladly, but are you sure Sharifa will not immediately perceive what has happened to you?"

I shivered at the thought that Sharifa might even get a hint of such an exploit. She was not like most Egyptian women, able to casually share their husbands in a reasonable way, even glad to have others share the burden of pleasuring their husbands.

"Selling her is out of the question," Yazid finally admitted, "at least for the next few years while she's in her prime. I only mentioned a price to get rid of your brother. I would never sell her, even if he could come up with that outrageous amount."

When I later explained to Jumoke that it was hopeless, carefully avoiding any mention of her exploits with Yazid, he gave me a weary look. He had not slept well for many days. Then he said the words I would never forget, but at the time, completely misinterpreted.

"Since I can't buy Nefertiti, I guess I have no choice."

The months passed. The pyramid inched higher, block by block, as Jumoke, Khaldun and Rashidi chipped away from dawn to dusk. The end of another season of Inundation approached and it was time for me to attend Yazid on his travels. The Pharaoh anxiously needed to replenish the royal storerooms, the pyramid expenses a great drain on the treasury. The Vizier had instructed his tax-collectors to be vigilant. On the first trip, to the north, we were away for twenty days. When we returned to Memphis, the city's low-lying environs still lay under water.

I usually spent the first hour or so with the children, Layla and Lateef, whom I missed almost as much as Sharifa. On this occasion, I saw from the drawn look on Sharifa's face that something had happened. I cut short my play, and took Sharifa aside.

"What is it?"

"Your brother, Jumoke."

I felt a sense of relief. My first thought had been that it was something to do with her, and the Pharaoh.

"He has left Memphis, and he's taken that Nubian slave girl, Nefertiti, with him."

I stared at her, unable to believe what I had heard.

"It happened not long after you and Yazid left."

I slumped down on a chair. "Amon. That idiot. Yazid will probably blame me. He'll hire men to find Jumoke, and when he does. . ."

"No one knows where they went," Sharifa said. "The tax-collector's servants said they saw him around the villa the night before Nefertiti disappeared."

"He just walked in and took the slave girl away? He stole her?"

"So it seems."

"She went with him willingly?"

"How would I know that? You talked to him. You've seen the girl. What do you think?"

"I think he's crazy and so is Nefertiti. They're in the Delta, that's certain. It'll be hard to find them there, but sooner or later they will."

"And that's not all that has happened," Sharifa said, after a moment of silence.

Instantly I was on guard, until she smiled and shook her head. "Femi is writing love letters to Chafulumisa daily. He has not responded. She is heartbroken, and angry, and may do something reckless. Again."

"I'll strangle her."

I started to walk away, needing a jar of the strongest beer. Sharifa gently placed her hand on my arm to detain me. When I saw her face, I knew what she was going to say before she said it.

"And I'm pregnant."

Such is life, that the good comes with the bad. I took Sharifa in my arms, and for a glorious few minutes forgot all about Jumoke, and Femi, and my demanding employer.

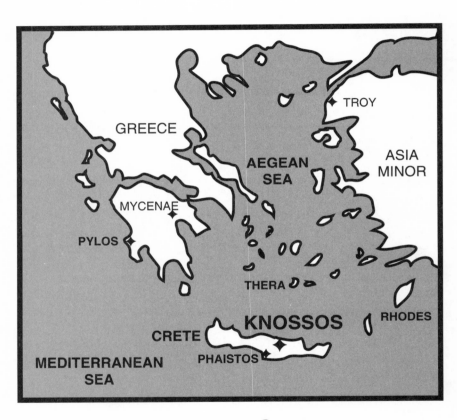

Knossos, Crete

III. Knossos, Crete
1500 BC

Five-hundred miles northwest of the Nile Delta, across the dangerous eastern Mediterranean Sea, the lively and creative people of Crete, lovers of nature, skilled seafarers, founded the world's first maritime empire. During an era of decentralization and decline in Egypt, the Cretans made use of fast sailing ships of an innovative design, to suppress piracy, and establish trading colonies throughout the islands of the Aegean Sea. In time, Crete gained a monopoly on sea trade in the eastern Mediterranean, and the island prospered.

By 1500 BC, Cretan sea captains traded with Mycenaeans on the Greek mainland, dealt with the powerful city of Troy on equal terms, traded with Babylon through Phoenician ports, and sailed into the mouth of the Nile to deal with the agents of Pharaoh Tuthmosis. Of the dozen or so cities sprinkled around the island, Knossos was the largest, its multilevel palace, home of the ruling priest-king, a splendid city in itself.

Perhaps as many as a thousand people lived in the Palace of Knossos, its massive five-story structure sprawled over a five acre hillside site. Unlike palaces in Egypt and Mesopotamia, the Palace of Knossos looked outward onto the world, with wide verandahs lined with stone bull's horns, and columns painted in rich hues. None of Crete's palaces had fortifications. Isolated on an island, with a strong navy, Crete feared no invasion.

The Bull-Leaper

1

I sometimes believed, with good reason, that one of the more mischievous gods had inserted my sister Filia into our family for the sole purpose of challenging my sanity. Whereas my brother Jason's folly with the bull-leaper Nephele was at least understandable, Filia's exploits often defied comprehension. Now she came to me with her latest typically blunt announcement and again wrenched my life out of its fine, straight course.

"I've decided to train as a bull-leaper," Filia said, leaning over the desk where I had been working undisturbed until she burst in.

"Are you serious?" I said, gently pushing her arm away from some papers that threatened to spill off the desk.

She started pacing around randomly, her eyes blazing with excitement. "What do you think?"

I laughed. "I think you've lost your mind. Does this have anything to do with Jason's madness?"

"Why would it?"

"Perhaps you expect that some rich trader will see you perform and sweep you away to some unknown island to live as a princess."

"Don't be stupid," she said, making a face. "I'm serious about this."

"Sorry, but I do sometimes wonder about your sanity."

"I suggest you wonder about your own sanity, Abderus." She

stopped in front of my desk in the tax-collector's vestibule off the main entrance to the palace. "Look at you. Slaving over these figures and numbers. What kind of life is that? I want to do something important."

"Leaping bulls."

"Yes."

"All right. Do as you like. I have work to do," I said, picking up a ledger listing the contents of one of the palace's many basement storage vaults, that particular one filled with waist-high jars of olive oil.

"I need your help," she said, grabbing my hand.

"Please. Some other time." I pulled my hand away. "Can't you see—"

"All right. All right. I'll be back later, when you're not so busy with your wonderful columns of numbers," Filia said, giving me a determined look before turning away.

"I'm sure you will be," I said, calling after her.

She looked over her shoulder and gave me a forced smile.

I shook my head and threw down the ledger. She had destroyed my concentration. After Jason disappeared with Nephele, I wanted to have nothing to do with the rites of the bull-leaper. Six months, and no word from my brother. No one had seen them. They were no longer on Crete, that was almost certain. They had probably slipped onto a trader, and fled to a Cretan colony on a distant Aegean island. My brother Kadmus thought they were on Thera, and said he would look for them when he next passed through Akroteri, Thera's capital, a two day sail from Crete. We once lived on Thera, near Akroteri, before my father decided to move us all to Knossos when I was seven.

My mother could not get over what Jason had done. I think, despite her protests, that Jason was always her favorite. She blamed Nephele for everything, calling her a skilled seductress, sorceress, and temptress, to recite a few of the labels she regularly heaped upon the girl.

I blamed Jason, and felt sorry for Nephele. He had torn her away from Knossos at the peak of her career. She had been famous, adored by every young man and woman in Knossos, envied by many, including my sister, apparently.

Filia would not leave me alone. She was back the next day, again leaning on my desk, expecting me to drop everything to talk to her. Despite her protests, I think she had Nephele in mind when she came to me with her latest scheme, in which I would have to play a large role. For one thing, the bull-leaper's vow of purity made my sister's announcement laughable. I had already arranged one abortion for her.

I gave up and pushed aside what I had been working on. "Filia, you're not a virgin, and you're too old, and also probably too tall. Where do you get such farfetched ideas?"

Filia started to tap a rhythm on my desk, an annoying habit of hers. A small crowd waited reluctantly outside to pay their taxes in kind, impatient to get back to their farms, vineyards, orchards, herds, ships, pottery factories, weaving shops, breweries. As one of a dozen palace scribes—the youngest at nineteen—I dutifully recorded all they brought in. Laborers collected and stored the grains and oils in the palace's vast cellars.

Filia's eyes blazed, daring me to contradict her. "You know better, Abderus. You can't be that naive. For a sufficiently rich offering, the priests will sanctify me at the cave-shrine on Mt. Ida, and I'll be as pure as any eleven-year-old virgin. How many virgin bull-leapers do you think there really are? And I'm not too old, or too tall. What nonsense."

"You're almost seventeen. Bull-leapers begin training at the age of fourteen, or younger."

"I'm sixteen still. What's a couple of years?" She gave me that pleading look, and her tone matched. "You can help me, Abderus. You have influence with palace officials. You can talk to the chief-trainer. Offer him something."

"You want me to bribe him? In the name of Zeus, you expect too much." I stood up, leaning forward over the desk. "Mother accuses me of having encouraged Jason, and claims I should spend all my time looking for him. You want me to bribe officials. You all ask too much of me."

Filia laughed, and patted my shoulder. "That's your role in the family. It always has been. You can't shirk your duties. You're the clever one, with your scribal training, living in the palace, rubbing elbows with the priest-king's high officials."

"I refuse to be constantly taken advantage of," I said, but I sensed that she was breaking my resolve, as she usually managed to do.

"Sit down, brother. It isn't good for you to get so riled up." She gave me that smile again, and I groaned. "I'll leave you to your tax-payers. Think about it. Promise me you will."

The argument continued, off and on, for days. Filia was not one to give up when she decided she wanted something, or someone. She needed my help, or else she wouldn't have bothered to come to me.

I eventually discovered a compelling reason for her new enthusiasm—a man, as usual. I saw them together, and recognized her new passion. He was the bull-leaper, Charybdis, a veteran of the bull-arena, almost four years older than Filia.

I confronted her, desperate to force some sense into her head. "What do you hope to accomplish? I know about Charybdis."

"Yes—so?"

"Do you think it'll be easier to gain his attention by making a fool of yourself in the bull-arena? And what of his vow of chastity?"

"I want to share my life with the man I love. We will remain pure."

I didn't believe a word of that, but held my tongue. If I had laughed, she would have probably struck me.

As usual, the family left Filia to me. I dared not bring the problem to my mother. And Kadmus was at sea, on a trading voyage with my father, not that either of them had much influence with Filia.

My father and brother had sailed five months earlier for Africa. Their trading voyage would take them to Lybia, Egypt, Palestine, Syria, Rhodes, Greece and a dozen of Crete's island colonies, ending with Thera where Kadmus vowed to look for Jason and Nephele. If all went well, they would return to Crete with their ship loaded with commodities worth considerably more than the cargo they departed with a half a year before. Jason used to sail with them, before he discovered Nephele. I did too, before I entered scribal school, but I hated the sea, the sickness never leaving me.

Kadmus had built a large villa near the sea, ten miles from Knossos, a few minutes away from the port at Amnisos. It needed to be large. My father and mother lived with them, my mother helping care for Kadmus's eight children. His wife Omphale needed the help.

Filia, of course, had moved out long ago. Now, alas, she lived with Sirena and me, and our two children, Lelia and Lethe—soon to be three—in our palace apartment.

2

Rasmus and Kadmus were three weeks overdue. This was not unusual, considering the uncertainties in the weather, and the difficulties in dealing with foreign trade officials. In Egypt, officials could be diabolical, Pharaoh Tuthmosis III's vizier personally reviewing every transaction. Cretan traders had almost no one to compete with, accept each other, so perhaps the Pharaoh had good reason to take care.

Crete and Egypt would have both suffered if trade had ceased. Crete would have had to seek other outlets for its surplus olives and olive oil, grapes and wine, cedar and cypress wood, pottery and wool cloth. And Crete's luxury minded aristocracy would have had to do without Egyptian ivory, gold, and alabaster. Without a ready source of papyrus, I would have had to go back to making marks in clay.

Weather, in the eastern Mediterranean, was less certain than profits, even in the spring and summer. Storms could arise unexpectedly to engulf ships in towering waves and screaming winds. No ship in the world could match a Cretan trader for seaworthiness, even the famous Phoenician coastal sailors. Yet, every year, tragedy struck one or two Cretan traders, unable to avoid a sudden storm.

When my mother and sister-in-law came to me with their worries, I told them that business had probably delayed their husbands on Thera. I didn't say that they were looking for Jason and Nephele. I didn't want to give my mother false hopes, or restart that argument.

"I'm certain they've halted at Akroteri," I said. "They like to fill up any remaining room on their ships with pottery. You know how father is." Akroteri was famous for its pottery, made from the fine volcanic clays locally available.

"It's been too long," Megara said, Omphale nodding worriedly.

"They were gone longer last year."

"This is different," Omphale said. "I've had dreams. Crazy things, which I can't interpret."

"And I too," Megara said, not to be left out.

As it turned out, their forebodings were justified, but in an unexpected way. Zeus did give us some strong hints, most notably in the smoke and fire that frequently billowed from Thera's volcanic peak. Theran natives believed the island's fiery summit was the throne of gods and reverently interpreted every rumbling utterance it made. Centuries ago, they had built a pathway to the top, an amazing engineering feat. I had climbed it, on several occasions. It was impossible to remain long at the summit when Thera's gods were speaking. The smoke and heat could overpower the inattentive climber in seconds.

The frequency and strength of Thera's eruptions noticeably increased shortly before we moved to Crete, more than a decade ago. Occasional explosions deep in the earth began to shake the island and knock down a few of the weaker buildings. It was no longer unusual to see Thera's cloudy expulsions from Crete's higher mountain shrines. But since it had gone on so long, everyone grew used to the occasional inconvenience. Most people ignored the religious fanatics who predicted that the volcano would soon erupt to punish its inhabitants for their lax religious behavior. I have always wondered whether my father had taken these warnings to heart when he dragged his family to Crete.

3

I finally gave in to Filia and agreed to talk to the palace priest in charge of the bull-leaping rituals. Sirena thought I was crazy, and said so.

"You continually give in to everything she asks for," she said, her hands resting on the vast bulge of her pregnancy.

"She wears me out. All you women do," I said.

Sirena gave me a hard, serious look. "It's too dangerous. Your mother will be furious with you. A bull-leaper was killed last year, another crippled for life. Is that what you want for your sister?"

"I've had all this argument with her. Let it be."

"You don't have to try so hard to get the priest's permission. After all, he has a reason to deny her."

"You and I, and Filia, are the only ones who know about the abortion. Are you suggesting I tell him?"

"Isn't it your duty?"

I had thought about that already. The bull-leaping ritual, with ancient origins, steeped in deep religious significance, had gradually changed over the years. Less a religious rite, it had become largely a sporting event, a demonstration of prowess. The crowds that lined the bull-arena loved the danger, the thrill of a flawless performance, the horror of the occasional accident, and idolized leading bull-leapers. The most skillful bull-leapers became celebrities, and grew rich from their exploits, mainly through gifts from Crete's nobility, though the priests frowned on this. Despite their solemn vows of chastity, made in the presence of the gods, many bull-leapers were no more pure than the rest of us. Some bull-leapers even secretly married and lived together, though outwardly they kept up the myth of virginal purity.

"It no longer matters," I said, and gave Sirena a look that said the matter was closed.

"I think you're wrong about that," she said. "You and Filia will have to learn the hard way." I could never get in the last word with her.

Sirena was six months pregnant, and did not enjoy it. She hated her bulbous and unwieldy body. Sirena had been, and still thought of herself as a sacred grove dancer. She wanted to dance again. I loathed the thought of it, for I remembered how it was before. Too many times, I had had to endure men scrutinizing her near naked body as she danced past them, each of them hoping desperately to find her alone after the event. I always had to make sure that I came to her first. It was nerve-racking, because I didn't always manage it.

But I could not hope to keep her from dancing. It was an essential part of Sirena's life before I married her, and it would continue to be until she was too old to participate. Almost all aspects of religion were demonstrative, reflecting an all-pervasive and ever-growing desire for active, physical displays of piety. Most involved dancing in one form or another, but even gymnastic performances had religious connotations. People of all ages took pilgrimages to the cave shrines that dotted the mountains, where natural stalagmite formations had sacred meanings as fertility symbols. Pilgrims brought votive offerings, or animals for sacrifice. Music and dancing always accompanied the rituals. Most remote of all were the shrines set on mountain peaks, the strenuous climb itself inherently ritualistic. In the palace's Pillar Shrines, a symbolic mimicry of sacred stalagmite caves, priestesses gyrated with snakes wrapped around their waists and shoulders, as priests anointed the fluted columns with oil.

Yet, the most visually alluring of these rituals was the grove dance, which I both dreaded, and adored. Women, some of them young girls just past puberty, danced amid ancient gnarled olive trees, eyes glazed in a trance brought on by the extract from the poppy plant. There was something magical about it, something unworldly, so startling was the contrast between the rough, twisted, grotesque trunks of the olive trees, and the lithe, smooth beauty of the dancers, clothed only in a wisp of thin cloth at their waist. This was what Sirena had a passion for, and how we met. Now I wished she would give it up.

I talked to the priest, and chief trainer, and readily convinced them to accept my sister, once I assured them that she was serious, and would not give up and change her mind, as she was prone to do. They knew her reputation. They also knew that she was one of the most beautiful women in Knossos, with the strong legs and slim, narrow-waisted build of a bull-leaper, though just a little too tall. They could not resist the chance to see her in the bull-ring. Filia was elated, but did her best to make me worried.

"Thank you, Abderus. I knew you wouldn't fail me. You never do." She came around the desk and embraced me from behind as I slumped, dejected over my tax-rolls.

"I'll worry about you, and mother will be furious with me if she finds out what I've done to get you installed," I said.

"You must not tell her."

"I won't, but she'll eventually have to find out."

"When I'm performing for the first time, she can come," she said.

"Behave yourself with Charybdis, or you'll never perform."

Though she was behind me, I knew she was smiling. "Of course, brother. I'll make you proud of your little sister."

4

My father and brother returned two months later. Kadmus came immediately to see me. He found me, as usual in my palace office, bent wearily over official records. He was thinner, and his face showed even more lines and creases. He looked in good spirits, but something clearly troubled him, something I had no doubt he would soon unload on my shoulders. We went out onto the Central Court where we could move about in relative privacy while we talked. It was early morning. The sun illuminated only the palace's western facade, its balconies tinged a reddish brown. We had the courtyard almost to ourselves, unlike later in the day, when visitors would swarm into the Palace of Knossos to gawk at its wonders. A few gymnasts practiced towards the far end. An artist and his two assistants refurbished a fresco adjacent to the entrance to a Pillar Shrine.

"It's good to return to Crete," Kadmus said.

"What delayed you?" I said, sensing that he was troubled about telling me something.

"We stayed six weeks on Thera."

"Why so long? Did you find them?"

He looked around, as if to see if anyone could overhear us. "That's what I need to talk to you about. We did find Jason. We ran into him in the market place at Akroteri."

I grabbed his arm. "That's wonderful. Why didn't you say so right away? Did you talk to him? Was Nephele with him?"

"Of course I talked to him. I wasn't about to let him get away again. He was alone, but we later went to his house on the hillside above the town. Nephele was there, and nearly as large as Sirena."

"He doesn't care if someone recognizes him, or Nephele?"

"What difference does it make if he never comes back to Crete?"

"He is still officially accused of abducting Nephele," I said.

Kadmus shrugged. "I told Jason that. He doesn't care."

"He is content, then? And happy to soon be a father?" I said.

"He seemed so. Jason works in a pottery factory. He does excellent work. I brought back several of his creations. They should sell well."

"So they'll remain on Thera."

"What choice do they have?"

We passed in front of the Grand Staircase that led up to the royal apartments. A lone servant was on his knees scrubbing the steps clean. It was a thankless job, taking many hours, and needing repetition every week or so. It reminded me of my own job, often just as monotonous, and also repeated endlessly.

"They could probably live in Phaistos," I said.

Phaistos was an independent city-state on Crete's southern coast, safely separated from Knossos by mountains. The two cities were friendly rivals.

"Perhaps," Kadmus said.

"Phaistos is the most beautiful city on Crete," I said, as if trying to sell Kadmus on the idea of moving there.

While Crete's northern coast offered many good harbors and landing beaches, the southern coast presented mostly a harsh face to seafarers, with imposing chalk cliffs that plunged into the sea, and few places to land a ship. But Phaistos, precariously perched on one of those cliffs, at the end of a ridge, occupied a site of incredible beauty, something the citizens of Phaistos constantly reminded visitors, especially those from Knossos.

"As they are both artists, Phaistos would be perfect for them," I said, becoming more and more convinced that my idea was good. "Did you say anything to them?"

Kadmus let out a sigh. "It was difficult. Father was angry, as you might expect. I had to get Jason alone. And then, when I suggested he come back, he got angry with me, reminding me that I hadn't stepped forward to help him when he was trying to find a way to entice Nephele away from bull-leaping."

"I'm not surprised. I suppose I'll have to go there and try to talk to him. Eventually."

"You'd better go soon," Kadmus said. "The mountain spoke to us again, while we were there."

"I know. Mother was worried. A priest returning from Mt. Ida told her he saw a larger than usual cloud hanging over Thera. And she has had dreams about it, which she takes seriously."

Kadmus laughed. "It was mostly smoke, some fiery emissions, and an ominous rumbling sound. A series of earthquakes kept our nerves on edge. Several houses in Akroteri collapsed. Not Jason's. He built it himself, with wood to reinforce the brickwork."

"It was that bad?"

"Jason wasn't concerned, but we had people clamoring to buy passage with us back to Crete. I think you should go there soon and have a talk with him. He'll only listen to you."

"I can't get away. This is tax season."

"I'll take you there myself."

"I'll have to think about it," I said.

Our talk turned to other things as I brought him up to date, the announcement about Filia saved until last. Kadmus didn't show as much surprise as I thought he would.

"She'll either kill herself, or become Crete's most famous, and richest bull-leaper," Kadmus said. "Does mother know? She didn't say anything."

"I haven't told her yet. I want to wait until Filia has completed her training. Maybe she'll fail, or quit."

Kadmus shook his head. "Mother will be furious with you for not telling her, but that's your problem. What about father?"

"Don't tell him yet."

"Has Filia begun to practice?"

"She's well into it. No sign that she's ready to give up. Not as long as Charybdis is with her."

I shouldn't have said that. Kadmus's face slowly grew red. "She makes me furious. There's always a man involved. I should have guessed, as soon as you mentioned it. How can she do this to us, to the family?"

"What do you mean to us, the family? It's me that she does it to. I have to deal with her, help her, get her out of her difficulties. You won't have anything to do with her. You even drove her out of your house, and into mine."

"She left of her own volition. She could have stayed."

"And taken abuse, every day."

Kadmus turned to face me, taking my arm. "I can see why she always comes to you for help. You're soft. You give in to everyone. How did she get approval from the head priest, and the trainer? That must have been your doing, also."

I shook my arm free. "Let's not argue over her. She would've found a way, whatever I said or did. You know that."

"This is not going to turn out well. First Jason, and now Filia is going to bring disgrace to the family."

I stared at him for a moment, shaking my head wearily. "I have to get back. This is a waste of time."

I expected him to follow me, but he didn't.

5

I went to watch Filia practice whenever I could get away from my endless tax rolls. That's where I first saw Germaine, though I didn't know her name at the time. I often allowed Lelia and Lethe to come along. They constantly clamored to see their aunt Filia practice with the bulls. Filia and the other noviciates trained in the bull-arena to the south of the palace. I usually watched from one of the lower palace verandahs. Lelia and Lethe always insisted on going down to the fence surrounding the arena where they could see better. Filia would usually come over to talk to them. Predictably, the kids both decided they would become bull-leapers when they were older.

From a distance, even from the arena fence, it was impossible to tell that she was three to four years older than the other noviciates. They wore the same short kilt, split at the side to the waist, boys and girls, and nothing more. The wide belt, almost a corset, made their waists seem unusually slender. It also helped protect their back from injury. They all had similar body shapes, as if formed in the same mold—slim, with long springy legs, narrow waist and, if females, small breasts. From a distance it was not easy to tell boys from girls. However, I could pick out Filia right away. She was half a head taller than the rest.

Filia first practiced on a fixed vaulting platform. When she mastered this she would progress to live bulls. The first bulls would be tethered with their heads tied down to keep their horns steady. They were trained to put up with such indignity. Eventually, in several months, maybe as long as a year, Filia would be ready to take on an untethered, but highly docile and dependable bull. Many would drop out before they reached this stage. Yet this was mere play compared to the real thing, when bull-leapers faced a wild bull's untamed fury.

The highly skilled hunters that captured those bulls took almost as much risk as the bull-leapers. They worked in teams of ten, and used huge nets to tangle the bull and bring him down without injuring him. Most of the injuries to the hunters came when they subdued the struggling animal. Hooves and horns flailed about with deadly force as brave men scrambled and dodged to hobble the bull. A horn raked across a hunter's midsection could easily cost the man his life.

The kids and I one day watched the noviciates practice for a while, vaulting over a platform about the shape and height of a bull's back. Filia waved to us, the children jumping up and down excitedly. She seemed to have no trouble getting over the platform. After an hour, the trainer called for a break, and his two assistants brought out a pair of bull horns to attach to the platform.

Filia grabbed Charybdis's hand and ran towards us. Charybdis seemed to always be there when Filia practiced, helping out in one way or another. He would pull her aside to whisper instructions. He would applaud her successes, and console her when she had trouble with a new exercise. He sometimes demonstrated the proper form. Charybdis helped others too, but it was obvious to any observer that he took a special interest in Filia.

My sister's body gleamed with the water she had drained over her head after the strenuous workout on the vaulting platform. It ran down between her breasts and darkened her practice kilt, making her look amazingly desirable. How could Charybdis resist her?

"You are doing well, it appears," I said, meaning it.

"Thank you, brother," she said, a little breathlessly.

She knelt down to kiss Lelia and Lethe through the fence rails, making them giggle, then gave me a sisterly hug. She leaned sideways on the rail of the bull-arena fence and took a deep breath, clearly satisfied with herself. Charybdis wrapped his arms around her waist, his hands clasped together over her lower belly. He looked thoroughly besotted.

"It's easy for me," Filia said. "In six months you'll see me per-form, with Charybdis. We'll be a team."

I almost said I thought they looked as if they already performed together, but resisted. "You'll make a good team," I said instead.

Filia smiled. "He has helped me a great deal."

They made a striking couple—young, healthy, with figures every Cretan would envy. They could be models for the fresco painters. Their hair was dark, long, curled, over the ears. Charybdis was deeply tanned, almost as dark as an Egyptian, a little shorter than Filia. She was light-skinned, signifying a life protected from the sun's burning.

"You haven't told mother about this," Filia said.

I smiled. "About you and Charybdis?"

"About the bull-leaping."

She glanced at Charybdis, who looked past me, trying to stay aloof from the conversation between brother and sister. Filia must have told him all about me, probably describing my cranky sarcasm, infatua-tion with words, and otherwise lovable disposition.

"As you wished, I haven't told her or father. I did tell Kadmus."

She made a face, and I turned to Charybdis. "She knows her older brother wouldn't approve."

"He's old fashioned," Filia said, looking at Charybdis.

He leaned towards her and mumbled something to her that I couldn't hear. She laughed, covering her mouth with her hands. A blush spread over her face.

That's the moment I saw Germaine, walking along the fence to-wards us, stopping about thirty paces away, watching us. I saw her over Filia's shoulder. She didn't see Germaine, but Charybdis did. I noticed him stiffen, and frown.

I don't know how to describe this female apparition. I had never seen such a woman as her before, even during the year I was at sea with my father. She had a tall, well-formed, muscular body, skin the color of bleached sand, and golden hair that flashed a myriad of shades as she swung her head. She wore the dress of an aristocrat, with her left breast and shoulder exposed, and her arms and neck richly bejew-eled. Oddly, her feet were bare.

Charybdis whispered something else to Filia and moved away from her. Filia turned to see the woman, and gasped. Charybdis walked slowly along the inside of the fence until he was opposite the woman. I could hear Filia breathing rapidly. I saw her white knuckles where she gripped the rail, but only momentarily, for I could not take my eyes off the woman, who leaned on the rail, waiting. Charybdis stopped next to her. I saw the woman smile at something he said.

"Who is that?" Filia said.

"I've never seen her before," I said.

Filia began to walk along the fence towards them. Then the trainer called her back. Charybdis stayed with the woman. They acted like old friends, or something more.

I turned away to watch the noviciates. A bull-leaper demonstrated what they next needed to practice. Trainers had attached the bull horns to one end of the vaulting platform, giving it the crude appearance of a small bull. The bull-leaper ran towards the horned end of the platform, grabbed the horns, and rolled a somersault onto the back of the platform. It looked easy, nothing like the midair flip they would eventually learn, performed over a live bull free to toss his horns at his whim.

Filia kept glancing back at Charybdis and the strange woman. I began to worry. I knew her anger. She was the third to try the new maneuver, the first two noviciates managing the roll without too much difficulty. The trainers kept them from falling. Filia wasn't so fortunate. She grabbed the horns and tucked her head to roll, getting a good push from her strong legs. Then something went wrong. Her legs swung to one side, as if she had lost her balance. She slammed to the ground with a yelp of surprise, sliding off the platform too quickly for the trainer to break her fall.

Filia lay on her back, not moving, except for her head that rocked back and forth, as the trainers gathered around her. Lelia and Lethe were yelling beside me, clamoring for me to do something. I leaned down and ducked under the fence rail and ran towards the circle forming around Filia. Lelia and Lethe followed me.

Hearing the commotion, Charybdis turned away from the mysterious woman and ran to join the crowd surrounding Filia. She struggled to her feet just as we both got there.

"Are you all right?" I said, but she didn't hear me, or notice me. She was busy staring angrily at Charybdis, as if it was his fault that she had fallen.

Charybdis and one of the trainers started to lead her away. She shook free of them, and turned back to the platform to try again. Charybdis went after her, grabbing her arm.

"Wait until you recover," Charybdis said.

"I'll do it now," Filia said.

"You're shaken up. Your back may be injured," he said. "There's no need—"

"Its fine. Leave me alone." She caught sight of me approaching. "Tell him to let me be," she said to me.

"Maybe you should listen to him," I said.

Filia yanked her arm away from Charybdis. "If you'd been here, instead of with that woman—"

"You're blaming me for your carelessness?" he said.

"Who is she?"

"Her name is Germaine. She's a friend."

"I'm sure she is."

Filia shoved him away and ran to the platform. She hesitated for a time, rubbing her back. Charybdis walked towards her. She waved him away. The trainer went to talk to her. She nodded her head. He said something more and then went to the platform to protect her against another fall. Filia ran slowly toward the platform, grabbed the horns and rolled onto the back without trouble. The vault was almost perfect. But afterward I saw the pain register on her face, and saw the way she kneaded her back with her fist. When Charybdis approached her, she turned and walked away.

I was proud of my sister, but had no opportunity to tell her. A messenger arrived to inform me in an overly excited way that Sirena's time had come. I grabbed Lelia's and Lethe's hands and dragged them along the fence toward the path leading up to the palace, shouting at Filia as I came near her.

"Sirena's having the baby."

She laughed and shouted for me to hurry. Everyone clapped.

6

With the help of a servant, Sirena had made her way to the Pillar Shrine, in the west wing of the palace. Peasants, if they could manage, climbed to nearby cave shrines to have their babies under the watchful eyes of the gods. After I arrived, a priest poured a libation of the purest olive oil on the central pillar, where it ran down grooves carved in the sides. Sirena lay on a wood-framed leather cot under a light wool blanket. She smiled a welcome.

"Are you all right?" I said.

"Fine."

"Can I get you something?"

Sirena grimaced and held her breath, gripping the side of her bed. I moved towards her. She violently shook her head.

"Is it time? Is it coming?" I said, trying to sound calm.

"Go away, Abderus. It'll take hours. I don't want you to hear me scream, and call you names I'll later regret."

"I should stay."

"Go. Please."

"Are you sure?" I said, rather more hopefully than I should have.

She waved her hand dismissively. I leaned over her and kissed her forehead and ran out of the Pillar Shrine, guiltily relieved. It had been exactly the same with the first two children. This time, however, I should have remained with her, or hidden outside the shrine in the palace courtyard and listened to the music of her screams. How different the future would have been if I had.

With no purpose in mind, I let my feet move of their own volition, my thoughts adrift, in a turmoil, looking for an escape, any sort of distraction. For the next hour or so I wandered about the palace, down halls, through courtyards, past reception rooms. I halted briefly at different shrines to make devotions, thinking they might help ease Sirena's pain. I intruded on artisans I knew, at work, until they nudged me on my way. I paused for a time on a verandah where I could stare at Mt. Ida, home of Zeus. Disturbing thoughts entered my head. Was the remote god really looking after my wife? Did he care what happened to her? I shivered and hurried back past the Great Hall and the Tri-Column Shrine to the corridor that led to our apartment. I wanted to rid myself of such thoughts, so I went to check on Lelia and Lethe.

The birth seemed to be taking longer than before, but I had no real sense of time. I should have repeated my steps around the palace, or sat with Lelia and Lethe. Instead I left the palace, exiting through the main entrance to the west. I found the West Court surprisingly crowded. People waited for a performance of some sort in the L-shaped Amphitheater to the north of the court. Dancers, or possibly a boxing match, I thought. Wrestling and gymnastics were also popular. I wandered closer, curious, welcoming the possibility of distraction.

Two hundred or so people crowded the amphitheater tiers. The overflow stood in the West Court and along the adjacent Royal Road that led to the King's Summer Palace. I had difficulty getting near enough to see anything, until someone pulled away and I managed to scramble into the opening. Gymnasts were performing.

Cretan gymnasts performed feats seldom seen anywhere else in the world. Their bodies were so perfectly formed, so graceful of movement, that to merely watch them walk onto the stage was a pleasure. I watched for more than an hour, a fortuitous diversion from worry. The performers were good, but not exceptional. Sirena had once been a gymnast, before turning to grove dancing, as skilled as any that performed that day, except the last. It became immediately clear why the audience was so large, for what had been an ordinary afternoon performance.

The audience fell strangely silent when the last gymnast, a female, walked—floated would better reveal her motion—onto the stage. Her appearance could only be described as shocking, for the uninitiated.

She had discarded the gymnast's short kilt. Her pale body, completely devoid of hair, glowed with an oily sheen. Her stark nudity oddly made her seem less an erotic symbol. She seemed pure, barely human, a character of mythology. She captured the crowd's attention so completely that the priest-king himself could have walked across the stage unnoticed. I'm ashamed to report that I instantly forgot about Sirena and her suffering.

I didn't recognize the gymnast at first. Then she twirled in an opening movement, her long golden hair flying out like a fishing net tossed onto the sea, and I remembered. It was Germaine, Charybdis's friend and Filia's nemesis.

Her performance differed from the other gymnasts, less wildly exuberant, more controlled. She combined flexibility and strength to bend and move in astonishing ways. She sometimes held agonizing, impossible poses for a half-minute or longer, every muscle still, seeming not to breathe, or even blink, frozen like a golden statue, her image forever engraved in every viewer's memory. Everyone seemed to hold their breath. It was not a long performance, but the audience probably could not have endured longer, the tension so great.

She finished with what I learned later was her specialty. Almost too painful to watch, she slowly bent backward, farther and farther, her back bowed in an impossible way, until her finger tips and then hands gently touched the pavement behind her. She formed a perfect half-circle, like the entrance to a cave shrine. Her golden hair lightly caressed the pavement. Seconds passed and she didn't move a muscle, and didn't seem to breathe. Then she moved and the spectators gasped, though most probably knew what to expect.

She moved lithely across the stage while bent in a circle, on toes and fingertips, like some sort of spidery animal, slow at first, then fast, first to one side of the stage then to the other, giving everyone a momentary upside-down stare. I felt her eyes touch mine for a fraction of a second as her gaze swept my section of the audience. I shivered. I did not believe she could be entirely human.

I turned back to the palace after the performance ended, immediately remembered Sirena, and felt guilty. I thought of her unheard cries and how I had forgotten her suffering while I savored the golden-haired gymnast's performance. Starting back, I shivered with apprehension. At the entrance I turned around without thinking and looked back. I don't know why. Perhaps some malicious goddess took a hand in my fate.

Germaine stood no more than fifteen feet away, talking to someone, perhaps her trainer. She had a skirt wrapped around her waist. Unconsciously, she ran a hand from her neck, over a breast and down to her belly. She looked at me for a second, then away. I turned and ran into the palace.

Sirena presented me with my second son. He was crying mightily when I saw him for the first time, cradled in his mother's arms. I looked questioningly at her.

"He's healthy," she said.

I sighed with relief. "And you?"

"I'm fine."

"You're wonderful," I said, and kissed her.

We named the boy Hephaestus, after an obscure god. By then I had forgotten the golden-haired gymnast.

7

Strangely, it was Kadmus that brought Germaine back into my thoughts. A few weeks after Hephaestus's birth, I met Kadmus accidentally in the city where we both went to get our hair trimmed. That was the one exceptional situation in which Cretan men were prone to gossip. Somehow, sitting around idly with a woman cutting away at their hair made even the quietest of men loquacious.

"Have you heard the story about that new dancer?" Kadmus said.

"What new dancer?"

"The one from the northern mainland. Germaine they call her."

"Keep your head still, please," the woman behind me said.

"What about her?" I said, the memories of the day of Hephaestus's birth filling my head, one image dominating all others—Germaine bent over backwards, staring at me for an instant

"Her story is remarkable," Kadmus said.

I closed my eyes and listened as my brother explained what he had heard about Germaine's origins. She apparently came from a wild and primitive land of forests and rivers to the northeast of the Aegean world, a place where civilization had not yet reached. A trader in copper brought her to Crete. He had found her in Cilicia, a slave to some local official. The trader bought her, taking pity on her sad plight and apparently as enamored of her unusual beauty as everyone else. He naturally freed her when he returned to Crete, where he could not keep a slave. She lived with the trader and his wife, treated like a daughter. They soon discovered her amazing athletic abilities, and introduced her to a gymnastic trainer.

"I'm surprised you've never heard of her," Kadmus said. "Everyone is talking about her."

"I've been working hard lately. And with Hephaestus only weeks old, Sirena and I don't manage get out much."

"If you hear that Germaine is going to dance again, let me know," Kadmus said.

I did find out when and where Germaine would perform, and made sure I was in the audience, but I neglected to tell Kadmus. I never grew tired of watching her. I was dangerously susceptible to the distractions of the human form, when it existed in such utter perfection, a beauty unmatched by any other object in nature. She was that. I was stricken, and she began to fill my dreams, day and night.

I also continued to see Germaine at the bull-arena. She never stayed long, always grabbing Charybdis's attention for a short time, making Filia's face darken with confused anger. Filia and Charybdis argued about it. It affected Filia's performance. At least that's what she claimed, focusing her complaints on me.

"He won't tell me why she comes," Filia said.

"Why not?"

"I don't know. Every time she's here, I have trouble. I fall, and make a fool of myself. She's a sorceress."

It was not just Filia. Everyone seemed nervous when Germaine made her appearance. They all knew who she was. A tense stillness would settle on the bull-arena, and even the skies seemed to change, the sunlight more intense. Filia had trouble doing vaults that before were easy for her. I watched her fall too often, and noticed the trainers talking to each other, but Filia refused to give up, bruise marks beginning to overlap on her chest, back and legs.

"Are you sure?" I said to her.

"About what?"

"You know. You look as if you've fallen down the side of Mt. Ida."

"It's her fault."

"He still won't tell you anything?"

Filia shrugged and rubbed the elbow that she had just scraped along the side of a horn, lucky to have only a minor injury. "He just says she's a friend of the family, but I know there's more."

Something else was happening to make the weeks and months after the birth of Hephaestus foreboding. The skies to the north, over Thera, increasingly displayed the fiery emanations of the island's unique population of deities. Small earthquakes rumbled through Knossos every few days, causing little damage, except to unnerve the population, always wary of the next disaster. My father and brother left on another extended trading voyage. Kadmus came to me before he sailed, on a day that we could see the cloud over Thera even from Knossos. Minutes after, another earthquake left people standing in clusters, whispering lest the gods hear their fear.

"This is serious, Abderus. You know what they're saying."

"About the warnings?" I said.

"We have to get Jason and Nephele off that island."

"These eruptions have happened before. I can't remember when we haven't—"

"Not like now. Why won't you come with us? I could drop you off on Thera. Jason will listen to you."

"We've talked about this before. I can't leave now at the height of the tax season. And Hephaestus is only two months old. Sirena hasn't been well."

Shortly after that, Germaine ceased to come to the bull-arena. She also ceased all performances in the West Court. She vanished from public view. I discreetly asked about her, but could get no answers, even from the trader and his wife that she had lived with when she first came to Crete. I was certain that Charybdis knew where she was, and what had happened to her, for he didn't look surprised when she no longer came to the bull-arena. When I asked him, he only shrugged.

Filia immediately came out of her trance. She began to vault with new enthusiasm, and the trainers no longer whispered together. Instead they applauded. The sense of doom lifted. Even the skies cleared and the earth fell still as the gods on Thera seemed to follow Germaine into an unknown exile.

The gods like to mislead us.

8

Filia looked happier than I'd ever seen her. She showed no signs of nervousness or fear, though she was about to attempt her first vault over a wild, untethered bull. This was still practice, but the word had spread and a large crowd gathered around the bull-arena fence. Filia had finally told her mother and father. They stood beside Sirena and I, silently angry that I had not told them sooner of Filia's new infatuation. Megara looked worried. Rasmus kept shaking his head.

Hephaestus stayed with his nurse, but Lelia and Lethe stood near us, next to the rail, excited to see their aunt perform. When Filia and Charybdis walked into the arena, Lelia and Lethe called out to them, much to Filia's delighted embarrassment.

After the trainer left the arena, and Filia and Charybdis had moved beyond the fence, the audience grew quiet in anticipation, all eyes on the gates to the holding pens. We could hear the handlers' shouts, the bull's accompanying grunts and snorts, furious at his confinement. A gate opened and Filia's bull charged into the arena. The audience gasped though everyone knew what to expect. Those near the suddenly flimsy-looking arena fence involuntarily edged back, us among them. Lelia and Lethe clung to my legs.

The bull charged around the arena in search of a way to escape, eyes ablaze, his senses fouled with human smells and sounds. It was as if distant memories of the rocky hills where he had been king were driving him to fury. Only weeks before, he had roamed free in his domain, unchallenged, except by other bulls. No one could doubt that he was as wild as the day the hunters captured him. Handlers had not limited in any way his freedom of movement. Nor had they dulled his three-foot wide horns. The crowd chanted their approval.

I heard my mother talk to herself, behind me. "Why must she do this? It's insane. She is too old. I don't think I can look. I shouldn't have come." She fell silent when Rasmus nudged her.

I felt equally nervous, although I had seen Filia's skill in practice sessions. Anything could happen, even to the most skilled bull-leapers.

Few completed their short careers without injury. Seldom did a year pass without a death in the arena.

The bull's wild initial charge eventually withered. This always happened. After a time, that varied greatly from one bull to another—a measure of their prowess, and danger—the bull would dimly realize there was no obvious escape from the hated two-footed creatures that had captured him. He would stop and snort and paw at the ground. It was as if the bull was planning and dreaming of revenge, should he ever get the opportunity. Soon he would. Those initial wild moments seemed to take forever with Filia's bull, and my anxiety increased. When he finally slowed to a walk, Filia and Charybdis returned to the arena.

The contest of wills began, the bull-leaper's grace and athletic skills pitted against the bull's savage power. Words cannot adequately describe this encounter. The daring and beauty, the harmony of action, the seeming cooperation between human and bull, shocking in its intensity, invariably left everyone drained.

Filia and Charybdis wore identical, short, brightly colored kilts, complete with codpiece, even Filia, a tradition reflecting the virginal, asexual character of the fertility rites. The audience knew what to expect, but Lelia did not.

"Look at what Filia is wearing," she said, in a remarkably loud voice. "Has she grown a penis?"

It did break the tension, as those who heard burst into laughter. I picked Lelia up and put my hand gently over her mouth.

"It's just a costume, Lelia. You must remain quiet now, so you don't bother aunt Filia."

Filia and Charybdis worked as a team. Charybdis began to circle closer to the bull to distract the animal, to induce it to stand still. Filia watched carefully. She studied the bull as Charybdis moved slowly into position facing the animal. The bull unusually nervous, kept shifting its head back and forth. Whenever Charybdis got too close, it charged. He expected that, but that didn't make it any less dangerous. His only means to escape was to wait until the last moment and then leap to the side as the bull brushed past him. His timing had to be perfect. Too soon, and the bull could follow him to the side. Too late, and the horn would catch an arm, or thigh as the bull swept by.

The quickness of the bull's first charge apparently took Charybdis by surprise. He waited an instant too long. The bull's horn tore a piece of his kilt away and left a bloody welt on his hip. The crowd gasped, sensing that this might not be an ordinary first vault. Charybdis never glanced at his injury. He returned immediately to stalking the bull. The next time the bull charged he was ready and his timing was perfect. The game kept on for an inordinately long time, until finally the bull grew tired of this frustrating contest and came to a halt. It was Filia's time. I found it hard to breathe.

She walked slowly toward the bull's lowered horns, eyes locked with his. He did not let her get as close as she needed before he again charged, sensing a new antagonist. She scrambled out of the way, but I could see the surprised look on her face. Filia again slowly approached the bull, and again he charged before she got close enough to begin her run. This happened five times with Filia, everyone in the crowd seeming to count the charges, a measure of the bull's tenacity. Each time, the tension rose, in and out of the ring. Each time she stepped aside at the last second, hardly moving, the horns brushing past her waist. On the third charge the bull left a scrape mark just above her kilt. She looked down at it, and then over to where Charybdis watched, as if to say that now she too was marked by the bull.

Finally the bull waited, curious, attentive, filled with explosive energy, at rest for a dozen seconds. Filia moved closer, rising up on her toes with each step, eyes fixed on the bull, as if she could mesmerize it into cooperation. Twenty yards away, the bull's horns lowered, a second away from a charge. Filia cried out something, a primeval animal sound that brought chills to the crowd though they had surely expected it. Lelia wrapped her arms around my neck. Lethe grabbed my leg and began to whimper. The bull froze with the sound. Filia broke into a sprint. Everything suddenly happened with violent speed, yet the next three seconds seemed to take an eternity.

Sunlight flashed on Filia's powerful and beautifully sculpted legs. Her long strides accelerated to a headlong, seemingly uncontrolled dash. The bull, momentarily mesmerized, lowered his head farther and pawed a front hoof. Unknowingly, he was ready to play his assigned role in the momentary fusion of bull-leaper and bull.

At what seemed certainly too soon, even for those who had seen a hundred bull-leaps, Filia left her feet in a high-arched, head first dive toward the waiting bull's horns.

I was afraid she had made a mistake. I tensed for disaster.

Arms outstretched, Filia managed to just reach and grasp the bull's horns. She curled her body and pushed off at the instant the bull violently lifted his head. The bull tossed her ten feet in the air where she spun in a somersault.

Filia's timing was perfect. But her landing on the bull's back was not quite as perfect.

Her left foot slid off the side.

I was sure she would fall beneath the hooves of the enraged bull. The crowd gasped as Filia struggled to stay on the bull's back. Charybdis raced out, prepared to distract the bull if she fell.

Filia's other foot slipped, and she fell to her knee, grasping at the bull's rough hide, trying to get a grip, slowly slipping.

The bull swung around in a circle, frantic to reach the creature clinging to his back.

The trainer shouted. The crowd began to cheer Filia's determination.

The bull gave a sudden lurch to the side where Filia had slipped. If she had fallen then, the bull would have trampled her. But she harnessed the movement, as she had the bull's head toss, to scramble back on top.

In an instant she was on her feet, her face radiant, hair swinging wildly about her head, sweat from the bull smeared over her breasts and thighs, deliriously happy.

Filia stretched tall, arms raised to the heavens, as the bull shook his head and the crowd cheered and pounded their feet. Tears streamed down Sirena's face and Lelia cried out because I held her too tightly. I heard my mother ask my father if it was safe to look now. Filia did a flip off the bull's back and ran to embrace Charybdis.

As if she had reached too close to the gods with her effort, the ground shook in another earthquake, the strongest yet.

9

Unfortunately for bull-leapers, Cretan bulls sometimes failed to cooperate. Even a slight twist of the head at the wrong moment, when the bull-leaper reached for the bull's horns, could bring disaster. Filia's happiness was short-lived. Two months later, Charybdis met up with a bull that refused, for a full hour to stand still for more than seconds at a time. He should have abandoned the attempt.

He began his run while the bull still moved, shaking his head back and forth, shifting his feet. Charybdis almost succeeded in doing the impossible. He managed to grab one horn. His leg caught the other.

The bull's horn ripped through muscle and Charybdis's blood splattered the arena floor.

Charybdis survived only because Filia managed to distract the bull, wild with rage at the scent of blood. Charybdis would never perform in the bull-arena again, and he would go though life with a limp to remind him of his reckless foolishness.

Hephaestus was one-year old when Germaine swept back into my life. I had gone to the town of Knossos to buy ink. She approached from the opposite direction along the main road through the city, crowded with people. Heads turned as she walked past food vendors' stalls. She took no notice, her eyes fixed straight ahead. She walked with a casual pace, but her long stride took her quickly past me.

As I turned and watched her move away from me something happened to me. I did something I never do. I went after her, almost running to catch up. I caught her as she turned a corner onto a side street.

"Wait, please. I want to talk to you," I said, a little breathless.

She turned, stopped and looked at me, but didn't say anything. She waited, a curious look on her face.

"I saw you perform, months ago. You were extraordinary."

"Perform? Where? You must be mistaken." Her accent was unrecognizable, her voice raspy, in odd contrast to her appearance.

"In the amphitheater. Your name is Germaine."

"Do I know you? You look familiar."

"I also saw you at the bull-arena, when you visited with the bull-leaper, Charybdis."

She narrowed her eyebrows in a quick frown. "How is he?"

"You've heard?"

"Only what people are saying."

"He'll never again enter a bull-arena as a performer."

"That's too bad. He was very skilled. I learned a great deal from him." Germaine said.

"He helped train you?"

She nodded. "I owe much to him. He was my first friend, when I came to Knossos."

"Why don't you perform any more?"

"I'm done with that life."

"Why?"

"I can't explain. I don't know. It's as if I have done everything."

We looked at each other in silence. I felt my heart begin to beat faster as she met my gaze. Her eyes were blue, and large. I could see her focus on different parts of my face. When they reached my lips, I had to wet them.

"I have to go," she said, turning away.

I didn't try to follow her, but I watched her until I saw her turn to enter a house. It was all I could do to resist the temptation to go after her. I slept fitfully that night, and dreamed strange fantasies, not at all erotic, but centered about Germaine. When I awoke, I knew I would try to see her again. I hurried to the Pillar Shrine and made a massive offering to Zeus, but fell silent when I contemplated pleading for release from Germaine's spell.

The next day, as if in answer to my failed prayer, Thera exploded. It happened in the early morning, shortly after dawn. Those outside, turned toward Thera, could see the flash and rising column of smoke and cinder before the sound arrived. In ten seconds, a booming shock wave rumbled across Crete, louder than anything anyone had ever heard, louder than thunder. Houses collapsed. The thundering violence stripped entire orchards naked of branches and leaves, as if a giant hand had swept over them. Animals, when they regained their feet, ran in crazy circles, panic stricken. Children wailed.

Seconds later an earthquake struck Crete. More buildings fell. The Palace of Knossos, built to withstand earthquakes, survived without serious damage. Beams that reinforced the bricks and stones of the walls, allowed the structure to give without breaking, and saved my family's life. Kadmus's villa suffered considerable damage, but no one sustained anything but minor injuries. For them, the worst was yet to come.

Unknown to us, a huge wave raced towards Crete, destined to reach us in minutes, traveling at unfathomable speeds. When the wave reached shallow water it rose up and slowed into an avalanche of water oblivious to everything in its path. Kadmus's wife Omphale told me later that she and her children had been outside, watching the great black cloud looming up over the horizon, when her eldest daughter pointed to the shoreline.

"The sea had pulled back for a half mile, at least. Ships lay on their sides in the mud. I saw Kadmus's ship. Then I saw him and Rasmus. They started to run towards high ground. It was horrible. They had no time."

The sea rushed back, swept over the headlands to engulf Rasmus and Kadmus, and every other moveable object—trees, fences, animals, boats, sheds, wagons—in a mad foaming nightmare. The wave overwhelmed Kadmus's villa. It destroyed everything the earthquake had left standing. There was nothing to indicate that a home had once existed there. The sea took Omphale and the children and carried them farther up the hillside, but the wave had weakened, and their ride was less violent. Only the youngest child drowned, trapped under a tree limb.

We never found my father's body. The retreating wave took him out to sea, where he had spent the last years of his life, and would now spend an eternity. Kadmus was more fortunate, grabbing hold of a tree limb and riding it to higher ground where it lodged between rocks, preventing the sea from taking him back.

Sirena, and the children and I fared embarrassingly well in the palace. My mother was with us. Everything fell off shelves, furniture toppled, plaster sprinkled over us, but we survived, unhurt.

The sky grew dark, day turned into night, as the ash and cinder cloud drifted over Crete. Ash started to gently rain down on the island. It continued for three days. In a few hours, we began to breathe ash-laden air. Ash and cinder soon covered everything. The landscape turned the uniform gray color of death. Plants withered. The harvest would be half what it should have been. The shock-wave, earthquake and tidal wave ended quickly. Those that survived suffered most from that insidious, quiet invasion from the sky.

Kadmus had stopped in Thera, but failed to get Jason and Nephele to leave. We did not know what had happened to them, and their infant son. We had little hope. In the weeks that followed the eruption, a few survivors from Thera made it to Crete. They were the fortunate few that had taken heed of the rumbling warnings that preceded the explosion a few hours and escaped to sea. Jason and Nephele were not among them. No one could tell us what had happened to them.

The tidal wave carried Kadmus's ship hundreds of feet above the shoreline, but otherwise left it largely undamaged. A month after the eruption, Kadmus went to sea again. He sailed to Thera, and I went with him. Where there had been a volcanic island, with a peak seven-thousand feet high, there was now a thin ring of small islands surrounding a circular bay. No one survived that had remained on the island. A hundred feet of ash covered the remnants of Thera, completely burying the city of Akroteri. If Jason and Nephele and their son had not escaped by sea, they were lost, buried forever.

Crete survived, but for years would remain crippled, like Charybdis. The palace of Knossos remained standing largely undamaged, but Thera's demise destroyed many others on the island. Crete's dominance in the Aegean began to wane. The Mycenaeans, trading partners on the Greek mainland, began to compete ambitiously with Cretan traders. For the first time in anyone's memory, rumors of a possible Mycenaean invasion reached Crete.

My family carried on, trying to maintain hope for Jason and Nephele, grieving for our lost father, my mother heartbroken, but resilient. The rains of winter washed the ashen shroud into the sea and the land began to renew itself. Kadmus rebuilt his villa, on higher ground. His eldest son, at fourteen, went to sea with him, another father and son team.

I had Sirena, Lelia, Lethe and Hephaestus, and my work as a scribe. Sirena occasionally gave in to an impulse to partake of the poppy and dance among the gnarled olive trees, while I worried and fretted. I made sure I was the first to reach her after she had finished. Then, sometimes, the rewards were worth the worrying wait.

Filia, as we expected, became one of Crete's most famous bull-leapers. But it did not seem to make her happy or content. That Charybdis could only watch and envy her from beyond the arena borders saddened her and began to eat away at their relationship. She suddenly quit bull-leaping, two years after the eruption.

I should have been content. But Germaine had infiltrated my secure, controlled, well-ordered existence. She had caught me in her innocent, reluctant web, and I could not escape. I was certain that some day she would insert herself back in my life, with both marvelous and disastrous consequences.

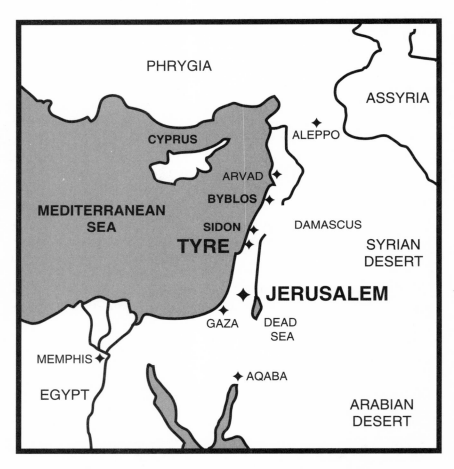

Tyre & Jerusalem, Canaan

IV. Tyre & Jerusalem
925 BC

Six centuries later and six-hundred miles east of Crete, in the land of Canaan, two cities of remarkable contrasts formed a close alliance, one of the world's first. Tyre was the most powerful of the Phoenician city-states. Jerusalem was the capital of the young nation of Israel. Tyre controlled a heavily fortified offshore Mediterranean island. Jerusalem lay in the desolate lands near the Dead Sea. Tyrians worshipped Baal and Astarte and some other lesser gods, who occasionally demanded human sacrifices. Jews claimed Yahweh was the true, one God. Yet, the two cities found reasons to link their destinies and overlook differences, growing rich through trade and commerce.

Late in King David's reign, he entered into an alliance with Hiram, the new King of Tyre, giving Israel access to the richest port on the Mediterranean, while the Phoenicians gained a prosperous trading partner and access to the Red Sea port of Aqaba. Tyre and Jerusalem prospered through the reign of Solomon, who renewed and strengthened the alliance with Tyre. Phoenician craftsmen helped build Solomon's palace and the first great Jerusalem Temple. Economic benefits took precedent over religious and cultural differences, leading to peaceful coexistence, instead of war.

The Arrangement

1

I wasn't sure where I belonged. Two cities, two lives, and two women tore me apart. I felt as if the gods—or *the* God—were toying with my life, finding ingenious and amusing ways to torment poor Avraham the scribe. No doubt the priests of Jerusalem and Tyre would have agreed that my self-centered nature knew no bounds. Yet, I perceived that everyone close to me staggered through life beset with untoward problems, not of my doing, but somehow invented to give me a permanent headache. They all came to me, my beloved family, baring their souls, seeking spiritual absolution, and practical solutions.

Even my eldest brother Kadar, the supposedly stable one, the man of strength, resolve, steadfastness and faith, had come to me, his back bent under the weight of false accusations. At least I believed they were false. I had to. I kept all the records and would have known of any discrepancies. King Solomon's vizier sought a scapegoat to blame for the delays on the palace. The blame should have resided with Solomon, who kept altering plans—adding and rearranging rooms, modifying decorations. If the ancient pharaohs of Egypt had acted like King Solomon, they would never have completed a single pyramid.

But my greatest problem was of my own doing. I could not blame anyone else for Germaine—my beautiful, mysterious, and irresistible dancer.

She appeared as if by magic. I nearly rode her down in my fast chariot, as usual in a rush to reach Tyre, carrying in my satchel a critical order for additional cedar for Solomon's palace. She walked at a fast pace, with long strides, and a heavily laden donkey plodding behind. The wiry little man was not with her. At the last moment I saw a flash of golden hair escaping the confines of her deep hood. I swerved to a stop.

I should have kept on, and never looked back. But how could I? She had inflamed in me the worst sort of passion and desire, the first moment I saw her perform in the market place near the Temple. A woman of the forest, the wiry little man called her, hair golden, tall and as strong as most men, a body lavishly exposed in a short Assyrian tunic, able to contort, flex and bend in impossible ways during a sensuous dance that left men sweating and woman shaking their heads. She seemed as wild and untamed as the uncivilized land she came from. I wanted her. I needed her, though I refused to admit it, and was greatly ashamed.

I was ready and sorely tempted to embrace adultery, as the Jews call one of the worst transgressions against the laws of their God, the one they call Yahweh. That I could so easily trample my wife Shifra's rights, appalled me during moments of sanity. I loved Shifra and our three children, Laila and Lufti, ten and seven years old, and young Hezekiah, just three. How could I not love a woman who had done so much for me, put aside her religion to worship the foreign gods Baal and Astarte? Yet here was Germaine, a temptation of the gods.

Had I *not* caught a sparkle of gold beneath her hood, I would have driven past, and probably never seen her again. Instead, I pulled up the horses, jumped down and threw the reins over a bush beside the road. She had stopped, and had one hand on the donkey's neck. I walked closer to peer at her face, nearly hidden beneath the hood. Germaine did not look as she did when she performed, the long, drab cape hiding most of her body.

"It *is* you," I said, idiotically.

She pulled back her hood a little, to free more of her hair. "What do you want? Why did you stop?"

"I nearly ran over you. Are you all right? Can I help you, Germaine?"

"How do you know my name? Do I know you?"

Her voice was lusty, as befitted such a marvelous woman. I felt a shiver of apprehension. An inner voice urged me to turn my back on her, climb into my chariot and drive on.

"I've watched you perform many times. I talked to you once in a street behind the Temple."

"Perhaps. I don't remember."

I had often seen her perform in Jerusalem's markets and squares, wherever the wiry little man could drum up a crowd likely to contribute a coin or two, to witness her impossible gymnastic dance movements. Germaine became well known, talked about, too well known it seemed. Everyone tried to guess where she came from. She looked different. No one could mistake her for a Phoenician or Jew.

Germaine turned away and reached for her donkey's halter. I backed up, ready to let her go on, and disappear again. Why didn't I? Some malicious god, probably Astarte herself, whispered in my ear and I spoke up, grabbing the loose sleeve of her coarse cape.

"Where is that little man who took care of you?"

She turned to look at me with suddenly harsh eyes. "What man?"

"Your trainer, I suppose."

"Trainer." She laughed. "Is that what people thought?"

I hesitated, somewhat shaken by her abrupt manner. "I've heard stories about how he found you in distant lands to the north."

Germaine waved her hand contemptuously, grabbed the donkey's bridal and started walking.

"Wait."

She slowly halted, as if undecided. She turned around, her cape falling partly open. I saw that she wore the Assyrian tunic beneath, nothing more, as if she had left Jerusalem hurriedly. My curiosity increased.

"What do you want?" she said.

"People say that he bought you from a northern trader."

She sighed and looked down at her feet. "Is this what you believe?"

"I don't know. Is it true?"

"What does it matter? He isn't here with me, is he?"

She started to turn again. I impulsively grabbed her arm. "Wait, don't go yet."

She yanked her arm free and stepped back, eyes narrowed, lips set. She shook her hair free of the cape's hood, the golden tresses flashing in the sunlight.

"Have you run away?" I said.

She hesitated, glancing back along the road. "Why do you want to know? Are you his friend?"

I hesitated, unsure what to say. "I just want to know why you're alone, on this road."

She looked at me with a furrowed brow, rubbing the side of her face with long slender fingers. She shrugged and even that careless movement stirred something in me.

"He's gone, and I'm alone. That's all that matters."

"Where did he go?"

She hesitated. "I don't know."

"You shouldn't be out on this road alone."

"I prefer to be alone."

"Where are you going?"

"Tyre," Germaine said. "People are different there, they say. Is that true?"

"They are different in many ways, and the same in many ways."

She shook her head vigorously, walking towards me. "I only want to dance. I pray that in Tyre, people will be pleased to pay to see me perform. I pray that the officials will not hound me. That the priests will not curse me. Then I can live in peace. I want nothing more."

I didn't know what to say. Germaine's gaze held me, her eyes hindering any attempt to read her thoughts.

"You can ride with me, until we reach Tyre," I said, at last. "It's only a few hours away."

She looked surprised. "I can walk. I've gotten this far."

"If someone is looking for you—"

"No one is looking for me."

"I'm sorry. I just thought—"

"I'm free to go wherever I want."

I shook my head. "Fine. Walk if you wish."

I had turned to my chariot and had a foot on a wheel spoke, ready to climb in when I felt her hand on my arm, surprised at the strength of her grip.

"Who are you?" Germaine said, her mouth close to my ear.

I turned around. She kept her hand on my arm. We were agonizingly close. I found it hard to speak. The day suddenly seemed distractingly warm.

"My name is Avraham, and I am a scribe."

Germaine raised her eyebrows and looked down at my hands, as if they were some miraculous tools to create the odd marks she would likely never understand.

"Well, Avraham the scribe, what do you want with me?"

"Nothing." I said it too quickly to be convincing, and I saw a smile play momentarily across her face. "I'm simply offering you a ride."

"I'll never again be a slave to a man. Any man."

Her hand squeezed my arm painfully, but I made no effort to pull it away. She had reason to be angry, if the stories were correct. For all but the first years of her life, since being taken away as a child from her mother, she had apparently lived, if not as a slave, at least controlled by one man or another. She knew no other life. She was adrift now, her owner, or trainer apparently vanished. How could she help but think that I wanted to take his place?

"You look tired. Accept the ride. I expect nothing in return," I said.

"Everyone expects something."

"Why won't you trust me? It's dangerous for you out here, alone on the road."

"I can take care of myself."

"You won't reach Tyre before dark, and what will you do when you get there? Do you know anyone?"

She looked at me curiously, skeptically, but made no further objection. I took the rope from her hand and tied the donkey to my chariot. I motioned for her to climb in. She hesitated a moment, pulled up her cape to expose the long, muscular legs I remembered, and swung herself into the chariot.

2

We were Phoenicians, my family—Tyrians really. My father brought us to Jerusalem when I was seven years old. With several hundred other Phoenician carpenters and sailmakers, he came to build ships at Aqaba, Israel's Red Sea port. We never returned to Tyre. My family, except for my middle brother Jacob, and my father who died two years ago, eventually settled in Jerusalem.

My eldest brother Kadar and his eldest son Butrus, supervised the stone-workers for Solomon's extravagant new palace. Most of the skilled workers were Phoenician, the majority from Tyre. Solomon was generous with his subject's wealth, extracted through the efforts of the world's most efficient army of tax-collectors. In the early years, Kadar worked on Jerusalem's famous Temple, a Phoenician creation that, not surprisingly, came to look remarkably like the Temple to Baal in Tyre. Phoenician styles in architecture fascinated king Solomon as much as Phoenician styles of clothing, hair, jewelry and foods fascinated the Jewish people. Jerusalem's wealthy nobility, especially the women, took great pains to copy the latest styles from Tyre.

King Solomon was famous as a great builder, not just in Jerusalem, but also in Hebron, Bethel, Beersheba and Mizpah, and in every one of Israel's twelve districts, homes to the original twelve tribes of Israel. But Jews did not love Solomon for his urge to build. Jews thrived on argument, and seldom agreed on anything, except their abhorrence of the heavy taxes required to pay for these edifices to Solomon's greatness, as well as his court's maintenance. Each month one of Israel's twelve districts had to provide all the food, oil and wine necessary to support Solomon's lavish court. This involved more than a wagon load or two of provisions. Solomon had thirty-five wives (by a conservative estimate), each with her own contingent of servants and personal attendants. Solomon's court was an enormous consumer.

Jews stubbornly insisted on the supremacy of their one God, while we Phoenicians maintained a rich pantheon, and, most abhorrent to the Jews, occasionally felt compelled, but only in times of great emergency, to resort to human sacrifice. I could never see the attraction of a single lonely God. If there was one, there must, logically, be more than one. And if you must limit yourself to just one, why make him, as the Jews made Yahweh, into such an intense, somber and fearful god, who shunned ornate rituals and joyous ceremonies, and spent all his time lecturing mortals on sin? Some Jews felt the same. They found Phoenicia's more vibrant, happy and expansive religion tempting. They fell prey to Baal, and secretly worshipped in one of Jerusalem's shrines to the Phoenician gods. Judaism never tempted me.

Although Jerusalem and Tyre learned to live with their religious differences, they threatened to tear my family apart. Kadar and Oma and their seven surviving children were staunch Baal worshipers. Shifra was Jewish, but she converted to Baal worship after I married her, much to her family's dismay. Her father was a priest. He never ceased in his attempt to recapture her. And he never forgave me.

My sister Fadilah married a Jew named Chanoch, and converted to Judaism. As a convert, she was more enthusiastic and tiresome than most people born to the Jewish faith. She, like my father-in-law, never gave up trying to convert me. Alas, her devotion to Yahweh subsided, at times of convenience. Fadilah was, if nothing else, pragmatic.

Then there was brother Jacob. The year before I met Germaine on the road to Tyre, I had gone there on palace business, papyrus and pen ready to record agreements and orders, numbed by nagging negotiations that Jews and Tyrians love to drag out interminably, as much a ritual as business. I managed to get away for a few hours and walked to the docks where the ferry landed. I only wanted to breathe some fresh air, listen to the gulls cawing and the waves lapping at the piers, and watch the workmen return from their labors in the factories and fields on the mainland.

I suddenly found myself standing beside a beautiful Jewish woman. We looked at each other at the same instant, in mutual astonishment.

"Nedivah," I said.

"Avraham isn't it? Jacob's brother?" she said.

"Yes, yes. Is Jacob here?"

"I'm waiting for him."

"We thought . . . why didn't he let us know?"

When Nedivah, a Jew, defied her powerful family to marry Jacob, the couple had no choice but to leave Jerusalem. They disappeared for a time, until we got word that they had boarded a ship headed for Crete, a desolate and unlikely place. We heard nothing further, for months. Kadar made a trip to Crete to find them, and he did. He returned to announce to the assembled family that we had a new member, my nephew Seraphim. A few months later, an earthquake struck Crete, causing much destruction and many deaths, and we heard nothing further from Jacob.

"You'll have to ask your brother that," Nedivah said.

"I will ask him that, and much more. But I can't wait. Tell me where you're living."

Two days later I managed to get away from my predatory employers for a few hours. I embraced Jacob, who at least looked a little guilty. Nedivah was not at home. They lived in a small second story apartment. The building, four stories high, crouched menacingly on a busy narrow street, in the heart of Tyre, the strident sounds and sinister smells of street vendors wafting through an open window. I knelt down to shake the hand of Seraphim, a serious looking boy the same age as my Hezekiah.

"When your mother and Kadar finally learn that you've lived in Tyre all these months since the earthquake, and didn't let them know, they may never forgive you," I said, after Seraphim had run off to play.

"I couldn't take the chance that Nedivah's family would find out. They're capable of anything."

"You could have gotten word to us."

Jacob shrugged and smiled. "Well, I didn't. Eventually I would have."

It was no use. Jacob would always be Jacob, a typical middle son, I suppose.

"How do you support your family in Tyre?" I said.

"I work in the dyeworks."

I laughed. "Is that what I smell? I didn't want to mention anything."

After that, I began to stay with Jacob and Nedivah whenever I came to Tyre. It was natural therefore that I would bring Germaine to my brother's house, when we finally reached Tyre, dragging her reluctant donkey behind us, like a ship with a sea anchor.

If I had thought, even for a moment, of the consequences, but that is not my way.

3

"I'm sorry Avraham, I can't talk here. Meet me in the Temple, tomorrow morning. Please."

With these words, my sister Fadilah ensnared me in another of her problems, and in another of her reckless stunts to solve them.

"I'm not a Jew. I can't enter the Temple," I said.

"Nonsense, Avraham. Anyone can go into the Anteroom. People do business there all the time. It's a good place to talk."

I hesitated. I feared this solitary Jewish God. He seemed so intense and somber, so human. Gods should be more godly.

"All right. But I'll wait for you outside."

The next morning, when I reached the Temple, Fadilah was not there. I thought I must be early, so I waited, pacing back and forth in front of the huge doors leading to the Anteroom. I was not alone. Jews from the most distant district of Solomon's kingdom came to the city on pilgrimages, as much to view the Temple, as to worship Yahweh at his principal home. The Temple's Inner Sanctuary held the sacred Ark of the Covenant, the origin of Israelite mysteries, which I didn't profess to understand.

After Solomon's unfinished palace, the Temple was Jerusalem's largest building, though it could not compare in size to larger temples in Egypt and Babylonia. The Temple's position within the crowded city, set on a shallow knoll, the city's highest point, combined with the building's unusual height and massive construction, made it appear that the Temple was presiding over the lesser buildings surrounding it. The beauty and detail of the decorations distinguished the Temple from any in the world. Solomon had spared no expense. I had recently braved the interior to get a glimpse. It was a marvel of cedar beams, cast-bronze pillars, and ivory-covered doors. The walls were paneled with cedar in beautifully matched grain, inlaid with gold.

I looked up at the massive statues that commanded the entrance and shook my head. It was too much for many Jews. Older, traditional Jews preferred the stark, plain interiors that existed in most of Israel's temples, where no fabulous riches distracted worship of Yahweh.

Emulating Tyre's temple to Baal, Jerusalem's temple consisted of three main rooms. An Anteroom, led into the Sanctuary, the main room for worship, and beyond to a smaller Inner Sanctuary that only certain of the priests could enter, where they maintained, with ancient rituals, the holy of holy Ark of the Covenant. I once saw the Inner Sanctuary, during the building of the Temple. Kadar took me there, before the priests had sanctified it. It still worried me that I had seen what most Jews would never see.

I was about to give up on Fadilah when she finally arrived.

"I'm sorry, Avraham. I couldn't get away from Chanoch. I had to massage his leg and rub the oil in to lessen the pain."

"I hate waiting here. I feel so out of place."

"I said I'm sorry. And you shouldn't feel that way. Look at all these men coming and going. Do you think they're all going inside to pray? They're doing business, meeting people, and waiting for their sisters, to help them in their time of great need."

I laughed, too loudly I thought, and frowned somberly. "That's what I was afraid of. Where's Chanoch? I thought he'd be with you."

She shook her head and frowned. She grabbed my arm and walked me quickly into the Temple, before I could change my mind.

It was early and visitors had not yet crowded the Anteroom. A steady stream of worshippers made their way into the Sanctuary, where I refused to go. Fadilah led me to a corner, and drew me close to her.

"Chanoch is the reason I need to talk to you."

"Is he all right?"

"He has good days, and bad days."

I guessed that this had been a bad morning. Shortly after they married, Chanoch fell from a scaffold at the palace construction site. He broke his left leg—a bad break, the bone exposed—and suffered internal injuries with deeper, long-lasting consequences. He was lucky. Others have died from similar falls. The leg mended improperly and left Chanoch with a severe limp, and constant pain. It also left him moody and unpredictable. I didn't enjoy his company, but Fadilah was devoted to him, I thought. I often wondered if it was guilt or love that kept them together.

"This is hard for me to say," Fadilah said.

"Then don't say it."

"Avraham!"

"Every time you unload one of your problems on me, I end up getting involved in schemes that lose me sleep, cause me embarrassment, and make Shifra think you hold me enthralled with some sort of magic spell."

It had started with the abortion I arranged for her when she was thirteen. Other mishaps followed regularly, year after year. Had I not intervened with the officials, used my position as royal scribe to get the Temple priests to accept Fadilah's conversion to Judaism, she could not have married Chanoch.

"If you don't want to help, just say so," she said.

"Some day, I might just do that." I took her hand to show that I was only exacting my price through complaints, a habit I'm not proud of.

Fadilah took my arm and turned me towards the corner. She whispered so softly I could barely hear her. "Chanoch can't manage to, you know . . . I mean, he can't perform. Or at least, he has great difficulty."

I looked into her eyes. She screwed up her face, imploring me to understand. I thought I did, but I wasn't about to let her off that easily.

"What are you talking about? Perform what?"

"Not so loud. Don't pretend you don't understand."

"Well?"

"If only I had another, more sympathetic brother."

"You don't, unless you'd rather talk to Kadar."

Fadilah leaned even closer to me. I could smell her perfume, something imported from southern Arabia, I guessed. "Chanoch can't perform in bed, when we are together, as man and wife. Now do you understand? Is that clear enough?"

Quite adequately clear. I looked up at the Temple ceiling, far above my head, and wondered if Yahweh was taking time to listen to our petty conversation.

"I tremble to ask why you must tell me this. What can I do?"

Fadilah looked at her feet. She seemed embarrassed, unusual for her. "Avraham, you are a man. You must know about these things. It upsets him so. I think he blames me, but you know—"

"Yes, I know of your sordid past."

"Avraham. Don't be cruel."

I suddenly felt the need to embarrass her. "What exactly is his problem? Where—at what point—does he fail?"

Fadilah caught my tone of voice and punched me hard in the arm. "I'm serious about this. I need your help. I want a child."

"I'm sorry. But what do you expect me to do? After all, we are brother and sister."

"My God, Avraham, will you be serious? I want you to talk to Chanoch. Maybe you can help, perhaps give him pointers."

I jerked away from her. "No, no. That I won't do. I have to draw the line somewhere."

"Don't say that. He'll listen to you. He trusts you."

"Fadilah."

"Who else can I go to?"

"Fadilah."

"It's your duty. You're my brother. I'd do the same for you."

I couldn't help laughing. "You'd talk to Shifra? You'd give her tips on how to arouse me? How to please me? Perhaps that'd be a good idea. Maybe, with your experience, you know a few things—"

"Are you going to help me or not?"

I sighed, and gave in, as she knew I eventually would. "I'll try, but I doubt I'll be able to help. He'll probably refuse to talk to me."

She paused and glanced at the heavens, as if worried about a thunderbolt from Yahweh. "If this doesn't work, I suppose I'll have to visit Astarte," she whispered, breathing into my ear.

"Have you lost your mind?"

"Can you think of a different solution?"

Astarte was Tyre's goddess of love and fertility, typically pictured with hands held to her breasts, spewing forth milk for the comfort of man. Her likeness in clay and bronze and ivory, were as commonplace in Tyre as the gulls that constantly stood guard on the seawalls. Women of all classes who wished to show their respect for Astarte and thereby gain her favor, prostituted themselves in the name of the goddess, lending their bodies to the temple priests to ensure their fertility. It seemed to work, for such women often did become pregnant not long after a temple visit.

"Listen, Fadilah—"

"Don't say anything. I have to go now. This would be a good time to talk to Chanoch, since I'll be away for the morning. The future of my marriage is in your hands." She left me slumped against the wall, my mouth idiotically agape.

Moments after I emerged into the bright light of day, I suddenly realized what I had promised. It was not a simple matter to bring up such a subject with your brother-in-law. I groaned, and cursed myself for giving in to her.

I went to their house. Chanoch was there, angry, upset, not at all in the mood to give away his darkest secrets to a nosy brother-in-law.

"What do you want?" he said, after begrudgingly allowing me to enter.

"How are you?"

"Wonderful."

"I just ran into Fadilah."

"In the market place no doubt."

"Actually, in the Temple."

Chanoch looked at me, while rubbing his leg. "What were you doing there?"

"She asked to see me."

"In the Temple? Don't tell me she's trying to convert you."

I hesitated. I couldn't do it. I had never been able to talk to men about such things, even my brothers. My throat choked up, my mind froze, and no words came.

Chanoch leaned towards me, curious now, and a bit suspicious.

"Yes, that's it," I finally said. "She's trying to convert me again. I'm not at all interested, of course. But she may ask you if I talked to you—about Judaism. I promised her I would. Just tell her I was here."

"I meant it as a joke," he said. "Why did she really want you to come here? What is she planning?"

"It doesn't matter. I see you're busy. Maybe I'll come back—some other time. I'd better go…"

He shook his head. "You're strange, even for a Phoenician."

I escaped as quickly as I could. Fortunately, I left Jerusalem for a two-week trip to Tyre the next day, and thereby managed to postpone further dealings with my sister. I moved up my trip one day to avoid her, but it only got me into worse problems, for otherwise I would not have nearly trampled Germaine on the road to Tyre.

4

With a fast chariot, and another change of horses, I could have reached Tyre in three hours, maybe less. I could travel as fast as I dared push my horses, for the road was well maintained. It had to be, since commerce between Tyre and Jerusalem was critical to both cities. It was impossible to travel the road without passing caravans of heavily laden wagons coming and going, those from Tyre most often loaded with cedar logs, many of them destined to find their way into Solomon's new palace. It was invariably a hot and dusty trip, the bleak desert scenery no distraction, and I was always relieved when it was safely over, particularly when the temperatures reached their extremes in the summer. But with Germaine's reluctant donkey holding us to a sedate walking pace, it took us most of the day, into late afternoon, to reach Tyre. It was maddening. I might have found it a pleasant journey, if Germaine had not slept practically the entire distance, after the first few awkward miles.

I had often dreamed of having Germaine to myself, guilty daydreams full of adolescent images. Now she sat beside me in the chariot, close enough to feel her breath on my arm when she turned toward me, and to smell the musty aroma of her old cape. When the chariot lurched over uneven places in the road, our bodies gently bumped, and a few times, when we negotiated sharp curves, she briefly took hold of my arm to steady herself. I should have enjoyed every moment with her, and yet, the time passed slowly, and I grew less comfortable, more nervous, the longer we were together.

At first, I tried to get her to talk about herself, with little success.

"Where did you live, as a child?" I asked.

"I don't remember much about it."

"Somewhere in the north, beyond Greece?"

"I don't know."

"You were young, when they took you?"

"Yes."

"That must have been terrible for you."

"Yes."

"And for your parents."

She shrugged.

There was more of this sort of one-sided conversation. I eventually gave up, and endured the uncomfortable silence. Germaine seemed content with the absence of discourse, and soon leaned back against the side of the chariot, and lulled by the swaying motion, fell asleep. I could have slept myself, and let the horses find their way to Tyre, but Germaine made me too nervous for that. I glanced at her frequently, slumped against the side, her cape partly open, legs swung over, arms folded, lips slightly parted. She seemed to me as sensuous in repose as she was swaying to the music of the lyre in Jerusalem's back street markets.

It was early fall, and the day was hot, the sun relentless. Germaine drowsily pushed aside her cape, freeing her legs, her tunic pulled up to her waist. She rolled over on her side, a languid movement, unintentionally sensuous, like a lioness stretching in the sun, and, distracted, I nearly ran the chariot off the road. A little later she awoke enough to remove the cape altogether, taking no notice of me. She folded it carelessly to make a pillow and slid serenely down on her back, sprawled on the floor of the chariot, her sandaled feet hanging over the front edge. This time the right wheels of my chariot did skid off the paved road into the sand.

The chariot lurched and bounced until I got it back on the pavement. Germaine shifted about, but didn't awaken. That's when I saw the knife. It had worked its way out of an inside pocket in her cape, and lay beside her makeshift pillow. It looked like a fisherman's knife, honed to quickly rip the guts out of fish. It could easily do the same to a man, and I shuddered to think how close I might have come to feeling its thin blade slip between my ribs. I wondered again about the wily little man's fate.

When we neared the first Tyrian guard station, I leaned down and placed a hand on Germaine's shoulder and gently shook her. She awoke with a start, grabbing my hand and sitting upright with such sudden force that she pushed me against the other side of the cramped chariot.

"Where am I?" she said, her eyes wide with fright, quickly getting to her feet.

"It's all right." I let go of the reins, trusting the horses to know the way as well as I, and took hold of Germaine's hands, turning towards her.

She looked at me with a quizzical expression for a few seconds, then smiled, showing white teeth, with a large, but charming gap between the middle two.

"Oh. It's you. How long have I been sleeping?"

"Most of the way."

"Are we near Tyre?"

"The first guard station is just ahead."

"Will they let me enter?"

I smiled. "It is not likely that they will have any qualms about letting you in. Whether you'll ever leave, is another matter."

Germaine frowned, taking me seriously. She picked up her cape. The knife, its point catching in the cloth, clattered to the floor and off the front of the chariot to the ground.

"Wait. Stop," she said, starting to climb out.

I slowed, and she jumped out before I came to a halt. I watched her run back along the road to pick up the knife, stuffing it back inside the folded cape. She climbed in and leaned against the side, clutching the cape to her chest, eyes fixed on me, judging me, alert.

"Are you going to tell me what that's for?" I said, after whipping the horses forward.

"Protection. What else?"

"Have you had to use it?"

She didn't answer.

At the station, the guard glanced at the paper I held out and waved us on without taking a second look at Germaine. She had put on the cape and pulled the hood over her head.

"You seem worried that someone will recognize you," I said.

"It's better if they don't see."

"Why?"

"I may not want to stay in Tyre."

"Are you still afraid of that man?"

"He's no danger to me any longer."

We rode on in silence for a few miles to reach the shoreline. I started to put away the document that I had shown the guard, the seal of Solomon's vizier prominently displayed.

"Can I see that?" Germaine said.

I held it out to her. She studied it for a moment, then shook her head. "You can write such things? And they mean something?"

"That's what I was trained for."

"You must be clever."

I laughed. "It only takes time, and a cruel teacher."

"It must be very exciting."

"Not really. Mostly hard work, and incessant traveling back and forth between Jerusalem and Tyre."

"I wish I could read."

"You would not find it interesting. At least what I write. Contracts, bills of exchange, receipts, lists of materials, accounts."

"But what do all those little marks mean?"

I looked at Germaine with amazement that such things would interest her. "Do you really want to know?"

Germaine shrugged. "It doesn't matter."

I held out the document and pointed. "These are letters, of an alphabet. There are twenty-two of them. Together they make up words. It's only a matter of learning the strokes, and memorizing a great deal." It inordinately pleased me that I had gotten her attention, in something at least.

Of course it wasn't as simple as I made out. Nor was the work of a scribe as complicated as it once had been. Well before Israel became a nation, some of my predecessors, scribes in the northern Phoenician city of Ugarit, invented a new way to write, putting an imaginative end to the promiscuous proliferation of pictographs that had before made the life of a scribal student so miserable. Centuries ago, Sumerian scribes learned to use combinations of pictographs to symbolize words instead of using a separate pictograph for each word. However, this still left hundreds of pictographs for students to learn, with the strong tendency for writers to create new ones whenever it suited them. The Ugarit scribes carried the process one logical step forward. They threw out all the pictographs, except twenty-two which they stylized into simple forms. They related each to a sound so that they could combine them to form any word of the language. It seemed a miracle that so much could be done with so few symbols.

My duties would have been extremely difficult without the alphabet. It made it possible for me to write several languages with the same set of symbols. It also made learning to write vastly easier than it once was, for there was far less need for scribal artistic dexterity and fewer things to remember. It was no longer unusual to find a ship's captain, ship's mate, port agent, merchant, or exporter, who could write with sufficient skill to keep track of his business. This gave the

Phoenicians a distinct competitive advantage. This also meant there was less need for professional scribes, such as me. Our numbers had dwindled, but on royal projects, such as Jerusalem's Temple and Palace, we were still indispensable.

"You must be very rich," Germaine said.

I shook my head sadly. "I wish it were so."

"But you have a skill that few have."

"More have it than you think."

"I don't understand any of those marks."

I turned to her then, and waited until she caught my look. "But you can dance, as no one in the world can dance."

She frowned, turned away, and fell silent again. She stared off to the side, her back to me. I wondered if I would ever understand her.

When she caught sight of Tyre, the portion built on the island, she came out of her stupor. The city, its striking setting, the environs so different from the harsh land surrounding Jerusalem, seemed to stir something in her distant memory.

"It looks as if the sea is about to swallow Tyre, or as if the city has just emerged from the sea," she said.

"It did, sort of. Tyre is built on two small islands, filled in to make one. The sea will not take it away." I offered my hand to help her down, but she ignored me and leaped out of the chariot.

After I settled my horses, and Germaine's donkey in a mainland stable, we boarded a ferry to make the short journey across the well-protected harbor to the city gates. A half-mile of open water separated the island from its mainland counterpart. Dozens of ships crowded the harbor, some just arriving, others loaded and ready to depart, and several under repair.

"Are those cliffs or the city walls?" Germaine said

"Walls. No army will ever capture Tyre," I said, feeling a sense of pride.

"I'm not so sure," she said. "Wouldn't the city soon run out of water."

"Not for a long time. King Hiram has built a huge underground cistern, holding enough water to allow Tyre to withstand a yearlong siege."

Germaine laughed and patted my arm, making my heart flutter. "You must be from Tyre, the way you talk."

I gave the boatman a coin, and another to the man I hired to carry Germaine's bundles. I swung my own small pack over my shoulder. I told the men to take her things to my brother's house, without asking Germaine. I guessed she had no place to go. She remained silent as we headed into the city, through the massive gates. She kept looking all around, taking in everything.

Tyre's narrow, crowded streets seemed to amaze her. She walked with her head back, looking up at the tall houses and buildings, many of them reaching six stories. I had seen the reaction of first-time visitors to Tyre before. Tyre's streets were canyons of masonry and stone. Sounds echoed in confusion, sometimes making conversation difficult.

Normally I would run into men at every other corner who insistently and loudly offered me the pleasures of a woman for the night. I always dutifully declined. This time they left me alone. One look at Germaine, and they decided I was well provided for. She had thrown open her dusty cape to let the sea breeze sweeping through the narrow streets cool her in the afternoon's lingering heat.

"Where are we going?"

"To my brother Jacob's apartment."

"Why?"

We walked side by side. She seemed oblivious to the stares she caused.

"That's where I always stay. He'll have room for you."

Germaine stopped. "I think I should find my own place."

"That isn't easy. Do you have money?"

"Of course."

"My brother has room to spare. Stay there for a while, until you find a place."

"Why do you want me there?"

"I don't *want* you anywhere. I'm offering to help you. Why is it so difficult for you to let me help you?"

"Because there's always a price."

"Not this time," I said, trying to sound as if I meant it.

"I don't believe you."

"As you wish. I can't waste any more time. I'll tell the man to take your things anywhere you want to go." I turned back to talk to one of the porters.

"I don't intend to ever again be any man's property," Germaine said.

"Fine. I accept that."

"Are you sure your brother won't mind?"

"Are you coming with me, or not?"

With obvious reluctance, she nodded her head.

When the porters dumped Germaine's bundles on the pavement in front of the four-story apartment building, and collected another coin, Germaine seemed to panic. She grabbed my arm in a grip that hurt. We were the same height so she could look me straight in the eye. I saw fear, and uncertainty, for the first time in her eyes. I wanted to embrace her, comfort her. My heart went out to her.

"I can't stay here."

"Why not?"

"I don't know anyone. Everything is so strange here."

"You've just arrived. Have patience."

"I should never have left Jerusalem."

She turned away from me. She ran her fingers through her hair and stared up at the sky, showing thinly between the buildings. I saw her shudder. Without thinking, I stepped behind her, took her shoulders and pulled her back against me.

With my mouth near her ear, I whispered, my voice shaking, "You'll get used to it. Everything. I'll show you the city, introduce you to people. I'll take care of you."

That I had said that, amazed me. How would I take care of her? What had I gotten myself into?

She twisted around in my arms to look at me. I forgot to breathe. She started to say something, lips parted, eyes searching my face, but remained silent. What I wanted to do, that moment, as I gazed into her pale blue eyes, her golden hair blowing in the breeze, her breasts pressing against the thin cloth of her tunic, I dared not think, much less say.

Germaine suddenly pushed away from me and glanced up at the tall building looming over her head. "But your brother doesn't know me."

"I'll tell him about you. It'll be all right for a day or two. Then I'll find you a place of your own. Where I can visit you."

My heart fluttered as I said the last, when what it might mean struck home. Germaine seemed to understand that too. It was what she was all too familiar with. I was just another man to take care of her, and use her.

"Only visit, nothing more," I hurriedly said, when I saw the look on her face. "You need never be a slave to any man, least of all me."

She smiled, and gave me a mischievous look that left my knees weak. "That's what they all say, at first."

It was afternoon and Jacob was still at the dyeworks. Nedivah came to the door, not surprised to see me, but outwardly shocked to see Germaine. The two women stared at each other in wonder, as Nedivah stepped back to let us in. They could not have been more contrasting. Nedivah was a dark-skinned beauty. Somewhere in her ancestry there was more than a trace of Nubian blood. She was also small, with tiny, elegant features, and nearly black eyes.

"This is Germaine, a friend who has no place to stay. Can she stay with you and Jacob for a couple of days until I find her a place."

Nedivah looked at me with a penetrating stare that made my face blush. She smiled and started to say something, then thought better of it. I looked firmly serious, my hand on Germaine's arm, an unintended gesture of possession.

"If it won't be too much trouble," Germaine said, pulling a little away from me.

"There's always room for another," Nedivah finally said. She took Germaine by the hand and started to lead her away from me, as if taking possession of her. "You look tired and thirsty. Let me get you something."

I started to follow. Nedivah stopped and turned to me. "But if you're staying here too, Avraham, you two will have to share a room." She looked back and forth between us to see how we reacted to this.

"I'll go somewhere else," Germaine said.

"No. I'll go. I know the city."

"I can't let you do that."

"I want to."

Nedivah started to laugh. "Enough, please. Forgive me. I was only teasing. Avraham can sleep with my son."

I started to thank her. With a raised hand, and suddenly solemn look, she interrupted me. "But only for a few days. Jacob and I are leaving Tyre."

"What? To where?"

Nedivah shrugged. "Anywhere but here. Probably back to Jerusalem."

"Why? I thought that was impossible. What has happened?"

"Has Jacob talked to you?"

"I've just arrived. I was going to go see him at the dyeworks. Has something happened? He hasn't lost his position, or had an accident has he?" I had good reason to wonder, considering my brother's tendency to stumble into predicaments, usually of his own making.

"No. And he doesn't approve of our leaving," she said, her face clouding. "It's my idea, you see." She took Germaine's arm again and headed for the cooking alcove.

"I don't understand," I said, mystified.

Nedivah glanced over her shoulder. "You will. When you talk to him."

5

I left Germaine in Nedivah's hands and took the ferry back to the mainland to reach the dyeworks. Nedivah smiled knowingly when I told her where I was going. I never visit the place. I hated the smell. She had guessed right. I *had* gotten an oddly frantic message from Jacob, urging me to see him as soon as I arrived. It worried me, because he said I should say nothing to Nedivah about it. Men always underestimate their wives' prescience.

Jacob looked pleased to see me, but worried. He took me to the shore, outside the dyeworks, away from the worst of the smell. "I'm sorry to make you come here. I wanted to see you as soon as you arrived."

"I hope it's important. If the wind shifts I'm leaving."

Fortunately, most of the time the prevailing winds took the smell away from the city. Otherwise Tyre's citizens would have long ago burned the dyeworks to the ground, even though it made the city rich. The wealthy elite of every country and nationality avariciously sought to acquire the city's famous textiles, made from imported cotton and flax, dyed in brilliant colors, from soft pink to lustrous deep violet.

"How can a few snails make such a horrible stench?" I said, suddenly trying to delay hearing Jacob's news.

The source of these unique colors and incredible smell was the murex, an insignificant appearing, spiny-shelled sea-snail. It was Tyre's astounding good fortune that the murices lived in abundance along the eastern Mediterranean shore, and nowhere else. It was however not the murices good fortune that the Phoenicians, centuries ago, had discovered their hidden secret.

I often wondered how that had come about, considering the efforts necessary to extract the snail's hidden wealth. The creatures had to be collected in huge quantities, smashed from their shells, and left in the sun to rot, where they gave up a few drops of yellowish liquid, accompanied by an atrociously repugnant and revengeful smell. Using secret additives, they heated the liquid for up to two weeks, varying the process to create an astonishing variety of shades. The deepest violet, called royal purple because it was so costly that only kings could afford it, required some sixty-thousand snails to fill just one small urn.

"That stuff you smell is ten times more valuable than gold," Jacob said. "That's why I get searched every day when I leave."

"What's so urgent?" I held my breath. Jacob, like Fadilah, had a talent for trouble he expected me to resolve.

"Nedivah wants to return to Jerusalem."

"Why?" I had decided not to tell him what Nedivah had said.

"She hates it here. She thinks we're all idolatrous pagans, doomed to Hell. She inadvertently witnessed a sacrifice. She wanted to leave immediately, even without me."

"What was the emergency?"

"A fleet of ships overdue several weeks. No word. Only two infants were sacrificed. Just my luck that Nedivah had to witness one of them."

The sacrifices helped placate Baal, Tyre's thunderous god of storms, a decidedly male god, identified with strength, violence, youth, and action. The victims were invariably infants offered up by their parents, brought in solemn procession to a place called the Tophet, where a priest first calmed the child, then quickly slit its throat, the child dying in the arms of a bronze statue of Baal as its blood drained into a fire below. Tyrians gained strength from such cruel sacrifices, carried out only in times of unusual trouble.

"What are you going to do?" I said.

"That's what I wanted to ask you, Avraham. Can you talk to her. Explain things."

"What things? Talk to her yourself."

"I've tried. She won't listen to me."

I thought about my recent attempt to talk to Chanoch, and shook my head. "I can't do it. It's a waste of time."

"She wants to be near her family, she says. But they've disowned her."

It was hopeless. I had no will power when it came to these sorts of things. It was easier to agree, than to argue. Also, I wanted him indebted to me, considering what I was about to tell him.

I sighed pretentiously. "I'll talk to her. I'll try to calm her down and get her to at least delay leaving."

"Thank you, brother," Jacob said, soundly surprisingly grateful.

As I was about to leave, I turned and spoke to him in a voice too excessively casual to escape notice. "By the way, I brought someone to stay with you, for a few days. You don't mind do you?" I dared him to object, after what he'd asked me to do.

"I guess not. Who is he?"

"A woman, actually."

"A woman?" He paused. "You obviously don't mean Shifra."

"Her name is Germaine. I met her on the road from Jerusalem. She's a dancer. At one time a slave, I think. She escaped, or something. She won't say."

Jacob grabbed hold of my arm and turned me towards him, a brotherly scowl on his face. "What are you up to?"

"Nothing. I'm just helping her out."

"I doubt it's only that. You have the same look about you as when you first saw Shifra, in the Temple Square."

"Nonsense."

Jacob stared at me for a few seconds. "I suppose she's beautiful, or else you wouldn't have bothered to stop to help."

"She was walking alone on the road, forty miles from Tyre. I would have stopped to help her even if she were as ugly as the donkey she was pulling behind her."

"Perhaps. But if she had the face of a donkey you wouldn't be trying to find a place for in the city. You'd have left her standing on the shoreline staring out across the water at the city."

"Will you give her a room for a few days, or not?" I said, growing impatient.

"I wouldn't miss the chance to meet this woman for anything," he said. "I'll delight in telling Shifra all about her the next time she comes with you to visit."

"Fine. I'll take her somewhere else," I said, starting to walk away.

"I'm only joking," Jacob said, coming after me, grabbing my arm. "I'll keep your little secret."

"There's no secret to keep," I said, yanking my arm away.

"Then why did you get angry when I joked about telling Shifra?"

"It was the way you said it."

"You're not going to tell her, are you?"

"I probably will, if I remember. It doesn't mean anything."

Jacob laughed annoyingly.

"Jacob, I'm this close to strangling you." I held my hands up a few inches apart.

He held up his hands in mock alarm. "All right. I'll reserve judgement until I meet your new friend."

6

I didn't get a chance to talk to Nedivah until the next day, after Jacob left in the morning for the dyeworks. Before he left, Jacob dragged me outside, pulling me into an alley that ran beside his apartment. I knew what he had in mind. He had met Germaine.

"You can't do this," he said, keeping hold of my arm, as if to keep me from escaping.

"I know what you're thinking. It isn't true."

"You're either lying to me, or to yourself."

I pulled my arm free and started to push my way around him. He blocked my way. "Leave it, Jacob. This isn't any of your business."

"You won't fool Shifra, you know. She isn't like Kadar's wife."

He was referring to Oma's calm acquiescence with Kadar's highly visible, but never spoken of, or explicitly acknowledged mistress, maintained in a convenient village a few miles from Jerusalem.

"Germaine is not my mistress."

"Not yet."

"She never will be," I said, with as much conviction as I could muster, which apparently wasn't much.

Jacob smiled and shook his head. "You delude yourself. You're no different than me when it comes to beautiful women. After my Nedivah, and Shifra, and maybe our sister, Germaine is the most beautiful woman I've ever seen."

"Now you sound jealous."

"And don't think for a moment that she is naive, innocent, or unaware of the effect she has on you."

I looked at him, to see if he was serious. "What're you talking about?"

"She is only waiting for the right moment."

"For what?"

"Do I need to spell it out?"

119

"I could barely get her to let me give her ride, or bring her here."

Jacob nodded his head and smiled maddeningly. I could have strangled him. "Yes," he said, "she is clever. I can see that. Everyone can, except you."

I pushed Jacob aside. "I don't want to hear any more of this."

"Be careful. That's my final warning. I won't ever mention it again."

"I'm going to hold you to that."

"And please talk to Nedivah after I've left," Jacob said, in an anxious voice.

"I said I would."

I was more successful than I expected with Nedivah. At first she was adamant about leaving, and angry that Jacob had asked me to intercede.

"I feel responsible for you two," I said. "If I had not arranged for Jacob to attend the banquet, you two would have never met."

"Have you witnessed a sacrifice, Avraham? Have you seen one of those tiny babies, their life just beginning, with the blood slowly pumping out of them as they struggle in the cold, stone arms of that horrible statue?"

I knew it was hopeless to explain, but I tried. "There are many crueler things in life than a baby's death. At such a young age, they're barely alive. They don't understand. It's all over quickly. And it's done before the baby's parents have spent time and effort raising the child. In a year, they can have another child anyway."

I thought I had explained it well, but Nedivah burst into tears and ran to take her own child into her arms. I started to explain that she had nothing to worry about. Seraphim was already three years old.

"I'm going to have another child," she said, the words screamed. "In a year I *will* have a baby just the right age."

I patted her arm. I understood. "If that's what you're worried about, be at ease. Mothers volunteer their babies."

"Jacob believes in these horrible practices. He's not a Jew. What if he decides, at the next crisis, to come forward and . . . I can't say it."

I tried to convince her that he would never do anything she didn't agree to, and in the end got her to at least agree to delay leaving until the baby was born. I reminded her of what they faced if they returned to Jerusalem. No Jew would employ Jacob, such was the influence of Nedivah's family. They might ostracize Nedivah as well. Worse problems faced the children, as they grew up.

"If Jacob promises me he will never suggest—"

"He'll promise."

"But if I see another mother start to hand a child over to those beastly priests, I'll grab the baby from her arms and run, whatever the cost."

After the lecture from Jacob, I decided to find Germaine a place to live without delay. I even postponed my business in Tyre, feeling justified since I had arrived a day early. When I told my plan to Germaine, she immediately bridled.

"I'll find my own place," she said, dismissing my offer.

"You don't know the city. I do. Why won't you let me help you?"

"I'm already obligated enough to you."

I felt like grabbing and shaking her like a willful child. Nedivah overheard and surprisingly stepped in. "Let him help, Germaine. He knows everyone in Tyre. And if you have any trouble with my brother-in-law, come and see me."

"I don't think I'll have any trouble," Germaine said, smiling oddly.

We found a small apartment on the fifth floor of a building near the harbor entrance. I spent half the day arranging things for her, and then took my leave to meet with suppliers.

"When will you come back?" Germaine said, as I was about to leave.

"In a month or two."

"No, I mean today. Tonight."

I stared at her, an idiotic look on my face.

She gave me that odd, indecipherable smile again. "There's room here. You don't need to crowd in with Jacob and Nedivah."

"I thought you said—"

"I meant it. I'm free, and intend to remain so." She hesitated, and looked away. I thought I saw a blush spread briefly across her cheeks. "This is different. You're not the same as the others."

She looked at me again, took a step nearer, and then stopped. I heard Jacob's warnings ring in my ear and shut my mind to them, angry at their intrusion. To show *my* independence, I took a step towards Germaine, so that we stood, somewhat foolishly, just out of reach, as if waiting for someone to come up behind us and shove us together.

"I've seen the way you look at me, Avraham the scribe."

"You mystify me, Germaine."

She laughed, covering her mouth with her hand. I craved to touch her lips with my fingertips, then with my own lips, to crush them, to taste her essence, to weld her to me, to make dreams a reality.

"This is torture," I said, my voice hoarse.

"I know. What are we to do?"

I raised my arm, reaching my hand towards her. She did the same, and our fingertips just met.

"Did you know that your brother warned me to stay away from you?" she said.

"He shouldn't have done that."

"It's made me wonder."

"About what?"

"About you. He said you're happily married to a wonderful wife with three children."

I dropped my hand and looked away. I didn't know what to say. At that moment I might have escaped. I even took a step back, as if retreating from the overwhelming heat of a fire.

"I don't understand," she said, moving towards me. "Is this all a game with you? Aren't you happy with your wife? Doesn't she please you any more?"

"No. I mean, yes. But this is different," I said, feeling like an idiot, my face burning with her fire.

She reached out and took my hand with both of hers. "I knew what was on your mind when you stopped to help me. I even remember seeing you in the Temple Square, watching me perform. What am I to understand about you?"

In answer, I broached the invisible barrier separating us and took her in my arms, as I had wanted to do from the first moment I had seen her. Our lips touched briefly. Then she moved her head aside, and I felt her breath brush against my neck. Hesitant at first, she finally allowed her arms to circle around my back. As her body pressed against mine, I could sense the strength in her dancer's thighs and her sculpted torso.

"Are you sure?" she said.

"No. I'm not sure. I'll never be sure," I said.

"This isn't right then."

I thought about Shifra and tried to break away, but it I couldn't find the strength.

"Is it wrong to feel as we do?" I said.

"I don't know."

She moved her shoulders and head back so that she could see my face, neither of us willing to let go. I pulled my hands from around her waist and brought them up to cup her breasts, feeling angry at the clothes that still separated us. She gasped, but didn't try to move aside. There was no turning back for either of us.

My business in Tyre got delayed. Germaine's athletic agility made love-making an innovative adventure. She was not submissive. She did not give in to me, merely to please me. She met me on equal terms. Germaine, a slave nearly all her life, had learned a lesson that even my dear wife Shifra had not learned—that a woman's role is to please, by pleasing herself.

I stayed several extra days in Tyre. I didn't tell Jacob and Nedivah, though I suspected they guessed. I moved in with Germaine, and we hardly ever left her two small rooms, except when we had to get food, or when, in the dim light of dusk, we felt safe to wander the narrow streets of Tyre, arm in arm, obvious lovers to everyone we encountered. My wholehearted embrace of adultery had begun.

7

I astonished myself with my ability to act as if nothing had happened, when I returned to Jerusalem, met my children and embraced Shifra. It amazed me that I could, so soon, make love to my wife. I tried desperately to not compare the two women. I tried to forget Germaine, and how I had done things with her that I would never think to try with Shifra. I kept my turmoil hidden, or thought I did. I didn't want this to be the beginning of a double life. I made a vow to end it that I knew I would likely never keep.

The guilt and self-repugnance were worse, almost unbearable, when I greeted my children, especially Laila. She was almost eleven. In a year or two she would reach maturity. She would be a tall, slender beauty like her mother, and the thought of some man taking advantage of her made me angry and ashamed.

Fadilah came to see me at the palace building site as soon as she learned I had returned. She waited next to the fenced yard where material was stored, a place where I could not miss seeing her, while the vizier's assistant had me record the latest of King Solomon's expansion plans. This time the king wanted more columns along the front portico, a relatively simple change.

"I couldn't manage it," I said to Fadilah after joining her. "I tried, but Chanoch was not in a mood to listen to me."

Fadilah smiled at me and shook her head. "I wonder how hard you tried. It doesn't matter now. I've given up on him." She fell silent for a moment as we stared at each other. "I don't have a choice. I have to try it. What else would you suggest?"

I knew what she was talking about, but pretended not to, trying to look perplexed.

"I want you to take me with you to Tyre the next time you go," she said.

"Why? You never go there. The city of sin you call it."

"You know why." She hesitated, and even managed to look a little embarrassed. "I told you before, and I meant it. I'm going to visit the priests. Those serving Astarte."

I sighed and shook my head. "You're a Jew now. How can you think—"

"No one needs to know."

"And if it doesn't work?"

"It will eventually. Remember, I know it isn't me."

"This is the maddest idea you've ever had. How will you keep it a secret? Chanoch will know the baby is not his."

Fadilah smiled. "I've thought of that. Sometimes he almost does it right. It's just a matter of timing, and a bit of playacting."

I continued to protest, halfheartedly, with little effect. She could find her way to Tyre without me, but I didn't want her traveling alone. What did it matter if she succeeded in fooling Chanoch? She would have her child, and he would have a far more content, less cantankerous wife. In the end I agreed to take her along, though I worried about how I would keep her from discovering Germaine. I had begun a life of duplicity that could only end in disaster, yet that certain knowledge could not deter me. Such is man's ultimate weakness.

Only a week later, Fadilah came to see me again, that time at the house. She looked excited, her face flushed, and then annoyed when she discovered that Shifra was at home.

"I need to talk to you," Fadilah said, to me, glancing and smiling at Shifra.

"What's the matter," I said.

"When are you next going to Tyre?"

I looked at Shifra and shrugged. "I have no plans."

"Not soon?"

"What has happened?" Shifra said, sensing my sister's alarm.

"I need to get to Tyre, as soon as possible," Fadilah said.

I knew why, of course, and felt like teasing her a little. "Have you been doing a little playacting?" I said, trying to sound serious.

"Playacting?" Shifra said. "What is this you're involved in now, Fadilah?"

Fadilah gave me an angry dismayed look that would have made Shifra even more mystified if she had seen it. "It's a surprise for Chanoch," she said.

"I'll say," I said, laughing, despite my best effort to keep a serious tone.

"What are you two up to?" Shifra said, getting angry.

"I think you'd better tell her," I said.

"All right, I will," Fadilah said. "First, tell me you'll take me to Tyre. Soon. At least within a week."

"I can arrange it," I said. "I'll see about it now, and let you two women talk over this little project Fadilah is working on."

Shifra was furious with me later, though she realized that there was nothing I could do to dissuade Fadilah. Shifra had also failed, despite her best efforts. Fadilah was equally angry with me for allowing Shifra to find out, putting her through an embarrassing afternoon of questioning.

Fadilah and I fumbled our way through another awkward moment when we reached Tyre a week later. I wanted to stay with Germaine, and avoid Jacob as much as possible, knowing the verbal assault he would put me through. But I couldn't tell Fadilah that. Fadilah also wanted to keep Jacob in the dark, for obvious reasons.

"I'll leave you to find your way to Jacob's house," I said, after the boatman had deposited us on the island landing place. "You know the city. I'll be here three days. Is that enough?"

She looked around nervously. "Where are you going?"

I shrugged. "I'll stay with a friend. It's easier. You can use Jacob's spare room."

"I don't want to stay there," she said, sounding a little panicked. "Can't I stay with you?"

"No, no. Not enough room," I said, feeling a bit of panic myself.

She looked at me oddly. I managed to avoid looking away. I think she suspected something, but didn't dare bring it up, considering what I knew about her.

"I'll find someplace to stay," she said. "Where will I meet you, three days from now?"

We agreed on a place and went our separate ways. That was when it really started, my life of deception with Germaine. The first time, it had been something of an accident, that the gods might have overlooked. This time, when I knocked on Germaine's door, I embarked on a journey I could not return from with my soul undamaged.

I eventually moved Germaine into a bigger apartment and found her work in the market place, selling produce. I didn't want her to have to dance for her coins. "I only want you to dance for me," I said.

"That's rather selfish of you," she said. "I don't know whether I'll agree to that."

"You know what will happen if you call attention to yourself. Someone will recognize you, eventually. There's no one like you, in either Tyre or Jerusalem."

"Perhaps I'll go somewhere else, farther away. Maybe Egypt."

I tried not to show my panic. "If you need more money, I can give you a little, though I'm not wealthy."

Germaine laughed. "We'll see how this works out."

She did well in the market place, her unique appearance attracting customers. I stayed with Germaine every time I went to Tyre, more often than before. Jacob and Nedivah I'm sure knew, but pretended not to.

Fadilah needed to make just two visits to Tyre to receive her gift from Astarte—a glorious pregnancy. Her playacting with Chanoch must have been superb, for the next time I saw him, he acted as moronic as any expectant father.

Life settled into a tense equilibrium for several months. I began to relax, uneasily. I accepted my adulterous dual life, unduly comforted that I had separated it in two cities. Two events soon shattered the calm.

First Kadar, of all people, came to me for advice, and to warn me. Always the stable, dependable member of the family, his worried face shocked me.

"Blame it on Solomon's vizier," he said. "He has accused me, and others, of intentionally delaying and slowing construction on the palace. He says we charge too much for the changes Solomon orders. He says we overcharge on supplies from Tyre."

"That's nonsense. I keep all the records."

"Which is why I'm here. You're in this as deeply as I. There'll be an official investigation."

"The vizier is seeking a scapegoat."

"The reason doesn't matter," Kadar said, increasingly agitated, unable to stand in one place.

"The vizier is only deflecting criticism from the king. Nothing will come of it."

"Phoenician contractors will take the blame, scapegoats for Solomon's excesses," Kadar said. "I could be that scapegoat. You could be too. Remember what happened during the construction of the Temple."

My face must have paled, for Kadar grabbed hold of my arm to steady me. "Three supervisors executed. It could happen again," he said.

Kadar had succeeded in making me as worried as he. The next day, I left for Tyre, where the second blow struck. Germaine welcomed me in her usual, no-nonsense, energetic way, and in a half-hour left me drained and spent, my hand lazily grazing over her gloriously naked body.

She took my hand and pressed it to her belly. "Your child is growing in here."

Athens, Greece

V. Athens, Greece
445 BC

Solon, the father of Athenian liberties, introduced reforms in 592 BC that launched Athens' slow, unsteady march to democracy, in an era when every other Greek city-state remained firmly in the hands of dictators. After his death, political chaos returned the tyrant Pisistratus and his sons to power. Thus began the battle that still raged a century and a half later, between the oligarchs and the democrats, the old landed aristocratic families against the growing middle class. Tyrants held control until the reformer Cleisthenes gained power in 500 BC, and instituted the most momentous reforms in Greek history, formalizing democracy and launching the so-called Classical Period.

Leadership of Athens' pro-democratic elements passed to Pericles in 459 BC, upon the assassination of his predecessor Ephialtes. Pericles would remain Athens' leading and most controversial citizen for nearly three decades. The era began with peace and prosperity, a result of Athens' remarkable victory over Persia (with Sparta's help). Most memorable was the Battle of Marathon on September 9, 492 BC, in which an outnumbered Athenian army brought everlasting fame to the city.

A Deadly Game

1

Germaine looked at me with her pale blue eyes, tears welling visibly, and I felt as if my life was crumbling about me. Gelasius stood at the side of his mother's chair, resting an arm on her leg, staring at me with near replicas of her eyes, only his dark hair giving a hint of my role in bringing him into that troubled world.

"What are we going to do?" Germaine said.

"I'll think of something. This isn't the end of the world. Try not to worry." Such useless words.

"How often can you come to Sparta, with the negotiations at an end?"

"Not often, I'm afraid."

"We'll hardly ever see each other again, unless—"

"I don't know whether I can do that."

Germaine picked up Gelasius, and set him on her knee. "What about your son, Abderus? Will you leave him too?"

"I won't abandon either of you."

"Then, what are we to do? You said this would never happen. That we would always find a way to be together."

I didn't think it would happen so soon. I didn't think it would ever happen. Sparta and Athens, against all odds, had agreed to a thirty-year peace treaty, something which had never happened before. Two Greek city-states agreeing on anything, except ways to defeat a common enemy was remarkable. In the case of Sparta and Athens, consistently at odds with each other, their systems of government and social conventions so diametrically opposed, it was nothing short of a miracle. I had thought that only an overwhelming common threat, such as another Persian invasion fleet sailing across the Aegean, could ever drive the two city-states together. But they had.

All of which meant that I would no longer have an excuse to visit Sparta. As an aide to the Athenian emissary, I had helped negotiate the details and write the terms of the historic treaty. My duties had brought me frequently to Sparta, and gratefully into Germaine's arms during every moment of freedom I could steal. I had learned to live with my adultery, accepting the pain of guilt and the cloak of shame as the price of the pleasures Germaine gave me. I stopped thinking about the consequences. My adultery became a habit, not easily conquered without some outside force. Now, perhaps that had happened. Now, unless I did something, I would rarely see my beloved Germaine, and our two-year old son Gelasius.

"Why can't I move to Athens?" Germaine said, after a long silence. "Why will it be different? Are you that afraid that your wife will learn about me?"

I shuddered at the thought. "You don't understand. She is different from most wives in Athens."

"Then you shouldn't have started this," Germaine said, suddenly placing Gelasius on the floor and standing up, her cheeks coloring.

"Don't be angry. I'll find a way," I said.

"Maybe I don't want you to. Maybe this is a sign that I've become too dependent on you. I sometimes feel that I've lost the freedom I fought so much to get."

"You shouldn't. If anything, it is I that has lost my freedom. In moments when I'm away from you, I sometimes think that I've become your slave."

She smiled at that and came to me, holding out her arms. I settled into a familiar embrace. Gelasius laughed gaily and clutched at my leg.

"I hereby give you back your freedom," Germaine said, whispering in my ear.

"I don't want it," I said, running my hand down her back.

My brother Jason and his beautiful, dark-skinned wife Nephele confronted their own crisis. She wanted to leave Sparta. He did not.

They had to decide quickly, for their eldest son would soon reach the age of seven.

"If we remain in Sparta," Nephele said, telling me something I well knew, "the authorities will take Sebastiano away from us, and install him in a military school where we'll never see him."

"It's not that bad—" I started to say.

"You constantly exaggerate," Jason said. "You talk as if Sebastiano will be locked in a prison. He'll come home for a visit once a month. A week at a time during holidays. And we'll still have Zeta. We should be honored that our son is Spartan by birth. Twenty or more generations of Spartan youths have undergone such training, with wonderful consequences. Sparta owes its success to—"

"I've heard all that propaganda a thousand times. That doesn't make it good for *our* son. And I don't want our daughter growing up in Sparta either."

"Why do you think it's so terrible? Food, clothes and lodging provided by the city, and an excellent education."

Nephele laughed, and looked at me for support. "They'll make him into a mindless hoplite, and then send him off to die in some equally mindless war."

They had argued off and on for months. My presence always brought the argument out into the open, both of them seeking my support. I tried to remain neutral, though my sympathies were with Nephele. I had dealt with the Spartans for years.

"Don't just sit there and stare, Abderus," she said. "Tell him what you think. I know how you feel about the Spartans."

"Abderus knows the value of a Spartan education," Jason said, warning me with a frown to mind my own business.

I had just come from seeing Germaine, and had my own troubles to worry about. Jason's and Nephele's problem seemed minor in comparison. I wanted to tell them that, but I feared what they would say. They knew about Germaine, though they never said anything to me about her, pretending that she didn't exist. Somehow that was worse.

"Try to think of it from Sebastiano's point of view," I said, hoping to end the argument.

"I am," they both said in unison.

I sighed, deciding I would have to abandon neutrality. "In Sparta, if Sebastiano is to succeed, he must resign himself to the system, and give up any free choice of expression. At least until he is well past middle age, retired from military duty. Take him to Athens, and his future remains in his own hands. He can be what he likes."

"That's where you're wrong," Jason said, grabbing my arm. "If we return to Athens, my son's future, as well as mine, will be in the hands of *her* father."

I glanced at Nephele and saw her eyes turn fiery. I knew an explosion was imminent.

"If you don't agree, Jason, I'll take the children and go alone to Athens," she said.

"Your family has disowned you."

"I don't care."

"Where will I find employment if your father decides to carry out the threats he made eight years ago?"

Nephele was on her feet, pacing. I shrank back on the couch, wishing I was somewhere else. Though not a citizen, Nephele's father was enormously wealthy. He owned hundreds of acres of olive groves, and exported olive oil all over the Mediterranean. Nephele's grandfather had fled Egypt eighty years ago, when the Persians reached the Nile, and Egypt lost its independence. As fiery and unpredictable as Nephele, her father violently hated Jason for thwarting his plans for his daughter. He had betrothed Nephele to an influential politician old enough to be her father the day before Jason and Nephele ran away to Sparta. Jason had abducted his only daughter, he told everyone, vowing revenge.

"I'll deal with my father when the time comes," Nephele said, her voice low and dangerous.

"How will you manage that?"

She shrugged, some of her confidence eroding. They stared at each other in silence, Nephele beginning to grow calmer, a look of hope creeping into Jason's expression, giving me a chance to break in.

"You'll have to decide this without my help. I won't be back in Sparta for at least a year, maybe longer."

They looked at me with an unspoken question and I knew their thoughts had instantly focused on Germaine. I stood up, pretending not to notice.

"What about *her*?" Jason said, still trying to avoid saying her name.

I continued the stupid charade, raising my eyebrows in feigned confusion.

"Germaine and your son," Nephele said.

I shrugged, and smiled guiltily. "I'll have to move them to Athens, I suppose."

Nephele gasped. "Sirena will make your life miserable."

"Only if she finds out," Jason said.

"And she will."

Sirena's temper, as Nephele artlessly reminded me, would vigorously assert itself if she found out about Germaine and Gelasius. Unlike most docile Athenian wives, who knew their place and understood men's special needs, she would not overlook her husband's adultery.

"I don't have much choice," I said. "I can't leave them here."

Nephele laughed wickedly. "That'd be inconvenient for you, wouldn't it, Abderus? You couldn't take your extramarital pleasures on such a regular basis. Jason, if you ever try anything like this, you'll never see me or your children again."

Jason flinched, then reached up to pull Nephele back down onto the couch beside him. "I'm not as wayward as my two weak-willed brothers. Besides, how could I ever find a more sensuous, delectable creature than you?"

"Don't try to talk your way out of this."

"I haven't done anything yet. Nor will I, as long as I have you. My brothers are fools."

"I think I actually believe you," Nephele said, the tension draining out of her.

Jason eased her into an embrace that threatened to turn embarrassing for me. They hardly noticed when I left. I went straight to Germaine's little house on the outskirts of Sparta and told her to pack her things.

"Are you sure?" she said, not reacting with the enthusiasm I had expected.

"I don't want to lose you."

"You may anyway."

"What do you mean by that?"

She shook her head. "I don't know. I just have a feeling that this isn't right."

"Everything will work out," I said. I smiled and took her in my arms, but she stiffened at my touch and I let her go.

"I suppose there's only one way to find out," she said.

Acting hastily during the few days remaining, and trying not to think carefully of what I was doing, I arranged for a ship to take Germaine and Gelasius to Athens one month later. That would give me time to return to Athens and arrange a place for them to live. A new life of duplicity was beginning. I tried not think of the enormity of my decision, but failed completely. I knew with hopeless certainty that I'd stumbled into a lake of quicksand, and yet I kept walking, blind to destiny.

2

"There's going to be trouble," Kadmus said, speaking quietly to keep from being overheard. "More and more people call for Calicrates to step aside. They even talk about ostracizing him. They accuse him of overcharging, delaying construction, outrageous profits."

I hadn't been home two days when my eldest brother insisted on burdening me with his own largely imagined problems. Kadmus and his wife Omphale with their seven children lived not far from Sirena and me. He and I often spent an hour or two in the evening slowly sipping wine and eating olives in a crowded wine-shop adjacent to the Agora, the famed Athenian market place, where anything from everywhere could be bought.

"That's typical in Athenian politics," I said, popping another olive in my mouth. "They want to attack Pericles, but it's easier and safer to blame his contractor. Calicrates only makes a normal healthy profit."

"His normal profit is bankrupting the city, they say."

I laughed and clapped him on the arm, trying to make light of his worries. "That isn't likely. Athens is rich enough to build three Parthenons."

It was a frustrating chore to make Kadmus understand the intricacies of Athenian politics. As an artist with an artist's mentality, his only desire was to chisel beautiful sculptures in public buildings.

Kadmus's worries centered on the Temple of Athena Parthenos, or the Parthenon as more commonly known, an architectural and artistic masterpiece under construction on the Acropolis to honor the goddess Athena, the city's namesake. The inner shrine's huge columns were already visible from almost everywhere in Athens. Stone-workers had begun to raise the outer columns, one cylindrical section at a time, locked with a wood shaft, rotated and ground into place to make the column seem a single marble block. When finished, the Parthenon would be Greece's largest temple, one of the wonders of the world.

"Calicrates is hardly ever at the building site," Kadmus said. "Pheidias oversees everything, especially the statuary for the frieze that Boreas and I work on. Ictinus is sometimes there, for an hour or two in the morning, talking to the crew, never to the artists."

Ictinus was Athens' leading architect. He had designed the controversial Parthenon. Pheidias was the lead artist, a fanatical perfectionist who would have preferred to carve every statue himself, if he could have lived three lifetimes.

"What's causing the delays?"

"The statue of Athena of course. It's only half complete, and already has cost several times the original estimate. Have you seen it? It stands twenty feet tall. The goddess's body is already sheathed with ivory. Eventually nearly a ton of gold will be needed to form Athena's robe."

I sipped some wine trying to think what I could say to deflect his worry. "With all that, it's rather ironic that Athena is the virgin goddess of wisdom and charity."

Kadmus laughed. "And that wise head of hers will soon be encased in a helmet decorated with a fortune in jewels."

I gave up trying to dissuade Kadmus from fretting. He was a worrier at heart, especially about things over which he had absolutely no control. And that was mostly politics, Athens' favorite pastime.

Pericles's political opponents constantly complained that the Parthenon would ruin Athens. The island city-states of the Delian League complained with equal, and perhaps more justifiable vigor that Pericles had purloined the funds set aside for the League's defense against Persia. He had of course. Everyone knew that. But Pericles, as skilled at politics as any man alive, blandly countered that Athens deserved the largess, reminding everyone that would listen that Athens had twice thrown back Persian invasions of Greece (conveniently forgetting the help from Sparta), but not before Persian armies sacked and burned Athens, systematically destroying every one of the city's temples and public buildings. Pericles, I'm sure, felt not a morsel of remorse in using Delian League funds to rebuild the city.

Nor did I feel much remorse when I met Germaine's ship at Piraeus. I arranged to transport her belongings to the small apartment I had rented on the eastern outskirts of Athens, as far from my house as I could manage. I didn't go with her. I had arranged with the manager of the building to see that she got moved in safely.

Germaine looked at me with near panic when I told her that. "You won't be coming with me?"

"I'll come and see you in a few days," I said, giving her a quick embrace.

But, I didn't. She had been right. Everything was different.

3

I dearly loved Sirena, more than I ever had. I told myself that I would never intentionally do anything to hurt her, or my children, especially thirteen-year-old Lelia, so remarkably like her mother they could be sisters. And yet, I had brought Germaine and her son to Athens, fully certain that Sirena would eventually learn about them—and thereby be deeply hurt.

What contradictions we live by. For I also knew that it was far from unusual for a man of even moderate means, such as myself, to have a mistress, or two. Sirena should not have complained, as long as I did not neglect her, as long as I honored her as my wife. But Sirena was different. She came from the same dangerous, but exciting mold that produced Aspasia, Athens' most notorious and envied woman.

Aspasia was unique, a liberated woman in a society which believed that women belonged in the home, raising children, and serving their husband. Women applauded her, but mostly in secret. Many men of prominence condemned her. However, a sizable minority, no doubt due to her special alliance with Pericles, gave her reluctant respect. She came from Milesia, a city-state on the coast of Asia Minor. Since she was not, and could never be an Athenian citizen, Pericles could not afford to marry her, and still maintain his political ascendance. The son she bore him, even if they had been married, could never gain citizenship, never hold office, or vote. Still, Pericles divorced his wife of many years to allow Aspasia to openly live with him.

Aspasia arrived in Athens five years ago, divorced or widowed, no one was certain which. She rejected the traditional Greek marriage's constraints and lived in unlicensed unions, even in outright promiscuity to realize her goal of equality with men. She founded a school of rhetoric and philosophy, and encouraged women to attend. This was how Sirena first met Aspasia, and fell under her influence. Soon Aspasia's intelligence, wit and beauty attracted men to her school, some quite prominent. Out of curiosity, I went, and continued to go, but seldom with Sirena. Aspasia's school grew famous. Her former students visited her at Pericles's home, an informal salon where people of great intellect argued every issue of the day. Pericles used her salon to maintain his influence and power.

I first met Euripedes at Aspasia's house. He was a talented and productive writer whose somewhat melancholy plays had gained critical attention in Athens, much to my envy. I also met Pheidias there, unquestionably the greatest sculptor in Athens, my brother Kadmus's employer. Anaxagoras, the philosopher was often in attendance, the controversial longtime friend of Pericles, who had the gall to claim that the sun was a molten, fiery rock rather than a god. The conservative oligarchic faction threatened him with actions for impiety. Less well known, was a young man named Socrates, still a hoplite in the army, but obviously an intellect of great promise, who easily held his own in conversations with more famous personages. Rumors persisted that Socrates was Aspasia's lover before Pericles came into her life.

Aspasia nearly reached her goal of equality with men, but she still could not hold public office or attend or vote at meetings of the Ekklesia. It was my opinion that she had gone too far. Men and women obviously should not and could not receive equal treatment under the law. Sirena believed otherwise, a source of contention between us. One such argument occurred shortly after Germaine and Gelasius arrived in Athens. I was on edge, nervous. I was having second and third thoughts about bringing them to Athens with the regularity of a bad recurring toothache.

The argument started innocently enough, when I stupidly asked what Aspasia had been up to lately. I normally enjoyed hearing about her more outrageous behavior.

"You haven't heard?"

"I've only been back three weeks," I said, seeing in Sirena's expression that I'd opened the door to a dangerous subject.

"Aspasia tried to buy a ring in the Agora, without Pericles, or any other man with her. The dealer refused to accept her money. It was above the limit, for a woman to deal with alone."

I shrugged. "That's the law. And a good one. It's for a woman's protection, to keep them from being cheated—"

"Ridiculous. Aspasia is right. Athenian society is sick. The segregation of the sexes is carried to an extreme." She sat down beside me, pushing my legs out of the way.

I leaned forward with my elbows on my knees, feeling the anger build in me, but unable to quell it. "Athens is more liberal than any other city in Greece. Be glad you don't live in Sparta."

"For all the times you've been there, you seem to know practically nothing about Sparta," Sirena said. "Aspasia says that Spartan woman can own and transfer property in any amount, in their own name, without a man to hold their hands, or give their seal of approval."

"Ownership is only one—"

"Wives and daughters of upright Athenian families seldom even stray away from their husband's home. You never go anywhere in public with me. You prefer your men friends, even your dull brother. Athenian society is unisexual. Women are servants, child-producers, and nothing more."

"I've never treated you that way." A flash of guilt shook me when I remembered Germaine.

Sirena gave in a little. "You're better than most men, I admit. At least you talk to me, ask my opinion on your plays, and are willing to argue."

"Right now, I'd prefer not to argue. Is there anything to eat, or do I need to find my dull brother and go to the Agora for food?" I smiled to try to release some of the tension, but Sirena was more incensed than I had imagined.

"Most husbands restrict their so-called intellectual life to the streets, clubs, and wine-shops of the city where the only women they come in contact with, and are willing to talk to are prostitutes."

"Now you *are* exaggerating."

"I'm not. Even you spend more hours with your men friends, fellow writers, in drinking clubs, in the market, in the gymnasium than you do with your family. At least I don't believe you have a mistress stashed away somewhere, like your brother has."

I felt my face grow hot, the argument straying into dangerous currents. "We have business to conduct, contacts to make. Without them, how would I ever get a play produced?"

Sirena scoffed at that. "That's not all that men talk about. What about certain streets, crowded with prostitutes, as easily available in Athens as a loaf of bread?"

"That's not what *my* friends talk about," I said, knowing it was only a half-truth.

"It better not be. These harlots create havoc. It's obvious why Athenian men avoid marriage as long as possible, then give in only under family pressure, often not until the age of thirty or older. Then they only want young brides. What would you say if a thirty or forty-year-old man came to ask for Lelia's hand in marriage?"

"I'd run him out of the house."

"Of course you would. At first. Until you learned how wealthy he was. But let Lelia slip up and lose her virginity, and—"

"Sirena, please."

"I only say what is true. Women must remain chaste, but men have seemingly no moral restraints. Even after marriage, an Athenian man of prominence may safely make use of a courtesan or keep a concubine without damaging his reputation. If I ever thought—"

"In the name of Zeus, let's end this. I'm too tired to endure any more of your harangue." I stood up and made a deep exaggerated bow to her. "I admit the grievous errors of my thinking. All men are selfish boors. Women are equal in every respect, except one. They have far more endurance for arguing. Now will you release me from your verbal prison so I can get something to eat?"

"I'm sorry," Sirena said, taking my hand and gently pulling me back down beside her on the couch, her anger subsiding as fast as it had risen. "I shouldn't have gone on and on like that. It's just that, when I hear Aspasia . . . never mind. Let me prepare you a hot bath, and scrub your back for you. You shouldn't eat while you're so upset."

She put her arm around my waist, beneath my tunic, low on my hip, her warm touch stirring me, as she pressed in close. She smelled fresh and clean, like a field of spring wild flowers. She felt familiar and comfortable. Why had I wanted more? I thought of Germaine waiting patiently for me to come to her, as I gazed into Sirena's trustful, loving eyes, and suddenly began to cry. I turned my head away so Sirena wouldn't see.

"What is it?" Sirena said, sensing my discomfort.

"Nothing. I'm just happy to be home. Why don't you join me? Then we can wash each other more thoroughly."

"I've missed you."

"And I you."

4

This one-sided argument still lingered in my mind a few days later, when Filia came to see me. She insisted for once that Sirena listen to her new troubles with Charybdis. Unfortunately, Filia's new complaints reopened our recent argument, taking it in new directions.

Filia looked as angry as I'd ever seen her. "Charybdis has bought a slave boy, a twelve-year-old child from Egypt or Persia, or some such place."

I hoped that I had not heard correctly. "You mean, a household slave?"

"To play with. I think you know what I mean."

This was one aspect of Athenian society, that Sirena had somehow failed to mention before, one that many citizens increasingly deplored, in private. But sexual inversion had gained placid widespread acceptance, if not official recognition. The harlots' chief rivals were the boys who participated in homosexual practice, officially immoral, but commonly overlooked. Merchants imported boys and sold them at auction. Their owners used them, and sometimes abused them, for a few years, and then discarded them into the vast general slave population.

It didn't take long before Sirena became as angry as Filia, and I became superfluous to the conversation, except to serve as the evil male closest at hand.

"He brought him home three days ago, and gave him a room to himself, where Charybdis can visit him whenever he wants," Filia said.

"You can't let him do that," Sirena said.

"I was too shocked. I wasn't sure at first. Then Charybdis slept with him last night, all night, and refused to talk about it this morning. The boy paraded around the house like a proud bird, with practically nothing on. Isadore came and told me. That's what made me most furious."

Isadore was Filia's three-year-old daughter, conceived after Filia sought the services of a stand-in for Charybdis, despite my strenuous warnings of where it might lead.

"That's terrible, Filia. You have to protect your daughter. You don't know what that boy will do, in front of her. Take the boy by the hair and throw him out."

"I just might do that," Filia said.

"Don't wait."

"Charybdis will be furious."

"Let him be. If he wants to play with boys, let him find them somewhere else. There are plenty of places."

"It's horrible to think about. Seeing the expression on that boy's face."

Sirena laughed. "If Pericles attempted to do something like that to Aspasia, she'd twist the boy's balls off with her bare hands and feed them to Pericles."

"Sirena," I said. "The children may hear."

"I don't care. They should know the truth about this dark side of Athenian society. I want them to know."

Filia turned to me. "Can I bring some sort of legal action?"

Sirena didn't give me a chance to answer. "Forget about the male-dominated courts and just throw the boy out of your house, and if Charybdis wants the boy that bad, throw him out too."

"You're both talking nonsense," I said. "Charybdis has the right to own a slave. And what he does with him is his own business. Learn to live with it, Filia."

Sirena and Filia looked at me as if I was insane. Sirena shook her head and took Filia by the arm. "Come on. We'll talk somewhere else."

Sirena never told me what plans they might have dreamed up, and I soon put it out of my mind. Then, three days later, Filia came storming back, pounding on our door not long after dawn, while we were still asleep. I got to the door first. Sirena stood just behind me when I opened it and Filia burst into the house, brushing past me before I could say a word, dragging a confused Isadore along by the hand. When I turned, Filia was already in Sirena's arms, and I had become the forgotten male again.

"What's happened?" Sirena said, looking accusingly at me over Filia's shoulder. "How did you get that bruise?"

Filia pushed back from Sirena, wiping tears from her cheek. "We had a terrible argument this morning. He again spent the night with the boy, but this was different. It was horrible. I could hear the sounds and voices. It was too easy for me to imagine exactly what they were doing. All these years I've always thought he was impotent. After last night I know different. It was only me. He prefers a partner with hair-less balls."

That left us speechless for nearly a minute. Sirena and I stared at each other, our mouths hanging open. Then she clamped her hand over her mouth to keep from laughing. I swung away, and pretended to cough.

"Go ahead and laugh," Filia said. "I can tell you it wasn't at all funny to hear them bouncing around in there."

"What happened to your face? Did he hit you?" Sirena said, getting control of herself.

"I lost my temper. The boy walked in on me bathing this morning. He had nothing on. He laughed at me and wiggled his penis, and started to urinate into my bath water."

"Zeus! I would have killed him," Sirena said.

"I very nearly did. In a way it was comical, I suppose, something Abderus could use in one of his more ribald plays."

"I don't write such plays," I said, but I listened carefully anyway.

"What happened?" Sirena said.

"I scrambled out of my bath, ignoring my own nakedness. He had the gall to laugh and point at me. I grabbed his penis, balls and all, and squeezed as hard as I could. Just like milking a goat."

Sirena grabbed Filia by the shoulders, laughing so hard that tears flowed down her cheek. "You did that? You really did that?"

I wanted to sneak away, my skin crawling with the image of that poor boy's private parts in Filia's strong hands. I almost felt the pain, as if it was me.

"It was glorious," Filia said. "I nearly yanked him off the floor. He screamed like a pig being slaughtered. Charybdis heard, of course, and came running."

"He saw you?"

"He nearly fainted. I grabbed the boy by the hair with one hand, kept hold of his penis with the other and dragged him out of the house onto the street, both of us as naked as the day we were born, while Charybdis limped after us, screaming almost as loudly as the boy." She looked down at Isadore and patted her on the head. "Fortunately, Isadore slept through all this."

"You're not making this up?" Sirena said, barely able to talk.

"Not a bit. I threw the boy into the gutter, nicely running with filth, and kicked him a few times before Charybdis got to me. He struck me in the face, so I hit him back just as hard and ran into the house. I barred the door. The last I saw of him, he was limping away, carrying the boy in his arms like a child."

Sirena grew serious, wiping the laugh tears from her face. "You must leave him. You have no choice now. You can come and live with us until you find a way to get rid of him."

Filia fell silent for a moment. She looked at me. "Abderus, have you told Sirena, about Isadore?"

I nodded.

Filia leaned close to us and whispered. "Charybdis knows that

143

she isn't his."

I wasn't surprised. "How did he find out?"

"He knew from the start. My tricks didn't fool him. Yesterday he threatened to disown her and accuse me of adultery if I made any trouble over the boy. I don't know what will happen. I don't know what to do."

For once, Sirena had no quick answer. A grave silence fell over us, until the two women looked, as one, at me, and I began reflexively to vigorously shake my head.

"Yes, Abderus," Sirena said. "You must talk to Charybdis, man to man. Tell him what *he* will suffer when he brings all this out into the open."

5

Filia and Isadore moved in with us, and for a time we had some peace in the family. I convinced Filia not to raise a fuss over Charybdis's undue interest in small, foreign born boys, and Charybdis realized that he was better off without Filia around, especially since his boy would never enter the house while she was there. It took me only a brief, one-minute conversation, while standing outside his door, horribly embarrassing for each of us, to convince Charybdis that doing nothing was best for everyone. But then, as I turned away to leave, he grabbed my arm. I reluctantly turned back, fearing he would try to explain his actions, the last thing I wanted to hear.

"I want to see my daughter," he said.

"I thought you said—"

"I know she's not really my daughter. I always have. But I love her as much as if she was. Why do you think I've never said anything?"

"You loved her so much that you brought a slave boy her age into the house to play with. Did they get along well?"

He looked at me for a long time, his lips set in a straight line. "I want to see my daughter."

"And what about your threat to reveal Isadore's parentage?"

"I was angry when I said that. I would never want to hurt Isadore. I insist on seeing her. Otherwise I will make trouble, whatever the consequences."

I shrugged. "You're welcome at our house any time. But leave the boy home."

A few weeks after Filia and Isadore moved in with us, Jason, and Nephele showed up at our door with a wagon load of belongings pulled by two tired donkeys. Sebastiano rode one of the donkeys, Zeta the other. Nephele had won the argument to rescue Sebastiano from his Spartan future. Without a place to live, they moved in temporarily with us. With five adults and six children, the house was as crowded as the Agora after a three-day rain storm.

I found it nearly unbearable, and not just because I couldn't work, and seldom had a moment alone with Sirena. I constantly worried that Jason or Nephele would let something slip about Germaine. I resolved to get them out of the house quickly, and if possible, housed an inconveniently long distance away from us.

It was also a tense time for Jason and Nephele. They worried about what her father would do when he found out they were back after an eight year absence. They couldn't decide what to do. Their indecision soon became a favorite topic of conversation.

"Don't do anything. Just leave him alone," I said, putting forth my general strategy for dealing with unpleasant people. "Find a place to live in a small Attica town outside of Athens, and he need never know you've left Sparta."

"They don't want to move away from Athens again," Sirena said. "How can you suggest such a thing?"

"It might not be a bad idea," Jason said.

"I don't want my children to grow up in some poor, miserable village," Nephele said.

"They'll probably be better off there than in Athens," I said, meaning it.

"That's nonsense," Sirena said. "They'll miss out on so much. And how will Nephele continue to dance, living off in the country somewhere. It's almost as if you're trying to get rid of them now that they've finally returned to the family. What will your mother say?"

What could I say after that? I shrugged and fell into an annoyed silence.

"Just do nothing. Ignore your father. What can he do really?" Filia said, speaking for the first time.

"He has a lot of influence," Jason said.

"So what? What do you think he'll do? Try to get you ostracized? Kadmus can always get you a job on the Parthenon," Filia said.

"I don't think that's a good idea," Sirena said. "Go and see him right away, Nephele, before he finds out from someone else."

Nephele nodded her head warily. "Do you really think so? That's what I've half decided to do, but I wasn't sure."

"And take Sebastiano with you. Yes, do that. He's never seen his grandson, has he?"

"What about Zeta?"

Sirena looked at me, her mouth briefly twitching into a scowl. "Take her along. It can't hurt. But your father probably won't give her a second look. Poor Zeta is only a granddaughter after all."

Sebastiano came running into the room, hearing his name. He looked around, expectantly, as everyone stared at him. "What do you want?" he said, hands on hips. Sebastiano was tall and slender, olive-skinned, handsome and reserved. He looked as if he had just emerged from an Egyptian relief on one of pharaoh Ramses's thousand-year-old monuments.

Nephele held out her arms. "We're going to visit your grandfather."

"I might as well repack the wagon," Jason said, listlessly.

"I'll help you," I said, and the three women scowled at us as they wandered out of the room, talking amongst themselves on how best to prepare Nephele for her crucial confrontation.

The next day I attended a meeting of the Ekklesia with Kadmus, at his urgent request. He said that a crucial vote would take place concerning expenditures on the Parthenon project, and he was worried about the outcome. I thought he was overreacting.

I met Kadmus in the Agora. The Ekklesia, to which every male citizen belonged as their birthright, met in a natural, open-air amphitheater nearby. It could comfortably hold six-thousand citizens, a quorum, the number necessary to vote an ostracism. We joined the crowd filing into the amphitheater.

"What do you expect to happen today?" I said, impatient at the thought of wasting a morning listening to boring speeches.

"The Boule has placed an ostracism on the agenda," he said.

"Good. That should be interesting," I said, trying to compensate for his glum mood.

"You would say that. Calicrates is the target, and if he's ostracized, I don't know what will happen with the Parthenon. They'll probably delay everything and dismiss half the workers."

"Look around you. From the size of this crowd I doubt they'll get a quorum."

Had the required six-thousand male citizens shown up, someone would have spent the next ten years of their life outside of Athens. Whoever received the largest number of votes, scratched on surplus clay pottery scraps, even if it was far less than a majority, would be expelled from Athenian territory. It didn't happen often, since it required a good deal of civic enthusiasm to manage the quorum. And it was not as harsh as it sounded. The ostracized individual kept his possessions and business interests in Athens. After ten years he could return, usually richer than when he left. When political passions were high, ostracism provided a convenient and peaceful way for citizens to choose between two leading politicians with markedly conflicting policies, and thereby put a halt to paralyzing conflict.

"What else is on the agenda?" I said, wondering how long I would have to endure the heat, standing out in the open. Fortunately, speeches were strictly limited in length.

"Pericles has been asked to defend his building projects, particularly the Parthenon. Others will speak against the unexpectedly large expenditures. I'm not sure what will come of it."

"I guess I'll stick around then. I enjoy listening to Pericles," I said.

His eloquence and intelligent grasp of the essentials of any issue always impressed listeners, though he did not speak in a particularly impassioned or inflammatory manner. Nor was his presence all that commanding. He was not a tall man, or even remotely handsome. His head was somewhat longish, and out of proportion. But we all listened carefully to what he said, and more often than not, agreed with him.

"Let's hope he's well armed with words of wisdom today," Kadmus said.

"If anyone can talk himself out of these accusations, he can."

The ability to persuade was the main source of Pericles's power, in a system of government where no individual had the power to enforce his will against the majority of citizens. The Ekklesia had the sole power to pass or reject laws, to decide whether to wage war or seek peace, to approve or disapprove alliances and treaties. And among its members, Pericles had only one vote, no more than any other citizen. Power was more concentrated and potentially more susceptible to Pericles's influence in the five-hundred member Boule. The Boule set the agenda for the Ekklesia, determined what laws could be voted on, what issues could be discussed, an extremely powerful function. But the members of the Boule were all chosen by lot. Fifty male citizens came from each of Athens' ten districts, serving for a single year, and no more than twice in a lifetime.

These randomly chosen individuals, not Athens' politicians, not Pericles, were the watchdogs of democracy. They met every day except festival days and days of ill omen to organize the business of the Ekklesia. Of equal importance, they also oversaw the activities of public officials and agencies, and brought legal actions to enforce their own decisions. Pericles had to win these men over to his views quickly, for in a year a new set would be randomly chosen. He had to work even quicker with the individual Prytanies, the regional contingents of fifty, which took turns serving as a standing committee for the Boule, for they only served for a tenth of the year. For power hungry politicians, it was a frustrating system to work within.

The path to continuing power was through the military. Athens' ten strategoi, generals of the army, were all elected. And unlike most other public offices, Athenian citizens could elect the same man to the office of strategoi, year after year, without limit. As a consequence, the commander-in-chief, the strategoi autokrator, was the most influential man in Athens. That was the office that Pericles had held for years.

However, even such a high office only provided Pericles the opportunity to be heard and listened to. The real power came from Pericles the man, not from the position he held, for the strategoi autokrator could only recommend laws, resolutions, and policies. He still had to convince the Ekklesia to vote for and approve his measures. And, unfortunately for Kadmus's peace of mind, he did not always get his way.

Such was the case that day. Despite Pericles's highly convincing speech, the Ekklesia passed a resolution by voice vote that required that Calicrates take immediate steps to reduce his expenditures on the Parthenon, even if it meant delays. I raised my voice against it, out of loyalty to Kadmus.

"That's what I was afraid would happen," Kadmus said.

"The vote only requires Calicrates to be a little more frugal," I said.

Kadmus laughed. "Calicrates has only one way to reduce his costs, and yet maintain his considerable profits."

6

A few days later, Nephele put her plan into action, dragging Sebastiano and Zeto off to see their grandfather. When she returned in less than an hour, we were all waiting, surprised at her quick return.

"I was shaking, I was so nervous," Nephele said. "Sebastiano and Zeta were wonderful."

"What did your father say? How did he react? I imagine he was shocked to see you suddenly turn up without warning," Sirena said.

"Surprised, and instantly furious of course. Then he saw the children, and it seemed that ten years evaporated from his face. That perpetual frown, that I remember, seemed to melt from his face. I think he's been miserable ever since I was born. Cursed with an only daughter."

"And now, a boy at last. An heir. I told you," Sirena said, looking mostly at me.

"Of course, he thought I had left Jason."

"You corrected him of that impression, I hope," Jason said.

Nephele looked at him, with a teasing smile. "I was tempted to let him go on thinking I'd abandoned you in Sparta. Later, we could have had a sudden reconciliation. My father would have been so happy, for a while."

"Nephele, please" Jason said, shaking his head.

"I eventually told him that the man who had robbed him of his daughter was back in Athens," Nephele said, laughing. "The scowl returned to his face."

"Zeus," Jason said, standing up in the crowded dining room where we'd gathered, and starting to pace back and forth behind his chair.

"Then I reminded him that you were also the man who produced a grandson for him," Nephele said.

"What did he say to that?"

"I think he was about to say that now that you'd done your duty, you should remain in Sparta where you belong. But he managed to restrain himself, no doubt seeing the look on my face."

"Did you tell him what we talked about?" Sirena said. I had no idea what thAT was, and from the look on Jason's face, he didn't either.

"I didn't need to. He guessed right away."

"Smart man, your father. What did he say?"

"He said, I suppose I'm going to have to accept that man into the family if I'm going to get to see much of this boy, and I nodded to confirm his guess."

Jason shook his head, not at all cheered by the apparent victory. "After your father has had a chance to think about it, he'll probably change his mind. He'll start scheming ways to get control of his grand-son. There *are* ways."

I saw his point. "Absolutely right," I said. "He's rich enough to hire a small army of lawyers and buy a few judges. He might claim that you're both incompetent to raise a child properly and get himself awarded legal custody."

"If he tries that, I'll kill him," Nephele said.

None of us said anything. I think we all thought that she would.

The conversation continued over dinner. We tossed around con-jectures on how the old man would deal with his newly accepted son-in-law, some amusing, some serious, none accurate as it turned out. The comments and suggestions got more and more outrageous as the evening progressed, not surprising considering the amount of wine we consumed in our need to celebrate. However, Jason got more and more morose, taking the suggestions all too seriously. For the rest of us it was a pleasant meal for a change, the tension drained from us, until Sebastiano wandered in from where the children were eating, with a chicken bone in his hand, and innocently chopped my legs out from under me with a few innocent words.

"Where's Germaine, and little Gelasius, uncle Abderus? I thought they'd be here."

My heart missed at least three beats, before lurching into action again. I might have gotten through his unintentional revelation if Nephele hadn't gasped and dropped her knife, and if Jason hadn't simultaneously grabbed the chicken leg from Sebastiano's hand and ordered him back to the children's room. I never learned why he took the chicken bone.

Sirena looked at the three of us, one at a time, ending with me. I had, stupidly, resumed eating.

"Abderus."

I looked up.

"Who is Germaine?"

I still might have made something up, except that Jason and Nephele had to make matters worse. They jumped up, abandoned food and drink and rushed into the house, leaving me at Sirena's mercy, while Filia looked on in amazement.

"Who is she?" Sirena said. "A woman I suppose, though the name is odd, foreign sounding. The other is her child, I would have to say."

Sirena was dangerously calm and controlled. I knew that what I said next would determine the course of my life. I didn't want to lose her. I would die without her.

"She's from beyond the Black Sea. A grain importer bought her when she was still a child, and brought her to Samos. He sold her to another man who taught her gymnastics. She showed great talent, with remarkable dexterity. Always a crowd pleaser. He brought her to Athens to earn money off of her."

Filia gasped, covering her mouth with her hands. "I think I've heard of her. She disappeared from Athens several years ago."

I gave Filia a hard look, quickly shaking my head.

"I think I'll go see what Isadore is up to," Filia said, knocking her chair over in her haste to get away.

Sirena's voice raised a pitch higher, as she leaned forward across the table, eyes locked on me. "Remarkable dexterity. A crowd pleaser. In other words, she brandished her female charms for every man in sight. No doubt well endowed, with that ugly sand-colored hair that men seem to adore, if it's true she's from the north. And naturally, when you saw her you immediately fell victim to her barbarian charms."

"It wasn't like that," I said, wearily.

"How was it, then?" Her look, her eyes seeming to redden in anger, dared me to attempt a lie.

I felt sweat running down my sides beneath my tunic. I knew my forehead must glisten damply in the last rays of sunlight to reach the courtyard. I didn't lie, but I skipped over a few things. "I came across her wandering along the road towards the harbor at Piraeus. She had escaped, I think. Never quite certain. I helped her reach Sparta and found her a place to live."

"What a charming story. I'm sure she was very grateful. You, of course, found time to check on her when you made your trips to Sparta. And no doubt helped her with a few coins to meet her needs."

I nodded forlornly.

"And that's all you have to say?" Her voice had subsided again, into a muted whisper.

"That's about it."

"What about the child?" she suddenly shouted, standing up. "Where did he come from?" I couldn't think of anything to say. "You became her lover, didn't you? That child is yours. Of course it is."

I managed to keep my eyes from darting away, but I couldn't get the word out.

"How old?"

"Gelasius is two years old," I finally managed to say.

Sirena turned away, to keep me from seeing her tears. She raised her hand to wipe her eyes. I started around the table.

"Don't come near me," she said.

I stopped. "Sirena. This is not so unusual. Many men have—"

"Don't you dare say that."

"You're not being fair."

"I'm not fair? You should be relieved you're not married to some-one like Aspasia. She'd be carving on you with a knife by now." She turned back to me, face hardened against emotion. "Where is she now?"

"Here in Athens."

"Dear Zeus! You *would* bring them here, now that you no longer have an excuse to travel to Sparta."

"Gelasius is my son. You don't expect me to abandon him?"

"No, of course not. Which means that you're also obligated to keep her as your mistress."

"I haven't seen her since—"

"I don't want to hear that. You've said enough. Do you think I'll ever be able to trust you again as long as they live in easy reach of your uncontrolled lust?"

I winced. "We've talked about this before. A man is different from a woman. We easily fall prey to more than *one* woman's charms. Man isn't by nature monogamous, and many a respectable Athenian sup-ports a concubine or two. At least she's not a boy."

"I warned you not to say anything more. Men are different are they, when it comes to sex? We'll see about that."

With that, she stormed out of the room, leaving me alone with a table full of food, and no appetite.

7

I escaped the house, and after wandering aimlessly around for an hour or more, found my way to Pericles's villa. Friends and support-ers crowded around, conversing excitedly, much of the talk related to the previous day's unexpected vote in the Ekklesia. I listened in for a while, trying to forget my problems. Pericles didn't seem particularly worried about the vote. He seemed convinced that Calicrates could find a way to satisfy the Ekklesia's demands and still keep the project on schedule.

I eventually wandered away, seeking solitude and anonymity. I spoke for a time with Euripidis and felt worse for it. He had found a producer for his latest play, a wealthy businessman who would put up the money, as a donation to the city. The businessman would gain nothing from it, except an enhanced reputation. Euripidis asked me what I had written lately. I told him that I'd just finished a new play, but when he inquired about it, I made an excuse and moved away. I saw Socrates, but went out of my way to avoid his tart, probing wit. I was not in the mood for that.

I ended up in a less crowded corner of the central courtyard, where I sipped steadily from a wine chalice. I had only a moment alone when a sly-looking man of about my age came resolutely towards me, someone I had never met. I tried not to make eye contact, but it didn't work.

"Excuse me. Are you Abderus, the writer?" he said.

I nodded, stood a little straighter, and took more interest in the stranger.

"My name is Eupeithes. I'm in shipping—principally grain from the Black Sea ports."

For a moment, I thought he might have something to do with Germaine, and took a deep drink of wine before responding. "You must be busy," I said, to make conversation.

"I heard Euripidis describe his new play. Sounds wonderful. Do you know about it?"

"He has mentioned it once or twice."

"He already has a sponsor."

"He is rather popular now. He could write any foolish play, and get a sponsor." I regretted saying that as soon as the words were out.

Eupeithes hesitated, less certain of his mission than when he first approached. He looked at me closely for the first time, frowning. He could no doubt tell that I was slowly making myself drunk, in a sort of methodical, and unenjoyable way.

"Euripidis told me that you have a new play, and might need a sponsor."

At that moment I could have embraced Euripidis like a long lost brother. Startled into alertness, a writer catching the scent of funding, I took a large swallow of wine. "Yes, that's most certainly true," I said. "I've just finished. A third writing."

Actually, I hadn't yet finished the play. The third act was giving me trouble. Sirena hated my first treatment, and I trusted her judgment. But that was no reason to discourage a possible funding source.

"I'd like to read it. What's it about?"

"It's a tragedy, a new twist on the Oedipus myth. I really shouldn't say too much more."

Eupeithes looked at me with new interest. "That sounds ambitious. When can I read it?"

Those were words every writer ached to hear, especially when the speaker wore a gold embroidered waist band around his tunic, and more gold on his arms and wrists than I owned. "Come around to the house some time. Any time."

"What about tomorrow? Say in the morning?"

"The afternoon would be better," I said, feeling my heart begin to race.

"I'll be there," Eupeithes said, and with a casual wave, disappeared into the crowd.

I grabbed another cup of wine and drained it with a single swallow. How wonderfully surprising life could be I thought as I made my way to the door, nodding and smiling to everyone I encountered, the problems with Germaine and Sirena momentarily pushed aside. If I had only known the diabolical forces I had unwittingly unleashed to further upset and rearrange my tangled life, I would have celebrated with less enthusiasm. But being a writer, I would have continued on anyway.

Sirena and I put our argument on hold. She understood the importance of a wealthy patron, whatever happened to our marriage.

"Get busy then," she commanded. "Rewrite that last act. Are you still going to argue about whether—"

"I'll do it your way."

"It's about time."

It took me until dawn. I had to replenish the oil in the lamp three times. Sirena slept fitfully, getting up every hour or so to see how I was doing. I drowsed off as she picked up my scrawled handwriting, nearly unreadable during the last hours. "Yes, that's better," I heard her say later, then oblivion.

It seemed like only seconds later, though nearly two hours had elapsed, when Sirena shook me awake. Even half asleep, I noticed the alarm in her voice.

"Wake up, Abderus. Wake up. You must do something."

I straightened up in the chair, trying to wedge my eyes open. They felt gritty with sand. "What the Zeus has happened?"

"There's been trouble on the Acropolis. Apparently some sort of riot."

"Kadmus?"

Sirena nodded. "That's what Boreas said."

"What happened?"

"I don't know. He was in too much of a hurry to say, except that Kadmus has been injured, and wants to see you."

I stood up wearily. "I know what happened. I was at the Ekklesia when they voted to force Calicrates to reduce expenditures. If I know Pheidias, he was behind this."

I learned the details later. Calicrates had demanded that Pheidias dismiss half his artists, to cut costs. Pheidias at first refused. He threatened to stop work completely. He assembled his artists that morning, and warned them. He aroused them, then let them down. Kadmus was among those Pheidias finally let go. His son Boreas was not. The dismissed sculptors refused to leave. They threw stones when Calicrates showed up. It turned into a riot when Calicrates asked Pericles to bring in the army to restore order.

"You'd better go see Kadmus and find out if you can do something," Sirena said.

"What about Eupeithes? He'll be here soon."

"I'll entertain him, if you don't get back in time." Those were fateful words, I would long remember.

Kadmus's house was unexpectedly quiet when I arrived. My brother sat slumped dejectedly in a chair with a bandage covering half his face, and with his arm in a sling. He looked beaten, and only grunted when I entered.

Boreas got up and offered me his seat. He looked just like his father—sturdy, broad-faced, with wide-set eyes that seemed sleepy at first, penetrating when you looked more closely.

Kadmus gestured with his good arm toward his son. "The fool resigned, as a useless protest. Now we have no one working."

"I won't work for them without you, father," Boreas said.

"I think they'll eventually take you both back," I said. "Calicrates and Pericles will get the Ekklesia to reverse itself. I heard Pericles talking about it."

Kadmus laughed. "It's too late now. Look at this." He held up his injured arm.

"What's wrong with your arm?"

"Not my arm, my hand. It's broken."

"Oh, well. It'll heal."

"That's easy for you to say. My fingers were crushed beneath the foot of one of Pericles's damned soldiers. The physician isn't sure I'll ever recover use of the hand."

"Nonsense. What does a physician know?"

"I'm finished, if I can't carve. It's all I have."

I turned to Boreas. "You've got to talk some sense into your father. He's always been this way—panicking at every slight misfortune. In a few days, everything will be back to normal."

When I returned home much later, exhausted from lack of sleep, I found Eupeithes still at the house. He and Sirena sat facing each other, in close conversation. I halted at the door, confused at the stranger in my house. I saw Sirena lightly touch Eupeithes's hand when she said something. He laughed, and patted her hand. What was going on?

I walked noisily into the room. They looked up, saw me, and straightened away from each other. Eupeithes stood up to embrace me.

"I enjoyed your play. Sirena has let me read it, or rather, she read it to me. Quite beautifully, I might add."

That was how it started. In the weeks that followed, Eupeithes visited the house frequently, ostensibly to converse with me about the play's production, but always disappointed if Sirena was not there. He brought friends, who stayed long into the evening. My house became almost as crowded and hectic as Pericles's. Sirena loved the excitement of it. I knew her intention, though she didn't say anything, except once, when I made a mild objection.

"We never have an evening alone," I said.

"If you want to be alone, go and spend an evening with Germaine, your Black Sea concubine."

The way she said her name made me wince. I didn't want to get into an argument with her. "I haven't been to see her since I brought her back to Athens."

"Why? What was the purpose in bringing her here? You waste your money."

I shuddered. I never realized she could be so cruel, so invective. Why hadn't I gone to Germaine? Perhaps because I was not the same person in Athens, as I had been in Sparta. When I left Athens on a trip, I left my Athenian life behind me. I could pretend all kinds of things. I could not do that walking across Athens.

"What's going on with Eupeithes? He comes here more often to see you than me."

Sirena smiled. She came to me and took both my hands and gently kissed my lips. "Are you jealous—finally?"

"Is that what you're doing?"

"No more than Aspasia does. I'm trying to develop the kind of atmosphere here that she has in Pericles's house. I think it'll be good for us, and will surely help you get patrons for your work. I think only of you."

I didn't feel reassured, but I dared not ask more. The thought of Sirena in another man's arms made me sweat and shake—murderously.

She let go of my hands and stepped back. "And then there is Lelia. We must think about her marriage. She was thirteen, months ago."

"It's too soon."

"Eupeithes brought his younger brother here, when you were out, yesterday. His name is Thersites. He is well-established in the trade business."

"I hope you're not suggesting—"

"He'd be a good match for her."

"How old is he?"

Sirena shrugged. "I suppose in his early thirties."

"He's too old. What are you thinking?"

Sirena laughed. "Do you expect Lelia to marry a fourteen-year-old boy?"

I didn't want her to marry anyone, but didn't say that. She was only a child to me. It seemed just yesterday that I had held her on my lap.

"What does Lelia think of this—Thersites?"

"I haven't asked her. She has met him, and I suppose has guessed why."

"I don't want to talk about this. I think I'll go out for a walk."

Sirena laughed, and gave me a little push towards the door. "A husband's way to escape every argument. Going for a walk. Wine with your men friends, and politics to take your mind off important things."

"Maybe I'll check to see how Germaine is doing in the new place."

"If you do, don't come back until you've been to the gymnasium to wash off her smell."

8

I started out towards the apartment I had rented for Germaine, but soon lost heart, and lost my way. That had happened to me several other times, which was why I had not yet managed to see Germaine since first bringing her to Athens. I was utterly incapable of walking away from Sirena, waving my farewell after embracing her, giving some excuse of where I was headed, knowing she knew the truth, to then march directly into Germaine's embrace. It seemed like betrayal to both women. I had felt comfortable, my guilt controlled, with Germaine in Sparta. I had been living different, non-overlapping lives, without conflict or competition for my time or devotion. I could justifiably feel that I was not cheating on either Sirena or Germaine then. But now, with them both living within an easy walk of each other, each knowing about the other, each knowing that when I was with the other, it was time I was stealing from her, everything had changed.

So I just walked, on and on, trying not to think. It was a pleasant, cool afternoon for a change, the sky cloudy, and the streets crowded with other aimless walkers. I went through the Agora, enjoying the anonymity of the crowds. I found a place in a wine bar, and drank the grapes from Athens' rocky hillsides and listened to the sophists discuss and argue the questions that have ever troubled mankind. I could have added some to their list.

Protagoras sat at a nearby table with a group of friends. I knew him slightly, but did not join them. Originally from Abdera in Thrace, Protagoras was one of the most influential of Greek sophists, Athens' greatest teacher, and a close friend of Pericles. He was famous for his often quoted and often puzzled-over statement, that *The human being is the measure of all things; of things that are, that they are; and of things that are not, that they are not.* As I looked at his balding head and scowling face, I thought of that assertion. One interpretation hit me immediately, and provided no comfort. I could not blame the gods for the predicament I was in, nor call for their help and expect any solution.

After sipping fruity, thick wine for an hour or so, I walked on, along the covered walkways bordering the Agora. I paused to admire the marble sculptures that lined the walk, mostly of men, but an occasional woman. I did not do this often enough, my life too busy, my pace always brisk. Kadmus delighted in explaining to me, or anyone else who would listen, the latest advances in the art of sculpture. The most recent statues—those created during the last couple of decades—

were no longer static, rigid caricatures of people. The goal now was realism, sculptures alive with movement and feeling. Statues of males, usually carved in the nude, showed such realism that a quick glance, a first impression could shock and elicit a sudden gasp from the unwary observer. Statues of females were usually a captivating study in the flow and folds of gowns and clothes.

I left the Agora and walked along a path that took me beneath the cliffs of the Acropolis. I gazed in envy at the Theater of Dionysus, one of Pericles's first projects, where I dreamed of having a play performed. I entered the amphitheater and climbed the marble steps to the top row and remained there for a long time trying to imagine what it would feel like if five-thousand spectators sat below me on the stone benches that climbed the hillside, listening to words I had created for the actors to speak. Many times before I had stood that way, dreaming, imagining such a wonder. Now it might happen.

I continued on around the Acropolis, and wandered aimlessly through streets I seldom entered, lost in thoughts about my play. I paid no attention to where my feet took me, at least no conscious attention. But some part of me was directing my feet. For when I suddenly emerged from my reverie I found myself outside Germaine's door.

Not allowing myself time to stop and consider my actions, I quickly went to her door and knocked. She was home and answered the door immediately, as if she had expected me. She looked at me as if I was a lost child who had suddenly returned home. I silently took her in my arms. I felt the strength, and relief in her embrace, and something else, a measure of reserve.

"You've been away from Athens?" she said, when we backed away from each other.

I shook my head. I didn't know what to say. "I wanted to come see you sooner. But I've been terribly busy."

She flinched as if I'd slapped her. She turned to keep me from seeing her face, and walked to the other side of the room.

"I didn't mean it to sound that way," I said, going to her, gently rubbing the back of her neck. "I have a wife and three children to worry about, and now my brother—"

"What about Gelasius?" she said, turning around to face me. "Isn't he your child also?"

"Of course. I didn't mean—"

"I know it's easy to forget your slave girl and bastard child when

159

you're so busy."

"Don't ever say that. You've never been a slave to me. You know that. And you know that I love Gelasius. As much as any of my children." I wondered if it was true. How does one measure love anyway? Another question for the sophists.

"She knows about me, doesn't she? That's why you don't come here any more, why you've abandoned us. Why didn't you leave us in Sparta, where I at least had friends?"

I hesitated, then nodded. "I should have come sooner."

Germaine wandered over to stare out a window opening onto a small enclosed garden. I went behind her and took her in my arms, and felt under her shift for her breasts. I began to feel the reluctant passion rise, and kissed her on the back of the neck.

"Let's talk about this later," I mumbled.

She didn't say anything. She let me lead her into her sleeping room. The slave girl I had bought for Germaine was there, playing with Gelasius. I told her to take the child for a walk. I was impatient now. Seconds after the slave girl closed the door behind her, I began to remove Germaine's clothes. I tore her shift getting it off. She made no comment. When we were both naked, I paused for a time to look at her. She was such a splendid creature, someone from another world, almost a curiosity in Athens with her pale skin and golden hair, with the soft barely visible fur on her arms, with the unusual strength in her long athletic legs.

I sighed deeply and went to her. She was oddly reticent at first, even a little shy, but then became immersed in the old game of pleasure. In Athens, the game seemed to have different rules. It was like the first time, except that we knew each other so well, every curve, every imperfection, every way to touch and caress. It also seemed like it might be the last time, the intense way we went at each other, trying to elicit every feeling we'd ever had together. At moments it was almost brutal, but never cruel, and always stopping short of punishment, although, in a sense, I was punishing myself just by being there with her, knowing how I would feel when I returned to Sirena.

Afterward we sat and drank wine, not bothering to dress, but separated from each other, she on the bed, I on a nearby couch. I felt guilty, as I never had in Sparta. We didn't have much to say to each other, and sat in silence for a long time.

"I'll come more often," I said, at last.

"I don't think you will."

She was right, of course. I didn't say anything.

"You've been kind to me, Abderus. Without you, I don't know what would have happened to me. You even gave me a child."

"You make it sound like it's all over." I felt a sudden panic—or was it hope, or both?

A stillness settled over the room. Germaine lazily got up and came to sit next to me on the couch. She hooked one leg over my knee, and let her hand lie limply on my thigh.

"I have met someone," she said, her voice unusually quiet, her eyes meeting mine.

"What do you mean you've met someone? A new friend?"

"I think you know what I mean."

"I don't. I've no idea what you're talking about." I got up, pushing Germaine's leg aside, and began pacing. I felt as if everything was sliding away from me.

"He's a mate on a ship. A sailor. He's from the north, like me. He comes regularly to Athens from some place beyond the Black Sea, twice a year, on a grain ship."

I walked faster, not able to look at her. "Tell me more. I know you have more to say."

Germaine approached me and reached for my arm. I brushed her aside and kept pacing, furiously back and forth.

"We're friends. Nothing more," she said.

I laughed.

"It's true," she said. "But it could be more."

"What do you mean by that?"

"I wish to go away with him, and return to my homeland. He has asked me. But I won't unless you give me your permission."

I stopped my pacing and slowly turned towards her. We were still both foolishly naked, which suddenly seemed comical to me, and I laughed.

"Is that so funny? That I should want something more than the fragile life you've given me?" she said.

I went to a chair and retrieved her dress and handed it to her. I watched as she slipped it around her shoulders and tied it in front, sensing that a door was closing on a part of my life. After she finished, I retrieved my tunic and slipped it on, while she watched me, perhaps the same thought in her mind.

"Did this sailor say who he worked for, who owns his ship?" I said.

"I don't think so."

"He never mentioned someone named Eupeithes?"

Germaine looked at me, mystified, shaking her head slowly.

I took a couple of deep breaths to calm myself, but my heart kept racing. "He's like you? Golden-haired, light-skinned, tall, and wonderful?"

She laughed. "He is. You'd like him. He seems kind."

"What about Gelasius?"

She looked worried. "You won't take him away from me?"

I shook my head, trying to hide my regret. I would never see Gelasius again, but *never* is a harsh, unforgiving word, and seldom correct.

"I have your permission? You will release me?" she said.

"You don't need my permission," I said.

I didn't stay long after that. Though she didn't want to take them, I gave her all the coins I had with me, and left quickly before we both broke into tears.

9

Sirena and I sat on our padded stone benches in the Theater of Dionysus, and watched my play performed for the first time. We sat near the highest row. I wanted to see the audience's reaction. We could hear perfectly, and I didn't need to see the actors' masked faces. I felt horribly nervous, and ached for it to be over, without some unspeakable disaster. It was like watching your child born, something I have only once done, with Lelia, never to repeat. This play was also my first major production. Eupeithes had not failed me. I was certain I had Sirena to thank for that. I still wasn't certain how far she had gone to insure his support.

"She has left Athens," I said, during the break between the first and second act.

Sirena took my hand.

"I suppose you'll get mad, if I say it's for the best?"

"Please don't."

"I could have left you," she said. "I nearly did. You could have lost us both. I think you deserved to."

"Some things just happen," I said.

"Don't blame the gods for what you do."

"I blame them for putting such temptations in my way," I said.

We looked at each other, and began laughing.

I ached to ask her whether it had been Eupeithes that had helped me out my entanglement, but dared not. Some things are best left unsaid. We waited in silence for the second act to begin.

Between the second and third act, we bought cups of wine from a boy who had finally made it to the top row. We drank in silence for a while, not wanting to say anything about the play yet, as if it might jinx the outcome.

"I've grown tired of having people around the house all the time," Sirena said, suddenly. "It's tiresome, don't you think?"

I squeezed her hand. "Let's leave that to the politicians. What about Eupeithes?"

"He's leaving for the north in a few days. He'll be gone for half a year. Maybe when he returns you'll have another play for him."

"Or maybe we can find another sponsor."

The play was a success. Eupeithes, as the patron, enjoyed as much praise as I did—perhaps more. He certainly gained more by it than I, his political, and therefore his economic future, dependent on such wise and popular largess.

On the subject of political futures, we got an unexpected visit from an exuberant Nephele after the play.

"Guess what," she said. "My father has surprised all of us. We all had it wrong." She referred to our predictions of what her father would do about Jason.

Though one of the richest men in Athens, he was unable to participate directly in politics since he was not a citizen. This must have nagged at him for years. Now he realized he could do the next best thing—promote his son-in-law's political career. Although Jason was not born in Athens proper, he was a citizen since he was born to citizens. Our parents had originally lived in Attica to the east of Athens, part of the greater Athenian city-state, before moving to the city.

"He can't be serious," I said, laughing.

I stopped abruptly when I saw the dangerous frown on Nephele's face. Jason in politics, speaking before the Ekklesia, elected to a skilled office not drawn by lot, perhaps in time gaining the high rank of strategoi? I couldn't accept it, but kept my thoughts hidden.

"Does Jason know about this?" Sirena said.

"Not yet."

Nephele sounded worried, and well she should. Jason might easily drag her back to Sparta to avoid a political career.

The play's success—and the other events that accompanied it—marked a turning point in the life of my family. Sirena and I worked to set aside the past, concentrating our thoughts on the children. Jason and Nephele found a house, half paid for by her father. Filia, ignoring our advice, went back to live with Charybdis, and his slave boy. Sirena and I again enjoyed moments of privacy, when the children were asleep or distracted. Not unexpectedly, Sirena eventually became pregnant with our fourth child, and my fifth. For a few weeks, we were intensely happy. Then family matters struck another blow—two blows.

Kadmus disappeared. His hand had failed to heal properly. He would never again grip a chisel, carve a muscle's form out of stone. Something died in him. Boreas went to look for him. He found his father working in Piraeus, Athens' port on the Saronic Gulf, loading ships. He refused to come home, and forbade his family to follow him. Boreas went to see him regularly. Kadmus sent back most of the paltry pay he earned, while he lived worse than a slave. Ironically, as I had predicted, Calicrates took back his dismissed artists. Boreas again worked on the Parthenon, without his father at his side.

Then another tragedy descended upon us. Sirena and I came home to find Filia waiting. She looked ghastly, face blanched, eyes darting, fearful, but no tears. My heart started to beat wildly. Sirena ran to her side.

Filia could barely speak. "Something terrible has happened."

We took her inside to a couch and got her wine. "Is it something to do with Charybdis?" Sirena said.

"He's dead."

Sirena gasped, reaching for Filia's arm.

"What happened?" I managed to say.

"Murdered. The boy too, his head almost cut off." Filia's hand shook so hard she spilled the wine on her dress. Sirena took the cup from her and handed it to me.

"You don't need to talk about it. Just try to relax. Breathe deeply," Sirena said.

"I found them both lying naked in his blood-soaked bed, hands clasped together. They had been mutilated. Someone had cut off . . . I can't say it." She gagged, and shook horribly, but still no tears. Sirena held her close. I sat back down and drank some of Filia's wine.

"Isadore, she's all right?" I said.

"She was with me."

"Thank the gods for that, at least," Sirena said. "Where is she now?"

"At a neighbor's house."

"Tell us which one. Abderus will get her. You two can stay here as long as you want. In time, everything will work out."

Filia looked up, eyes wide, like a frightened deer. "No. No. It'll never be all right. They think I did it."

Rome, Italy

VI. Rome, Italy
AD 175

In the first centuries of the modern era, the Romans accomplished what no other nation had before, or has since—linking under one authority all the lands touching the Mediterranean Sea. This commonwealth of nations reached its quintessence during the reign of the 16th emperor, Marcus Aurelius. Under his rule the sense of unity, the reconciliation of peoples, the uniformity of prosperity, reached a height never since surpassed. The Empire stretched from the shores of the Caspian Sea to the Atlantic coast, from Hadrian's wall in Britain to the southernmost outposts of Egypt and Syria.

In every corner of the Empire, and in every aspect of life, the "Roman way" had taken root: in justice and administration; in uniform building standards for aqueducts, baths and temples; in a well-maintained road system that connected every province. Latin was the language of government and commerce in every land bordering the Mediterranean and beyond. Roman citizenship was the highest calling of men everywhere, even among the barbarians across the Rhine and Danube, clamoring for entry—and often succeeding.

The Betrothal Banquet

1

The magistrate dismissed the accusations against Felita for lack of evidence. But that did little to alleviate my sister's worries. Chryses's brothers railed against the decision. They believed that Felita had murdered and mutilated Chryses, and they openly vowed revenge.

"They'll come after me again, when they find a way," Felita said, during our muted celebration of the magistrate's verdict. "The family is wealthy. They can buy whatever they want. Even witnesses ready to perjure themselves."

"The authorities may find the murderer," I said.

"There's a lot of money at stake also," Felita said. "Chryses's share in the family grain business has passed to me. They want it back, at any cost."

Serina gave birth, without difficulty, despite her age, to a beautiful baby girl we named Helen. She was tiny, half the weight of our other children at birth. We worried about her constantly for the first year. When she began to walk at just eleven months, and soon after ran, keeping her nurse happily busy, we began to relax a little. We had been fortunate. All our children would apparently survive the perils of childhood, a rarity.

"Helen will be our last," Serina announced, when she was still recovering from the birth trauma. I didn't argue. Our eldest daughter,

Lelia, at fifteen, was old enough to be my youngest daughter's mother.

And, indeed, it was time Lelia married. Tithonus, the younger brother of Euphorbus, who produced my first serious play—a financial flop, though critically acclaimed as a *new brilliant adaptation of the Oedipus theme*—had finally proposed marriage. Serina and I argued over Tithonus. Serina liked him, since he was well established in business, with good family connections, and entirely moldable by any halfway expert wife. I objected to him. At thirty-seven, I thought that he was too old for Lelia. But I had another reason for disliking Tithonus that I dared not mention to Serina. He reminded me of his brother Euphorbus who came into our lives just after Serina found out about Germaine. Euphorbus was good for my career, but a further threat to my marriage, already at risk, thanks to my weakness for German gymnasts. Serina's successful efforts to make me jealous nearly drove me mad. Even after it ended with Germaine's departure, I could never stop wondering whether Serina had actually had an affair with the wealthy trader. Irrational though it was, I could not abide the sight of the man, despite the fact that he had produced my first play.

Lelia readily agreed with me about Tithonus, for her own reasons.

"His nose is too big," Lelia said. "And I don't like his dark, bushy eyebrows. And he hardly ever smiles."

Serina shook her head at us both. "Tithonus is only the third proposal we've had, and the first that is suitable."

"But I don't like him," Lelia said.

"His business is very risky," I threw in, though neither of them paid me much attention.

"Lelia, trust me that you'll learn to like him, sooner than you expect. You'll get used to him, like I got used to your father."

"What do you mean you got *used* to me?" I said.

Serina waved my question aside. "We've suggested the names of several other young men we might open negotiations with, and you've found objections to them all."

Lelia walked over to the pool of water at the center of the atrium and sat down on the ledge, elbows on knees, chin in her hands, eyes downcast. Her light summer stola draped around her, the pale blue color in perfect harmony with her light complexion and wavy dark brown hair. I caught sight of her sandaled feet, tapping the tile floor, the only sign of impatience. She had always been the most obedient, accommodating of children. I hated to see her grow up and leave the home. I would miss her dearly. Serina was much more rational than I.

In private she expressed her worry that if we didn't do something quickly, Lelia would be too old to attract a suitable husband.

"Someone will come along, mother," Lelia said. "Can't we at least postpone a decision about Tithonus. It's not that I don't see his good qualities, despite his nose and eyebrows, but I think—"

"She can do better," I said, finishing her thought.

Serina groaned impatiently. She got up from her couch, shaking her head, and came to sit next to me, giving me a quick kiss on the forehead. "No man will ever be good enough for your daughter." She turned to Lelia. "You'll need a better reason than his nose and eyebrows to reject Tithonus. This time we may have to insist. I think we know what's best for you."

"Mother, please." Lelia gave us a pleading look, head cocked to the side, that I was helpless against, and even Serina could not often withstand.

We agreed to postpone a decision, and delay giving an answer to Tithonus, ostensibly to allow Lelia time to get used to the idea, time to get to know Tithonus better. Lelia had other plans for the reprieve.

Tithonus's chances vanished the day Lelia brought home a young man we had never seen before. "This is Dominico. A friend," she said, firmly gripping the young man's hand.

She said friend with special emphasis. Serina and I exchanged glances. Lelia had obviously not just met Dominico. And they were obviously more than friends. Serina looked Dominico over with embarrassing intensity. He was young, not much older than Lelia, twenty-four we soon learned. He had a robust appearance, with perhaps a touch of Celtic blood in his veins, his face rounder than most Romans. He smiled with calm assurance as Lelia brought him to each of us in turn, ending with my mother, who had recently moved in with us. Lelia chose her words of introduction carefully, obviously rehearsed.

"This is my mother, Serina, who you may soon mistake for the Emperor's inquisitor." I winced when she said that, though there was truth in it.

Dominico made a short bow, speaking with a flourish that nearly made me laugh. "You can't be Lelia's mother. You're too young. You must be an older sister, masquerading as her mother."

Serina raised her eyebrows at me, and let Dominico briefly take her hand. I knew that kind of flattery would not win over Serina, and that she remained silent with great difficulty. Lelia sensed this too, for I saw her wince when Dominico made his greeting.

"And this is my father, the great dramatist, Absyrtus," Lelia continued. "You may have seen his latest play, *A Celtic Death*, not to my taste, but very popular. His shorter plays are quite funny." She referred to my ribald skits, filled with sex and intrigue, which found ready audiences at banquets, and provided a decent and steady income.

Dominico looked at me with a serious expression. "I thought *A Celtic Death* was excellent, highly realistic and moving. You have a great talent."

And you have a certain talent for words, yourself, I thought. I didn't believe for a second that he had viewed my play. "I wish the critics had the same opinion," I said.

Unlike my first play which received praise from the highest circles, and made me no money, *A Celtic Death* earned my no plaudits, but attracted audiences like the Tiber attracted Rome's refuge. Roman audiences, attuned to gladiatorial contests, loved the violence and sex, a certain formula for financial success.

Lelia pulled Dominico over to a couch in a cool shady section of the Atrium. "This is my grandmother, Malache, who provides me with a safe haven whenever my loving parents abuse me with too much affection."

Dominico knelt down and patted my mother's hand, bringing a cracked smile to her lips. "I can see where Lelia and her mother get their beauty."

"She's *my* mother," I said, with a certain relish.

That didn't phase Dominico in the least. "Yes, of course, now I see the resemblance," he said, with an expansive gesture.

A lengthy moment of silence ensued. Lelia looked pleadingly towards her mother. Serina sighed, glanced my way and stepped towards Dominico. "Why don't you come with me, Dominico, and I'll show you our garden."

Sirena took the young man firmly by the arm and walked him through the arcade into the peristylum where she could question him at her leisure. I looked at Lelia, who blushed happily. Her expression changed, a moment later, familiar frown lines appearing between her eyes as she watched her mother leave with Dominico.

"Don't worry," I said. "I think he's more than capable of surviving even your mother's interrogation." I took Lelia by the arm and gently led her to a bench along the atrium wall, to get out of the direct sunlight.

"How is it that we've never met Dominico before? And don't tell me you just met him."

"I did. Well, only a couple of months ago. We met at the Baths of Trajan."

"I see. I thought the Emperor, in an astute attempt to make himself horribly unpopular, abolished mixed bathing?"

"Not *in* the baths. It was after Resanna and I finished with the tepidaria. She wanted a massage. I didn't, so I waited for her in the library."

"You never read."

"Father! I sometimes read. I like to read your plays."

"Not the serious ones. So is that where you met him?"

Lelia nodded. "Shouldn't we go and rescue him from mother?"

"Give her a little more time. So Dominico walked into the library, caught sight of you reading, flush from the tepidaria, and instantly fell in love. With your intellect, or perhaps you were still wrapped only in a towel."

"Father!"

"And you saw this manly creature looking down at you, and dismissed Tithonus forever from your mind."

"It wasn't at all like that. We talked. We agreed to meet later. That's all."

I patted Lelia's knee, and nodded my acceptance. "That's more or less how your mother and I met, accept that I didn't get up the nerve to talk to her until we crossed paths a dozen times. What does your cousin think of Dominico?"

"Resanna? She hasn't met him."

I raised my eyebrows in exaggerated surprise, like one of the actors in my latest ribald skit. Resanna was the eldest daughter of my brother Kasen. She was the same age as Lelia, about the only thing they had in common. Resanna had already gained a dismaying reputation, her behavior, especially in regards the opposite sex, bordering on the scandalous. Despite their difference in temperament, Resanna and Lelia were the best of friends. It didn't please Serina and me, but we had long ago learned that saying anything negative about Resanna, or decrying her bad influence, only brought out in Lelia one of her rare angry outbursts.

I blamed Kasen for the way his daughter had developed. He had fled from responsibility just when Resanna entered her teen years. Kasen remained in self-imposed exile in Ostia, Rome's port at the mouth of the Tiber river. His fall from a scaffold, his hand crippled, a career in stone-carving at an end, had left him in despair. He could not face his family. He could barely live with himself. His wife Oma remained loyal, though she had to cope alone with her large family. She was certain he would one day return, and refused to consider divorce. Boreas, her eldest son, supported the family. He carved replicas of Greek statues that commanded high prices from wealthy Romans, who liked to sprinkle them around their villas. Boreas was the only stable member of the family, it seemed. His brother Benedetto raced chariots, much to Oma's dismay. He was as wild and undisciplined as Resanna. The other four children seemed destined to follow in Benedetto's and Resanna's footsteps.

"You'll have to introduce Dominico to Resanna soon," I said, intending levity. "She'll want to approve of him, and will probably have more questions than your mother."

Lelia frowned, but said nothing.

2

Not long after Lelia introduced Dominico to us, I met Nebulia in the Forum, quite by accident, or so I thought. I had been standing in a small crowd who had nothing better to do than to listen to an inept poet recite his latest efforts from the rostra, the speaker's platform. I had a different excuse. I was doing research, looking for memorable characters for my next play. The poet was a likely candidate. To get ideas, I had to venture out, away from my desk, and wander Rome's crowded streets, stare at people, listen to their conversation, watch and absorb. Rome's business, legal or illegal, reputable or disreputable, ordinary or novel, took place in the city's streets, squares, and taverns.

The Forum was not crowded on that day, probably because of the direction of the breeze, which was wafting strong sewer smells across the square. They didn't particularly bother me. I viewed them as an inevitable fact of city life. However, the sometimes overly pungent fragrance of Rome's air could overpower even long time residents. People complained of too few latrines, and of sanitary laws not adequately enforced. But Rome was one of the few cities in the world with a sewer system running beneath its streets, constructed centuries ago. If only people made better use of it. Romans simply shrugged and did what was most convenient. Good citizens dutifully hauled their wastes in open buckets to the nearest sewer facility. Others, regardless of the law, dumped their night soil out the window, which gave me and everyone else ample reason to avoid early morning walks.

I also tried to avoid the close of Senate deliberations, for similar reasons. I could withstand Rome's smells easier than I could endure the sight of the three-hundred or so pompous, self-righteous senators emerging from the Curia, like maggots from a dung heap, all monotonously dressed in white togas, the uniform of respectability, except for a few that held office and could add a purple stripe to their hem. Their prideful carriage was a joke, since none of them had real power, all decisions emanating from the Emperor. The Senate was a relic of the days of the Republic, centuries dead.

On the other hand, I went out of my way, sometimes embarrassingly so, to unabashedly scrutinize the women of Rome, for they dominated my plays, and without their mystique I would have been a pauper. I never hesitated to follow them, stand nearby, and listen to their conversations. My plays invariably portrayed such aristocratic women—exaggerated naturally—as well as a liberal dose of the lowest borne women of the streets, for accent, like salt on food. No austere, unadorned white attire hid the notable Roman woman's graceful form. Her stolas, finer tailored versions of the men's togas, were brightly colored, of the finest wool, the rich material caressing her proud figure to sketch a shape, and hint at what was beneath, a shoulder bare, a breast half-exposed, ankles and calves swinging into view with each sedate stride.

Jewelry provided the accent that advertised the wearer's wealth. Centuries ago, in the ancient days of the Republic, Cato the Censor attempted to restrain public demonstrations of wealth, the wearing of excessive gold jewelry in public. Aristocratic women took to the streets in protest. A near riot ensued, and Cato revoked the edict.

When I had enough of the poet, I turned away and saw Nebulia standing beneath the portico of the nearby Temple of Saturn. There was no mistaking her, dressed as richly as the Empress, her statuesque dancer's figure not in the least diminished in the decade I'd known her. She was looking directly at me, as if she had been watching me. I raised my arm in greeting and walked towards her.

My middle brother Janus was a fortunate man. After enduring the isolation of exile for years, he and Nebulia now seemed to have few cares, riding the crest of a wave of prosperity. Their son Sebastianus was nine years old, a handsome lad, with a complexion that more and more took on the deep tones of his mother, an Egyptian beauty with Nubian blood in her veins. Their daughter Zezili, three years younger, would one day rival her mother in beauty. Janus's father-in-law, a wealthy Egyptian businessman named Polydorus—reconciled with the pair thanks to Sebastianus—promoted Janus's political career with great enthusiasm. When Janus first met Nebulia, she was a dancer of some renown, much to her father's dignified dismay. Her career ended when she and Janus returned to Rome, but apparently the desire to perform simmered beneath the surface, as I would later find out, in a rather dramatic way.

Nebulia came slowly down the steps of the Temple to meet me. We embraced, something that always made my heart flutter a bit, as she was the kind of woman who took her embraces seriously, even when casually greeting her brother-in-law.

"You look wonderful," I said, my standard greeting, one that always brought a smile to Nebulia's face. Why is it that beautiful women never grow tired of hearing people tell them that?

"You're looking a little tired, Absyrtus. Have you been writing into the wee hours of the morning, or is Serina keeping you awake?"

"Just worries. Not all of us in the family are as well off as you and Janus. Those gold bracelets must have cost my politician brother a fortune."

"Actually, they're a gift from my father. But did you know that the Senate is expected to appoint Janus to a high city office, probably one of the four Aediles?"

"Polydorus has been whispering to one of the Emperor's counselors."

Nebulia frowned. "What did you expect? How else can you get ahead in Rome?"

"I agree. The only way. Which areas of civic life do you suppose Janus will watch over? Brothels perhaps?"

"Absyrtus!"

"How about saloons, or public games?"

"I hope he's in charge of theaters. Then you'll have to show your brother some respect."

"Perhaps he'll enforce the Emperor's edicts, instead of turning a blind eye to Romans' love of getting around the laws."

The extremes of Rome's infamous social life had tempered under Emperor Marcus Aurelius's reluctantly and partially accepted reforms.

Besides supposedly abolishing mixed bathing in public baths, he forbade fights to the death in the gladiatorial arena, introduced reforms in the treatment of slaves, and reduced pay to actors, the last of some use to me, if enforced. Romans loved their emperor, but cared little for certain of his laws, which they found ways to ignore. Mixed bathing was not completely eradicated, and I still had to pay my actors outrageous fees.

Nebulia took my arm and turned me away from an enormously fat priest who had sauntered out of the Temple of Saturn, squinting in the bright sunlight. "Let's go someplace where we can talk," she said, in a strangely alert whisper.

I took this as a warning. "I should be getting back to the house. Serina is expecting me to bring her some special foods—I have a long list—from her favorite supplier in Trajan's Market."

Serina, our four children, my mother, and I lived in a small crowded house near the Tiber, almost directly beneath the Appian Aqueduct, which was why we could afford it. We preferred that to living in the huge, block long, multistory tenements that held the bulk of Rome's central city population.

"Fine. I'll go with you. And help you find what she wants."

"Why don't you tell me right now what's on your mind, and save me a lot of suspense?"

Nebulia punched me lightly on the shoulder. "You don't like my company."

"You make me nervous. All beautiful women do."

"Except Serina?"

"She too, sometimes."

"You're an odd sort of person, Absyrtus. I suppose that's why everyone loves you and goes to you for advice."

"I'm a playwright. I deal in human emotions, conflicts, personalty defects."

Nebulia laughed. "Especially the last, for which you're an expert."

My business, as a dramatist, was to entertain, and for this I had to dredge deep in the sludge of mankind. I had much competition, for Rome never lacked entertainment. Rome's notables felt compelled, in the interest of public contentment, to mark every holiday with a public spectacles—dramas, orations, chariot races, gymnastic competitions, boxing matches, gladiatorial contests, or if everything else failed, a public execution.

Fortunately for my career, Romans loved to eat and drink, and insisted on entertainment while they did—a Greek poet to recite verses, a troupe of clever actors to perform a short ribald skit, a bevy of scantily dressed dancers and liquid acrobats to amaze and awaken the sleepy guests, all of which I could arrange, for a price.

That was what Nebulia had in mind. She leaned close to me and whispered. "You often arrange dancers for banquets, don't you?"

"Only because it's necessary to get my plays included." I turned to look at her, and saw a rare blush color her face. She began to nod, seeing my shocked expression. "You want to start dancing again?"

"Can we talk about it?"

"Does Janus know about this?"

She hesitated, her face coloring slightly.

"You haven't told him, have you?" I said.

"I'm considering it. I haven't yet decided."

He didn't know. And she had no intention of telling him. I shook my head, sensing trouble. Janus and Nebulia's well-ordered lives were about to hit stormy seas, and I would be asked sooner or later to quiet the waters.

"I think that's a crazy idea. But I will say this. You're as beautiful now as you ever were when you were dancing."

She gave me a kiss on the lips, hugged me again, and danced away with a wave of her hand. She called back to me, "We'll talk again Absyrtus, when you have more time."

3

Benedetto had driven in at most a dozen chariot races, never at a major spectacle, never finishing better than third. Then he unexpectedly got a chance to race during a four-day spectacle honoring Marcus Aurelius's successful Rhine campaign. I asked Janus if he had anything to do with it. The Emperor had appointed him Aedile, as Nebulia predicted. He and his three colleagues oversaw everything from chariot races to prostitute fees. He assured me, with a newly cultivated pomposity, that he had not.

Janus the Aedile did however reward the family, who turned out for the event en masse, with an excellent viewing area in the Circus Maximus. We stood, uncrowded, in a roped-off section reserved for us, directly above the start and finish line. Even Emperor Marcus Aurelius, in his enclosed, well-appointed Imperial box high above us, did not have a better view, only one more comfortable.

The stadium looked full, an indication of the importance of the race. The Circus Maximus held up to a quarter-million spectators. There were twenty-one of us, including my mother, who hated chariot races and didn't quite understand why we had dragged her to the Circus Maximus. Only Kasen was missing.

Before Benedetto's race started, Felita pulled me aside, away from the others. I reacted impatiently, until I saw the familiar anxious expression, one I had seen on the many occasions she had come to me for help, the first time when she was only thirteen, and I had to arrange an abortion.

"I just heard from a friend that works for one of the magistrates. It's so terrible, I can hardly say the words. I have to take it seriously. I knew they wouldn't give up."

"What is it?"

"They're going to charge me with murder again."

"Chryses's family?"

"Of course. Who else, in the name of Zeus?"

"I thought the charges were dropped."

Felita looked around, eyes wide with alarm. She ran her fingers through her hair, and smoothed down her stola. "They've found one of our slaves, the one who disappeared after the murder. I told you about him before."

"The one you think did it. Then what do you have to worry about?"

She laughed, a harsh chuckle that made me shiver. "They'll make him talk. Not to confess to the crime, but to accuse me of it."

"The emperor has outlawed torture."

"Don't be naive, Absyrtus. Chryses's brothers want his estate bad enough to try anything, legal or not. They may even try to take Imogene away from me."

"Felita, things have changed. I'll talk to Janus, and he can find out what the magistrate intends to do with the slave—"

"You're not listening to me," Felita shouted. I saw Serina turn and start to walk towards us. I waved her away. "Chryses's father has the slave locked away somewhere, in secret. They'll torture him, or pay him off. He'll say whatever they want, when he's brought before the magistrate."

I hesitated, trying to think of something positive to say. "That isn't enough to convince a magistrate. Only the word of a slave."

Felita shook her head. "They're not that stupid. I've heard that they have another witness. I don't know who. He'll swear he saw me with blood on my hands. I did have. After I found the bodies, and touched Chryses, before I knew he was dead."

"That's easily refuted."

Felita grabbed my arm. "Absyrtus, think! You know how it is. Chryses's father was once a Praetor. He is one of the most powerful men in Rome. He can buy enough witnesses to convict you of the crime."

An exaggeration, but not far from the truth. Rome's legal system was the most advanced the world had ever seen, but everyone knew that its enforcement had many imperfections. Too often, the strong, powerful and rich could bend the law to their own devices.

"You need a lawyer," I said.

"I need a patron. Can't you help me?"

She was right. The average Roman's best defense was to seek and cultivate a patron, someone rich and powerful to watch over their rights. Every man of influence had many clients he protected in this way, in turn gaining their subservience and support.

"You should have told me this sooner," I said.

"I just found out."

The race was about to start. "Let's go back," I said. "We'll talk afterwards." I started to turn away.

Felita grabbed my arm. "I'm worried about Imogene. I'm afraid they will abduct her and hide her away somewhere."

"You can't be serious. She's not even Chryses's daughter."

"I've told them that. They don't believe me. You may have to help me hide her."

Felita began to cry. I held her, as Serina looked on, curious and worried. Felita left before Benedetto's chariot race started. I went to stand next to Serina.

"More trouble?" she said.

"I'll tell you later. Let's watch the race."

The three-horse chariots had already lined up, four to a row, in eight rows. The race would be for the standard twenty circuits around the pylons that marked the two ends of the track. Benedetto was in the inside of the third row, a favorable position.

The starter dropped his arm and the charioteers whipped their horses into a gallop. The crowd roared with approval, the sound cascading around the Circus Maximus like rolling thunder. I gripped Serina's hand and felt my pulse quicken. Nothing in the world was more exciting than a chariot race. It was impossible to sit and quietly watch. Before the first chariot reached the first pylon, everyone was on their feet screaming themselves hoarse, and Serina and I and the rest of the family were no exception.

We dutifully called for the gods to keep the race running without mishap, while secretly thrilling whenever a pileup occurred, as it inevitably did several times in every race. Remarkably, lives were seldom lost. With the chariots packed tightly, the first turn could easily bring the race to a premature halt in a pileup of chariots, horses and drivers. That day the lead row made it through. The next two chariots however locked wheels, one of them making too tight a turn.

One chariot's wheel ran up on the other's. The first chariot tipped on its side. The charioteer hung onto the reins, his best chance to avoid serious injury. His horses dragged the tipped chariot and the driver, wide around the turn. Three handlers jumped into the arena to pull the horses off to the side, and rescue the driver. The race continued, the minor mishap only enough to stir the crowd's anticipation of something more dramatic.

Several more similar mishaps occurred in the first four laps. Benedetto drove well, with surprising caution, and had worked his way into fifth place. Then disaster struck.

The lead chariot hit one of the stone pylons, lurched sideways, bucked and threw the driver out. He hit the ground hard and failed to hold the reins.

The next chariot ran over his legs.

Another caught an arm and tumbled him about as the audience groaned, and women turned their heads. The next two chariots missed him. Then Benedetto came on him.

He made every effort to miss the driver. At least I thought so. He swerved so abruptly that he nearly lost control, riding on one wheel for several stricken heart beats.

Benedetto's right wheel struck the driver's head a glancing blow. It happened right below us, near the starting line. We could not hear anything, but I could easily imagine the sound that made.

I clearly saw the driver's head snap to the side at a grotesque angle. Lelia gasped and grabbed my arm.

"He's killed him," Serina said.

"He tried to miss him."

The audience fell oddly quiet, as the race thundered on. Three men dashed out to drag the driver away. Unfortunately for Benedetto, the dead driver was a crowd favorite, a veteran of hundreds of races, a man whom people recognized in the streets of Rome.

Benedetto gained on the leaders, only half the original chariots still in the race. The crowd began to berate him with derisive calls when he passed. This seemed to drive Benedetto to race with more abandon, and more brilliance. We cheered, and some others did too, when Benedetto took the lead, but we could hardly hear ourselves above the abusive din.

Benedetto went on to win. When the jeers continued, he raised his fist in defiance. I feared a riot. Race officials quickly escorted Benedetto out of the Circus Maximus through an underground passage.

We had planned a family celebration, another excuse for a banquet, at Oma's large house. Benedetto showed up late, in a foul mood, and already half drunk. We tried to congratulate him, but it seemed only to make his mood darker. We all left early.

4

Lelia was relentless in her campaign to get her mother and I to accept Dominico as a legitimate suitor. Every day, it seemed, Lelia came to us with another marvelous revelation about the young man, as if it was something she had just found out, instead of a calculated scheme to keep him constantly at the forefront of family business. Lartius found his sister's infatuation increasingly annoying, and devised ways to mercilessly ridicule everything she said about Dominico.

After Lelia bragged at length about Dominico's military career, Lartius made a casual remark that nearly caused a fight. "That's why Lelia likes him. He's used to taking orders."

"He gave orders, you fool," Lelia screamed, swinging at Lartius, who easily ducked out of the way, laughing gaily. "He was a commander, or something. Served with the Emperor in Gaul. Fought the Germans."

"He was probably in charge of the Emperor's horse," Lartius said.

We had to pull them apart. After that, Lelia never talked about Dominico when Lartius was around.

In this piecemeal way, we got to know Dominico, or thought we did. As I had guessed, he had Celtic blood in his veins, a grandmother on his father's side, who still lived somewhere in northern Italy. Dominico joined the army at the age of eighteen and served his six years in the Legions, part of the time on the German front along the Rhine. His family was not wealthy, a minor problem for Serina, of no consequence to me, and something that Lelia looked upon as a distinct advantage. Dominico's father was a baker, the fourth generation to carry on that noble trade. It would end with him, it seemed, for Dominico told us emphatically that he did not intend to spend his life pounding dough. What he did intend to do remained something of a mystery.

We reluctantly gave in to Lelia's insistent campaign and met with Dominico's father, unlike his son, a quiet and subdued man. His powerful hands and flour-speckled hair gave away his trade. We concluded a betrothal agreement in record time. Dominico's father was elated with his son's good fortune.

"I've met your daughter," he said, in a rare outburst of extended speech. "She's beautiful and charming. So much more cultivated than all the other women Dominico brings home. I'm so pleased to see him finally settling down. He's always been so wild. Maybe now, with a good wife to urge him on, he'll find a trade that pleases him, or come into the bakery with me."

Serina gave me a withering look, as if it was my fault. I shrugged. What could we do?

Lelia and Dominico would marry in two months. I promised Lelia a modest dowry, as much as I could afford, a safety net in case the marriage went bad. Dominico's father insisted on helping them with their first apartment in one of the new large tenements near the Tiber. It was all set, Lelia's future well in hand, or so we thought. I began to plan a lavish betrothal banquet.

Then Lelia and her cousin Resanna visited the Baths of Trajan one too many times, and Venus stepped in to assert her hegemony over all matters of love.

They picked an appropriate place for such a misadventure. The Baths of Trajan were the largest and most lavish in Rome, in area five times the size of the Coliseum, in every sense of the word, a palace, richly decorated inside, with murals, tiled floors, statues, fountains, and gardens. Only a quadrans, one-sixty-fourth of a denari, was required for entry, a sum that even the lowliest beggar could usually dredge up on occasion. The opening bell was one of the most welcome sounds in Rome. Only Christians and philosophers—who proudly boasted of bathing once a month—denied themselves the pleasures of the Roman bath.

Almost any imaginable service was available, certainly any bath temperature you could desire, with steam rooms, hot pools, tepid pools, and cold pools. There were exercise rooms, massage rooms, game courts, gardens, and libraries for relaxed reading. The Baths of Trajan was as much a haven for spiritual cleansing as bodily cleansing. It was also a place for assignations, for gossip, and for love to coalesce or veer off course.

Exactly what happened when Lelia and Resanna visited the Baths, that last time, became a matter of quiet debate in my family. What follows is based on Lelia's version, with a sprinkle or two of Resanna's comments as counterpoint, and colored with my admittedly prejudiced interpretations.

They said little in the dressing room, while slaves removed their clothes, and brushed Rome's grime from their bodies. In appearance, the two young women differed as much as they did in personality, except in one respect. Both cousins were strikingly beautiful, enough to turn heads, even in a pool only filled with women. Where Resanna was dark, tall and angular, Lelia was lighter complexioned, shorter, and more softly silhouetted.

Finished with preliminaries, Lelia, with a towel wrapped around her waist, and Resanna, probably with the towel dragging behind her, entered the frigidarium, a pool held at the cool temperature of the unheated aqueduct water that constantly replenished it, a refreshing place to begin on a hot summer day.

The separate room for women annoyed Resanna. "No men, as usual. Just a bunch of fat old women to look at. What's the point of coming here?"

"It's not so bad," Lelia said, laughing.

"There's more camaraderie with men around," Resanna said, sinking down to her chin in the water, and shivering deliciously.

"I suppose. But it's not as relaxing."

"Who wants to relax?"

"I heard that on certain days, certain hours, the men arrange to come in here, despite the edict," Lelia said, lowering her voice.

"We must find out when."

After a half hour in the frigidarium, they moved on to the tepidaria, a warm bath almost body temperature. That was my favorite pool, where the skin tingled and a delicious lassitude settled over bathers. For a long time, they lounged back in silence, only their heads out of the water, resting on a ledge. Lelia finally broached the subject that had been on both their minds since they entered.

"Resanna, I have to tell you. I'm betrothed. I'll be married in two months."

"So I've heard."

"Who told you?"

"My mother. His name is Dominico, right? What's he like? Why haven't you brought him around to meet me?"

"I did. You were away somewhere."

Resanna smiled skeptically. "You didn't try very hard. I think you were afraid to show him to me."

"No, not at all. What a thing to say."

Resanna shrugged. "So, is he handsome?"

"He's tall and strong, with good features. Light coloring. He is kind and considerate—"

"Kind. Considerate. I want to know if he's any good in bed. If he isn't I won't let you marry him."

"Resanna! I won't answer that."

"You don't know, do you?"

"Of course not. And you wouldn't do that either, despite what you say."

Resanna smiled wickedly. "Don't be too sure. I look forward to meeting him. Maybe I can find out for you."

"I'm not sure I should let you near him until after we're married."

That conversation, more or less agreed upon by Lelia and Resanna, was a great shock to me as Lelia's father. I had no idea that young women talked that way. Serina laughed at my naiveté when she heard. What happened next was even worse for a father to hear.

Lelia and Resanna eventually emerged from the tepidaria, towels wrapped around their waists. Lelia started for the hallway leading to the calidarium, the steam room. Resanna grabbed her arm to hold her back.

"Why don't we see if we can get into the men's calidarium?"

"Are you serious?"

"Of course."

"I don't think that's a good idea."

That was what Lelia claimed she said, but Resanna's story had it a little different, with Lelia not at all objecting to the idea.

Resanna laughed. "We'll have towels around our waists. So will the men, most of the time. And the room is filled with steam. They won't even notice us."

"Something will happen."

"Good. Where's your spirit of adventure? Live a little. You'll be a married and have three kids to look after before you know what's happened to you."

However they decided, eventually the two young women wrapped their towels more securely about their waists and headed for the men's calidarium.

They could barely see when they got inside, the steam wafting about like winter fog over the Tiber. They heard men's voices, deep mumbled words, an occasional laugh. Lelia was ready to bolt, she claimed. Resanna held her firmly by the arm and propelled her forward.

They passed near three men who sat slouched, towels draped across the laps of two of the them, the third less modest. The men saw Resanna and Lelia, and smiled happily. The man without a towel on the end slid down and invited Resanna and Lelia to sit in between, but Resanna pulled Lelia along.

"They're too old," she whispered.

"I want to get out of here."

"Courage, dear cousin. This is fun."

They walked farther into the calidarium, and two seated young men emerged from the steam, towels draped over their thighs. Lelia was behind Resanna and didn't see them at first.

Resanna turned briefly to Lelia and intentionally spoke in a normal tone of voice. "These are suitable. They look friendly." She immediately sat down a few feet away from the nearest man.

"Are these places taken?" Resanna asked, leaning toward the closest young man, no doubt giving him a pleasant shock.

Lelia sat down next to Resanna, away from the two men, without looking at them. Just as she sat down she heard the man near Resanna speak.

"No, they're most certainly free," he said. "And you're welcome to use them any time."

"Thank you," Resanna said "We may just do that, if we know you and your friend will be here."

Lelia gasped. She tugged at Resanna's arm. Resanna ignored her.

"I didn't know the Emperor had finally repealed his edict," the man said.

"You won't tell him will you?"

The man laughed. Lelia frantically pulled at Resanna's arm.

Resanna leaned towards her. "What *is* the matter?"

"We have to get out of here. That's Dominico, next to you."

Resanna broke into a loud laugh.

"What's so funny?" said Dominico, trying to see beyond Resanna at the other woman.

"Please," said Lelia, pulling back behind Resanna.

"A wonderful coincidence. Let Venus rejoice," Resanna called out loudly.

"I'm leaving," Lelia said, starting to slide away into the steam.

Resanna turned toward Dominico, slid closer, grabbed his arm and practically pulled him around to face Lelia. "Here is your intended wife."

"Lelia?"

"I'm sorry, Dominico."

"There's nothing to be sorry about," Resanna said. "Lelia wanted to introduce me to you, and so here we are. I'm Resanna, Lelia's wicked cousin."

"I'm Dominico. And this is my friend, Carneades." The friend, obviously embarrassed, only nodded.

"Lelia has told me about you," Dominico said.

"I'm not surprised."

"Resanna, we have to leave," Lelia said, her voice taking on a pleading tone, according the Resanna.

"Go if you wish. I want to get to know your future husband." Resanna turned back to Dominico, again sliding a little closer. "Lelia, it seems—at least as far as I can tell in this steam—has much better taste in men than I'd imagined."

Lelia didn't say much more about the horrifying experience, as she called it. She was not a prude, or unduly timid about her body (she said), but trapped practically naked next to her future husband, her cousin in between, conversing happily with both of them, her remarks designed to shock, her hand stealing little pats on Dominico's thigh, must have been difficult to bear. It was hard enough for me to listen to them describe the remarkable scene, although, I have to admit, that I was tempted to use it in one of my ribald skits.

Venus continued her playful game with these three mortals, for in time, as Lelia put it, Dominico came to look less and less embarrassed, and more and more intent on the woman next to him, so that at last it seemed to Lelia that he had forgotten her.

After a half-hour, that seemed a lifetime to Lelia, Resanna said,

"We'll join you in the massage room, shall we?"

Dominico smiled and shrugged. He was all for the game now. Lelia tried to get his attention. He seemed spellbound, mesmerized was the term Lelia used to describe his state of mind. I wished that I had managed to talk to Dominico for yet another point of view about this remarkable encounter. If it had been someone else's daughter and niece involved, I would have found the investigation amusing and educational.

"I left them," Lelia told her mother and I. "I'm not even sure they noticed me leave. I skipped my massage, got dressed and left. I don't think I can bear to see either of them again."

But Venus took pity on Lelia, and deigned to restore matters almost to what they had been before her playful interference.

The next day, Resanna came to see Lelia. She acted as if nothing unusual had happened.

"What happened to you?" Resanna said.

"I left. You two didn't even notice."

"What do you mean? Dominico couldn't stop talking about you while we were having our massage. He kept saying how wonderful you were, how lucky he is. It got quite sickening." Resanna laughed. "I *do* approve, by the way. He is beautiful. And I'm fairly sure he'll be great in bed."

"I'm surprised you didn't test that assumption," Lelia said.

"I was tempted."

Later in the day, Dominico found his way to our house. I was at my desk editing a short skit for the betrothal banquet. They were shy with each other initially. I listened shamelessly. I wanted to be sure I wrote a play to some purpose. In minutes they talked as before, chums again. Neither of them mentioned Resanna. I should have seen the danger in that.

5

A week before the banquet, Nebulia came unexpectedly to see me. She had Sebastianus with her. Every time I saw him, he seemed to grow more handsome. He stood tall and confident, and seemed much older than his years. My son Lartius was three years older, but seemed less mature than Sebastianus. They played together as equals. Sebastianus could already read Greek and had the potential to become a great scholar. I wasn't sure how Lartius would turn out. I listened with skepticism to his tutor extol on Lartius's writing talents.

After the boys ran off, I instructed a slave to bring us wine, and some cheese to nibble on. Nebulia's dark sulkiness had not diminished over the years. She was only twenty-four, and looked no more than eighteen, if that. Janus was a lucky man.

Nebulia casually asked me about my plans for the banquet, particularly the entertainment, the play I was writing.

"It progresses. I can't decide just how sexually explicit to make it. Guests love scandalous talk and outrageous antics from actors, but this is my daughter's betrothal banquet, and you know how sensitive Lelia is."

Nebulia stared off toward the fountain that bubbled in the center of the peristylum, overhung with elm trees. I leaned forward as the silence dragged on. She focused suddenly on me. "I want to dance at the banquet. Remember when we talked about that?"

"I remember."

I also remembered a decade back, when she had danced at a famous banquet put on by Rome's Censor. She was only thirteen, but looked five years older. She danced in the nude, with shocking skill, silencing everyone in the room. We all thought she was a slave, her skin a light ebony color, her features angular, hinting of Nubia. We had no idea she was the daughter of Polydorus, a well-known Egyptian businessman. Her family knew nothing of her dancing. Janus was there, and fell in love with her. Now she wanted to dance again. It seemed an ominous request.

"Why?"

"I told you before. Because I'm bored. I have slaves to do everything for me. Sebastianus and Zezili are growing up. Janus is busy with his political career. I hardly see him. I must do something, or I'll become like all the other Roman notable women, spending hours in the baths, idle afternoons in the Forum, spreading rumors to combat boredom."

"That's enough for most women," I said, smiling.

"It is not. Ask Serina. Why do you think there are so many adulterous scandals amongst the wealthy of Rome? That is my other alternative. You're lucky you have kept Serina so busy with children."

I didn't miss the implication. If Serina did not have little Helen around, she might find her way into another man's bed, out of sheer boredom. I still wasn't certain about her and Euphorbus, but my old affair with Germaine would not permit me to inquire.

"My play doesn't include a dance."

"You can work one in at the end."

"I suppose so. Have you said anything of this to Janus?"

She looked at her feet. "I want it to be a surprise. He'll only try to talk me out of it."

"Are you sure about this?"

"Please, Absyrtus. Do this for me."

I smiled. "If you can dance half as well as you did as a teenager—which I will never forget—you can have a place in *all* my plays."

Nebulia laughed, and stood up. She whirled, swung a foot up to shoulder height, inches over my head. "Would you like to see a demonstration?"

A messenger arrived shortly after Nebulia departed. The note was brief. I read it three times, in disbelief and shuddering alarm.

In one week they take their case before the magistrate. I'm afraid for Imogene. I'll kill Imogene and myself before I let them have her! You must take her. Hide her somewhere, but don't tell me where. Please do this for me. I will find a way to escape my pursuers and meet you at the north end of the Fabricius bridge, opposite the Theatre of Marcellus. At noon tomorrow. Please, Absyrtus, dear brother, don't fail me this last time.

6

I reached the bridge a few minutes before noon. I stared down at the Tiber flowing peacefully towards Ostia to merge its brown waters with the blue Mediterranean, and morosely thought of all the bodies thrown into the river in the thousand years since Rome's founding. I worried about the frantic tone of Felita's letter, mirrored in her scrawling handwriting, barely legible. She was, I knew with utter certainty, capable of carrying out her threat. When Felita didn't arrive at noon, my worries increased with every minute that she was late, my imagination screaming off in all directions. I tried to tell myself that Felita was always late. It did little good.

I jumped a foot off the pavement when Felita tapped me on the shoulder and said, "There you are. Have you been waiting long?" She had unexpectedly come across the bridge from the Tiber Island. She had taken a long circuitous route to escape her pursuers.

"You're late as usual," I said.

"Sorry. We took a long walk, didn't we Imogene?" She was trying to sound bright and cheerful, but her expression gave away an inner turmoil.

"I'm tired. I want to sit down someplace," Imogene said.

"Say hello to your uncle."

"Hello, Uncle Absyrtus," Imogene said, giving me a quick bashful smile.

Imogene was a plain-faced child, rather tall and thin for her age. She didn't look much like my sister, except in the color of her hair, a dark brown, with streaks of lighter color. Her nurse, a sad looking Greek woman, had a firm hold on Imogene's hand, and looked determined enough to ward off a half-dozen abductors.

"Hello Imogene, how are you?"

"I'm hungry too. I want something to eat."

"We didn't have time. Can you get her something?"

"Am I going with Uncle Absyrtus?" Imogene said, with sudden interest.

"You're going to stay with him for a while."

Imogene looked at me intensely as if trying to decide whether that was a good thing or not. "Can we go now? I'm hungry."

"In a minute," I said. "I need to talk to your mother for a moment. Why don't you take your nurse and go over there and look at the river? See if you can see any boats."

She gave her mother and me a curious look, clever enough to know something unusual was happening, and marched off to the bridge wall, pulling her Greek nurse along.

"Thank you, Absyrtus, for doing this. You've saved our lives."

"Your note frightened me. I couldn't sleep last night. It can't be as bad as you say."

"That lawyer you found me said the magistrate could easily rule for Chryses's family. He seemed to imply, in his lawyerly obtuseness, that the best I could hope for was exile. In which case, they'd take Imogene."

"If it's that bad, you should get away from Rome. I can put you both on a ship for Spain."

Felita shook her head, and her dark hair, hastily combed, brushed her shoulders. "I can't do that. I don't want to run. I'm innocent, why should I be the one to ruin my life?"

"Perhaps justice will prevail."

Felita laughed. "You'd better take Imogene and go. Don't tell me where. I've brought some of her things." She handed me a satchel with a shoulder strap. Imogene had carried a small bag too, probably toys and such. The nurse had her own bag.

"Wait a minute," Felita said, and ran to Imogene.

I watched, my eyes moistening, as Felita gave her daughter some last instructions, Imogene nodding vigorously, her eyes locked on her mother's face. Felita quickly embraced her daughter and led her by the hand back to me. I tried to smile, as if we were about to go on a happy afternoon outing, but Imogene knew something momentous was happening.

Felita embraced me, and whispered in my ear. "If I never see you again, Absyrtus, thank you for being such a wonderful brother."

Before I could say anything, she pushed away from me, gave Imogene another quick kiss, whispered something in the nurse's ear, and ran back across the bridge. Imogene watched her mother carefully, standing on tiptoes, until she lost her in a crowd. She looked up at me and smiled. "Can we eat now?"

I bought honey-cakes and sausages in one of the open markets along the Tiber. Then I surprised Imogene, getting her to laugh happily. We embarked on a boat for the five hour trip to Ostia. I had decided to take her to stay with my brother Kasen. He knew nothing about this, as I had no time to even send him a message. I had not seen him for months. I hoped I wasn't making a mistake.

Kasen looked surprised to find the three of us sitting outside the door of his modest house when he arrived late from the docks. He stared for a moment at Imogene. He didn't recognize her.

"What are you doing here? Is this your daughter?"

Kasen, at one time almost a father to me, had never lost his gruff manner when he talked to me. Since his exile, his manner had become even more abrupt. He hardly ever smiled.

"This is Imogene, Felita's daughter." Imogene made a little curtsy, staring with interest at Kasen, whom she didn't remember. "Imogene, this is your Uncle Kasen."

"I don't remember you," Imogene said.

"I've been away a long time," Kasen said, amazing me with a lazy smile. "What brings you here? On an outing, are you?"

I looked at Imogene, wondering whether to send her away again, and decided that she had a right to know what was happening, at least part of the truth. "Can she stay with you for a while?"

"With *me*? What's wrong? What has happened to Felita?"

"She's having legal problems with her former husband's family. They want to get control of the estate. The magistrates are involved. It could get messy. Felita thinks that Imogene will be better off away from it, where no one can get to her, if you know what I mean."

"This sounds more serious than a few legal problems," he said, looking at me suspiciously.

"I can't tell you now," I said, glancing toward Imogene.

Kasen shook his head. "Leave Imogene here. They'll never find her. And if Felita comes here, I'll see that she too is safe. Tell her that."

Imogene was amazingly brave when I left her with Kasen, in a strange house in a strange city, with an old uncle she didn't know. She held me for a long time before letting me go, and then ran to take her nurse's hand. It helped when Kasen told her he would show her the docks and let her climb aboard ships from all around the world.

7

The guests arrived in the early afternoon at the banquet hall that I had rented, at a cost that made me shudder when I thought of it. Slaves took their shoes at the door, and their cloaks, if they wore one. People put aside the formalities of daily life when they attended banquets. Guests wandered into the triclinium, our expansive dining room, and took couches arrayed around food tables. Slaves—my own, and several I had to rent—stood ready to serve everyone's whims. The betrothal banquet would cost me a fortune.

Nebulia, looking exuberant, found me soon after she arrived. "I'm ready. You haven't forgotten have you?"

"I have you as the evening's final entertainment, right after my skit. My guests will be ready to see something beautiful and artistic. Does Janus still know nothing about this?"

"Don't say anything. I want to surprise him."

"What about your father?"

"What about him?"

"Does Polydorus know you're resuming your dancing career?"

"Don't tell me you invited him."

I saw her face cloud over, the joy drain away. "Janus asked me to."

She sighed and shook her head. "He never liked my dancing, even when I was younger."

"I remember well. You can still call it off."

Nebulia shook her head harshly. "Father will have to accept it. He can't run everything in our lives."

Resanna arrived with her mother and her brothers, Boreas and Benedetto. Resanna seemed wildly excited, her face flushed. Her gold embroidered stola clung to her, every curve of her body accentuated in a highly distracting way.

"You look enchanting, Resanna," I said, always ready to pay homage to female beauty.

"Thank you, uncle." She gave me a hug with excessively lingering contact, leaving me looking foolishly ruffled. "I promise to behave myself tonight." She sauntered away, gathering the studied glances of every man in the room.

I had doubts, and said so to Boreas and Benedetto.

"I'll keep an eye on her," Boreas said. "As long as she doesn't drink too much, she'll be all right."

Benedetto laughed. "If she wants to cause trouble she will. I hope you made a generous offering to Venus, uncle."

Suddenly alarmed, I tried to change the subject. "I've heard that the official investigation determined that the driver's death was accidental. You did everything you could to miss him."

Benedetto waved his hand dismissively. "There shouldn't have been an investigation. I nearly flipped the chariot trying to miss that overrated has-been. He should have retired years ago. The panel's decision did more harm than good. Now the ignorant street scum of Rome think I bribed my way to a favorable decision."

"Not everyone," I said. But he had left, following in the wake of Resanna.

"He's determined to keep racing, whatever the consequences," Boreas said. Then he too wandered away.

Slaves brought the first courses and covered the tops of the food tables with steaming dishes that filled the room with enticing smells. We had the usual fruits and cheeses, breads and soups, but the specialty of the cook I had hired was exotic seafood. He had fixed jellyfish scrambled with chicken eggs, which a number of my guests fought over. I didn't even taste it. I did however taste his sea urchins, marinated with spices, honey, and oil. It was edible.

Lelia and Dominico lounged happily on adjoining couches as slaves brought them whatever they asked for. Guests came in small groups to talk to them, and congratulate them. Musicians played a lively melody to get people in the mood for an equally lively evening. Everything seemed normal and I began to relax for the first time in days.

I turned to Serina, standing next to my couch. "No disasters so far," I said, intending a joke.

Serina leaned down to give me quick kiss on the cheek. Her smile abruptly snapped. "Look at Resanna," she said.

I turned. Resanna had gone to see Lelia and Dominico. Guests were resting, gathering their strength for the next onslaught of food. Slaves cleared away the debris from the first courses, while others began to bring in the second courses. Serina and I watched as Resanna lightly embraced Lelia, hesitated a moment before Dominico and embraced him too. I saw the close look Lelia gave her cousin, and wondered. I shrugged and turned away.

I heard a chorus of favorable remarks as the main dishes began to arrive on large platters. The room soon filled with new smells. We had deer roasted with onions, and covered with a wonderfully sweet sauce made from Jericho dates, raisins, oil and honey. To satisfy other tastes, my cook fixed my favorite dish—ham boiled with figs and bay leaves, rubbed with honey, baked in a pastry crust. He surprised me by sending out a platter piled high with doves, boiled in their feathers. Serina said it was a rare delicacy. I only shook my head, thinking of the expense.

The serious dining began. Slaves scurried to keep plates and goblets filled. Talk became louder, laughter more frequent. Musicians accompanied the first dancers, slave girls bare above the waist.

I looked over at Lelia and Dominico. Resanna hadn't left. She had taken permanent possession of the couch next to Dominico.

I arranged for my short play after the main courses were complete, and before slaves refilled the tables with desserts. I wanted some attention for my skit. I had hired only professional actors and actresses, at considerable expense. I signaled to Nebulia, and she slipped away from Janus and headed towards the dressing room.

Everyone loved the skit. The roars of laughter satisfied my ego, though I knew it was no great work of art. The idea with such skits was to surprise and shock, to break through the wine-besotted haze that by then had dimmed everyone's perceptions. Mistaken identities played a role, and at one point two lovers began to actually carry out the act, when the man discovered that the woman beneath him was also a man, as for just a second, his erect tool seemed to sway before the audience. But it was only a clever illusion. There were limits after all, especially since it was my daughter's betrothal. I knew the guests would talk about the skit to everyone they saw, bringing me more commissions.

During the play's climactic moments, when the two former lovers chased each other around the room, in between couches, and even managed to knock over a wine goblet or two, I looked at Lelia, Dominico and Resanna. They were oblivious to my actors' antics. They acted their own, far more dramatic scene.

Lelia had sat up on the edge of her couch. She reached across and had possessive hold of the shoulder edge of Dominico's toga. Dominico seemed not to notice. Resanna sat on the edge of Dominico's couch and was whispering something in his ear that brought a shocked flush to his face, clearly visible from across the room.

Resanna pulled away, letting her hand stray along Dominico's thigh, laughing gaily. At the same moment, Lelia yanked Dominico's toga and yelled his name loud enough to make my actors pause momentarily. Resanna settled back on her own couch, as if nothing had happened. Lelia and Dominico, his toga pulled off his shoulder, engaged in an intense whispered interchange that seemed to draw the attention of more of my guests than my actors did.

After one final collapse into a scramble of legs and arms, that nearly knocked over one of the empty food tables, my two actors crawled out of the room in opposite directions. Everyone applauded. Slaves ran out to clean up the mess and refill everyone's drinking mugs. I paid no attention. I was watching the other play, as the first act drifted towards a climax.

Lelia brushed a tear away. Dominico took hold of her hands, and raised them to his lips. He kept shaking his head. I saw Lelia glance toward Resanna, who suddenly stood up and walked over to kneel before Lelia and Dominico, making a close, intimate triangle. Resanna's back was to me. Whatever she said, it made Lelia and Dominico suddenly laugh. Resanna had one hand on Lelia's knee, the other on Dominico's thigh, like a priest ready to pronounce a blessing. Resanna leaned in close, drawing Lelia's and Dominico's heads together. She said something to again make them laugh. Simultaneously, she squeezed Lelia's knee and darted her other hand up Dominico's thigh, beneath his toga, to briefly explore, like a physician checking her patient's vitals. Dominico jumped and grabbed Resanna's hand. Lelia, with her head back, didn't see. I noticed. A moment later, their first act ended as Resanna wandered back to her couch and Lelia gave the flustered Dominico a quick kiss on the forehead.

I started to say something to Serina, but then Nebulia sauntered in, and the room suddenly fell silent in anticipation of my next surprise. I turned to watch Janus's reaction. He slowly sat up on his couch. His mouth fell open, eyes widened. He leaned stiffly on his knees. He looked as he had when he first set eyes on Nebulia, nearly a decade before, transfixed by her beauty. Except now, I was convinced, she looked even more desirable.

She wore beads, a waterfall of them, but apparently nothing more. They draped in long strands around her waist, hundreds of them in vibrant colors, hanging down to cover her about as well as the short tunic of a gladiator, but far more precariously. It was difficult to avoid watching those dancing beads, to see how faithfully they would do their job. Her breasts were bare and looked as youthful as that of an eighteen year old. She began her dance to the haunting sounds of a double-flute. My guests grew quiet. I glanced back at Janus every minute or two to see how he took it. His face grew red as Nebulia's dance became more fluid, more athletic, more seductive, as she wound her way around the couches.

Polydorus, sitting near Janus, looked as if someone was strangling him. I was certain he was about to have a seizure. He sat up and whispered something to Janus, who shook his head vigorously. After a particularly seductive back bend, I heard Polydorus say loudly to Janus, for all the room to hear, "You must stop this! I won't have it!" Janus shook his head.

"If you don't stop her, I will," Polydorus shouted.

I saw Nebulia hesitate for a second, then keep on. Serina grabbed my arm. "You have to do something. Go talk to him."

I stood up and started across the room—too late.

Janus jumped up and tried to grab Nebulia as she came near him. She danced out of his clutches. To the loud cheers of my besotted guests, Janus pursued Nebulia in a dance around the couches and tables, making an utter fool of himself. He finally caught her, picked her up and carried her out of the room. I'm sure most of the guests thought he was part of the act. Polydorus didn't. He got up, started to go after them, glanced murderously at me, and stormed out of the house.

Serina grabbed my arm. "Why didn't you tell me about this? How could you think to let her dance like that?"

"I didn't know what she would do."

"You should have."

"Everyone will forget by tomorrow."

Serina groaned. "You can be remarkably naive sometimes."

I didn't answer this, because I had just noticed Lelia sitting alone, a perplexed look on her face as she searched the room. Dominico and Resanna had vanished.

Serina, also noticed. "Where have *they* gone?"

I shuddered to think.

Some semblance of order returned. Slaves brought out the desserts and refilled the tables. The selection was delectable, my cook finishing with a flourish of sweets to tempt everyone. I nibbled on some dates, fried in honey. Slaves poured more wine for everyone, and handed out cloths to wash faces and hands. It was time for me to toast the betrothed couple, but only Lelia was in sight, increasingly angry, and lost.

"I'm going to find out what has happened," Serina said.

She got up, but Lelia suddenly rose and strode out of the room through an archway into the peristylum. Serina followed her, and I followed Serina. Wind-tossed torches lit the garden paths. Columns and statues sent out long flickering shadows in every direction. We couldn't see which way Lelia had gone.

We heard a scream, then another, higher pitched.

Someone shouted a curse.

We hurriedly followed the sounds along another path.

We heard more shouts. Another scream. Something ripped. Around a hedge we came upon them.

Lelia and Resanna rolled on the ground, their elegant stolas tangled and torn, bunched around their waists. They punched and scratched, grabbed at hair, used elbows and knees. Dominico was trying halfheartedly to pull them apart, with little effect.

For a moment Serina and I watched, shocked, unable to believe what our eyes revealed—our sweet, calm, controlled daughter writhing on the ground in a clear attempt to murder her cousin with her bare hands.

Serina and I managed to pull them apart. Dominico stepped back, out of the way, looking remarkably calm. I had my arms around Resanna, pinning her arms to her side, her torn stola down around her waist. She relaxed against me, breathing deeply. Lelia continued to thrash about in Serina's arms, angry tears running down her face.

"I found them together," Lelia said, her voice choking. "He had her in his arms. If I hadn't come along, in another minute they would have coupled like farm animals in the dirt."

"You see Lelia, what kind of a man he is," Resanna said, calmly.

"I see what kind of a friend you are. I'm not going to marry him. I'm never going to marry anyone. And I'll never speak to you again."

8

I reached Kasen's house in Ostia just as he returned from the docks. I watched, heartened, as he embraced Imogene, who then came to give me a hug. The girl looked well. She immediately asked about her mother, and I said she was fine and that she missed her, and hoped to see her soon. Imogene tilted her head and frowned, but asked nothing more.

Kasen gave me a cup of wine. "What's happened? You look terrible."

"I haven't slept much lately. There are times when I envy your isolation."

I told him about the banquet, and the consequences. Kasen listened, trying hard not to laugh.

"The wedding is off. Lelia and Resanna will not speak to each other and neither of them will have anything to do with Dominico. Resanna claims she was only trying to show Lelia the kind of man Dominico was, how she would suffer married to him. Serina, at least, is happy that the wedding is off. But Lelia claims she'll never marry anyone."

"Time will heal this," Kasen said. I wondered if that applied to his troubles too.

"Janus blames me for Nebulia's dance. Nebulia blames me for inviting her father, and they too do not speak. Janus's career is in jeopardy. Lelia never leaves the house. Serina blames me for everything."

"But what about Felita?"

I sighed, and checked to see that Imogene was out of the room. "That's really why I'm here. They won. Chryses's family. The slaves testified, and lied."

"The magistrate took their word over Felita's?"

"He was probably indebted to Chryses's family in some way. It could have been worse. The magistrate banished Felita from Rome for only five years. That was all the punishment he dared inflict based on only a slave's testimony."

"Where? When?"

"She's already gone. To Sicily. Imogene will need to remain here a little longer, until I can arrange for her to join her mother."

"Do you have any good news for me?"

I thought for a moment. "I'm getting more commissions now, as a result of the scandalous reports about Lelia's ill-fated betrothal banquet."

With every tragedy some good comes to those who look for it. I forget which Greek philosopher said that.

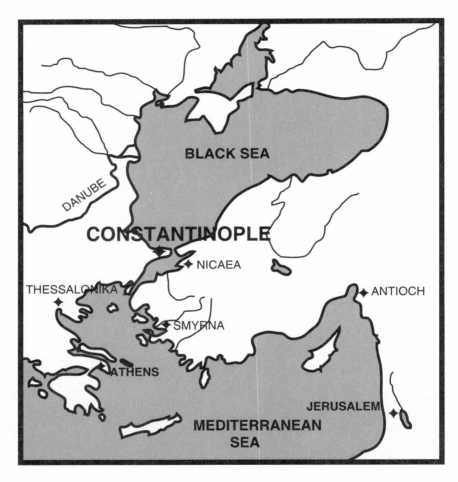

Constantinople

VII. Constantinople
AD 1015

The ancient Greek city of Byzantion stood at the gateway between Europe and Asia for at least a millennium when Roman Emperor Constantine chose it for his new eastern capital. He dedicated Constantinople in May of AD 330, and not long after decreed that everyone in the city must convert to Christianity, as he had—the first emperor to do so. During the next two centuries, Constantinople prospered, while the western half of the Roman Empire relentlessly declined. When Rome fell, the surviving eastern half became the Byzantine Empire.

Constantinople held out for centuries against potential conquerors from all directions—the Visigoths, Huns, Ostrogoths, Bulgars, Persians and Arabs, to name the most prominent. The greatest and most stable era of Constantinople's history came during the two hundred years of the Macedonian Dynasty founded by Emperor Basil I in 867. All the world's wealth seemed to flow through Constantinople, the focal point of trade routes to India, China, Africa, and all the lands to the north, including the vast areas that would one day constitute Russia. By the closing years of the reign of Emperor Basil II in the second decade of the eleventh century, the Byzantine Empire extended from the eastern reaches of the Black Sea to the Adriatic, and from the Danube to the Euphrates. Constantinople had become the world's richest city.

The Student

1

Jason drained his wine and slammed the goblet down hard enough to shake the table. He needn't have done this to show me that something troubled him. That stricken look, one I remembered well, like a captain watching his ship go down, gave him away.

"You don't understand, Abderus, you never have. You have everything, a loving wife, the University, children to take pride in. Everything comes easy for you."

I smiled and shook my head. "You conveniently forget, but I won't try to match you trouble for trouble. I prefer to look at what's right, and you have much to be thankful—"

"I don't want to hear again how fortunate I am to have Polydorus as a father-in-law."

"It's a fact. Polydorus is the city's most powerful official. Except for the emperor. And what does that make you, as his assistant?"

Polydorus held the office of eparch, or prefect, under Emperor Basil II. He combined the roles of chief justice and chief of police, with dictatorial power over Constantinople's elaborate guild system. He was the highest official in the city's military-like civil service. Officials, including Jason, even wore uniforms with badges and a highly visible military-style belt to mark their office and rank. The belt was so distinctive that taking or leaving a civil service position was referred to as *taking the belt,* or *giving up the belt.*

"I still say you're fortunate. Where would you be without Polydorus? You're his chief assistant. You attend guild meetings where everyone fears you, where your word can make, or ruin a man's."

"I didn't ask for it. I hate every aspect of the job."

"Almost any man in Constantinople would gladly exchange positions with you."

"You wouldn't."

"I'm not so sure of that."

"You'd never have the patience to deal with the constant petty squabbles that arise in these insufferable guilds. The system is nearly unmanageable."

I couldn't argue with that. On the other hand, I did believe that Constantinople's prosperity owed a great deal to the city's elaborate guild system. Twenty-one separate autonomous guilds controlled the city's trades and professions. They regulated wages, hours, and the location allowed to each artisan or tradesmen, thereby keeping peace and order in the city's commerce, a great benefit to stability. Yet, when pressed, I had to admit that some of the hundreds of elaborate regulations had become severe, even cruel, as Jason hinted. No man (women of course were excluded) could belong to more than one guild in his lifetime, and a son automatically followed his father into the same guild, the same trade or profession. Someone expelled from a guild could not return, and had no opportunity to enter another guild. Expulsion meant a lifetime of forced retirement, or employment as an unskilled laborer.

"How would you like to have a hand in ruining your own brother's career?" Jason said.

"That wasn't your fault."

"That's not the way Omphale sees it."

"What do you expect? She's lost a husband."

Our elder brother Kadmus fell from a scaffold while refurbishing a mosaic in Hagia Sofia, the largest cathedral in Christendom. Partially crippled, he had to give up his place in his guild, and no other guild was open to him. Rather than live off charity, or his sons' labors, Kadmus left Constantinople, left his family, abandoned everything, to find work in a remote village to the north on the Black Sea.

"You have a marvelously talented son in Sebastiano," I said, growing impatient with Jason. "Your daughter Zeta will someday marry well, and you have a wife the envy of every man in Constantinople."

Jason snorted and shook his head. "Nephele has left me, or have you forgotten? She refuses to give up dancing. I'm caught between Nephele and her father. Did you know that he has disowned her?"

"I didn't know it had gone that far."

"If I want her back, I'll have to give up everything. Or she will. Perhaps if she apologizes to her father and gives up dancing, everything will be as before. Will you talk to Nephele? Reason with her? I think you owe me that much."

I held up my hand. I didn't want to hear again about Lelia's disastrous betrothal banquet, which launched Nephele's return to dancing, ended my daughter's betrothal to Damocles, and made me resolve to never write another play. Lelia entered a convent two years ago. Resi Annys, her once-loved cousin, shocked everyone by marrying Damocles. I took a position teaching rhetoric at the University of Constantinople, where I thought—mistakenly as it turned out—that I could not get into trouble.

"I doubt if it will do any good, but if it makes you happy, I'll talk to Nephele." This wouldn't be the first time I had intervened in their troubles. Why should I break an old habit?

Sirena eventually forgave me for the banquet travesty. She was thankful that Lelia was free of Damocles. Lelia began to work in the hospital associated with the monastery of St. Savio Pantocrator. Employing ten doctors, one a woman, it was the largest hospital in Constantinople, with fifty beds and separate wards for surgical cases, medical cases and for women. Lelia worked as an assistant, and hoped to become a doctor, the only profession open to her.

Marriage did little to tame Resi Annys, Kadmus's eldest daughter. Scandals followed her around, like puppies followed their mother. Damocles, though he had vowed not to, and remained sorely discontented, had no choice but to follow his father in the baker's guild. Sirena, forever bitter, claimed with glee that Damocles and Resi Annys deserved each other.

2

Emperor Basil II had recently won a great victory over the Bulgarians at the Battle of Balathista, ending an eighteen year war against King Samuel, and returning Greece and Macedonia to the Byzantine Empire. Our eldest son, Lethe fought in that famous battle, and received a promotion and the Emperor's recognition for his bravery. After years wondering what would become of Lethe, caught in the shadow of his sparkling sister Lelia, he surprised us with his sudden determination to pursue a military career. I gave thanks to God that he survived that bloody battle. Sirena, Lelia, Hephaestus, Helene and I joined the throngs lining the Triumphal Way when Emperor Basil II rode through the Golden Gate at the head of his victorious army. We cheered when we saw Lethe. Helene, perched on my shoulders, discovered him and shouted "there he is," bringing smiles to everyone around us.

After the army came thousands of prisoners, destined for the slave markets. Emperor Basil, to discourage King Samuel from further military adventures against the Balkans, had sent several thousand other captives back to their king, conveniently blinded. It was said that King Samuel died of shock, but I doubted that. The campaign's other spoils rolled by in wagons, riches the emperor had confiscated from pillaged towns and cities.

The family celebrated Lethe's return. He regaled us with stories of the battles, the long marches, the disease and suffering that attended the glories of warfare. I was proud of him. Sirena later said she thought it had gone to his head, and lamented that he didn't have a safe profession and a normal life, whatever that was.

Resi Annys and Damocles came to the celebration, the first time since the ill-fated betrothal banquet that Lelia, Resi Annys and Damocles found themselves in the same room. I watched them closely as they encountered each other. After the initial, perfunctory greetings, the three kept their distance from each other. Resi Annys left Damocles alone, with no one to talk to. He looked uncomfortable as his wandering wife took charge of her cousin, Lethe, and sat arm in arm with him as he told of his adventures. Resi Annys encouraged him, spurred him on, heaping praise upon him. Damocles, whom the family had never quite forgiven, sat in somber silence, much as Lelia did, for different reasons.

I don't think anyone else noticed it at first, but I did. As a writer, it was my duty, my curse perhaps, to observe everything, to see what others overlooked. Everyone else's attention was on Lethe, and his companion for the evening. I saw Damocles look towards Lelia, an odd expression on his face. I saw her glance towards him, and linger without feeling. I saw him nod, and her turn away, refusing to acknowledge him, except that a flush stole over her face. She looked distinctly flustered, and Damocles seemed to notice, smiling broadly.

My God, I thought, does a flicker of love still linger in Lelia's heart? I mumbled a quick prayer that my senses had deceived me. There was no other contact between them that evening, no other brief meeting of the eyes, that I noticed. Lelia went out of her way to avoid Damocles, while he spent much of the evening stalking her with his eyes, or so it seemed to me. Thank God, neither Resi Annys nor Sirena seemed to notice.

Jason came to the banquet accompanied only by his son. Sebastiano was tall for an eleven-year-old, and looked exactly like a male version of his mother. Nephele had not come, despite my invitation. I had hoped to bring a reconciliation. I had talked to her, as Jason had asked.

She lived in a crowded tenement to the north of the Holy Apostles church. It was not a desirable neighborhood, the streets crowded and trash-strewn, harsh smells permeating the air. It was an area I seldom visited, and it shocked me that Nephele had to live there. She was not at home, but an old lady that managed the tenement said she was at a local tavern. I found her sitting with another woman and three men at a table, drinking beer in large tankards. She got up when she saw me.

"Let's walk," she said, taking my arm. "This place is too disreputable for a famous University teacher."

We walked down the hill towards the waterfront, past Constantine's ancient walls which the city had long ago outgrown, and through the Phanar Gate to reach the shoreline. The air got fresher and the streets cleaner. Along the shore, the houses were large, home to wealthy traders and factory owners.

"What are you doing Nephele? This is crazy, living like that, giving up your family. Do you ever see Sebastiano and Zeta?"

Nephele shook her head angrily. "I have to beg him to see my children, to spend even a few hours with them."

"It seems such a waste, the two of you separated like this—"

"Is that why you came to see me? I guessed as much, as soon as I spotted you. Jason has always depended on you."

"He misses you terribly."

"I miss him too, and my children, and a clean place to sleep."

"Why then? I don't understand."

Nephele didn't answer right away. I was ready to argue, implore, try to convince her to give up this crazy idea of a career. She was a woman. She should be with her husband, serving him, raising their child. When I said this, she laughed at me.

"You sound like my father. You sound like every man, except Jason. Or rather, the way Jason used to sound."

We sat down on the sea wall, letting our legs dangle over the water below. The delicious sea breeze refreshed me greatly. I felt suddenly optimistic that we could work out something to bring them back together.

"When Jason first saw me, I was a dancer, much to my father's displeasure. When I went away with Jason, he said I should keep dancing. You didn't know that did you?"

I shook my head. "But you stopped, until a year ago."

"I had Sebastiano, and soon after Zeta. They were enough, then. Perhaps Jason and I should've had more children, like you and Sirena. I must do something else with my life. Jason would agree, if it weren't for my father. He thinks he can control everybody, and everything."

"You can't live like this. How will it end?"

Nephele shrugged. "Jason will have to choose between my father and me."

"He'll lose his position."

"He doesn't realize it, but that'd be the best thing for him. He hates what he does."

I invited her to the celebration, but she refused to come. She said she was a family outcast and would remain so, until Jason rescued her.

3

I met Tanya for the first time in the Augustaeum, the wide expanse of perfectly laid, brilliantly clean, blue marble slabs, that marked the center of the city, the center of the Byzantine Empire. I was not in a hurry, comfortably early for my class. I watched the sweepers and scrubbers patrol the square, heads bent seeking the smallest blemish, pouncing on one when found, as if they'd stumbled upon a priceless treasure. The massive Hagia Sofia loomed on one side, the Hippodrome opposite, a contrast of spiritual and worldly pursuits. Hagia Sofia, the Church of the Holy Wisdom, was Christendom's largest cathedral, over five-hundred years old, the fourth church built on the site. Constantine the Great built the first. The Hippodrome, past site of chariot races, now entertained visitors with spectacles of all sorts, most notably horse racing, the city's most cherished sport.

I meandered past both looming edifices, hardly noticing them, towards the gilded gates marking the entrance to the Imperial Compound, my thoughts on my classes, as impervious as usual to events taking place around me. I would not remain absent minded for long.

The Augustaeum was the site of great and small events, the former rare, the latter occurring by the hundreds every day. That was where the select Imperial troops raised their newly elected emperor on a shield to receive the crowd's acclaim before entering Hagia Sofia for his formal coronation. That was where orators of great distinction held audiences spell bound for hours. That was where thieves stole the purses of wealthy traders, and were later hanged. That was where I met Tanya.

She was with her brother, Myron, one of my students. He was on his way to the University, as I was, a building within the Imperial Compound. I caught sight of them walking in the shade of the colonnade that surrounded the square. They had just paused to watch two old men playing dominoes. I paused too, a hundred paces behind them, pretending to watch an odd chess game between a young boy, no more than seven or eight, and an ancient graybeard old enough to be his great-grandfather. Perhaps he was. When Myron and the girl moved on, I did too, suddenly desirous of catching up with them, and dangerously curious.

I had reason to be curious about Myron and his female companion. He was, in a real sense, my most important student. The University of Constantinople was free to any youth who qualified. But Myron could well afford to pay, if necessary. His uncle was a high-ranking priest, a candidate for bishop. Myron's father had died in a battle somewhere—I never learned where, or when—leaving the youth, and a large inheritance, in the charge of his uncle. The boy was not however one of my better students, an embarrassing problem for me. Church clerics had a powerful influence over all aspects of society, especially the University. It mattered little that the Emperor appointed every priest and bishop. The Church had an amazing degree of independence, as long as it did not tread on Imperial toes. In effect, Myron's uncle, whom I had never met, and only knew by reputation, was one of my employers.

Myron's mediocre to poor performance was no idle matter, to him, or me. Education was a virtue and a necessity among all classes. To be uneducated was to be disgraced, something to be ashamed of, and a great handicap, at least for men. Everyone, even young girls, received some education. To advance in government or the Church, a higher education was imperative. The University of Constantinople, revived and reorganized in the last century, was one of the world's leading institutions of higher education, and one of the oldest.

I caught up with Myron and his companion before they reached the Imperial Gates. He looked surprised and pleased that I would condescend to speak to him outside of class. Then he noticed me staring at the girl.

"This is my sister Tanya," Myron said. "She wants to see where I study." He didn't sound pleased to have her tagging along.

I looked at the girl more closely as I took her hand briefly. She nodded and smiled and looked down at the ground. I judged her to be fourteen or fifteen. She was tall and angular, with eyes that darted an intelligent glance before looking away. She had reddish hair, and a pale complexion. They were a Russian family, immigrants like my family, like a good percentage of Constantinople's population.

After walking in silence for a time, Tanya suddenly turned to me. "My brother says that you're the best teacher in the University."

Myron gave his sister an angry look, and pretended not to notice my amazed reaction. I patted him on the shoulder and said, laughingly, "That's good to hear. I only wish your uncle felt the same."

"I'm sure he does," Myron said.

"Why are you interested in the University, Tanya?"

She hesitated, looking uncertain. "Myron keeps talking about it, and I'm just curious, I guess."

Myron laughed. "She wants to attend the University too."

That surprised me. What did a girl want with such an education? She could have no use for it. Some girls did receive a smattering of education. Lelia had received enough to allow her to work at the hospital. The medical profession was open to Tanya, but rhetoric and philosophy and other subjects were useless to her.

"I don't see why I can't," Tanya said, looking defiantly at her brother.

Myron laughed. "Don't be ridiculous."

"It's not fair."

"You're just a girl."

Tanya stopped, head bent. She suddenly looked younger, more vulnerable. I didn't know what to say. Myron sighed, gave me a knowing look and went back to her. He took her hand. "I'm sorry. Come on. I'll show you where I study. You can go that far."

Tanya went with her brother, hand in hand. I followed along behind, increasingly curious.

We came to the gilded gates, standing open at that hour of the day. The Imperial Compound extended down the promontory to the Bosporus, the narrow channel that connected the Sea of Marmara to the Black Sea and separated Europe from Asia. Although only the most influential visitors gained entrance to the Imperial Palace, the adjoining Imperial Gardens were a different matter, open to the public during daylight hours. The Gardens had everything the world's wealthiest emperor could desire: summer pavilions, churches and shrines, a stadium, an indoor riding school, a polo field, several swimming ponds, as well as the building housing the University. Central to everything was the Imperial Palace, with its vast reception rooms and throne rooms. The riches that those contained, the gold, silver and precious jewels obtained from all over the world, were said to defy description.

Sirena and I often took advantage of the Emperor's generosity and strolled through the Imperial Gardens on a late afternoon after my classes ended. Tree-lined paths meandered from one peaceful terrace to another, down the slope to the sea, a dramatic sculpture at every turn, past a dozen or more fountains, no two alike (one that dispelled wine on special occasions), many centered in sedate lily ponds. We often stopped to watch rare birds, such as the ibis, peacock and pheasant, that made those places their homes, all of them gifts to the Emperor from the world's leaders. Along one path was the Porphyry, a small pavilion where royal births took place. Purple tiles covered the building's walls, from whence the phrase "born of the purple" arose. The Garden's lowest levels adjoined the Imperial Harbor, its beautiful marble quays, dotted with sculptures, and home to the fabulous royal barges and yachts.

When we reached the University building, I hesitated. This was as far as Tanya should go, without arousing a clamor among the boys. Myron hurried on ahead, a casual wave of dismissal to his younger sister. Tanya stared up at the marble building.

I came up beside her, hesitating, still early for the class. "How old are you Tanya?"

She looked up at me, surprised that I had spoken to her. "Almost sixteen."

"I have a son about your age."

"I know."

I raised my eyebrows, and she looked away embarrassed. "I know your daughter, Lelia. She comes to Hagia Sofia often, where I see her. We talk about many things. She says your son—Lethe, I think—is a great military hero."

I laughed. "He's done well. What else do you and Lelia talk about?"

I could imagine them in the church's gallery, jabbering away, as most women did, much to the annoyance of their male relatives, who congregated below in the main sanctuary. Women were required to sit in the gallery, from whence they supposedly could not give offense or distract men from their religious duties. However, it was impossible to ignore the low murmuring chatter that emanated from above. Other worshippers even less privileged, such as penitents suffering from excommunication, had to remain in the vestibule.

"We often go there when there is no service, to take pleasure in the portraits of the saints."

That surprised me. Lelia had never mentioned that to me. "The church's mosaics are masterpieces of the art form," I said. "My nephew has a permanent job cleaning and repairing them."

"Lelia talks about a lot of things. She talks about her work at the hospital, and about you, and your teaching. She agrees with my brother."

"You're embarrassing me. You two must occasionally talk about more mundane things, like the latest fashions in clothes, in hair styles, or what singer is drawing the largest crowds in the bazaar."

Tanya wrinkled her nose and didn't say anything for a moment. She looked a little disappointed with me.

"I'm sorry," I said. "I didn't mean that to sound as it did."

"It's only what most men think."

Tanya seemed much older than her years. She was clearly more intelligent and sensitive than her brother, and I could see what Lelia liked in her. She was not beautiful. But she had wonderful eyes, a pale greenish color, and a wide, oddly sensuous mouth. Her hands constantly moved, gesturing as she talked, her long thin fingers also unexpectedly sensuous.

"I must get to my class," I said, suddenly in a hurry to get away.

"Thank you for talking to me. As a person." She meant as a man but refrained from saying that. "I wish I could sit in your class, and just listen to you. Nothing would give me more pleasure."

The way she said pleasure stirred something in me. "I'd like to talk to you again, and hear why you're so interested in an education," I said, not properly thinking of the consequences. I hesitated, unsure of whether to take the next step.

Tanya looked startled, even a little frightened. Then she smiled in an odd shy manner that made her look even younger.

"I'll finish my lecture in two hours," I said. "We could meet in the Forum of Theodosius for a bite to eat."

"I'd love that." She reached out and touched my arm with three fingers for a brief moment, like the probing of a curious butterfly. Then she backed away, and gave me another shy smile. "I'd really love that. Thank you." She turned and ran away, dodging in and out between late arriving students. I watched her until she disappeared from sight.

4

I didn't see her at first, and thought she might have changed her mind. The Forum was unusually crowded, and I wondered if it was some holiday that I'd forgotten about. In Constantinople, it sometimes seemed as if the whole city had taken to the streets, that every building must be vacant. Much of the city's business took place outside, in the Forums, an indication of its present Greek heritage and Roman traditions. I shouldered my way past throngs of traders, bureaucrats, lawyers, merchants, all doing business, making deals, negotiating contracts, arms and hands waving expressively to reinforce their arguments, searching for the most advantageous deal for client, for self.

Not everything was business and commerce. As I searched for Tanya, I also maneuvered my way past aristocratic women, flaunting their husbands' wealth, street musicians playing for their bread, bearded priests walking with a studied gravity, harlots plying their wares, and children of all ages doing what they do everywhere.

Tanya found me before I found her. I felt someone pull on my coat sleeve and turned to look at a stranger. Her red hair was no longer visible, hidden beneath a scarf wound about her head, the end draped over her shoulder. A pale blue cloak covered her tunic, the hood pulled back. I recognized her half-moon shaped earrings, and her eyes, which she could not hide. But even then, I pretended to not know her, frowning.

She gave me puzzled look, forehead wrinkled.

"Do I know you?" I said, trying to keep a straight face.

"I'm Tanya. Myron's sister." She stepped back and put her hands on her hips, her eyes never leaving me.

I relented. "I know. But at first you surprised me. You look ten years older."

"That's a woman's prerogative."

I laughed. "You're a philosopher. Tell me other female prerogatives." We stood where she found me, in the midst of a stream of traffic passing through an archway leading to a nearby bazaar.

She put on a serious expression, pretending to ponder the question. "To pick a place to eat, and to suggest that we move away from here before we're trampled."

"Come on," I said, taking Tanya's arm. "I'm famished. Filling those thick-headed boys with knowledge makes me hungry, and thirsty." She laughed with delight.

As we jostled our way through the throngs, the sounds of dozens of languages played like a strange music in our ears. We saw in the faces that drifted past us, every human variation, from dark-skinned, black-haired Africans, to fair-skinned, redheaded Russians. We stopped at a slightly less crowded sidewalk cafe, and shared a table with a foreigner who could have been a Greek, Bulgar, Khazar, Turk, Armenian, Jew, Russian, or Italian.

After we slumped into our chairs and caught the supercilious look of the stranger, we both laughed. "I must have wine, a large glass," I said. "What about you?"

"The same." Her pale green eyes sparkled and danced a challenge to me as her mouth set in a straight line. Her expression seemed to say, here we are, so now what? Is there something you can teach me? Will you test to see if my brain is as dull as my brother's?

I signaled the waiter with a raised hand and pantomimed pouring wine. He understood and moments later hovered above us, holding forth a bottle, eyebrows raised, two glasses grasped in his other hand.

"You've saved our lives," I said. He poured quickly, filling the glasses to the brim. "And something to eat. Whatever you have ready and quick. We're famished."

He ran off in mock panic as Tanya laughed, showing sparkling white teeth, head back, eyes nearly crinkled shut. She was suddenly beautiful when she laughed.

We talked for a time of inconsequential matters, probing each other's state of mind, drifting towards something that neither of us could predict. We nibbled on small pieces of salted fish. In a short while we drank two glasses of wine, and ordered a third. Tanya noticeably relaxed. She leaned back in her chair and looked around at the crowded tables. The man that had shared our table left, never saying a word. I watched Tanya, intrigued, wondering what it would be like to have her in my class at the University, thinking of the scandal it would produce.

"Will you teach me what you teach my brother and the others?"

"How did you know I was thinking of that?"

Tanya shook her head. "That would be giving away female secrets."

"Nonsense."

"You were looking at me a certain way."

"What kind of way exactly?"

She hesitated, suddenly looking embarrassed. "You seemed to be trying to look inside me, to evaluate what I'm capable of." After a brief pause, she said, in a rush, suddenly leaning forward across the table so her head was close to mine, "Do you really think that women are inferior to men? Less intelligent, I mean?"

I didn't feel serious enough—or maybe it was the wine—to answer her question honestly. I whispered confidentially, leaning even closer to her, so that I could see flecks of blue in her green eyes. "Of course women are inferior, at least most of them. Why else would women put up with the lives they lead? No man would. Well, maybe some."

We looked into each other's eyes. She frowned, then smiled when she realized I was teasing her. We were so close that, with a slight movement, I could have planted a kiss on her nose. I moved away quickly, wondering if she read that in my look also.

Tanya sighed. "I sense that I'll never get another serious word from you now. After three glasses of wine."

"And an afternoon with my thick-headed students."

Tanya shook her head. "Some of them must be intelligent."

"I think you could hold your own against any of them." That had just come out, the words erupting from some depth in my brain, surprising me as much as they did her.

"Do you mean that?"

"Yes, I think I do."

"Then will you teach me? Anything. Everything."

It was tempting. "I don't see how I can."

"I don't mean in the class. I know that's impossible."

"What are you suggesting?" I knew exactly what that was, but wanted her to say it.

She hesitated. "If we could sometimes meet, like we are today, and talk. I know it's a lot to ask. Just tell me a few things you tell your class. I only want a taste. I only want a hint of what it would be like if I'd been fortunate enough to be born a man."

"I'm glad you weren't born a man."

She looked at me surprised, and for the first time blushed.

"I'm sorry," I quickly said. "I didn't mean that the way it sounded."

"It doesn't matter."

"A little knowledge will only make you crave more."

"Is that bad?"

"For you it might be."

Tanya shook her head. "I don't think you really believe that."

I hesitated. I stalled, taking a long drink of wine. "No, I suppose I don't."

"Then where shall we meet?" she said, suddenly excited, forcing me to make a decision. "What about right here, at this exact table? Where we first sat down together beside that grouchy old Russian?"

I began to have second thoughts. "Perhaps it's not a good idea."

"Are you afraid to be seen talking to a woman?"

"No. Of course not."

"I'll buy the wine. At least the first glass. That's all I can afford. My uncle doesn't give me much."

"You don't need to do that."

"Can we meet on the days that you have my brother in your class? We can meet in the Forum of Theodosius, as we did today. Then we'll come here, or find another cafe somewhere, perhaps different every time." She laughed happily.

I had let it go too far. I had to give her a chance, though I sensed a disaster in the making. "We'll try it a few times."

She gave a little cheer and reached out and gripped both of my hands for just a moment before pulling back. "Thank you," she said, in a formal way. "I'll try to be one of your best students."

We left shortly after that. She walked with me part of the way, keeping a safe, respectable distance off to the side, sometimes getting temporarily separated by the crowds, then rejoining, like two ships navigating dangerous, stormy waters. We didn't speak until we arrived back at the Forum of Theodosius.

"What was so wonderful about this Theodosius that he should get a Forum named after him," Tanya abruptly said, skipping ahead, then turning and walking backwards to face me.

"You've never heard of him? Don't you know any history? Watch out! You're going to bump into someone."

Tanya glanced over her shoulder and dodged around an elderly couple walking slowly arm in arm. She laughed, a pretty sound I would often hear in the weeks and months to follow. She slowed, to let me get closer to her.

"Don't you see?" she said. "I'm like a dry sponge, waiting for you to drip knowledge on me. Please don't ask me what I know, or don't know. Assume I know nothing."

"Theodosius was the Roman Empire's last great emperor, the last to briefly rule a united empire, more than six centuries ago. He had a daughter named Galla Placidia, who, like you, regretted having been born a man. She led a remarkable life, which I'll tell you about some time. For more than a decade, she virtually ruled the Empire as her son's regent."

"There," Tanya said, briefly touching my hand, lingering just a second, making me shiver "You've begun. I'll always remember this first drip of knowledge."

"You should be a poet," I said, meaning it.

"Then you'll have to explain to me what poetry is."

That's how it started. We met almost every day that I had her brother in my class, usually at the same small cafe. I didn't attempt to teach her everything that I touched upon in my class, just a few ideas to make her think, to give her a feeling of what worlds were open to men. I wasn't ever sure that I was doing her a favor.

It was not all facts and lectures. We talked of many things, and I soon found Tanya to be more intelligent and receptive to learning than most of my regular students. Once, and only once, Lelia showed up with Tanya, greatly surprising me. I felt strangely self-conscious with my daughter present. Lelia too, did not feel entirely at ease.

"Tanya has overwhelmed me with praise for your teaching, father. I had to see for myself," Lelia said, after we had greeted each other.

I thought I understood what she really meant—that I had never given her the same attention. "I pass out a few tidbits of knowledge to her, much as I would hand coins to a beggar."

"Father. What a thing to say." Lelia looked at Tanya, who had displayed a puzzled frown.

"That didn't come out the way I meant it," I said, feeling annoyingly nervous. "Actually, I try out things on Tanya, to help me get through to the idiots in my classes."

"He likes to exaggerate, but you must know that," Tanya said.

Lelia nodded. "It's difficult to know when to take him seriously."

"I'm always serious." This made them laugh, and relieved some of the tension.

"He used to write plays you know, most of them quite disreputable," Lelia said.

"I didn't know that. Tell me about them."

"Well, there was one that he wrote for a certain betrothal banquet that didn't quite work out."

"Lelia, don't," I said.

"It caused the couple to break up. The marriage never took place."

"The play had nothing to do with that," I said.

"I think it did. But it's just as well. And Tanya knows all about it anyway."

"Oh, that betrothal banquet," Tanya said, trying to make light of the strange conversation. "That must have been quite a play."

Lelia nodded. "I'll tell you later. I don't want to embarrass my father any further than I already have."

"I'm not embarrassed, and I'm not at all ashamed of that play. I'll tell you exactly what it was about, Tanya."

But then I looked at Tanya and saw the way she leaned toward me expectantly, her wide, intriguing mouth set in a serious line, and I couldn't go on. She seemed suddenly years younger, a child. And with my daughter sitting beside me, I couldn't speak of such things as my plays focused on. I was too embarrassed to go on, and equally embarrassed to admit that I couldn't.

"Well, maybe another time," I said. "It's getting late."

Tanya looked disappointed for a second, then smiled and nodded. I felt grateful that she seemed to understand. We remained in the cafe only a short while longer, talking of inconsequential things. The nervous tension never left me. Lelia must have realized that she was in the way, an unwanted third party, though it pained me to realize that, for she never came again with Tanya.

5

We received word that my mother had died. She had lived with my brother Kadmus for two years, helping him look after my niece

Isadore, while Filia remained exiled on Crete. Kadmus returned to Constantinople with her body. After my mother's funeral in the small church of St. Mary Panachrantos, we buried her next to my father, who had died ten years earlier.

After leaving the grave site, the family gathered in Kadmus's and Omphale's large house, the first time we had all been together for at least two years. Seeing my brother and his wife talking quietly, hand in hand, heads bent towards each other, made me determined to keep them together. I took his son Boreas aside and told him we had to do something to keep his father in Constantinople now that he had returned.

"I have an idea," I said. "Let's talk to Jason."

My suggestion did not entirely please Jason. "Just because I have some limited authority over the guilds does not mean that I can blithely break all the rules."

"This is a minor thing, Jason. He was not ejected from the guild. He only dropped out, while in good standing, because he thought he couldn't work any longer. It was a mistake. You only need to reinstate him. No one will object."

Jason took a deep breath. "What will he do? He can still barely walk, and has little strength in his right arm."

"He'll work with me," Boreas said. "There's much he can do."

"I doubt you'll convince Kadmus of this," Jason said.

I jumped on this. "But if we do, you'll see that he's reinstated?"

"I suppose so."

Boreas and I hurried off to find Kadmus.

If it had been anyone but Boreas urging this menial position on Kadmus, he would have refused without giving it a thought.

"If this is charity, you'll soon see the last of me," Kadmus said, his face grim.

"It isn't," Boreas said, holding his father's gaze.

Kadmus looked at me. "This was your idea, wasn't it?" I nodded. "What about Isadore? Is it safe for her to return to Constantinople?" Kadmus had become fond and highly protective of his niece during the years that she had lived with him.

"Charybdis's family is content with getting his inheritance back, and getting Filia exiled. They've had their revenge."

"Isadore will remain with Omphale and I," Kadmus said, leaving no room for argument.

Omphale seemed dazed to suddenly have her husband back, after a five year absence. They weren't quite strangers. She had managed to visit him three or four times a year. Now she also had ten-year-old Isadore to add to her large household. But I was certain she would rise to the occasion and make Isadore feel a part of the family. With Kadmus back, I began to feel optimistic about the future, that the family's turmoil and troubles were behind us.

Then Tanya told me about Damocles.

We sat facing each other in the cafe where the proprietor knew us well. He gave us the best table, and the cleanest glasses without our needing to ask. Tanya looked troubled, and acted withdrawn, her usual wit at rest.

"Something is troubling you," I said.

"I'm sorry. There is something. I don't know if I should tell you."

"You don't need to."

We fell silent. Then we exchanged a few inconsequential words on another subject. A couple walked by, lovers, arm in arm, heads leaning towards each other, and Tanya looked at them, wistfully I thought.

"Is it a boy, a man, that's troubling you?" I said.

She looked away from the couple. "Yes, it is. But not what you think. I have no men friends, except you."

Our eyes met, and I saw something I had not seen before, and it frightened me—an attraction that had nothing to do with intellect, or witty conversations. I felt as if I had strayed too close to a fire, and yet found it impossible to pull away.

"I was thinking of Lelia," she said.

"What about her?"

"I shouldn't tell you this. I promised her, but I'm worried. She's my best friend, and I don't like Damocles."

"Damocles?"

"She's seeing him. He comes to the hospital, brings bread for the patients, and stays to talk to her, sometimes for a long time. I see them together. Something is going on. But he's married to her cousin, I think. And besides, I don't like him. He is stupid, self-centered, and not good enough for Lelia."

"You know that they were going to be married."

"Yes. And then the famous betrothal banquet."

I tried to control my anger and disappointment. "Have you seen them together, anywhere but the hospital?"

"No."

"Maybe there's nothing to it."

Tanya shook her head. "If you saw them you wouldn't say that."

"I think we'd better call this off today," I said.

"I understand." Tanya reached out and patted my arm, as if comforting a child. "I'm sorry to have upset you."

We headed back towards the center of the city, to reach the largest of the city's open-air bazaars, sheltered under brightly colored canopies as protection against the sun. We wandered from stall to stall looking idly at products from all over the civilized world, checking prices, an habitual practice not easily overcome. In Constantinople, everyone—from the peasant making his annual trip to the city, to the aristocrat out for a stroll—avidly sought the greatest bargain.

"I shouldn't have told you about Lelia and Damocles," Tanya said. "Now you'll be worried, perhaps for nothing. Are you going to talk to Lelia about this?"

"I don't know."

"She'll be angry with me for telling you."

"I'll find a way to keep you out of it."

It must have been when our aimless walk took us near Hagia Sofia that her uncle saw us together. It was not long after that my peaceful world began to crumble. It started with Nephele.

6

Nephele came to me, unexpectedly, distraught and angrier than I had ever seen her. She looked ready to murder someone. I soon found out who her intended victim was.

"You must stop him. He can't do this to Sebastiano. It's my father's doing. I swear I'll kill them both," Nephele said, after bursting through the door to my house without knocking.

"My God. Calm down. What is he trying to do? Enroll him in the military? Marry him off?"

"If that were only the case. Jason has lost his mind. There's no other explanation. He wants to have Sebastiano castrated."

"Oh! I see."

I knew it happened. Castration was not uncommon. Though curious reasons were sometimes given for the practice—increased mental ability, for example—everyone knew it had to do with the Emperor's extreme, but justified, sense of personal insecurity. Few Byzantine emperors died a natural death. Succession by assassination was common. As a consequence, eunuchs held many of the higher administrative offices, an oriental influence, and an obvious comfort to emperors who so frequently got assassinated by their successors. Eunuchs, unable to launch a dynasty, posed no such threat.

Consequently, there was absolutely no disgrace to castration, and fathers sometimes had their sons castrated to advance their careers. Even patriarchs of the church and many Imperial generals were eunuchs. The law permitted only eunuchs (or women) to doctor women. Tanya's uncle was a eunuch, which didn't make him any less tough-minded and ruthless, as I would soon learn.

"You must talk to Jason and stop this insanity," Nephele said, grabbing both my shoulders when it seemed that I was not taking the news seriously enough.

"It's not unlawful. I can't stop him, if he insists."

Nephele pushed away from me and began pacing. "He's the only son we have. If he was the third or fourth son, without any prospects for inheritance, perhaps it might make sense, though even then I don't think I could stand it."

"Have you talked to Jason?"

"Of course. He doesn't care what I think. He's bitter because I refuse to obey him like a slave. He's under the spell of my father, who pretends I don't even exist."

"I'll try to talk to him, but he rarely listens to me any more."

"If he insists on going through with this, I'll do something to stop him. And if I fail to stop him, I swear I'll kill him."

"You don't mean that."

"You'll see."

It was highly unusual for an only son to "go under the knife." I found it hard to believe that Jason would promote such an idea, or that Nephele's father would suggest it of his only grandson. And yet, in Constantinople, where a high-ranking Imperial office inevitably meant prestige, power and wealth, anything was possible.

Unfortunately, my own tightly knit world blew up before I could talk to Jason, and Nephele and her problem fled from my mind like water through a broken crock. I returned home early that afternoon from the University. Tanya had not met me at our cafe. I waited for an hour before giving up, feeling both disappointed and worried. I arrived out of sorts with the waiting.

Usually Hephaestus and Helene played outside the house in the small front courtyard facing the street, but that too was silent and empty. When I reached the door, Sirena opened it as I reached for the handle.

"Sirena, you startled me. Where are the children?"

She stood staring at me, her face blank, but grim.

"What's the matter? Aren't you going to let me in?" I laughed.

She shook her head. "I probably shouldn't, but you have a visitor."

"What do you mean you shouldn't? What's happened? Who is here?" For a second I thought it might be Tanya.

Sirena slowly moved aside, a half-smile twisting her face, reading my mind. "It isn't who you think it is."

A priest stood in our reception room, a scowl on his face blacker than the robes he wore. He had his arms folded, his hands hidden in the sleeves of his robe. I noticed mostly his eyebrows, and his eyes, as piercing as Tanya's, but far less friendly. He didn't wait for Sirena to introduce him.

"I'm Vasyltso, Tanya's uncle. And you are Abderus, the teacher of rhetoric."

I nodded, remaining silent, feeling the cloud of disaster sink around my shoulders.

"I've told your wife what you've been doing to my niece."

"What are you talking about?"

"Don't try to deny it. I've seen you together. I've had someone following you."

I glanced at Sirena. She stood to the side, a hand covering her mouth, her eyes fixed on me. I tried to keep my voice steady, to control my simmering anger. "I'm not doing anything to your niece."

"You're together almost every afternoon, meeting clandestinely. Tanya tells no one about these meetings. She refuses to talk to me about them. Your wife didn't know about them. What purpose can they have, except that which I dread mentioning in front of your dutiful wife? And Tanya, in any case, has been betrothed since the age of five."

Sirena took her hand away from her mouth, set in a hard, straight line. I remembered that look, the hint of subdued rage, last seen when I told her about Germaine.

"It's not what you think," I said, speaking mostly to Sirena. "Tanya is a smart young woman, the sister of one of my students. She wants to learn, but can't attend the University. I teach her a few things when we meet. That's all there is to it."

"You never mentioned anything." Sirena said.

"I'm sorry about that. I should have."

"Why didn't you?"

Tanya's uncle broke in. "You two can work out your own petty differences later. I've come to deliver a simple warning. Don't see Tanya again, for any reason at all, or I'll bring charges of impropriety before the University authorities and have you dismissed."

"There's nothing—"

"I'm not finished. I've also forbidden Tanya from having anything to do with your daughter. I've seen them together, and with this baker, Damocles, who is apparently married to your niece. Damocles acts entirely too friendly to both girls, and your daughter leads him on. Since you can't seem to control your family, I've no choice but to take action myself."

I took a step towards the priest, who raised his formidable eyebrows in defiance. Sirena took a firm grip on my arm. "I won't allow you to talk that way about my daughter, about my family," I said, my voice shaking. "Lelia and Tanya have done nothing wrong. They're both sensible girls, and I won't do anything to keep them apart. As for teaching Tanya, if she continues to ask me, I'll continue to teach her."

The priest gradually turned red as I said that. He brushed past me, and made for the door. With the door open, and sunlight streaming in, he stopped and slowly turned.

"I understand your sister murdered her husband, and your sister-in-law dances half-naked in taverns, and your nephew races horses in the Hippodrome. I don't think the University students are safe in your custody."

A heavy silence descended on the room after the cleric left. I shivered. Sirena stared at me, shaking her head.

"You do believe me," I said.

She slowly nodded. "Is this true about Lelia and Damocles?"

"I'm afraid so. Tanya told me, some time ago—"

"Another thing you neglected to mention."

"I'm sorry. I didn't want you to worry."

Sirena started pacing, never a good sign. "What are you going to do about it?"

"If Tanya wants—"

"Not her, for God's sake. Lelia, and that baker."

I had meant to talk to Lelia. I had seen her several times since learning about Damocles, but couldn't bring myself to mention it, before she did, and she hadn't. But on this day, I was not destined to make my own decisions. Before I had a chance to say anything, Lelia burst into the room, Tanya on her heals. They must have been outside, waiting for Vasyltso to make his exit.

I stumbled back into a chair, dazed.

Lelia came to stand over me, hand on her hips. "You can't let him do this."

I groaned. "You sound like everyone else. Your Aunt Nephele shouted the same words at me this morning."

"What does Aunt Nephele have to do with Tanya's uncle?" Lelia said.

Sirena broke in. "What's this about Nephele? You didn't tell me she came by."

"I had to rush off. I was going to tell you. Her son is to be castrated, and she is opposed, to say the least."

Sirena stared at me. "And you didn't bother to tell me. What are you going to do about it? Jason must have lost his mind. Sebastiano is their only son."

"I'm well aware of that. I am going to talk to him, but as you can see, a few other problems have intervened on what was once a peaceful day."

"Father," Lelia said. "Are you going to keep teaching Tanya, or not?"

I looked at the angry cloud wafting over my pretty daughter's face, and wanted to embrace and comfort her. I could never deny her anything. Tanya stood behind, staring with narrowed eyes, her thin arms crossed, oddly like her uncle.

"I'll teach her when I can. But Tanya, it's best that you come here to my house." Preferably when Sirena is at home, I thought.

Tanya looked down, fiddling with a dish of pine needles on a small table. "I'm sorry for that. I didn't mean to cause trouble for you."

I laughed, trying to ease the tension. "A little trouble adds some spice to life." They all looked at me as if I was crazy. I shrugged. "Keep in mind, Tanya, that if your uncle decides to carry through with his threats, you might find yourself on a ship destined for Crete."

"Will he do something to you?" Tanya said.

I shrugged. "He'll probably try."

Sirena interrupted. "Lelia, what's this about you and Damocles?"

"I didn't come here to talk about him."

"You came here to scold your father. Now it's your turn to explain."

Lelia looked at Sirena and me, suddenly united in this new concern, and started to back away, bumping into Tanya.

"You told him," she said, to Tanya.

"Her uncle told me," I said, only slightly misleading Lelia.

A silence fell on the room. Lelia bit her lip, and tears formed at the corner of her eyes. I dreaded what I was about to hear.

Tanya spoke first. "I'd better go."

"You can stay. I want you to know," Lelia said.

"Know what?" Sirena asked, her voice brittle, controlled.

"Damocles no longer loves Resi Annys. He doesn't want to stay married to her. He wants to marry me."

"Lelia! You can't mean—"

"I'm going to have his baby."

7

I didn't remember my promise to Nephele until I met my two brothers at the Hippodrome to watch Kadmus's son, Bellerophon ride. By then it was too late.

Thank God for the horse races. It was the only opportunity for my brothers and I to get together, without our families, or I should say, without the female members of our families. That was a man's sport. Our wives cared not at all for it, and we didn't encourage them to cultivate a taste. Occasionally we brought along a son or two, but mostly it was just the three of us—with a little gambling, much wine, and ample time to talk without a woman to interrupt. And of course we also enjoyed the excitement of the races, the greatest spectacle in Constantinople, especially when the Hippodrome was filled to capacity with 100,000 screaming spectators, cheering their favorite horse and rider around the half-mile track.

I liked to entertain and shock my students with stories of the spectacular and often deadly chariot races, that long ago took place in the Hippodrome. Those early events became much more than entertainment, much more than a distraction from life's troubles. A few centuries ago supporters of the main chariot teams, called the Greens and Blues, had developed such wide-ranging organizations that they were like competing governments, a threat to the Empire. Once they nearly launched a revolution. The growing influence of the Church in every aspect of Byzantine life finally halted the barbaric chariot races, a relief to the Imperial peace of mind. Horse racing took their place.

Bellerophon was growing comfortably wealthy racing horses, although he could not completely shake off the scandal that resulted from his first great victory. That he was innocent of the charges made no difference in many people's minds. Bellerophon remained unmarried and consequently attracted throngs of admiring females. Fathers, who hoped to arrange a marriage for their daughters with Bellerophon, approached Kadmus almost daily.

Kadmus complained to Jason and me, as we awaited the start of the race. "I laugh at them. As if I have any influence over my son. Boreas is different. He I can talk to. Bellerophon leads a life of depravity. I hear things about him that I dare not tell Omphale. The all-night parties, emulating Roman practices. The women he takes up with, and discards as easily. The gamblers he associates with. I fear for his future."

I decided that it was not a good time to inform Kadmus that his son-in-law had impregnated his niece. I still hoped that I could somehow resolve the problem without destroying the family. I couldn't kill Damocles, my first grandchild's father, although it would have given me great pleasure to do so. I couldn't force him to divorce my niece to marry my daughter, and was not at all sure I wanted that anyway. If I didn't mind the scandal, I could have gotten Damocles excommunicated, but that would only get me in worse trouble with Vasyltso. I could think of only three realistic solutions: a quick, secret abortion; or an equally quick marriage to some unfortunate soul who wouldn't mind raising another man's offspring; or temporary exile and adoption.

Sirena and Lelia rejected the first solution out of hand, and I didn't much care for it either. Sirena and I liked the second solution, but Lelia would have none of it. So I concluded that Lelia must accept seven or eight months of exile. Lelia didn't agree.

"Damocles will divorce Resi Annys and marry me. He loves me. He knows that Resi Annys was a mistake."

"Tanya is right," I said. "He isn't good enough for you. He'll cheat on you, as he has on your cousin."

"He isn't like that. He made a mistake. You don't understand him. No one does."

I couldn't believe that my otherwise intelligent daughter could speak such nonsense. I had trouble keeping my patience. "Does Resi Annys know any of this?"

"I don't know. I never see her. Maybe she does, and doesn't care. It's all her fault, anyway."

"It's equally his fault," Sirena said. "You've forgotten what happened at your betrothal banquet. I'll never forget seeing you groveling with Resi Annys in the courtyard, like two street whores, Damocles looking on with a pleased smile on his face."

"It wasn't that way. And everything has changed now," Lelia said. "I want my baby to have a father. Is that too much to ask?"

We had no answer. Soon after, Lelia left, so ending our first attempt to solve the problem in a rational manner.

"Leave it for now," Sirena said. "She has to have time to think. Knowing Damocles, he'll probably do something stupid to alienate her again."

"You're far more optimistic than I am."

That was five days before I met my brothers at the Hippodrome. We'd heard nothing from Lelia since then. I asked Kadmus, offhandedly, about Resi Annys and Damocles.

"They seem happy, when I see them together, but who can tell? Resi Annys hasn't changed. She's as unpredictable as ever. Damocles hates his work in the bakery, and it shows. But he has no choice if he wants to remain in a guild. No children on the way, apparently."

"No children on the way," I mumbled, shaking my head, sorely tempted to tell him. I resisted.

Jason had not participated in the conversation, except perfunctorily. Kadmus noticed this first. "What's wrong with you Jason? Did you even see the race that just ran?"

Jason looked at us, then down at his feet. I remembered that I had promised to talk to him—two weeks ago. Had he already done it?

"How is Sebastiano?" I said.

He stared at me, and his face slowly turned a light shade of purple. "How did you know? Has Nephele talked to you? Did you help her? If you said anything to her . . ."

"What are you talking about?"

"Nephele and Sebastiano. They've disappeared."

"And Zeta?"

"Yes, of course Zeta."

"Where? How?" I didn't need to ask why.

"If I knew that, I'd probably know where they are. Are you sure you didn't have something to do with this, Abderus? You have a way of meddling in everyone's business."

"Do you think I want to? You all come to me every time you have a problem, which is nearly constantly. I'm getting fed up with it."

"Calm down, Abderus," Kadmus said. "Jason is obviously worried to distraction. He didn't mean that. What *did you* mean, Jason?"

"I'm sorry," Jason said. "I only want to know if you've heard anything."

I hesitated. "Just the reason."

"She did talk to you."

"She was worried that you would really do it."

"What are you two talking about," Kadmus said.

I stared questioningly at Jason. He shrugged. "He was going to have Sebastiano, his only son and heir, castrated to advance his career in the Civil Service. Nephele, for some odd reason, known only to mothers, didn't entirely approve."

Kadmus looked stunned. "Have you lost your mind?"

Jason shook his head in exasperated anguish. "I had changed my mind, for God's sake. I wasn't going to do it. Not ever, really. I only mentioned it once, after Polydorus suggested it, and I don't think he was serious either. I was angry at Nephele. It was a stupid thing to say."

I should have kept quiet, and left well enough alone. "She was horribly upset. I've never seen her like that. She was ready to kill you, and her father too, if you went through with it. I think she meant it."

"I'm sure she did," Jason said, lethargically.

"She mostly blames her father. Polydorus has too much influence over you. He owns you. Even this insane suggestion, you took seriously."

"I've told you. I didn't really take it seriously."

"But you made Nephele think so."

"How could she think such a thing?"

"You have to ask that?" I could not hide the disgust I felt.

"I've lost her, and my son."

"And your daughter."

"What am I going to do? Polydorus will answer for this. What good is a career, without them?"

Kadmus, who had abandoned his family for five years, because of a setback in his own career, looked at me, then away.

8

For the next few weeks, Tanya came to my house once or twice a week for lessons, on any subject I felt like teaching her, more enthusiastic than ever. She was insatiable. The third or fourth time she came, Lethe was present, and I introduced them. Tanya extended her hand and Lethe took it awkwardly, a nervous smile briefly playing over his face.

"Lelia's brother, the military hero. Your sister has told me all about you."

Lethe blushed. "Lelia exaggerates." He had forgotten to let go of Tanya's hand, and looked doubly embarrassed when she tugged it free.

"She's proud of you, nevertheless."

Lethe looked around, as if seeking some means to escape. He finally blurted out, "My father has told us that you're his smartest student." I hadn't actually said it in that way, but I let it go, increasingly amused by their reaction to each other.

It was Tanya's turn to look embarrassed. She glanced at me, as if to confirm what Lethe had said. I contented myself with ambiguously raised eyebrows. "I know so little," Tanya said. "I'm just beginning, but I'm afraid it will not last long."

"Why?"

"My uncle. He prefers that I remain ignorant. Your father hasn't mentioned him, I see."

Lethe glanced at me, looking puzzled.

I decided it was time to step in. "Tanya's uncle has forbidden her to come here, or meet me anywhere for lessons. She is a woman, after all, as you've no doubt noticed." They both looked embarrassed at that. "And she is betrothed, it seems, since the age of five, to some aristocratic landowner, I'd guess. Is that right, Tanya?"

"Yes, but I'm not going to marry him."

"You may have no choice."

"She doesn't have to marry anyone she doesn't want to," Lethe said, in an angry rush.

"I hope you're right." They both stared at me, standing side by side. "Are you going to stay for the lesson too, Lethe?" He made some excuse and quickly escaped.

After that, Lethe seemed to always be around when Tanya came to the house. He never stayed during the lesson, but was always there when it ended, offering to walk Tanya home. He was stricken with her, I could see. With Tanya, it was harder to be certain. She was always polite with Lethe, and sometimes did let him walk her home, but not always. I could see that she was intent on maintaining some distance between them.

Every time Tanya came, Sirena asked about Lelia, who had avoided us since we argued over what to do about Damocles's baby. Each day that passed increased the risk that her pregnancy would reveal itself. Her days at the hospital would end instantly. Resi Annys would also find out, and a family crisis of monumental proportions would ensue.

"She hasn't told Damocles," Tanya said.

"He still comes to see her?"

"Not as often."

Sirena turned to me. "You must have a talk with him."

"A lot of good that'll do," I said.

"Ask Lelia to come and see us, Tanya," Sirena said. "We have to decide what to do. She can't just pretend it hasn't happened."

"I'll try. She still hopes that Damocles will leave her cousin, but he comes less and less frequently. I suspect the reason."

"The bastard," I said.

A few days later, I received a rare letter from my sister Filia, exiled on Crete. Filia wrote, in her usual caustic and cryptic way. *What is going on with this family? Will all if its women end up on Crete? Who will be next?* She had written nothing more specific, but it was enough. I now knew where Nephele and her children had gone, and something else too.

"Sirena," I said, "I have the ideal place to send Lelia. The island of Crete. We'll let her aunt Filia take care of her, and see to placing the child with a family."

"Crete is so far away. I wanted to be with her when the baby arrives."

"She'll be well taken care of. Nephele and her children are also there, it seems."

Sirena sighed, shaking her head. "Do you plan on hiring someone to forcibly drag Lelia to Crete?"

"I'll escort her there myself. I'll talk to Damocles and demand that he tell Lelia the truth. That he hasn't the slightest intention of leaving Resi Annys."

"What about your classes at the University," Sirena said.

"I'll think of something. Perhaps find a substitute."

I didn't need to. The next morning the University director called me in and said an investigation had started into my misconduct with the sister of one of my students. He suspended me without pay, pending the outcome.

I went to confront Vasyltso, but he refused to see me, after keeping me waiting for more than an hour. When I got home, in an angry daze, unable to believe that the powerful priest had acted on his threat, I found Lethe storming about the house.

"That miserable eunuch uncle has sent Tanya away. You've got to do something."

I swore a few oaths, and slammed my books down on the floor, but that didn't help. "I shouldn't be surprised. He'll do anything to keep control of her."

"Can't you do something?"

"What do you expect me to do? He won't even talk to me."

"Why didn't she just refuse to go?" Lethe said.

"He's capable of sending her away by force."

"He can't do that."

"I'm afraid he could. Do you know where he has sent her?"

"No, but I'm going to find out. Then I'm going there, wherever it is. And bring her back, if she'll come."

I grabbed his arm and turned him towards me. "Don't do anything stupid. Vasyltso is a powerful man."

Lethe slumped down onto a chair and put his hands over his face. I had no idea he was that taken with Tanya. And I could see no good coming out of it, especially since I knew she didn't feel the same about him.

"He's probably sent her to Crete," I said, with a bitter laugh.

"Crete?"

"Your aunt Filia is right. Soon the whole family—as well as a few friends—will be residing there."

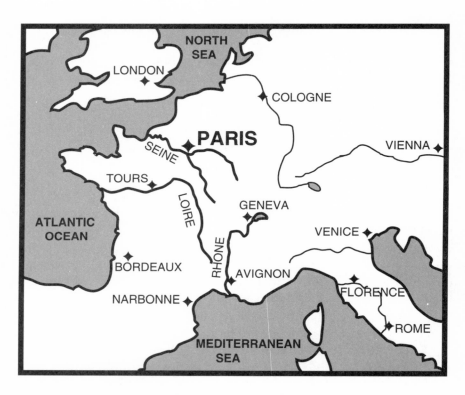

Paris, France

VIII. Paris, France
AD 1252

When King Philip II ascended the throne of France in 1180, he inherited a insignificant nation, surrounded by enemies on all sides. England's King Henry II controlled territory on the continent three times that ruled by King Philip. Germany held most of Burgundy. Flanders and Provence had broken away. King Philip's capital, Paris, was a backward city of no consequence. By midway in his reign, Philip had reconquered Normandy, Brittany, Anjou, Maine, Touraine and Poitou to make France an international power, and secure his unchallenged leadership over France's rebellious aristocracy. He defeated the Great Alliance of England, Germany and Flanders, led by King John of England, who, in the aftermath, destitute in defeat, reluctantly signed the Magna Carta.

Philip's son and heir, Louis VIII, accomplished little accept to marry Blanche of Castile, one of history's most formidable women, and sire Louis IX, later canonized as St. Louis. He completed the job that his grandfather began, absorbing Provence and Aquitaine. By the closing decade of his thirty-five year reign, France reached from the North Sea to the Mediterranean, from the Atlantic to the Alps, with peace and prosperity unknown since the days of Roman Gaul. Paris took its place among the great cities of the world. St. Louis even had time to lead Crusades to the Holy Lands—unfortunately.

The Knights

1

It took months, but France finally raised enough money to ransom King Louis from the Egyptians, who held several thousand French troops captive, including my son Lothair and nephew Brigliodoro. It was a miracle that they survived, for which Silana and I thanked God in our daily prayers. If anything had happened to Lothair, I would have been sorely tempted to seek well-justified revenge against Tilly's uncle, a meddlesome, narrow-minded and dangerously ambitious Notre Dame priest. A little over two years ago, he sent Tilly away—to Marseilles, we later learned—to get her out from under the influence of my tutoring. Lothair, infatuated with the girl, within weeks joined the King's ill-fated Crusade.

What a waste. If he had waited but a few more weeks, his romantic remorse would have ended with Tilly's unexpected return. I don't know how she did it, a young girl, barely sixteen, traveling alone from Marseilles to Paris during one of the coldest springs in memory. She showed up at our house three days before Easter. I barely recognized her when I opened the door. It was dusk and raining hard. She had a black cloak pulled over her head, tied under her chin, only a portion of her face showing.

"Yes, can I help you?" I warily said, always conscious of the danger of opening the door to strangers on dark nights in Paris.

"Avenelle, don't you recognize me? I'm Tilly. I've come back." Her voice shook from the cold.

"Tilly?" I said, foolishly looking at her more closely, as if someone would pretend to be her.

"Can I come in?"

I came to my senses and extended my hand. "My God, Tilly. What are you doing here? How did you get here?"

As I was helping her out of her rain-soaked cloak, she collapsed in my arms. I carried her, light as a child, into our sitting room. Silana jumped up when she saw me. "Who's that?" she said, her face taking on a worried expression.

"Tilly."

"Impossible."

"She's wet to the skin, trembling."

I laid her down on a couch. Silana went to get something hot for her to drink. I began to remove Tilly's cloak. When Silana returned, she said, "You'd better let me do that. Go get a blanket to cover her."

An hour later Tilly was sitting up, awake and cheerful, having made a youthful recovery. She had her feet pulled underneath her, huddled at one corner of the couch nearest the fire, the blanket embracing her up to her neck, only her hands and head showing.

"I couldn't live with my great-aunt and her spinster daughter," she said, "not to mention their five cats. I felt like their slave. They treated the cats far better then me. I had to leave. I was determined to reach Paris before Easter, and I made it."

"I don't see how you managed," Silana and I said, in unison.

"People were wonderful in the countryside. Always willing to help. I got rides with farmers sometimes. I found lodging in the most remarkable places. I had a little money."

I suspected that she suffered a great deal more than she would ever admit. "Does your uncle know you've returned?"

"Not yet."

"Aren't you worried about what he'll do?"

"He knows he can't imprison me in Marseilles. He can only bar me from his house, and cut me off without funds, which I suppose he will."

"Where will you stay?" Silana said.

Tilly leaned forward and dropped the blanket down a bit, freeing her shoulders. She looked at me, then at Silana, then back at me. A sheepish smile briefly flickered across her face. "Is it possible," she said, in a quiet voice, "that I can stay here, at least for a while?"

"You want to live with us?" Silana said, glancing at me. I was determined to remain silent at all costs.

"I'll work to earn my keep. I don't eat much. I'll gladly sleep in the attic with the servants, or anywhere else you choose. I don't take up much room, as you can see."

Silana looked at me. "Avenelle?"

What did she expect me to say? Should I refuse the homeless girl? If I welcomed her, would Silana later curse me? What further revenge would her pious uncle inflict on me? I looked at Tilly. I looked at Silana. They both waited for my astute decision.

"Lothair's room is vacant. I suppose she can use it until he returns, God willing that he does, safely."

"Lothair is away?" Tilly said.

With the wisp of a smile playing on her lips, Silana said, "Shortly after your uncle sent you away, Lothair joined King Louis's Crusade. I suppose you can guess why?"

Tilly looked away. Silana looked hard at me. "I suppose that someone might as well use the room."

Tilly jumped up to give us a hug, forgetting at first to hold the blanket in place, giving me a brief glimpse of a well-shaped thigh, and a premonition of trouble ahead.

King Louis's Egyptian Crusade, though a wasteful failure by any standard, brought honor to my family. My eldest son Lothair was a squire, his reckless cousin Brigliadoro a knight Templar. They fought bravely in the miserable, disease-ridden lands of the Nile delta, even after the advance stalled and the French army found itself surrounded, the Saracens attacking at will.

Lothair was one of twelve squires to receive the King's greatest accolade—the bestowing of a knighthood. In a religious ceremony that I found astonishingly tedious but his mother found tearfully fulfilling, Lothair declared his solemn oath before the Bishop of Paris to "maintain and defend the holy Catholic faith, and uphold and defend his earthly lord, the king." The day before, Lothair and the others had confessed their sins, fasted and spent the night in solitary vigil in Notre Dame cathedral. Clothed in white robes belted narrowly at the waist, wearing newly bestowed gilded spurs, the tiresome ceremony ended when the Bishop tapped them on the shoulder with a sword.

Lothair's friend Hugh received the same honor. Silana and I met Hugh when the two new knights joined us in front of Notre Dame after the ceremony. They were a contrasting pair, Lothair dark-haired, short of stature, with intense, nearly black eyes, Hugh a tall blond Norman with a quick smile and greenish blue eyes. He reminded me of Germaine.

Silana, wiping away tears, embraced Lothair after I had shaken his hand. Hugh patiently waited to be introduced, hanging back a few paces. Finally managing to pull away from his mother, Lothair accepted the accolades of his young brother, Hamilton, and ruffled the hair of Héloïse. Only his elder sister Lealia could not be there.

Lothair waved for Hugh to approach and introduced his family with a proud flourish. "This is Hugh, my closest friend. We battled the infidels in Egypt side by side. Without each other, neither of us would have survived."

Hugh bowed towards me and dropped to one knee in front of Silana, much to her amazement. "I am enchanted to make your acquaintance at long last. Lothair failed to tell me he had such a beautiful and charming mother."

Silana raised her eyebrows, suppressed a smile, and extended her hand. Hugh kissed it with unduly lingering care. "We are delighted to meet you," she said, with studied formality. "Please rise."

Hugh held onto Silana's hand and remained kneeling. Lothair laughed and grabbed Hugh's shoulder. "Get up friend. You always carry chivalry too far."

"Oh, but I am serious in this. If I may be so bold as to say it, your mother is one of the most beautiful women in Paris."

"You're too kind with your flattery."

"It isn't flattery."

"Then I thank you for the compliment."

Lothair slapped his hand on Hugh's shoulder. "Enough Hugh. Let us be off, away from these crowds. We must find Brigliadoro. He promised to help us celebrate."

Hugh stood up, reluctantly releasing Silana's hand. "I pray that we may meet again dear lady."

"I'm sure we will," Silana said, inclining her head in a ridiculously coquettish manner, like an actress in one of my silly plays.

Lothair gave his mother a kiss on the cheek, bowed to me and waved to his brother and sister as he ran off. I frowned at Silana. She broke into laughter. "Is Hugh not the perfect knight?"

"He plays a chivalrous fool. What nonsense. It amazes me that those two could be such close friends."

237

"You don't think his compliments are well deserved?"

I took both her hands and pulled her close. I whispered, conscious of Hamilton and Héloïse watching us. "You are the most beautiful woman in Paris, but I'm too old to get down on my knees to say it."

Silana laughed, planted a quick kiss on my lips, and broke away to turn her attention to our two youngest children.

The formalities, introductions, and congratulations over with, Lothair and Hugh, with the skilled guidance of cousin Brigliadoro, went off to celebrate in a knightly fashion, which meant wine, women and gambling, in that order. I was not too old to remember what that would be like. My niece Rosemarie told me a few days later that they arrived at her tavern shortly after dusk in a state of jubilant intoxication.

"They staggered in, your son and his friend still in their white robes, my brother herding them along like wayward sheep. I couldn't help but laugh. I knew what they sought."

And I knew whose face Lothair would visualize as he lay in the arms of one of Rosemarie's whores. We had invited Tilly to join in watching Lothair knighted. She had declined as I had expected. When Lothair returned from the Crusade, dispirited, in ill health, underweight, resentful of the King's military ineptness, he took Tilly's presence in our house badly.

"She has lived here for two years?" Lothair said, after I had explained the situation.

"Tilly returned soon after you left. She had nowhere else to go. She is still estranged from her uncle."

"Mother didn't mind?"

"Why should she?" I said, getting angry.

"It doesn't seem . . . right, somehow."

"What are you implying?"

"Nothing. Are you still tutoring her?"

"Yes. What difference does that make?"

Lothair shook his head. "None, I guess."

"If you're worried about your room, she said she will leave. She is earning some money copying books."

Lothair shook his head wildly. "No, no. She can stay here. It's time I found my own place."

I had almost as much trouble with Tilly, who didn't want to force Lothair to go somewhere else. "He wants to," I said.

"Are you sure?"

"Ask him yourself." I had lost patience with those two. "I don't understand. You two have hardly said a word to each other since he returned. You know he left because of you?"

Tilly nodded sadly. "I know. But you see, there's more to it." She hesitated, unable to look at me. "Before my uncle sent me away, Lothair asked me to marry him."

"What?"

"I told him no. He took it badly."

"I had no idea." I should have guessed. All the signs were there.

Tilly looked at me then. "He thinks the reason I refused him is . . . that I love someone else."

I was afraid to ask her who that might be.

"He said some awful things that I won't repeat, then later apologized. He vowed to never give up on me."

2

What Rosemarie eventually did should have surprised no one. My brother Kalman's eldest daughter inherited her aunt Filicia's wild, sometimes self-destructive unpredictability. She could also be as vindictive and determined as Ninette, my brother Jasper's wife, who abducted her two children and ran away to join Filicia in a remote village in Brittany. When Rosemarie heard that her cousin Lealia had also joined Filicia and Ninette in Brittany, and the reason, she naturally came to me to verify the rumors.

"Tell me the truth, uncle Avenelle. Is Lealia pregnant?"

"Who told you that?"

"What difference does it make? Is it true?"

"Yes."

"That bastard. I'll kill him."

I tried to calm her down, but she had learned what she wanted. She was certain her husband Donatien had impregnated Lealia. She left as suddenly as she had come. I took her threat seriously and expected a worse disaster to soon unfold, until I learned the means she chose to exact her revenge on Donatien. She recruited as a formidable ally, Paris's powerful guild system.

Paris's one-hundred and twenty guilds closely regulated commerce, in every aspect, for the public's protection. The baker's guild was the most stringent, for bread was Paris's most essential commodity. The slightest rise in price awakened the Paris mob's explosive resentment. Scarcity of bread could bring hunger to thousands.

Besides prices, written regulations specified the weights, sizes and ingredients of each of a dozen categories of bread. But bakers, like other artisans, tended to fall prey to the temptation to cheat on those rules to increase their profits, an unfortunately common practice. Rosemarie alerted guild officers. They inspected Donatien's bakery and found what Rosemarie knew they would find—underweight loaves with doctored ingredients. Donatien spent a day in the pillory, his neck, wrists and ankles locked, the offending loaf of bread hung from his neck, while the neighborhood boys heaped scorn on Rosemarie's humiliated husband. During the night, Rosemarie crept up to her husband, spat in his face, and hung another object around his neck—a sign with ADULTERER written on it. When the guild officers released him, Donatien fled Paris.

"I did this as much for Lealia as for me," Rosemarie later told me.

"Donatien deserves much worse. I'd have gladly seen him receive twenty lashes." We hadn't heard from Lealia since she left for Brittany, and I wasn't in the mood to be kind or forgiving.

"I'm glad I took him away from Lealia. She deserves better. I hope she finally realizes what a bastard he is."

I winced when she said that. She put her hand on my arm. My first grandchild would be a bastard. "What will you do now?" I said, to change the subject. "Will you live with your parents?"

"Hardly. They'd never take me back. In their eyes I've disgraced my family. Only you and dear Lealia, a saint, will talk to me."

"If you need money . . ."

I made the offer, though I was far from wealthy. My position as Master at the University of Paris, though wonderfully prestigious in the minds of some people, paid little, my students usually poor. My books, the popular fabliaux, humorous short stories in verse, which I churned out as fast as I could, gave me a steady, but modest income. They were effortless to write, all variations on the same theme, the same stock characters: the merchant, usually older than his wife, cuckolded, swindled, beaten; the young man, often a student, who outwits the husband; the lecherous priest, a favorite character, the student's rival for the wife's affection; the wife, treacherous, lustful, beautiful and faithless, who always manages to get the better of everyone.

"Do you mean that you'd be willing to lend me money?" Rosemarie said.

I nodded warily, already regretting my impetuous offer.

"Would you like to go into partnership with me?"

"On what?" My worry increased. I am utterly inept at turning down people, especially beautiful women.

"I've found a tavern I want to buy."

"A tavern?"

"What's wrong with that?"

"That won't make your father and mother any happier with you."

"It's a respectable business."

I laughed. "That depends on what you sell in your tavern."

"Uncle, please be serious. Do you want to join me in this venture or not?"

I gave in, after much discussion, and much stalling, though I was certain that I would live to regret it. Rosemarie's tavern, La Caverne, with its dark, cave-like interior, rapidly became the Left Bank's most infamous brothel and gaming establishment—much to my dismay. It made us a steady, healthy profit, but I prayed that no one would find out I was a full partner. I dared not ask Rosemarie whether she participated personally, though I had my suspicions. The Church condemned such places of inequity. Priests enthusiastically preached of the hell that awaited any sort of sexual aberration, from prostitution, to abortion, to even rudimentary forms of birth control. They also preached against every sort of game, and even physical sports. Yet, games flourished even in King Louis's court, and prostitution was rampant and tolerated as a necessary evil.

When Rosemarie described my son's drunken arrival at her tavern to celebrate his knighthood with his friend and cousin, I knew exactly what the three warriors were after.

"I hope they behaved themselves."

"I won't give you the details. They left of their own volition, well satisfied, pleased with my merchandise."

I sensed that she had not come to just tell me this. I waited nervously.

"Hugh is quite handsome. He looks like a Viking and is quite the chivalrous knight. I was tempted . . ." She halted, raised her eyebrows, and suffered a rare blush.

"By the way," she said. "He talked a great deal, in quite flagrantly amorous words, about Silana."

"Silana?"

"He said he would be willing to lay down his life for her. He said she was far more desirable, than my girls."

"Only words. Chivalrous affectation."

"I'm not so sure. I afterwards talked to one of the girls he was with. He talked to her about Silana."

"What exactly did he say?"

"He said, among other things, that he would give all his inheritance and sell his soul to the devil to spend one night in your wife's bed."

3

Paris had grown rapidly during King Louis's reign, well beyond his grandfather's fortifications, to both banks of the Seine, the Ile de la Cité, sandwiched in between. The northern Right Bank was new, home to wealthy merchants and traders. The older Left Bank, where Silana and I lived, portrayed a different character. Many buildings were hundreds of years old. Streets and cafes were aswarm with students who lived in Church-run hospicia, residence halls. Though without an official building, the Left Bank was the home of the University of Paris. It was also the favored location for convents and monasteries.

Three and four story wood frame houses encroached and leaned over narrow alleys barely wide enough for a single wagon. Everyone walked, sharing the alleys with dogs and cats and honking geese and peddlers crying their wares. Animal dung and garbage odors mingled with cooking aromas. Fortunately, we did not live near any of Paris's most odoriferous sections, where the fish merchants, linen makers, butchers and—worst of all—tanners plied their trades.

We lived in a narrow four story house of indeterminate age. It leaned alarmingly, and required frequent repairs, but I preferred it to sharing a newer house. We rented out the lower floor to a cobbler. The second floor was our living area, with a large, double-sided fireplace always burning, one side facing the kitchen. Our bedrooms were on the third floor. Our servant slept in the attic.

Parisians made up for the looming, precarious oppressiveness of their houses in a typically French way—painting them in distinct, loud colors, most often shades of red and blue. Tradesmen added to the colorful hilarity with signboards displaying distinctive images of commerce—a shoe for the cobbler, a loaf of bread for a baker, a hammer for a blacksmith.

In the pursuit of knowledge and its dissemination, France was the leading light in Europe, and the focus of that light was Paris. Every cathedral had a school associated with it, many of international renown, attracting students from all over Europe. The most famous was the University of Paris, of which I was proud to be a Master. The University began as a guild of master teachers under the authority of Notre Dame cathedral. The number of masters grew to such an extent that specialties emerged in the form of four faculties—theology, canon law, medicine, and the arts. I was a Master of the Arts, sometimes called professor. The arts students made up the largest group, since every student first entered this faculty to gain their initial exposure to higher education before going on to the advanced studies of theology, canon law or medicine.

There were no official University buildings, and students paid their teachers directly. We taught wherever we could—out in the open along the Seine, or in a wealthy merchant's courtyard, or in a hired hall, or in the cloisters of Notre Dame, St. Genevieve, and St. Victor. Popular teachers gained the largest following and consequently earned more money for their efforts. I did reasonably well, with a good following. My popularity, or should I say notoriety, increased dramatically after the controversy that nearly ruined my career—when I dared tutor Tilly. The University did not accept female students. Her uncle claimed I had subverted the rule, which I suppose I had, and pressured the University provost to dismiss me. My students, as they too often did, took matters into their own hands. They carried out a well-executed riot that left dozens of bloody heads, littered the streets with broken chairs and tables, and burned down a hall often rented for lectures. The provost reversed his decision, reinstating me.

Tilly's uncle didn't give up. I was one of only a few professors reviled by name in the priest's sermons. He waited hopefully for me to make a mistake, using students to spy on me. It didn't help matters that I continued to tutor Tilly after she defiantly returned from her brief exile in Marseilles.

The University's influence was formidable, out of control in the Church's opinion, students and masters forging intellectual directions that made the Papacy, once the University's greatest supporter, wonder what it had created. They cringed when masters quoted the controversial dialectician Pierre Abélard, who wrote: *The first key to wisdom is assiduous and frequent questioning . . . for by doubting we come to inquire, and by inquiry we arrive at the truth.*

The University's most popular lecturer was the famous Albertus Magnus, a lover of knowledge and a great admirer and promoter of Aristotle. He made it his life's work to survey and interpret the great works of the Greek philosopher and scientist. Aristotle became almost a god to Parisian students. They began to question everything, much to the Church's dismay.

The Church fought back. As early as 1210, a Church council in Paris forbade the reading of Aristotle's recently translated Physics and Metaphysics, which naturally made the works hugely popular among rebellious students. Twenty years later, Pope Gregory IX gave absolution to offending scholars, but continued the edicts *provisionally, until the books of the Philosopher have been examined and expurgated.* Despite these efforts, Aristotle's works were an unofficial requisite to a complete education at the University of Paris. I enthusiastically taught them, much to the annoyance of Tilly's uncle.

4

Justice is blind. It is also frequently slow and halting. Seven cruel years elapsed before we could prove that Filicia did not murder her husband. A condemned murderer, hours before execution, confessed to the earlier crime. This happened during Lealia's confinement. Filicia delayed her return to Paris to remain with Lealia in distant Brittany.

Filicia and Lealia and my grandson, a bastard the Church would say, arrived in Paris in late fall. Silana and I went to meet the coach. We brought along Filicia's daughter Iva, whom Filicia had not seen since the girl was five.

It was a tearful reunion. We made a thorough spectacle of ourselves. Filicia smothered Iva with kisses. Silana and I engulfed our daughter and grandson. Soon the baby nestled in Silana's arms and I saw something in her eyes I had not seen in years.

"What have you named him?" I said.

"Alexandre. Do you approve father?"

She knew I would. My grandson, named after a Greek conqueror, would need his namesake's profound ambitions and daring to make his way in the world. I grew less exuberant when I thought of this.

"What are you going to do, Lealia?"

"You mean about Alexandre?"

I nodded. Silana moved close to Lealia and me, rocking Alexandre.

Silana and I had talked about nothing else since we got word of the baby's safe birth.

Lealia hesitated. I saw her glance toward Filicia, and I knew. "I'm not sure I should say yet, until Filicia has had a chance to talk to Iva. If Iva agrees, Filicia will keep her. I'm going back to the convent, if they will have me."

Silana, I knew from our conversations, was hoping for a quite different answer. I was relieved. We fell silent, watching Alexandre. I heard Filicia saying to Iva, ". . . and perhaps we will travel, to Italy or Spain, or maybe even England."

They would have the means to do it. The Court ruled that her husband's family had to return the estate she had inherited from her husband, confiscated when Filicia suffered exile. In the intervening years, her properties had tripled in value as the city expanded outward. Filicia had suddenly become one of Paris's wealthiest women, soon to be the target of every fortune hunter in the city.

Lealia reentered the Convent of St. Genevieve. Filicia bought a house on the Right Bank, and moved in with Iva and Alexandre, and about a half-dozen servants and nurses to tend to their needs. For a time, Silana spent as much time at Filicia's house as at home.

Lealia went to see her cousin Rosemarie soon after returning to Paris, determined to eradicate past differences. Thus began one of the strangest friendships I have ever known—between a nun and the half-owner of one of Paris's most notorious taverns. They met regularly, always on neutral territory, often at Filicia's house where they both overlooked Alexandre's progress.

Occasionally they met at our house, and Silana and I had a chance to observe their peculiar friendship. Their conversations, often heated, but friendly debates, ranged over every controversial subject of the day, from abortion to Papal infallibility. Lealia did not try to reform Rosemarie, and Rosemarie did not try to extract Lealia from her convent. They were evenly matched.

5

Tilly was less than three years older than my son Hamilton. They were alike in many ways, both intelligent and curious, both energetic and vocal. When Tilly returned from Marseilles and moved into Lothair's room, Hamilton began to sit in on my talks with Tilly. Soon, they conversed and joked as equals, like brother and sister, or so I thought. Hamilton would never have had this opportunity if Lothair had not joined King Louis's Crusade. For two years, Hamilton had Tilly to himself. By the time Lothair returned, Tilly was eighteen, Hamilton fifteen, and a dangerous rivalry was in the making.

Hamilton had an insatiable appetite for knowledge. From the youngest age, as long as I could remember, he asked questions, and not just childish things, but pointed incisive questions that made me think and sometimes squirm to give him an honest answer.

I had apprenticed Hamilton to a book copyist and illustrator. Hamilton wanted to be a writer. I wanted him to have a good-paying skill to back it up, writing being what it is. Copyists were in great demand, to not only reproduce the books that commanded escalating prices, but to act as secretaries, both for illiterates and for those who sought fine handwriting. Writing out a two-hundred page book, word for word, was an arduous task requiring many weeks, deserving of a fair reward. Not surprisingly, many copyists, including Hamilton, added their own comments at the end of their ordeal, such as *Finished, thank God!* or *For the pen's labor, may the copyist be given a beautiful girl!*

Lothair emerged from a different mold. Before the Crusade, Tilly's dark beauty induced him to occasionally sit in on my discussions with her, but he took little interest in what was said, and when he did, embarrassed himself with his ignorance and naivete. He also embarrassed me. Like too many young men in Paris, for whom the military was the highest calling, Lothair was proud that his education mostly consisted of the manly skills of riding, hunting, hawking, jousting, and gambling. I did insist that Lothair learn to read and write, an advantage he had over a good many of his fellow knights. Hugh, I quickly discovered, could not write anything more than his name. A copyist wrote the letters Silana began to receive from him.

I should have noticed the jealousy that began to grind its way into my family, intent on dividing my two sons. They were both attracted to Tilly, from opposite ends of the age scale. Tilly remained open and friendly with both my sons. She showed no favoritism. Unfortunately, she sought neither of them romantically. This she focused on me.

I mistook her attention for the innocent student-teacher adoration I sometimes had to put up with, until Lealia bluntly told me, "Father, you must be careful. Tilly has fallen in love with you."

"What! Nonsense. I'm old enough—"

"What difference does that make? Take care that you don't lead her on. You could destroy her."

"I think I know how to handle this. You need not instruct me, Lealia," I said, exasperated.

I began to worry, nevertheless. I began to observe small things in Tilly that made me think that Lealia was correct. Tilly brought me small presents, almost every day we met, such as a small sweet cake she had made, or a booklet she had bought in one of the Left Bank book stalls. Once she brought me a white rose that I didn't know what to do with. I dared not ask her what she intended by it. She blushed whenever I complimented her on her appearance. She had matured into a beautiful woman during the three years I had tutored her. Most suggestive, she seemed more relaxed when Silana was not around, and seemed to want our conversations to never end when she had me to herself.

One such day, when Hamilton was off somewhere copying a book, she asked in studied innocence, "Do you suppose that we could sometimes meet outside, along the Seine, when the weather is good, as you do with your University students?"

I relished the idea. The house, though comfortable, resounded with too many distractions, especially six-year-old Héloïse and the servants that chased after her. Silana, no longer worried about Tilly, was content to get us out of the house.

"We can try. Shall we go today?"

"Yes, yes. Let's go right now."

I laughed at Tilly's enthusiasm. It didn't occur to me that neither Lothair nor Hamilton had come in yet, and that her haste might have something to do with that.

We sat on the grass beneath a tree on a knoll overlooking the Seine near Notre Dame. Tilly wore a bright green linen tunic with laces at the wrists. Over this she had fastened a mantle at the neck with a gold broach. She removed the mantle as the day was warm. She liked to part her hair in the middle, the style of the day, with long braids half way down her back. She had a slender, somewhat angular figure, with barely formed breasts, and skin as white as snow on ice as the poets say.

Everything seemed different. I had a hard time concentrating on what I had intended to talk about, my mind wandering as my eyes strayed over her youthful, lounging body. I noticed the way other students looked at us as they walked by. I knew what they thought, but I didn't care. Getting away from the house dangerously liberated me.

It also liberated Tilly. She was a toucher—a person who felt the need of such tactile interplay, even during ordinary conversation. As we talked, she edged closer to me, so that at last she lay sprawled on her side before me, looking up, one bare calf showing alarmingly, her hand within easy reach of my knee, or arm, or hand, to touch in emphasis of everything she said.

I had no intention of repeating the tragic error I had committed, at a far younger age, with the Prussian girl Germaine. But Tilly made me feel young again, a dangerous pleasure for a middle-aged man.

We met like this, innocently, every third or fourth session. Tilly would suggest it every time she had me alone, every time Hamilton had to absent himself for his copyist duties, and Lothair failed to show up. It became a welcome diversion, a means to refresh our minds, bring in new ideas. So I told myself.

Though I knew nothing of it at the time, Silana had her own youthful diversion. Hugh had taken to writing her with a skilled copyist's assistance, notes and letters and short poems, elaborating his admiration for her, extolling her wonderful qualities, her beauty, her desirable attractions.

Silana told me much later that, at first, she had enjoyed the novelty of being the focus of a young man's attentions. Hugh began to call on Silana when I was not at home. He would pretend to accidentally encounter her in the street and offer to carry a package or conduct her to a destination. I first learned of this from Lothair.

"I need to talk to you, father, about something delicate," Lothair said.

"You haven't gotten one of Rosemarie's girls pregnant have you?"

He gave me a disgusted look that shamed me into an embarrassed smile. "Did you know that Hugh has been here?" he said.

"I saw him yesterday, when you two—"

"I mean, at other times, when you're not here."

I looked puzzled. "How do you know this?"

"Hugh tells me everything, not that I want to hear. Mother hasn't told you of Hugh's visits, of his letters and gifts?"

I shrugged. "Why should she? Hugh is only playing his chivalrous games with her. It doesn't mean anything."

He had, however, planted the seeds of worry. After stewing about Lothair's warning for a few days, I brought it up with Silana, without considering the consequences, my choice of words less than circumspect.

"I hear that you've been entertaining Hugh here."

I received the fiery look I deserved. She didn't reply.

"He's been sending you letters and gifts?"

"Avenelle, are you jealous of this ignorant, but quite handsome, knight? Do you think that I'll fall prey to the words of his well-paid copyist, and welcome him into my bed, as you took in that Prussian girl?"

I sighed, the husband's eternal obligation. "Not at all. I was just curious, and wondered if he was annoying you. That's all." I wanted to end it.

"Do I complain when you disappear for hours with Tilly, who is even younger I might emphasize, than Hugh, and the subject of both your son's affections?"

"I'm tutoring her. I take her to the Ile de la Cité where I meet with my University students. How can you think there is anything more to it?" Naturally, my far too vigorous protest immediately heightened her suspicions.

"Lealia tells me she is—how can I say it without offending you, or building up your ego—taken by your charming intellect, and mature countenance."

I waved my hands wildly. How had the conversation turned on me? "This happens with every student, even the boys. She looks to me as a surrogate father. That's all."

"Nonsense!" She laughed and left the room.

So nothing changed. I went on seeing Tilly, sometimes alone, most often with Hamilton hanging about, occasionally with Lothair also present. When my two sons and I all paid homage to Tilly, the mood could switch from jovial camaraderie to sullen silence in a matter of moments, and then sometimes back again, depending on Tilly's ability and willingness to juggle the conflicting emotions that roamed the room. Tilly inevitably found reasons to cut these sessions short.

Meanwhile, Silana made no effort, that I could discern, to discourage Hugh in any way. She often invited him to dine with us, and not just when Lothair came home for a meal. I could not understand how Silana could endure the young man's silky attentions. His intentions seemed obvious to me. But I ceased saying anything. Matters would have to take their own course. Silana, I thought, was playing with fire.

She was not the only one.

6

The trouble between Lothair and his cousin Brigliadoro erupted out of nowhere. It started out nonsensically, and remained that way until the end. If we had taken it seriously, we could easily have avoided the tragedy.

I first learned of the growing animosity between the cousins from brother Kalman. He sent one of his younger sons to fetch me, much to my annoyance. I went with him to his father's glass shop where Kalman and his sons designed and assembled their highly acclaimed stained glass windows. They made their fame with glass for Notre Dame, and sealed it with their work on King Louis's beloved Sainte-Chapelle, completed in time to see the king off on his ill-fated Crusade. The stained glass windows in Sainte-Chapelle extended from floor to ceiling, between every column, a stunning effect. King Louis built Sainte-Chapelle to house his prized relics, among them, Christ's crown of thorns. The king, they said, paid three times as much for that single relic as he did to construct the chapel.

Kalman led me upstairs to a large sitting room where a fire burned, and his younger children played. He sent everyone out of the room, even Ophelia. We sat near the fire, not for the warmth, but to enjoy some light. Kalman didn't like to waste candles or oil in the daytime.

"It's about our sons," Kalman said, with his usual directness.

"Which ones?" I had two, he had five.

"Brigliadoro and Lothair, our two knights. There's trouble between them."

"Trouble? What kind of trouble?"

Kalman hesitated, rubbing the side of his lame leg. "It began when the king knighted Lothair and the others."

"I don't understand. I saw no sign of animosity between them. Brigliadoro helped them celebrate afterwards."

Kalman sighed. "It has simmered for months, a hidden volcano ready to erupt. Now it seems—"

"Just tell me the reason."

"Brigliadoro belongs to the Order of the Temple. It means something. The Knights Templar have defended Christianity for well over a hundred years."

I could have commented on Knights Templar motives. Because of privileges and contributions, the Temple had become one of the wealthiest establishments in Christendom, after the Church, supposedly with one purpose—to supply men and money to battle the infidel in the Holy Land. In reality, the Knights Templar operated a lucrative business, owning property all over Paris, in some sections, entire streets. The Temple's commandery resided in a towered fortress on the Right Bank, enclosing a chapel built to resemble the Church of the Holy Sepulcher in Jerusalem. Temple Knights took monastic vows, but lived the lives of soldiers, in every respect, on and off the battlefield.

"I don't see what you're getting at," I said.

"I enrolled Brigliadoro in the Temple at the age of nine. For years he has trained for the privileges of knighthood."

"I see. And Lothair only risked his life on the King's foolish Crusade." I started to get up.

"Wait. Let's not argue. I only want you to know the reason for Brigliadoro's bitterness."

"Bitterness? What's going on?"

Kalman looked around the room. "Here, last night, they argued with such violence that I feared they would draw their swords. It erupted suddenly, as if it was an old argument resumed. If Ophelia and I had not been present, I'm not sure what would have happened."

A week later I again heard about Brigliadoro and Lothair, this time from Rosemarie.

"I thought you should know—"

"I hate it when someone begins that way."

"If you don't want to hear."

"Tell me!"

"I had to throw Brigliadoro and Lothair out my tavern last night, for fighting. They nearly killed each other."

"A woman?"

"No. It started with some disagreement over dice, but I'm sure it goes much deeper. This isn't the first time, either."

She had succeeded in alarming me. I told her what Kalman had said.

Rosemarie shrugged. "It could be that. They shouted something about Egypt and the Crusade. Maybe it was something that happened over there." After a pause, Rosemarie said, "This never happened when Hugh was with them."

"Hugh wasn't there?"

"He never comes to the tavern. I guess you know why."

"I do?"

Rosemarie leaned her head to the side and gave me a pitying smile. "I wish I had someone that handsome as devoted to me. He says he will not look at another woman until Silana gives in to his—what was his word? Persuasion."

"He has nerve. What exactly does he mean I wonder?"

"You may well wonder." She laughed as she strode out of the room, only to turn back and stick her head through the door. "By the way, our profits are up again last month."

Lothair, when I demanded an explanation, claimed that it was nothing. "Your students fight more than we do. We've had some differences, a few arguments, that's all. Brigliadoro and I get along fine, most of the time."

I wasn't reassured.

When I mentioned to Silana what Rosemarie had said about Hugh, she too sloughed it off as nothing. "It's done all the time. He sends me notes and comes to visit. What harm is there? It's only a game, not like the love-sick attentions Tilly bestows on you."

7

Jousting had lost the overwhelming popularity it once held. What replaced it was no less dedicated to the glories of warfare. Mock battles with dulled swords and lances, a wild, unpredictable melee of two opposing forces of knights, had gained ascendancy in Paris.

At the spring fair, when the city's population swelled by tens of thousands, the tournament drew record crowds, one-third women, dressed in their finest, ostentatiously flirting with their favorite knight. Brigliadoro and Lothair had ended up on opposing forces. Hugh was with Lothair. I didn't want to attend, but Silana insisted, with strong support from Hamilton and Héloïse.

Before the melee began, in the preliminary parade before the packed stands, Hugh reined in his horse below us and raised his gloved hand in salute. "Fear not, fair Silana," he cried out. "I absolve you from worry, oh gracious beauty. I pledge to protect your son with my life, and if he falls captive, I will ransom him with my last coin."

He took a handkerchief from the sleeve of his mail armor, hooked it on the end of his lance, and extended it up to us. The crowd laughed and applauded as Silana took off the handkerchief and held it to her lips. I shook my head in dismay.

The knights fought their mock battle in quest of ransoms and spoils. If a knight fell into the hands of the opposing force, they could hold him for ransom, and seize his horse, weapons and armor. Victors reaped great financial rewards for their efforts. Losers suffered more than humiliation. Though injuries were frequent, deaths were rare, since unlike the deadly version of the game, victors did not dispatch fallen opponents.

The opposing sides donned their chain mail armor at opposite ends of the field, and at the King's signal raced towards each other, lances swinging to horizontal. A roar went up from the crowd as the knights slammed into each other. I lost sight of Lothair in the melee. Lances clanged noisily against armor plate. Unhorsed knights cried in rage and pain, and attempted to get up and fight on foot, before someone took them prisoner. Horses wailed. The crowd screamed for their chosen favorites. Silana clung to my arm.

"We shouldn't have come," she kept mumbling. "It's terrible. I can't watch this. Someone will be killed."

"If I remember, you insisted," I said.

"I didn't know it would be like this."

The battle spread over the field. Without the distinctive colors draped over their shoulders, it would have been impossible to tell the sides. Knights raced away to turn and charge back at any enemy they could find. Impromptu jousts, challenges taken up, grabbed the attention of the spectators. Brigliadoro raced into the open, unscathed, his lance held vertical, looking around. He saw Lothair, and screamed his name.

Silana painfully gripped my arm . "They're going to fight. I don't want to see this."

"Stop worrying. They'll only knock each other off their horses and both get themselves captured."

Brigliadoro charged and Lothair spurred his horse, taking up the challenge. It seemed to take them forever to reach each other.

"It isn't fair. Brigliadoro is too good," Silana said.

Brigliadoro did something with his horse at the last second and his mount jolted to the side so that Lothair's lance missed its target by a wide margin. Brigliadoro's lance hit Lothair full in the chest, sending him crashing to the ground. The crowd let out an appreciative cheer and turned to look elsewhere as Brigliadoro started to dismount to take Lothair captive. Lothair lay still.

"Oh my God. Is he dead?" Silana whispered, painfully gripping my arm.

"No. He's just stunned. Stop worrying." I didn't feel as confident as I sounded.

We didn't see Hugh, nor did Brigliadoro. Hugh caught Brigliadoro with a hacking sword blow that clanged loudly on his mail chest armor, just as the knight swung off his horse, one foot still in the stirrup. Brigliadoro fell with his foot still caught. His horse bolted, dragging him along the ground. The crowd laughed and cheered. It was the most humiliating thing that could happen to a knight, though, arrayed in full armor, little harm was likely to come to him. Hugh, when he saw Lothair stagger to his feet, raced after Brigliadoro, swinging his sword in the air, yelling merrily.

Then it happened.

Later, when it dominated conversations in every tavern in Paris, few could say they had ever seen it happen before. Some compared it to a lightning bolt on a clear day.

Brigliadoro's helmet pulled off, a rare happenstance in itself. His horse crashed into another horse, reared up, stumbled, front hooves flailing the air.

The crowd gasped, and then fell strangely silent. It seemed like only a glancing blow from the horse's hoof, but Brigliadoro's head snapped to the side and his body went limp. Later they said he must have died instantly, his neck broken.

Brigliadoro's death spread a blanket of sorrow over our family. Kalman blamed Hugh and indirectly Lothair for his son's death. He would not speak of it to anyone. He turned in on himself, another form of exile. We became strangers.

Hugh took it badly. The Knights Templar accused him of cowardice in his surprise attack on Brigliadoro while the latter was dismounting to claim his rightful captive. Hugh left Paris, another self-imposed exile.

Lothair gained unwelcome notoriety from the tragic incident. He had managed to recover his mount, and went on—callously many said—to capture three knights with their horses and equipment, while squires dragged Brigliadoro's body from the field.

The tragedy of sudden death has a way of altering the outlooks of those who survive. In many it infuses the need to live quickly, to take advantage of the time they have left. In some it releases inhibitions, unlocks doors of convention that seem pointless in lives that can end so abruptly. I would have preferred to claim that Brigliadoro's death did this for me, but I could not pretend such naivete. I had resolutely headed for the abyss of love's entanglement long before this tragic accident.

8

It happened a little over a week after Brigliadoro's funeral. The spring day was cloudy, threatening rain, but Tilly and I went anyway to our favorite site on the Ile de la Cité. We had the ship's-bow-shaped end of the island practically to ourselves. I found it impossible to talk sensibly about Aristotle's thesis that *character is subsidiary to action*, my mind wandering like some rudderless ship. Tilly seemed equally distracted. She didn't punctuate my discourse with questions as she usually did. She seemed not even to listen.

I fell silent. It took Tilly a half-minute to realize that I had stopped speaking. She turned to me, eyebrows raised. We had spread a blanket on the wet grass. I sat, leaning on one elbow, a translation of Aristotle's *Poetics* in my hand. She sprawled on her side facing me, ensnared in a heavy cape borrowed from me. It was much too large for her.

"What's the matter, Avenelle?"

"I can't think straight today."

"It's the accident, isn't it?"

"I don't know. Yes, probably."

It wasn't entirely. I felt disquieted in an odd uncertain way, difficult to identify. Tilly must have read something in my eyes, a desire I was only vaguely aware of. She scooted over close to me and raised herself to a sitting position, pushing the entangling cape to one side. She put a hand on my knee and watched me closely. I didn't object, or try to pull away, or divert my gaze from her eyes. She carelessly ran her hand up my leg a ways, enough to make me notice. I remained passive, as if watching two other actors in a play, curious to see what would happen next.

"Hold me, please," Tilly said, her voice registering a great need that I could never in a thousand years deny.

I held her, running my hands around her waist inside the cape. I slowly pulled her towards me, as I slumped down beside her on the blanket.

"Hold me tighter," she pleaded.

"Tilly—"

"Don't say anything. Just hold me."

I could not *just* hold her. I felt her breasts press against my chest, and sensed the beat of her heart, accelerating in time with mine. She still had her head pulled back so that she could watch me. Her gaze ensnared me, like some sort of invisible leash. Her lips parted as she breathed more rapidly, sliding her hips in closer. When her tongue swept around her lips I kissed her, tentatively at first, then with crushing intensity, as if I could end the passion with pain.

Tilly groaned and sagged backwards, pulling me on top of her. I lifted my head. I had to see what message her eyes gave. They were closed. When she opened them she said, "I love you, Avenelle."

"No, no. Don't say that."

"I love *only* you," she said again.

I tried to pull away, but she gripped me with a strength I did not know she had. She had kept her legs firmly together as I half straddled her. Now she reached down and touched me. When I gasped and involuntarily pulled away, she swung her legs apart. With a dismal sigh of defeat, I settled between her legs, all hope of restraint fleeing with the breeze that had suddenly begun blowing across my back.

"We can't, here—" I managed to say.

"I want you," Tilly said.

It began to rain. I felt it spattering on my back. I watched the drops hit Tilly's face. She smiled happily and licked the rain off her lips. I kissed her again. Our bodies began to gently move against each other. It began to rain harder.

When I pulled back, her eyes suddenly opened wide, focusing on something or someone behind me. She began to struggle beneath me, but I mistook her movement as something else.

"Let me up," she said.

"What is it?"

I was slow to release her. She pushed me back, both her hands on my chest. "Hamilton is here."

"What?"

Tilly shouted past me. "Hamilton! Wait, don't go."

"Oh, my God."

I rolled off Tilly and sat up. Hamilton was slowly backing away, arms folded across his chest. He looked small, as if shrunken. He stared at Tilly and me, eyes wide, head slowly shaking back and forth, trying to deny what his eyes revealed.

I remained shamefully silent, unable to find the words to explain the unexplainable. Tilly, got up and went to Hamilton. His eyes followed her, and I saw that he fought a battle between love and hate. She stopped two feet away from him and held her arms out to him, pleading, inviting. He slowly unfolded his arms, and they moved together, into an embrace. I could hear Tilly whisper something to my son, but not what she said. Hamilton looked over her shoulder at me with an expression that slowly changed from shock to acceptance, then to pity. I never learned what she said to him in those priceless moments.

As Tilly whispered to Hamilton, the rain ceased as quickly as it had begun and the sun broke glaringly between the clouds. Tilly released Hamilton and glanced back at me for a moment. I saw tears in her eyes. I could guess what they meant. She had lost something that day—her impossible dream. She took Hamilton by the arm and walked away.

I didn't return to the house for hours. I wandered the rain-soaked streets of Paris, wet to the skin from the rain that came and went. I was certain that I had destroyed everything, lost everything. When I got to the house, Silana was waiting. She knew what to expect. Without saying a word, she handed me a blanket and pointed towards the fire, then disappeared into the kitchen. She came back with a steaming cup of hot cider.

"Thank you," was all I managed to say.

"Tilly has left."

I nodded dumbly.

"Hamilton has gone with her."

"Where?"

"I don't know. Maybe to stay with Filicia."

I dared to look into Silana's eyes and saw terrifying pity. "They told you?"

"They didn't need to."

"I'm sorry."

"That isn't good enough."

"I know."

Florence, Italy

IX. Florence, Italy
AD 1490

During the 15th century, Italy, the former heartland of the Roman Empire, consisted of dozens of independent city-states, fragments of a nation free to consume themselves in war. Out of this chaos the Renaissance arose. The lack of a centralized, all-powerful government encouraged competition, in commerce, and in the arts. Cities and princes rivaled each other in cultural patronage, seeking to excel in architecture, sculpture, painting, scholarship, poetry and drama.

Florence embraced the Renaissance like no other city in Italy. Even before the Medicis brought order, Petrarch, Boccaccio and Giotto anticipated the Renaissance with their trend-setting creations. In 1434, Cosimo de Medici ended the Albizzi family dominance by appealing to the masses against the wealthy oligarchy, beginning three centuries of Medici family ascendancy. In a fragmented Italy, diplomacy was the politician's greatest skill, and in this game of promises and threats, Cosimo and his grandson Lorenzo the Magnificent excelled. They achieved a balance of power between Venice, Naples, Milan and Florence which gave Italy four decades of almost continuous peace. The last half of the 15th century, up to the death of Lorenzo in 1492, marked the height of the Renaissance in Florence, when geniuses such as Leonardo da Vinci, Donatello, Ghiberti and Michelangelo thrived.

The Preacher

1

My niece, Rosalie, had always been headstrong, wild and unpredictable. My daughter Liliana was just as headstrong, and almost as unpredictable. In every other way they differed as much as any two people could. Yet, despite astonishingly contradictory life styles, they were the closest of friends. Liliana was a nun, housed in a small convent on the outskirts of Florence. Rosalie was a cortigiane oneste, one of Florence's most famous and costly courtesans, a companion to the city's wealthiest and most powerful men, including, it was rumored, Lorenzo de Medici. She also ran a tavern that doubled as a plush brothel, and in this venture I was her silent, and slightly embarrassed partner.

My niece and daughter turned heads when they walked arm in arm through the streets of Florence, Liliana encased in her nun's habit, without makeup, but beautiful nonetheless in a dark Sicilian way, Rosalie, tall and elegant, her silk gown costing a fortune in flagrant defiance of Florence's sumptuary laws, makeup accentuating a haughty, mysterious countenance. Rosalie had no children, legitimate or otherwise, that I knew of. Liliana's illegitimate son, Alessandro, lived with her aunt Filomena and Filomena's daughter Isabella. Liliana visited two-year-old Alessandro as often as she could, as did Serena and I. We had learned to overlook the undeniable fact that our only grandchild was a bastard. At Liliana's insistence, Filomena raised Alessandro as her own.

After my abruptly terminated affair with my protege Tullia, before it had hardly gotten started, Tullia and Herminius sought refuge with Filomena, who had a large townhouse overlooking the Arno river. Filomena took in Tullia, but sent Herminius back to us, properly scolding him that his place was with his family. Tullia and Filomena quickly became the best of friends. My sister soon began to teach Tullia things that I could never teach her. As a result, Tullia grew even more self-confident, and self-reliant, ambitious to succeed in a man's world.

Helen, our youngest, turned thirteen not long after Tullia moved out. The occasion, celebrated in a muted fashion since Luigi and Herminius studiously avoided all but the most rudimentary conversation with me, marked the beginning of our campaign to find her a suitable husband. Serena and I vowed to not make the same mistake with her as we did with Liliana. The secret to success, we decided, was to marry her off quickly before she could get romantically entangled with some unsuitable youth. It was one of the few things we agreed upon.

Unfortunately, conversations with Serena, on almost any topic, often ended in arguments, one dangerously sensitive subject leading to another as we grasped at ways to punish each other. Serena could not easily forgive me for my transgression with Tullia, not so much because she was jealous of my former student, or feared a repetition, but because of what it had done to our family. Besides further eroding Serena's trust in me, and alienating me from Luigi and Herminius, it brought out into the open my two sons' escalating competition for Tullia's affections.

For my part, I had to put up with Hugo, who had returned to Florence after the controversy over my nephew's death had subsided sufficiently. I could not abide by Hugo's continued visits to my house, even when I was home, but especially when he played the dashing courtier to Serena when I was away. Though edging into middle age, Serena was still beautiful, by any standards. Her figure had thickened inevitably, but in a pleasing way. She could still turn men's eyes, as she attracted Hugo's attentions.

Serena's behavior embarrassed me. Except for famous courtesans, such as Rosalie, or the matriarchs of the aristocracy, society expected women to remain secluded, quiet, and display little independence. A Florentine merchant once wrote that *A woman is a light thing and vain, and if you have women in your house, keep them shut up as much as possible. Return home often and keep them in fear and trembling.* I could not agree more. However, Serena would never stand for such treatment from her husband, and I would never dare quote such a remark to her. Yet, her efforts to get back at me by toying with Hugo's affections led me to constantly make injudicious remarks.

Once, after we had a reasonably quiet discussion about Helen's future, a servant brought in a message from Hugo, which made Serena laugh. As usual, I spoke without thinking. "If you want to ensure that Helen does not repeat Liliana's mistake, stop this childish business with Hugo."

"What are you talking about?"

"I've seen the way Helen greets him, the way she looks at him, and the looks he returns."

"He comes to visit with me."

I laughed. "Of course he does. How well I know that."

"Are you accusing me of behavior in any way as vile as what you've been guilty of—twice in our marriage?"

"It doesn't matter what you do. It's appearances that count."

"Look to your own appearances."

By this time, I was on my feet pacing back and forth, my heart racing. "What I'm trying to say is that Hugo—whatever he is doing with you—also has his eyes set on our youngest daughter."

"She has more sense than that. If you want to worry, concern yourself with Herminius and Luigi. I saw them with Tullia again."

"We're not talking about them."

"I am. Their troubles are your fault."

"The three of them are just friends," I said, knowing that it was more than that. "What am I supposed to do about it?"

"She leads them both on."

"What of it? They're adults. I've done nothing to encourage them to fall in love with the same woman. If that's what it is."

"Herminius is only seventeen. He broods over her. He writes her letters and poems."

"How do you know that?" I said.

"Because he talks to me when he knows his father will not be around."

"He's a writer," I said. "That's what writers do. And he shows great promise."

"I doubt he is writing to Tullia only to improve his poetic skills.

There'll be trouble between Herminius and Luigi some day, especially when they learn that Tullia still seeks to get you installed between her legs."

"Serena! My god, I hardly ever see Tullia any more. That's over. It never actually began."

"Fine. Think what you like. I know better."

"She lives with my sister. The only time I go there is with you, to visit our granddaughter. How can you dare make such accusations when you entertain Hugo as often as Rosalie entertains her most frequent paying customer."

"You go too far, Aberto. Have you forgotten the four years you spent fornicating with that German girl, siring a bastard? And then Herminius finds you encamped between Tullia's spread legs, and you dare accuse me. I've never done anything to shame this family."

She began to cry. I sighed, knowing that I would feel miserable for days for my hasty words. I reached for her and she slapped my hand away.

"Get out!" she said. "Leave me alone with my shame at putting up with such a husband. Any other wife in Florence would have long ago banished you to your mistress."

I threw my hands into the air, looking at the ceiling, as if I expected some long dead pagan god to come to my rescue. "I can't talk to you. You're irrational and vindictive." I grabbed my coat and headed for the streets of Florence where it seemed I spent more and more of my time.

2

The freak training accident that killed my nephew Bertrando had far reaching consequences for my family. My eldest brother Kajetan blamed Luigi and Hugo for his son's death. He pressed to have both of them tried for murder, which made me furious and led to painful arguments and confrontations. But Luigi obviously bore no blame, and the magistrates quickly dismissed all charges. Still, the damage had been done.

Luigi soon thereafter retired from the military. He had no other occupation to fall back on. He would not let me help him. He rented a small room in a disreputable section of Florence, getting by on small jobs wherever he could find them. He would have never found his future, but for his friendship with Tullia. She saw him often, far more than I did, helping him get through this difficult period, keeping him from sinking further into despair.

Kajetan failed with Hugo too. The magistrates cleared the arrogant, but well-connected lad of any responsibility in Bertrando's death, even before Hugo returned to Florence. Serena and I thought the decision justified, but Kajetan did not, and this drove a wedge between us that took years to dislodge. Kajetan said I was a fool to continue to allow Hugo to present himself at our house. I agreed with him, for different reasons, but could do nothing about it. Hugo remained in the military, and much to our amazement, was soon promoted to officer rank. He obviously had strong support from someone with political influence of the highest sort. It seemed that his future was secure as long as Lorenzo de Medici retained power.

Once, when I found myself uncomfortably alone with Hugo, while we both waited for Serena to return from visiting her grandson, I questioned him about this.

"My family has supported the Medicis for decades," Hugo said, "Even when they were not in power. Even when the Pazzi family attempted their coup. I was only fifteen years old at the time."

It seemed that his family had bet heavily on the right family, always a dangerous gamble in Florentine politics. The crisis he hinted at had erupted twelve years before. The Pazzi family, frustrated with their lack of success with more peaceful means, resorted to the ultimate political weapon—assassination. It was rumored that Pope Sixtus IV knew of, and approved the plot.

"Everyone knows what happened," I said. "An ill-planned coup, anyway. Doomed to fail from the start."

"Why do you say that?" Hugo said, sitting up. "It very nearly succeeded. My father and I were in the Cathedral de Santa Maria del Fiore, that Easter Sunday, sitting not far from the Medici brothers when the attack took place."

"I suppose you're going to tell me that he stepped in to stop Lorenzo's attacker?" I sat up too, feeling increasingly annoyed with Hugo's pompous tone.

"That's exactly what happened. My father and I saw the priest first attack Lorenzo's brother Guiliano, quickly stabbing him in the chest and neck three or four times before anyone could do anything. There was blood everywhere, women screaming. Guiliano must have died almost instantly. He had no time to react. We were only fifteen feet away from them. Someone grabbed that priest, but another attacker went after Lorenzo. He wasn't taken by surprise. The attackers had failed in their timing, or Lorenzo would have been instantly killed also. My father shoved me back and went to help Lorenzo, who was struggling with his attacker."

"I was told that several men came to Lorenzo's assistance," I said.

Hugo laughed. "Of course, that's what everyone claims, but it wasn't true. Once my father and Lorenzo had the attacker—another priest, by the way—on the floor, subdued, everyone jumped in to get in a kick at the man, and take credit, and give themselves something to brag about for years. My father was the first to get to the attacker, and for his trouble he received a gash along the neck that came close to severing an artery."

"You saw all this?"

"I tried to get to them, but friends of my father held me back. I saw it all."

I wasn't sure I believed that, but I didn't say. Eye witness accounts of any great event tended to get embossed and exaggerated with each telling.

"There was more," Hugo said. "My father went with Lorenzo to the Palazzo Vecchio, to show his support, despite the mobs that were roaming through the streets, attacking every prominent Medici supporter. It took great courage, especially as he was injured."

"I'm sure it did."

Coinciding with the attempted assassinations in the cathedral—one of which had succeeded—the Archbishop Salviati with additional Pazzi followers, invaded the Palazzo Vecchio, killing Medici supporters, momentarily taking control of the government.

"Where were you when all this was going on? Barricaded in your house?" Hugo said, getting angry.

Since that was exactly what I had been doing, I didn't answer right away. For once I wished that Serena would hurry home to relieve me from entertaining Hugo.

"It was the general population, the common people, the workers, that really saved Lorenzo," I said. "If they hadn't stood by him when he came to the Palazzo Vecchio to confront the Pazzis, the results would have been different—whatever your father did."

Hugo shrugged, giving me that insipid smile that I so greatly loathed. "My father was at Lorenzo's side when he retook the palace. It was a very bloody affair. You should come by the house some time and let him tell you the story. He loves to talk about it."

Now he was teasing me, of course. I nodded, seeming to consider the offer. That had been a bloody day for Florence. In less than an hour, Francesco de Pazzi and the Archbishop hung by the neck side by side from a palace window, dripping blood on the pavement below for the dogs to quietly lick. Meanwhile, a mob murdered Iacopo de Pazzi, the family head, and dragged his naked body through the streets of Florence before tossing it like a bag of garbage into the Arno.

Even this did not end the conflict. The Pope, who supported the Pazzi cause even if perhaps he didn't approve of their methods, excommunicated Lorenzo de Medici and Florence's magistrates, suspending religious observances. When Florence refused to give Lorenzo up to Papal justice, Pope Sixtus and King Ferdinand of Naples declared war. That's when my family first got caught up in the controversy. Luigi volunteered—as did Hugo—when Lorenzo raised an army to defend the city. Bertrando was already an officer.

"I was personally able to show my support for Lorenzo after the war started," Hugo said.

"So did my son, and my nephew."

"I know," he said, smiling again. "I saved Luigi's life—twice."

I had also heard that many times. He was apparently not exaggerating. But they were all fortunate to survive. Florence's army, though it battled valiantly, met defeat after defeat at the hands of Alfonso, Ferdinand's son. In the end, it was Lorenzo himself who saved Florence.

With Florence's survival at stake, Lorenzo gave himself up to King Ferdinand, risking a quick execution. Ferdinand delayed, uncertain what to do with Lorenzo now that he had him. This gave Lorenzo the opportunity to try his hand at diplomacy, with amazing success. That debate between two of Italy's most skilled negotiators lasted several months, while Lorenzo wondered each day whether Ferdinand would tire of the arguments and hand him over to his executioner, or to the Pope. Lorenzo eventually convinced Ferdinand that it would not bode well for Naples if Florence's dominions fell into the Pope's clutches. It was the old question of a balance of power. They signed a peace treaty that halted Ferdinand's participation in the war in exchange for a number of secret concessions on Lorenzo's part. Lorenzo returned to Florence, while the Pope fumed and threatened further military actions.

Coincidentally, Mohammed II, Constantinople's Turkish conqueror, invaded southern Italy. The Pope was forced to reluctantly forgive Florence when Lorenzo agreed to equip fifteen galleys to help turn back the Turkish threat, which they did. Then, in the aftermath, to tie everything together, Lorenzo linked Florence by treaty to Milan, Venice, Naples and the Papal States in an Italian League, unified against outsiders. That was probably the greatest feat of diplomacy in Italy's history. It led to decades of prosperity for Florence. And it ensured that the Medici family would retain power as long as Lorenzo lived.

"So Lorenzo has shown his gratitude towards your family by looking favorably on your military career," I said.

"I think that I've well earned my promotions," Hugo said. "And Lorenzo was wise enough to know I had nothing to do with Bertrando's death."

"I'm sure he did," I said, pleased that I'd managed to anger him a bit.

Serena finally came home, with Helen, to save me from further need to talk to Hugo. "What have you two been talking about," she said, giving me a long look.

Hugo stood up quickly. "I was telling Aberto how fortunate he is to have such an alluring wife, and such an equally spellbinding daughter. You two look like spring flowers set to bloom."

I groaned. "We were only talking about politics." Serena and Helen didn't seem to hear me.

3

I gave up tutoring students after rumors about the dismal business with Tullia began to spread through Florence. Fortunately, I soon gained employment with the Medici family. I spent most my days at the Villa de Medici, a country villa near the tiny town of Cafaggiolo, an easy hour long ride from Florence. The sprawling complex of buildings and gardens, modified and expanded many times, had been the Medici family home for seven generations. Visitors from all parts of Europe invariably crowded the villa, the mix of professions—artists, scholars, diplomats, businessmen, traders, bankers—a tribute to Lorenzo's wide ranging interests. The villa also served as a residence for artists, writers, and musicians, such as the young Michelangelo, who made Florence their home for extended periods, and contributed to the city's outburst of creative energy.

All of my duties at the Medici villa related in some way or another to books. I served primarily as the curator for Lorenzo's vast book collection, one of the world's largest. He was a fanatic about books, and collected classics from anywhere and by any means short of theft, copied if needed. Lorenzo regularly sent the Florentine writer Politian—famous for his lyric drama, *The Fable of Orpheus*—far and wide to acquire books. Politian once brought back two-hundred manuscripts from the monastery at Mt. Athos Lascaris. They kept me busy for months.

I also vigorously participated in the discussions and debates of the Platonic Academy, an association of men absorbed in Plato and his writings. The Platonists met regularly, dining, reading aloud, discussing the Greek philosopher's writings, arguing meaning and significance. We celebrated his November 7 birth (and death) with near-religious fervor.

Lorenzo made his library available for the use of scholars and other educated Florentine citizens, including an occasional woman. Tullia was a frequent visitor. After our moment of weakness, as she once referred to it, she avoided me when she visited—at least at first—unless she needed my direction to find a particular work, which was rare. However, a few days after my latest argument with Serena, she came to the Medici villa specifically to see me. I sensed that was no ordinary visit when I saw her striding toward me across the Greek style atrium, her heals clicking a pattern on the tile floor.

"I need to talk to you, Aberto," she said, as usual touching my arm for emphasis.

"What are you looking for?" I felt wary, thinking of Serena's accusations, knowing how close I had come to validating them, realizing that despite my resolve, it could happen again.

"It's not about a book. Can we go somewhere to talk? Perhaps in the garden?"

"Why not here?"

Tullia looked around. Five other people shared the reading room near the alcove where I had my small desk. "We need to be alone."

I didn't like the sound of that. She sensed my unease. "Don't worry, Aberto, I'm not going to thrust myself upon you."

I nodded, feeling my face grow warm, and led her quickly outside. It was mid afternoon on a summer day and maddeningly hot as usual. We made for a bench under a large cypress tree. As she sat down, Tullia shook off her sandals and pulled her dress up to her knees. Her bare legs and feet dangled below, eliciting my attention.

"I heard about your uncle," I said.

Tullia's uncle, a prominent priest, and my nemesis, had died a week earlier. It was not unexpected. He had been ill for many months. I had heard that he left Tullia, his only surviving relative, a substantial part of a modest fortune. The rest went to the Church.

"I suppose you're relieved," she said, smiling to indicate that she didn't intend any criticism. "He was hard on us both, but I like to think he had good intentions."

"Some of the worst crimes are perpetrated in the name of good intentions."

Tullia laughed. "I wholeheartedly agree." After a brief pause, she said, "We used to talk about such things. I miss our conversations."

"I do too."

"Maybe some day, when things are different . . ."

I shook my head. "Some things time will never heal."

"That's sort of why I'm here, Aberto. You've done much for me, and I'm grateful. You've opened my eyes, my mind, to a world of ideas. But, I want to explore more."

"I can't tutor you any longer."

"I don't ask that." She paused again, frowning. "I want to attend meetings of the Platonic Academy, if only to listen."

"Tullia, it is for . . . we have only men."

"Why can't you have *one* woman?"

I shook my head. The thought was horrifying, worse than having a woman join you in a bath. "It cannot be. No one would come."

"I won't say anything. I'll only listen. They'll hardly know I'm there."

I laughed at that. "You've never sat silent for five minutes at a time in your life."

"Aberto!"

"I'm sorry. It's impossible. Forget the idea."

"Ask Lorenzo. Please."

"I know what he'll say."

"Ask him anyway. Let me talk to him. Arrange an interview. Please."

I finally said I would try, just to quiet her. I knew it was no use. We sat for a while longer, side by side, Tullia swinging her legs, humming a tune, lost in thought.

I broke the silence. "Tullia, answer me something."

"If I can." She turned towards me, smiled, pulled an ankle under her knee and put her hands in her lap.

"What are your intentions with my sons?"

"Intentions?"

"I'm concerned, as is Serena. If Herminius deigned to talk to me, he would probably ask me to arrange a marriage with you. We know that Luigi has similar ambitions, at least he once had."

"They're so different," Tullia said, turning to face me. "It's amazing that they could both be your sons. Herminius is a romantic, a budding poet. Luigi has the mind and temperament of a businessman, something I keep trying to tell him."

"I agree that they're utterly different, except in one respect. Their infatuation with you."

"I love both your sons." Tullia stood up and walked a few feet away. She turned to face me, hands on her hips, a familiar pose that brought back memories of past happy interludes. "But not in the same way . . . as I love you."

"Tullia, Tullia! My God!" I shook my head and looked to see that no one had heard.

"I'm sorry." She came over to sit close beside me. "But you must have known. Your sons I suspect do, though I've never told them so."

"Choose one of my sons, and have done with it. Put them out of their misery. We can never . . . I already have a wife." I laughed, trying, without success, to make it all seem like a humorous mistake.

Tullia put her hand on my thigh, slid it to the inside slightly, a quick tease. She leaned toward me so her face was inches from mine. "Someone of your status, of your position in society, deserves a mistress."

I looked around nervously. "You don't mean that."

"How do you know?"

When I didn't say anything, Tullia stood up, straightened her shift, and spun around on the walkway. She stopped in front of me, hands on hips. I held my breath. She could be utterly unnerving at times.

"I've no intention of marrying either of your sons. I'll not marry anyone. I refuse to devote my life to caring for a brood of screaming children, tending to a house, ordering servants around, gossiping with other old women who have nothing important to talk about except the price of bread, or their husband's latest mistress. I want to be free to do everything a man does."

I stared at her dumbfounded as she narrowed her eyes at me, a challenge, daring me to utter a negative word. "Have you let my sons into your bed?"

"You've no right to ask me that."

"I want to know."

"You're not my father."

I got up and started to walk away. She came after me, grabbing my arm so I had to turn to face her. Her face was flushed, her eyes glinting gold.

"If I say yes will you be jealous?"

"Definitely."

She laughed. "I wish I could lie with the skill of most women, about such things."

"Tullia!"

"There's only one man who I'll ever allow to part the sheets of my bed. And he, alas, is the rarest of Florentine commodities—a faithful husband."

She turned and walked away with studied dignity.

4

Despite Lorenzo de Medici's opposition, the preacher Savonarola returned to Florence to remind the city's populace of their profligate ways. Hoping for a confrontation with authorities, he preached a sermon in the piazza adjacent to the Palazzo Vechio. Curiosity led me to attend, as it must have done many of the thousands that packed the piazza, the crowd spilling into adjoining streets, all traffic at a standstill. Savonarola's voice thundered, ranging the scales from a low rumble to a high-pitched scream, as he explained in damning details what awaited sinners, which in his mind included all but the poorest of Florence's citizens. I felt an uneasy foreboding.

Near the platform, aides had cordoned off a section for church officials, including a row of nuns. I recognized Liliana, despite the anonymity of the nuns' habits. I saw her brush tears from her eyes. My uneasiness increased.

Savonarola's theme was what he referred to as the blatant paganism, corruption and immorality of Florence's leaders and leading citizens. He spared no one his fiery rhetoric, stabbing with his sharp words at the clergy and laity alike. And he did not hold back from lambasting Lorenzo himself. He devoted a special passage to condemn the well-paid courtesans and their patrons. I thought of Rosalie and my disquiet further increased.

I knew a little of Savonarola's remarkable history, and consequently was not too surprised at his invective. He came from a family of physicians, but rejected that employ when the decadence of the University of Bologna's students drove him away. He wrote bitterly of his experience, one phrase I always remembered: *If you live chastely and modestly, you are considered a fool; if you are pious, a hypocrite; if you believe in God, an imbecile.*

He horrified his family when he entered a Dominican monastery, where his mentors discovered Savonarola's oratorical skills. A decade ago he came to Florence to preach in San Lorenzo church. He was not popular, his style too obtuse and theological. Five years later, in Lombardy, he discovered a new voice a means to arouse crowds, to draw audiences to his sermons, with his denunciations of immorality, and the horrors that awaited sinners. His return to Florence provided Lorenzo with an enemy more dangerous than the Pope.

When I mentioned this to Serena, she waved her arms in dismissal. "He'll be like all the other street preachers. Popular for a few days, then on his way to milk the foolish and naive in some other city." I resisted the temptation to argue.

A few days later, when Tullia came to see me at the Medici villa, I learned that she had also heard Savonarola's harangue. She too had fallen victim to irresistible curiosity. She had listened to Savonarola from the base of the speaker's platform, trapped, unable to break away before he had finished, as I had.

"I was so close to him, I got sprayed with his spittle when he got excited, which was most of the time. His huge hooked nose and tight-lipped sneer will haunt my nightmares for weeks. I'll never go to listen to him again."

"You sound frightened."

"His vehemence and violence would frighten anyone, whether you agree with him or not."

I nodded. "Yes. I felt that too, though there was little I could agree with."

"That's because you're part of Florence's male-dominated aristocracy."

I laughed. "I'm only a caretaker for Lorenzo's books, an occasional tutor, and a hopeful writer."

"You know what I mean."

"If I'm an aristocrat, then there are few in Florence who are not."

Tullia had stood leaning forward over my desk so that we could whisper and not disturb two bearded scholars engrossed in a stack of Lorenzo's yellowing manuscripts. She came around the desk, put a hand on my shoulder and bent down to whisper in my ear.

"You should warn Liliana's cousin about Savonarola."

"Rosalie?"

"Who else? Your partner."

"You know about that?"

"Liliana tells me everything. She has a great deal of trouble with your involvement in such a business, as you might imagine."

I shook my head in exasperation. "Rosalie is her friend."

"She can easily forgive a friend anything, but a father must adhere to higher standards. As must a husband."

"And what of a wife?" I said, getting angry.

"That's different. A wife must have greater freedom to enjoy amorous advances whenever she can." Tullia laughed loudly, lifting the two bearded heads,

"Tullia, try to control yourself."

"I'm sorry." She patted my shoulder and moved away. I watched her, mesmerized as always by her youthful presence, and the indelible memory of what it had felt like to briefly embrace her.

"Your brother should be equally worried," I said, when she turned back to face me.

"He is."

I had attempted to teach Tullia's brother Mario the intricacies of Italian grammar and found his mind nearly impenetrable. Thus it didn't surprise me when he entered the banking industry, which nobly suited him. He seemed destined to reach the highest echelons of Florence society, and thus had good reason to worry about Savonarola.

I had hoped that Luigi would go into banking, though it was considered a disreputable business by many people, and barely tolerated by the Church. Yet no one, except perhaps Savonarola, would dare attempt to suppress the business. It was absolutely critical to Florence's continued prosperity. It was no accident that Florence had more banks than any other city in Europe, seventy-five, all independently owned. Most of course, were small. The Medici family had long ago grabbed the lead in this business, boasting of Florence's largest bank. They had also established branches in Rome, Venice, Milan, Pisa, Geneva, Lyons, Avignon, Bruges, and London. The business was as dangerous and risky as trade with the Muslim world, bank failures common.

Florentine banks took in deposits from all over Europe, with innovative schemes to ease the flow of money and credit, such as the use of checks (an idea borrowed from the Arabs) and letters of credit. They also loaned money to governments, and fixed rates of exchange between Europe's currencies. They had become indispensable, an often dangerous position, which Savonarola sought to use to his advantage.

"Did you hear about the riot?" Tullia said, coming back to the desk. I had. "I almost got pulled into it," she continued. "A mob formed after the sermon, a small fraction of the crowd, but enough to make trouble. They went looking for suitable victims to make good Savonarola's threats, chasing a few well-dressed people off the streets. They found a man escorting a woman, obviously a courtesan, and pelted them both with horse dung."

"That I hadn't heard about," I said, smiling at the image.

"Rosalie should take care. You should talk to her."

Before she left, Tullia looked back over her shoulder and asked in a voice loud enough for everyone to hear, "Have you spoken to Lorenzo yet . . . about me?"

I leaned forward over my desk, and let my head sink into my hands.

"You promised," she said. "Are you going to, or not?"

I knew she wouldn't leave until I agreed, so I nodded without looking up.

5

To escape the turmoil of uncertainty that swirled around my life, I fled the Medici villa and returned to the streets of Florence. I walked without direction or purpose, letting my feet lead the way, my mind wandering, my senses taking in the sights, sounds and smells of the city. I had much to worry about. My eldest daughter seemed to have fallen under Savonarola's spell. My niece and business partner was in danger from the same source. Tullia was again finding ways to alarm me with her attention. My sons would be dangerously disappointed if they continued to seek Tullia's hand in marriage. Serena seemed intent on tormenting me with Hugo forever. Amazingly, I had overlooked the one worry that would almost immediately become a reality.

I headed towards the center of the city, where you could still detect a remnant of the carefully organized Roman town of Forentia.

Outside this orderly center, an erratic sprawl marked the growth of the city during the last millennium. I crossed the Arno on the Ponte Vecchio, the city's oldest bridge, rebuilt many times. Floods had carried away bridges over the Arno on a regular basis. I finally reached an area of shops catering to the wealthy, where I wandered around looking at things I couldn't afford to buy.

Remembering Savonarola's words, I noticed Florence's rich merchants, especially their wives, who insisted on advertising their wealth through the extravagance of their clothes, and the rarity of the jewels that adorned them. They unfortunately gave strong ammunition to the fiery preacher. They also flagrantly disobeyed the sumptuary laws designed to restrain the impulse to flaunt fortunes. The laws regulated almost everything capable of excess, from the fineness of dress material to the number of courses served at banquets. Most people viewed the laws as too silly to obey. Savonarola considered them too lenient.

In an attempt to forget my nagging concerns, I entered the church of Santa Maria Novella seeking solitude. For a while, I got what I sought. The first half-hour or so, I walked around the nearly abandoned chapel examining the frescoes, paintings and sculptures that adorned every wall and alcove. The city's prosperity had made it possible to generously support the arts, and churches had greatly benefited. It was said, with more than a grain of truth, that greed and guilt enriched the arts. At a time when great wealth often aroused jealousy and suspicion, art could be a convenient outlet for excess wealth. We even built monuments to our artists, especially our painters, such as Giotto and Fra Filippo Lippi.

Patrons had influenced the course of art with their commissions, putting to rest forever the dismal, dark styles of the past, in favor of a more realistic, modern approach. Public awareness brought a healthy dose of praise and criticism to elevate standards, and with it, inevitably, a large element of rivalry and competition. In the art world as in the business world, competition drove progress.

Florentine artists reigned supreme in the art world, just as its bankers dominated the financial world. Leonardo da Vinci, who I had known slightly, made his reputation in Florence, though he had since moved to Milan. Sandro Botticelli became famous for his painting of *Madonna of the Magnificent* in which Lorenzo and his brother Guiliano appear as boys of sixteen and twelve. Verrocchio's bronze statue of *David* stood guard at the head of the main stairway in the Palazzo

Vecchio, the city's most famous tourist attraction. With the aid of a promising young student named Michelangelo, the aging Domenico Ghirlandaio recently completed his stunning painting of the chapel in the church where I had taken refuge. Lorenzo was so certain Michelangelo would one day accomplish great things, that he had moved the talented lad into the Villa de Medici and had given him a regular allowance of five ducats a month.

I was so completely absorbed in Ghirlandaio's painting that I didn't at first take in what I was hearing. Only slowly did the voices penetrate my brain to register their familiarity, although I couldn't quite make out what they were saying. I didn't want to believe what I was hearing. I turned around, but could see no one. In the Santa Maria Novella, sound could carry in odd ways, making it appear that voices were coming from speakers right next to you, when they were in reality standing at the opposite end of the chapel.

I edged slowly out into the center of the nave and looked around. The voices were dimmer. I started up the aisle, moving with great care, looking from side to side. I stopped abruptly when I saw them, Helen and Hugo, standing in the lee of a marble column, close together, hand in hand, absorbed with each other, speaking quietly. They looked like lovers seeking a moment of respite from their own insistent emotions. They looked as if they belonged together. I retreated a few paces, my contentment, my escape at an end. For a long time I stood still, out of sight, still hearing Helen's high voice and Hugo's deep voice exchanging what seemed like intense phrases, though I couldn't get the content. I thought about trying to get closer, but quickly shoved that idea aside.

I couldn't just walk away though. I had to confront them in some way, to at least let them know that I had seen them. I decided to wait outside the church, and, when they emerged, pretend that I was just about to enter. As I started toward the door, I heard Helen's voice raised higher, and the words took on a meaning that alarmed me.

"Hugo, no. We can't do that here. Please."

I froze, my fists clenching, my heart racing madly. I didn't know what to do. I listened with such concentration that I think I could have heard a mouse running along the roof of the church.

"As you wish," Hugo said, or at least that's what it sounded like, his voice not as intense as Helen's. "Let's get out of here then, and go somewhere less confining."

I quickly darted into a pew and sat down, bending my head in mock prayer. I could hear their voices, again quiet, as they slowly made their way up the aisle. So involved were they with each other that they would have walked past without noticing me if I hadn't raised up just as they came abreast of my pew. I turned towards them, as if getting ready to leave.

"Father!" Helen said, when she caught sight of me.

"Oh, hello," I said, probably looking as foolish as I felt. "What are you two doing here?" I nodded toward Hugo, about as friendly a motion as I could dredge up. "Is your mother here too, somewhere?" I looked around suddenly, as if Serena would pop up from one of the pews as I had.

"We just happened to meet," Helen said. "Is mother supposed to be here?"

I was happy to see that Helen looked at least a little discomfited. Hugo, after the first shock, had again assumed his imperious look of self-satisfaction. I couldn't bear to look at him.

"I don't know. With Hugo here, I only assumed that your mother would be close by somewhere. Why else would Hugo enter a church in the middle of the day." It gave me pleasure to talk about Hugo as if he weren't standing right in front of me, still holding onto Helen's arm.

She seemed to notice that and pulled her arm away. I allowed myself a glance at Hugo and saw his face set in a scowl. He suddenly made a little bow and stepped back.

"I'll leave you now, Helen. Your father can, I think, see to your safe return home."

"Don't leave," Helen said.

"Another time," he said, turning and walking away. We watched him stride down the aisle, his footsteps ringing off the walls.

"I didn't mean to interrupt anything," I said, trying to sound innocent, and failing.

"You didn't. We just . . . met here, by accident."

"I didn't know you came here. It's a long walk from our house. It's also an odd place to find Hugo. The last place, I would have thought. That's why I asked about your mother, since Hugo takes such an interest in her."

She looked at me closely. "What do you mean he takes an interest in her? You make it sound like something horrible. Are you implying that mother is acting improperly by allowing Hugo into our house?"

"No. I didn't say that."

"He comes to see me too. Is that also wrong?"

"Yes. I think it is," I said, unable to restrain myself any longer. "He's wrong for you, and for your mother. The man is a false, pompous—"

"I won't listen to this." She put her hands over her ears, like a child. "You never understand. You don't want to understand. You're just jealous." She turned and ran out of the church.

6

I did nothing about Helen and Hugo, or any of my other long list of worries. Too many things impinged on me, so I ignored them all. I spent more and more time at the Medici villa, or aimlessly wandering the streets of Florence, or seeking the companionship of a bottle of wine at an obscure shop where no one knew me. I would always regret my inaction, my cowardice to face my family's dilemmas as they raced toward deadly confrontations. As each event piled upon the next, I became more immune to disaster. I closed my mind and my heart. I emulated the sobering life of a Christian hermit, holed up in a cave.

Yet, all the news was not bad. My grandson Alessandro, who would always know me only as Uncle Aberto, continued to escape the various illnesses that took the lives of a third of Florence's infants. Serena and I spent time with him nearly every day. We sought these hours with Alessandro as much to quiet our own souls as to enrich his. Nowhere else could I sit beside Serena, take her hand with ease, share a laugh or a smile, exchange words without double meanings. We forgot everything else when we were with Alessandro, his innocence repelling the sordidness of life. We forgot how to argue, how to take offense, how to worry. Alessandro saved our marriage.

We also most often saw Liliana at my sister's villa. She could not spend as much time there as we did, her increasing responsibilities at the convent keeping her busy. I felt sorry for her self-made predicament—the need to pretend that Alessandro was only her cousin. I once asked her, "Will you never tell him that you are his mother?"

She thought about this for a long time, as if it had never occurred to her before. "He has a wonderful mother in Filomena. I don't see what purpose it would serve . . . and yet, it is hard."

"Perhaps when he's older," Serena said.

Liliana smiled. "Perhaps. You would equally like to acknowledge him as your grandson, I think." Then she turned to me and placed a hand on my arm, the first sign of affection I had had from her since the episode with Tullia. "Alessandro most needs a father," she said. "A grandfather is the next best thing, but an uncle may have to suffice."

I took her hand and would have embraced her, but Alessandro, sensing he was no longer the center of attention, let out a squall of protest and the moment escaped. I glanced at Serena as Liliana snatched up her child and saw a look in my wife's eyes I had not seen for ages. For a brief moment we reclaimed each other's affections.

It was also uplifting to see my sister Filomena so happy, after her years of exile. She had enlisted my aid with a wealthy Florentine merchant. She wanted me to negotiate a marriage contract for her daughter Isabella and the merchant's son. Filomena had urged haste since Isabella, at fifteen, was growing old, and had matured into as wild a creature as her mother had been at her age. She had ample evidence of what could go wrong in marriage. For once I was able to succeed in a family assignment. Isabella and the merchant's son were betrothed without difficulty, without protests from the principals, both happy in the selection, a marvelous rarity.

Another family member gained a push towards a successful career without my help. My nephew Sebastiano, Joannes's and Natala's son, gained acceptance as an apprentice to one of Florence's leading physicians. I learned from Natala that it was largely Lorenzo de Medici's doing.

"I couldn't have been more surprised," Natala told me, looking around nervously. "He has used this physician, and thinks highly of him, and apparently has some influence with him."

I couldn't help laughing. "Lorenzo has influence with everyone, even his enemies. It's good to have him on your side, as you seem to. After Sebastiano finishes his apprenticeship, Lorenzo will make sure that he's immediately inducted into the physician's guild."

That wasn't an automatic occurrence in a city where influence was a priceless commodity. The medical profession was among the most prestigious of Florence's seven professional guilds, which included judges and notaries, cloth importers and refinishers, textile manufacturers, retailers and silk merchants, bankers, and furriers. I had once thought about trying to gain admittance to the notary guild, but, after seeing what they did, decided I'd rather take my chances with the uncertain life of a writer. Florence also supported fourteen craft guilds—the butchers, shoemakers, blacksmiths, carpenters, second-hand dealers, wine dealers, innkeepers, salt, oil and cheese sellers, tanners, armorers, iron workers, girdle makers, wood workers, and bakers. It was an indication of the times that girdle makers and bakers held equal esteem in society.

A high percentage of the male working population belonged to one guild or another. And a kind of balance of power existed between the fourteen craft guilds and the seven professional guilds, each showing the other a grudging respect. Together, they were one of the most powerful political forces in Florence, the only voice the average citizen had with the governing aristocrats. The city magistrates, including Lorenzo de Medici, did not dare ignore their needs.

Natala smiled, and took hold of my hand. "I haven't told Joannes—I mean about Lorenzo's influence. So please keep this to yourself."

"Has Joannes's jealous fever begun to rage again?"

"It has hardly ever subsided. Mostly he fumes and fusses by himself, when he sees me dancing in the Villa de Medici."

"He hasn't lately jumped up and dragged you from the dance floor?" I said, with a laugh.

"Don't even joke about such things."

"And what of your poor overlooked daughter, Zeta?"

"She isn't overlooked. I'm giving her dancing lessons, along with a few other selected students, and she is doing well."

"I must come see her some time. Joannes doesn't object?"

"Not yet." I heard uncertainty in her voice.

Tullia delivered the last bit of good news before the deluge. She found me at my desk in the Medici villa reading room. I had been trying to avoid her since I had not yet had the nerve to suggest to Lorenzo that he include a woman in the deliberations of the Platonic Academy.

"Uncle Aberto. There you are," Tullia cried, disturbing two scholars who had fallen asleep over their books, and startling me out of a reverie.

"What do you mean, uncle?" I said.

"Everyone else calls you uncle, so I shall from now on. Maybe you'll be nicer to me and not try to hide every time I come here."

"I haven't."

"You have, and I know why."

"Tullia—"

"I know. Lorenzo is adamant. I accept it. At least you tried, for which I shall give you a niece-like kiss—"

"Don't you dare!"

"Uncle Aberto. You're too cruel," she said, her voice rising an octave, making her sound like a twelve-year-old.

I had to laugh. I had seldom seen her so effervescent. She bounced around in front of my desk, unable to stand still. With a brightly colored a scarf around her head, and wrapped in a simple peasant's dress, she could have just jumped from a farmer's wagon on the way to deliver produce to market. I loved her more than ever.

"What has happened to you?" I said, standing up and coming around the desk, intending to lead her away where she wouldn't disturb my readers any further. She allowed me to take her arm, and walked meekly at my side, but I sensed energy ready to explode.

"I'm going into the textile business. What do you think of that?"

"Textiles? How?"

"Luigi and I, together."

"Luigi?"

"I told you Luigi had a head for business. I finally convinced him. I got a bunch of money from my uncle, more than I've let on, because it embarrassed me so, especially after I was so mean to him."

"I hope you didn't do something foolish, Tullia."

"We've bought a textile mill."

"Luigi doesn't have any money. And he didn't come to me." We had reached the gardens. I had forgotten my hat, and the sun made me squint. I felt as if I was experiencing a waking dream.

Tullia laughed. "Of course he didn't come to you for money. He never would have. I put up the money, the Medici bank the rest. Luigi will run the mill. I'll give him a woman's advice whenever he needs it."

"Astonishing."

"Yes, isn't it. I thought you'd be happy."

"I am utterly befuddled by the news. Does this mean that you two are going to get married?"

Tullia made a face at me, wrinkling her nose. "Never. Sorry. You'll have to find someone else to provide you with another grandchild."

"But—"

"I've told you. I won't marry anyone, ever. I might be someone's mistress, but you know about that."

"Tullia! We agreed not to talk of such things."

She laughed. "I'm going to kiss you anyway." And she did.

For once I had something happy to relate to Serena when I got home—or so it seemed. The news pleased her, for Luigi's sake, but she quickly saw the dark side.

"What did she say about Herminius? He'll be jealous."

I sighed and shook my head. "She says she won't marry either of our sons."

"What do you suppose Herminius will say, and do, when he hears Tullia has become his brother's business partner?"

7

A few weeks later I got the answer to Serena's question. Herminius confronted his brother. Words turned to violence. They ended up brawling in a crowded tavern, like a couple of streetfighters. Herminius nearly killed Luigi. So many people told me the details that I felt as if I had been there. And yet, I could still barely believe that it had happened.

Tullia had met Luigi in their favorite tavern. It was where they always met, almost daily, in the late afternoon. Unfortunately, the tavern faced onto the popular Piazza del Duomo, the site of Florence's famous domed cathedral. From the tables and chairs that spilled out onto the piazza, patrons could sit and study the nearly century old bronze doors of the Baptistery, the small octagonal building that seemed to guard the main entrance to the cathedral. The doors were one of the first things visitors to Florence came to see. For a few coins, they could listen to a guide tell them the story of the great artistic competition between the two most famous artists of the day, Filippo Brunelleschi and Lorenzo Ghiberti. Even from the tavern tables, you could hear the guide loudly announce, with a twinkle in his eye, that Ghiberti won because he could carve the nude figure with a more rigorous classical form and detail.

The tavern's prominent location meant that any argument that escalated to violence would rapidly become public knowledge. Friends delighted, for weeks afterwards, in giving me their versions of the fraternal clash. I didn't trust any of them until I managed to find Tullia and ask her. To avoid any possible misunderstandings, I asked her to come to the house and explain it to me, in Serena's presence. Tullia reluctantly agreed, clearly still shaken by what had happened.

Serena greeted Tullia in a civil but cool manner. She blamed me for the earlier entanglement, but blamed Tullia for leading her two sons on. Tullia sat on the edge of her chair, nervously anxious to get the testimony over with.

"It pains me to talk about this," Tullia began, her hands clenched. "I feel that it's all my fault."

Serena nodded her head in agreement. We had talked before, and Serena had promised not to argue or scold Tullia, to get a clear report of what had happened.

"Luigi and I sat quietly discussing our textile factory—how to improve production, increase sales, cut costs. We've discovered more problems than we'd originally foreseen. Many of the looms are in need of repair for one thing. We may have to borrow more money."

I could have warned her about this, but she wouldn't have listened. The Florentine textile business was dangerously risky for the naive and inexperienced. More than a hundred textile factories operated in Florence and neighboring towns and villages, all privately owned. Ambitious entrepreneurs often made fortunes. But many failed. The competition was harsh.

The textile industry was also Florence's largest employer. The process that took raw wool to finished textiles involved dozens of steps and as many teams of specialized workers. Everyone benefited, when the textile business thrived, from the farmers and herdsmen who supplied some of the raw material, to the bankers who supplied financing, to the traders and merchants who imported raw wool from Spain and Britain and exported and sold the finished product all over Europe. Failure of the textile industry would bring ruin to Florence's economy.

"You weren't arguing?" I asked, something that a few observers had mentioned.

Tullia frowned at me. "We talked out things. We didn't argue. I suppose Luigi is surprised that I've taken such an interest in the business."

I laughed. "Luigi no doubt expected you to remain a silent partner. I could have told him differently."

"Let her tell what happened," Serena said.

Tullia sighed. "Herminius showed up at our table suddenly. He seemed calm, in control, but I sensed trouble. I asked him to sit down. He started to, then something passed between him and Luigi—a look, a word I didn't hear. I'm not sure what it was. They started to shout at each other. Luigi stood up. Everyone stared at us. It was horrible."

"What were they arguing about?" Serena said.

"That's what made me furious," Tullia said, leaning forward, her face flushing at the memory. "They both claimed that I belonged to them, that I'd promised them in some way. That's when I got into it. I couldn't help it."

"You don't see why they could come that conclusion?" Serena said.

Tullia didn't seem to hear, or else she ignored the provocative question. "I jumped up and planted myself in between them. I was so angry I didn't care who saw me, or what they thought."

"Good for you," Serena said.

"I told them I wouldn't marry either of them, that they were both children, that if I ever married, and it wasn't at all likely, it would be to a *man*."

A disquieting silence fell on the room as first Serena, and then Tullia looked at me. After a moment, I found my voice. "What happened then?"

"I started to leave, pushing past Herminius. I'm not sure what happened, but by the time I reached the edge of the piazza, your sons had begun to shove each other about. When I heard the shouting I turned to see. They were like children. But of course, as you've heard, it got worse."

"Didn't anyone try to stop it?" I said.

Tullia shook her head angrily. "Everyone urged them on, delighted in the diversion. I heard two fellows bet on the outcome, when Herminius hit Luigi, and Luigi lunged at Herminius knocking him back over a table, spilling drinks everywhere."

"We heard that Herminius nearly killed Luigi. How did that happen?"

"That was my fault too," Tullia said, slumping back in her chair. "Luigi had Herminius down on the floor, just holding him there, trying to calm him, I think. I tried to pull Luigi away, and before I knew what had happened, I was knocked back under a table and Herminius had his hands around Luigi's neck, choking him and pounding his head into the floor."

"My God!" Serena and I said, in unison, both of us now sitting on the edges of our chairs.

Tullia spoke softly, almost in a whisper, as if to keep anyone else from hearing the horror of her words. "I'm convinced he would have killed his brother if someone hadn't pulled him away. I've never been more frightened in my life."

"Oh no! I can't believe that," Serena said.

"I'm sorry," Tullia said. "I've been a fool not to see what was happening."

"Indeed you have been. But you're not alone in that enterprise," Serena said, giving me another sharp look.

"Herminius has left Florence," Tullia said. "He talked to me before he left. He apologized, but he said he couldn't live here any longer. Luigi is all right. He's strong, like you Aberto. And he has the textile mill to keep him more than busy."

"And you two . . ." I said.

"We're business partners, and will never be anything more."

"Luigi accepts that?" Serena said.

Tullia hesitated, sighed, looked uncomfortable. "I'm sorry. He doesn't. Not really. He has vowed never again to speak to you, Aberto. He's wrong about blaming you, but—"

"He has good reason," Serena said.

"I'd better go," Tullia said, standing up abruptly. When I started to escort her to the door, she waved me away. When I turned back, Serena was half way up the stairs to the bedrooms.

8

Troubles come in threes they say. Mine came in droves. I had lost my sons. I had lost Tullia, I surmised, judging from the way she looked at me as she brushed me aside and fled the house. I had lost a part of Serena, a vital part, without which I wasn't sure our marriage meant anything. What more could go wrong? I shuddered when I posed the question to myself.

After giving Tullia a few minutes to make her escape, I too fled the house. It was drizzling, but I took no notice. I wandered down along the wharves that nestled the embankments of the Arno. I watched boatmen poling skiffs across the slow-moving river. I watched men sing and laugh as they unloaded bales of wool from long pointed barges. I envied their simple existence. Why had I become a writer? There was something inevitably tragic about the profession, a consequence of the damnably sustained thinking that writers must constantly foster.

I turned my back on the Arno and nearly ran along rain soaked streets to reach Filomena's townhouse. My sister was not there, but Liliana was. Liliana had Alessandro in her arms, rocking him gently back and forth when the nurse led me into my grandson's room. Liliana looked up and smiled and put her finger to her lips. I tiptoed up to her, kissed her on the forehead and looked at Alessandro, sleeping contentedly, his little hands curled into fists. I sat down on the couch beside Liliana and for perhaps fifteen minutes the three of us sat in silence, the most pleasurable quarter-hour I had spent in months.

Later Liliana and I talked, something we had not had a chance to do for a long time. I told her what had happened with her brothers and Tullia. She seemed not at all surprised. Maybe Tullia had already confided in her. Then she said, making my eyes moist, "You know, you've been a good father, to me, and my brothers and sister. And you've been a wonderful friend to Tullia. She owes everything to you. Don't blame yourself for everything bad that happens. It is God's will. As mortals we can't expect to understand everything. Accept the pain, and look to the future."

My daughter, explaining life to me, her hand on mine, looking intently at me from the depths of her nun's habit, was undoubtedly the most stirring miracle I had ever experienced. "Thank you," I said, brushing away a tear and embracing her.

"I'll talk to Luigi. He'll eventually forgive you, though he has nothing really to forgive. Herminius will, with God's help, find his way, and one day return to us. Tullia is strong, and will always thrive. You must look to Helen. I worry about her."

"I do too," I said, "I've seen her with Hugo—"

"I know. Talk to her kindly. I know what she's feeling."

"I don't want her to—"

"End up like me?" Liliana laughed. "You shouldn't feel sorry for me."

"I don't. Not any more."

"Most of all, you must be patient with mother. Treat her kindly, and in time, all will be well between you two."

I wished I could believe that. I nodded and said I would, and started to get up to leave.

"I'm most worried about Rosalie," Liliana said. "Savonarola's preaching will eventually spur Florence's rabble into violence, I fear, in a misguided attempt to rid the city of evil, by perpetrating worse evils."

"She can take care of herself," I said, too hastily.

"I'm not at all certain of that." She paused, looking hard at me. "I am still amazed that you would help her set up such a . . . misguided business."

"She talked me into it. I regret it, but it's too late."

"You can talk to her. Warn her."

"Yes, I'll do that."

Liliana lifted my spirits tremendously. When we left Filomena's house and went our different ways, I walked with a new spring in my step, my mind filled with enterprises, a positive look to the future when the family would reunite. I should have gone immediately to Rosalie and forced her to pack her things and leave the city for a time.

Instead I hurried home to make peace with Serena. Alas, my resolve was not up to the task. Helen was with her. I found them in front of the fire in the sitting room, talking quietly. They stopped when they saw me.

"I've been to see Alessandro. Liliana was there."

"Are they well?" Serena said.

I nodded.

"We've been talking about Luigi and Herminius, and other things," Serena said, glancing at Helen, who still had not spoken.

"I hope you've been discussing Hugo," I said, instantly regretting it.

Helen grabbed Serena's arm. "Mother, you promised."

"It's settled," Serena said, giving me a look I didn't correctly interpret.

"You mean she's not going to see him again?" I asked, after which I stupidly added, "and what about you, Serena? Will you cease seeing him too?"

"Mother!"

"It's all right," Serena said, patting Helen's arm.

"Hugo is my friend, and I'll continue to see him if I wish," Helen said.

"I thought you said—"

"For once, be quiet, Aberto. You'll only make things worse, as you always do."

I couldn't help myself. "And I suppose you'll also continue to entertain Hugo, as *your* friend, in *your* bedroom, beneath *your* sheets."

"Aberto! For God's sake, think before you open your mouth."

I saw the stricken expression on Helen's face and sagged down on a chair, realizing what I had said.

"Do you think I care for that pompous man-child?" Serena said, her voice chilling. "I just wanted you to feel what I felt, when you surrendered into that German woman's arms, and when I heard what you had done to Tullia."

"I'm sorry," I said. "I wasn't thinking." Neither of us took any notice of Helen, listening to all that.

"He's never touched me," Serena said.

"What about Helen? He's wrong for her."

"Terribly wrong, as I have already told her."

"He'll hurt her, if she isn't careful. Ask Rosalie about Hugo. She'll tell you the way he treats some women—not you apparently. She's seen him in action."

We realized what we were saying too late. Helen had heard us all too well. "Stop it!" she said. "I can't stand this—what I'm hearing." Tears streamed down her cheeks. "You seem to hate each other, and blame everyone else."

"No, Helen. It isn't as you think," Serena said. Helen had stood up. Serena tried to reach for her, but Helen stepped away.

"I don't believe what you said about Hugo. He isn't like that—with me."

"You don't know—" I said.

"I won't listen to this any more," Helen cried, running towards the door.

I tried to stop her, but it was no use. She shook my arm free and dashed through the door. We waited up late into the night, and slept hardly at all. Helen didn't come back. The next day one of Filomena's servants brought us a note from Helen, that said, in clever simplicity, *I have left, lest you need to endure the man you hate—the man I love."* She had spent the night with Filomena and then left early in the morning with Hugo. We didn't know where they went. And we weren't sure whether to hope they had married or not.

9

Savonarola's inflammatory sermons attracted increasingly large and violent crowds. Lorenzo could not silence him. Savonarola went after every aspect of Florentine society, all of it corrupt in his mind. He attacked Lorenzo personally, without specifically naming him, saying in part, that *tyrants are incorrigible because they are proud, because they love flattery, and will not restore ill-gotten gains. They hearken not unto the poor, and neither do they condemn the rich.* But he kept his most inflammatory words for the kept women of the wealthy, courtesans like Rosalie.

I learned later that Liliana had urged Rosalie to leave Florence. I had forgotten my promise to do the same. She tried to warn her about the mob hysterics Savonarola could elicit with his words. Liliana, initially taken with the fanatical preacher, had turned against him, and in her quiet way, tried to spread her own calm words to counter his uncontrolled passion.

Rosalie refused to take the warning or danger seriously, although she did promise Liliana that she would hire some guards.

I was at the Medici villa when the mob formed following on the heals of one of Savonarola's more strident speeches. Later I told myself that if I had been in the city, I could have done something to stop the tragedy. But could I have? Or would I have? Those were questions I would forever ask myself, and never be able to answer.

Liliana had the courage to act. She confronted the mob at Rosalie's door. I don't know how she got there, how she heard of what was planned, why she did not seek help. I suppose I never will. Rosalie's guards, if she did hire any, were nowhere in sight.

I don't know what Liliana said to the mob. If they listened, it was only to mock a nun who dared to protect a prostitute. She delayed them long enough for Rosalie and her girls to escape through a back window. When the mob grew bored, they shoved Liliana aside and stormed past her. They broke into Rosalie's famous house and ransacked it mercilessly, furious that the famed courtesan had escaped.

When the mob leaders stepped back into the light of day, they found the courageous nun that had thwarted their bloodlust lying on the steps, her neck broken. They dispersed in shocked silence. The mob that had started the day intent on ridding Florence of all of its courtesans, had instead rid it of perhaps its most pious citizen.

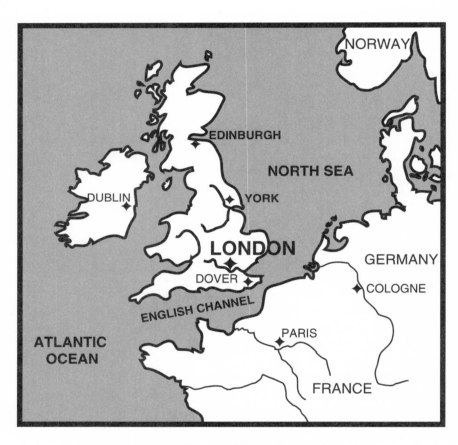

London, England

X. London
AD 1600

When the first Queen Elizabeth ascended to the throne of England in 1558 at the age of twenty-five, she inherited a nation in deep trouble. She had to deal with serious religious conflicts between Catholics and Protestants that had begun during the reign of her father, Henry VIII, and continued during the reign of her half sister Mary, better known as Bloody Mary. The economy was mired in a deep recession, and war with England's perennial enemies Spain and France seemed close at hand. She had to battle to hold her thrown against the claims of Mary Stuart, Queen of Scots, great-granddaughter of Elizabeth's grandfather, Henry VII. If the Spanish Armada had sailed thirty years earlier, England would have likely fallen.

Elizabeth met every challenge during her nearly half-century reign, to create a Golden Age rightfully named after her. It was an age populated with luminaries such as Shakespeare, Bacon and Marlowe, and with adventurers such as Hawkins, Drake and Raleigh. Elizabeth opened the door to the Renaissance in England and set the stage for the explosive growth of the British Empire.

The Birth

1

It is with great difficulty that I pick up my pen again. Reliving the death of our eldest daughter Louella, though the tragedy occurred several years ago, has halted my writing for months. How could I possibly describe the way I felt when I saw her youthful body lying in a coffin in the nave of St. Paul's cathedral? There is nothing more saddening than to bury your child. Why her? Why not me, I kept thinking? I have lived long enough, I shouted in my despair. She had so much to give, so much to live for. But I cannot abandon this writing. The stack of pages haunts me. They call out to me. I must finish this thing.

It seems horrible to attribute anything positive, anything beneficial to the death of a loved one. But Louella's tragic death on the steps outside Rosalie's pub unleashed forces that drew my family into a tight bond, just when it seemed destined to splinter irretrievably. Our mutual shared grief brought Sherri and me together again, our differences suddenly insignificant. We could not have endured the horror of the days following Louella's death without each other's support. As happened after my nephew's death during a military training exercise many years ago, the family pulled together, reunited and strengthened in tragedy.

"We have to find a way to get in touch with Helen and Heathcliff," Sherri said, after we returned from viewing Louella's body.

"It'll be difficult. We've no idea where they are."

"They should be here . . . when we bury their sister."

The horror of Sherri's words made me gasp. I was far from accepting what had happened as anything but the work of a cruel God.

"Talk to Twyla," Sherri said. "Maybe she knows where Heathcliff has run off to. I'll talk to Ludlow. He might know where Hugh and Helen are living."

I was surprised that she would encourage me to see Twyla, for any reason. She noticed my surprise. "I trust you can talk to Twyla without falling victim to her youthful charms."

"I'll try, though the sacrifice is great."

We fell silent then, appalled that we could offer such light-hearted banter at such a time.

Twyla still lived with my sister Filberta and niece Isabel, who would soon marry. Filberta was my grandson Alexander's guardian. He had now lost his mother, and would never know his father. Twyla had been one of Louella's closest friends. She looked as if she had been crying for days.

"I'm so sorry," Twyla said, when she saw me. In a moment we were in each other's arms and I felt her tears on my cheek. Once before we had embraced in this way, but rather for a purpose other than to comfort. When three-year-old Alexander wandered in, demanding attention, and we saw him look at us with Louella's eyes, it was almost too much for us to endure. We took time out from our grief to play with my grandson, who had learned to call me Uncle Averill, making my name sound like it had four-and-a-half syllables. It always brought a smile to my face. On that day, to be able to smile even for a moment, for any reason, seemed like the gift from a God who had begun to regret what he had done to us. But of course I didn't voice such a blasphemous thought.

A little later, with Alexander sitting on my lap I asked Twyla about Heathcliff. "Sherri and I want him to be here. He needs to know what has happened."

"Well . . . he has written me."

I looked surprised at this.

"Several times. I haven't answered him," she continued.

"Did you keep his letters?"

"No."

"Do you remember where they came from?"

"He's in London."

"That doesn't help much."

"I didn't pay much attention." After a pause, she continued more uncertainly, as if reluctant to reveal a confidence. "There may be a way to find him. The last time he wrote he said that every day at noon he would wait for me at the exact center of London bridge."

"He won't give up on you, will he?"

Twyla looked at me with a crooked smile, shaking her head. "Don't say it. I know I'm being selfish and egotistical to want my independence—"

"Will you go and meet him, if he comes?" I asked. "If I go, he'll probably flee as soon as he sees me."

"I doubt that," Twyla said, "but I'll try."

I didn't know whether Twyla had been successful until the day of the funeral. It was a befittingly bleak day, a light snow falling, bringing curses to the lips of every Londoner who had to get somewhere fast. We hurried inside, to the pews near the head of the nave where Louella's coffin sat perched on dull black trestles. The family filled the first three rows. Behind gathered the nuns from Louella's convent, and behind them, acquaintances and friends. The size of the turnout surprised me.

Sherri and I stood in the aisle quietly greeting everyone that arrived. My eldest brother Kendrik and his wife Olympia with four of their younger children arrived first. Their eldest son, Brock, a sought-after London portrait painter arrived next with his young, pregnant wife. Jasper and Nelwina arrived on time for a change, arguing as usual as they descended the aisle. I could guess what it was about. Nelwina wanted to take a role in one of Shakespeare's plays, *Much Ado About Nothing*, but she would have to pretend to be a boy playing a woman. She would try anything. Jasper as usual worried about the effect on his chances for winning a seat in Parliament. Their daughter, Yetta, was with them, looking uncomfortable. Their son Sebastian and his wife arrived late.

My sister Filberta arrived with Isabel and Isabel's fiancé, a handsome youth from an aristocratic family from the north. Twyla was not with her, which made me wonder. Filberta was leading Alexander by the hand. When the boy saw Sherri and me, he broke away and came running up to us. I picked him and told him he could sit with his aunt and uncle, wishing I could say instead grandmother and grandfather.

I turned to Filberta. "Where's Twyla?"

"I don't know," Filberta said. "She's been acting strangely the last three days. She left just before noon, saying only that she was going down to the river."

I smiled and patted Filberta's arm. "That's good. She's only trying to locate Heathcliff."

My son Ludlow arrived alone, looking glum and distracted. Some new labor problems must concern him, I thought. His factory operated eighteen hours a day, making him and Twyla, his not-so-silent partner, increasingly rich. Ludlow had fully embraced the business life. When he saw Sherri and me, he immediately shook his head.

"I suppose that means he couldn't find them," I said.

"He told me hasn't heard from Hugh for five or six weeks," Sherri said. "They've moved, he thinks. His letters are returned."

"That worries me."

Ludlow embraced his mother and warmly shook my hand, no longer upset over my aborted relationship with Twyla. "I had no luck with Helen and Hugh. They seem to have disappeared. I got in touch with the naval unit that Hugh was attached to. They said Hugh had been discharged. They wouldn't say why, but I gathered there was some sort of scandal."

"I'll bet I know what kind," Sherri said.

After weeks of silence, Helen had sent a terse message that she and Hugh had settled in Portsmouth. Hugh had intended to remain in the Royal Navy. He and Ludlow had served on the *Victory* under the command of Sir John Hawkins, architect of England's near miraculous defeat of the Spanish Armada. That had been a tense time for the family, with both my son and nephew at sea. As it turned out, once we learned the facts from Ludlow and Bentley, Hawkins victory seemed rather more inevitable than miraculous. Hawkins' revolutionary ship design had guaranteed England's victory against otherwise overwhelming odds. Smaller, faster, lower, they were able to sail circles around the lumbering Spanish Man-O-Wars, while firing broadsides into their enemy's fat underbellies, impervious to the return fire that sailed almost harmlessly overhead. Ludlow, Bentley and Hugh had all made good names for themselves during the war. Only Hugh had made a career of the navy. Now it seemed, the Royal Navy had seen the true side of Hugh's nature. My worry about Helen dramatically increased.

We were about to sit down when Twyla and Heathcliff rushed

through the door and down the aisle. They were holding hands, I noticed, immediately. I looked at Sherri and she raised her eyebrows, equally surprised.

Though I had last seen Heathcliff only a few weeks before, he looked older, more mature. Maybe it was because he looked angry rather than despondent. He saw his mother and I waiting for him and nodded. Twyla raised her free hand in a muted wave. When they reached us, the four of us stood looking at each other in oblique uncertainty until Heathcliff broke the silence.

"How could this have happened? What was Louella doing trying to stop a mob? It doesn't make sense."

"Death never makes sense," I said, wishing I hadn't the moment the words left my mouth.

"Where is Rosalie? What has she got to say about this? She's responsible. She as much as killed her."

Sherri took Heathcliff by the shoulders, pulling him away from Twyla. "Don't say that! Don't let your sister's death embitter you."

Heathcliff started to say something, then stared off to the side. Ludlow had risen from his seat and was approaching slowly from the front.

Sherri kept hold of her son. "Heathcliff, please. Don't say anything. This is the time for reconciliation, a time for the family to pull together."

Heathcliff looked back at Sherri, then at me, and gave us a quick elusive smile. "Don't worry. I won't try to throttle my brother again." He glanced at Twyla and I detected a message of some sort pass between them.

Ludlow and Heathcliff shook hands silently, then awkwardly embraced, much to our relief. Ludlow led Heathcliff and Twyla to a place he had saved for them in the second row.

The last of the family to arrive was Rosalie. Sherri and I had already sat down and the organ had begun playing some suitably dismal music. Something made me turn around. Rosalie was walking slowly down the aisle, head held high, tears streaming down her cheeks, her face blotchy. She didn't see me at first. When she did, she stopped, and I thought for a moment that she would turn and go back. I saw her mouth the words, I'm sorry, and keep on, head bowed. She sat down four rows behind me, with no one around.

Rosalie had been the first to reach me after the mob stole Louella's life. Sherri had not been at home. Later, I had to tell my wife that a mob had murdered her daughter, without doubt the most difficult words I've ever had to utter. I said some terrible things to Rosalie then, barely stopping short of Heathcliff's damning words. Rosalie made no attempt to argue or defend herself. Nor did she ask for forgiveness. But when I finally fell silent, she had whispered, in a shaking voice, words I would never forget.

"We both must take some responsibility, Uncle Averill . . . my silent partner."

2

The fortunate and successful liked to claim that London was a city where anything was possible, where daring entrepreneurs made fortunes every day, where everyone could earn a living, and live a productive life. That was an amusing exaggeration, true only if you had money, or fame, or royal blessing, or a link with Parliament. In my search for Helen, begun with foreboding after the funeral, I learned of the dark side of London. I had become convinced, for no rational reason, that Helen had returned to London.

The city was crowded beyond belief. Pedestrians, peddlers, beggars, vagabonds, soldiers, sailors, children, dogs, cats, carts and coaches swarmed streets too narrow, invariably muddy or dusty. Every time I ventured out to search for Helen, an enterprise that everyone in my family, except Sherri, thought insane, I would return almost too filthy to be allowed back into the house. To get anywhere fast, I used the Thames, London's main thoroughfare, running through the city, carrying barges, ferries, pleasure crafts, water taxis, and an occasional body. Only the four-century old London bridge, always crowded, linked one side of the city to the other. The bridge was a favorite spot for pickpockets, peddlers and prostitutes, however. I found it almost as quick to take a water taxi across the river—and much safer.

South of the Thames, London erupted every evening in exuberant celebration, the source of every sort of pleasure imaginable, and some beyond imagination. It was the former site of Rosalie's pub. Every block had at least one pub where you could sit for hours listening to aging sailors tell stories of the defeat of the Spanish Armada. They were also wonderful places to get information. I didn't miss any of them in my search for Helen. South London was also the site of the world famous London theaters, where William Shakespeare's plays attracted enthusiastic audiences, and where a few of mine had occasionally made me a profit.

People with money, position, or title lived well in London. Writers didn't expect to. Our house was in the center of London, a crowded neighborhood, but not as bleak as some. Less than a decade old, the house had three stories, built of brick and stone, with a safe tiled roof. Bay windows projected from the upper stories, giving a good view of the street below. In the alcove of one of those I wrote these words. Family life, when the children visited, took place in the great hall where a comforting fire always burned, wood only, with coal still forbidden in London to protect the air. The house was modern, with glass in the windows, and an indoor bathroom. If it proved to be practicable, and if we could find the money, we planned to install a new device which Sir John Harington, the queen's godson, invented a few years ago—a toilet that flushes itself clean with just the touch of a handle.

In my endless quest for my daughter, I didn't neglect the north, though it was an unlikely place for her to end up in. Commerce ruled London north of the Thames, and with the economy booming, the rule was tyrannical. Offices were scarce, real estate prices escalating. Businessmen even used the nave of St. Paul's as a temporary office, with clients meeting their lawyers and agents amidst more serious worshipers, exchanging money, signing agreements, while outside in the courtyard hawkers sold bread, meat, fish, fruit and ale. Not surprisingly, the Queen and Parliament had long ago escaped to the neighboring town of Westminster.

One day, a few weeks after the funeral, while I sat in my alcove trying to find the energy to write another bawdy play for a slightly disreputable theater in Shoreditch, located strategically just out of London jurisdiction, I saw below my window an unbelievable sight— Queen Elizabeth riding by in a gilded coach pulled by eight magnificent matched horses. That had never happened before. At first I thought her coachman might have gotten lost, but I soon laughed at the idea. The queen sat proud and erect, looking neither to the right nor left, implacable, ruler of a nation that had survived every calamity to become a world leader. That brief, fleeting image changed my life. I cannot explain it. Louella would have said something about God's will.

Elizabeth, the Good Queen Beth as her loving subjects called her, had already ruled for an amazing forty-two years. She was in the twilight of her reign, a remarkable age that had seen England blossom into a world leader, in every area of life. It was impossible to adequately describe the impression that she made. I had once seen her up close, when she made an appearance at one of Shakespeare's plays that I also attended. Even at the age of sixty-seven, she presented a striking figure, still slender and tall, olive-toned features only slightly marred with the lines of age. Her hair was a deep auburn color, though some gossips claimed it was not her own. She still wore it swept back, her high sweeping forehead a symbol of the age.

After a lifetime of ignoring the reigns of power I became fascinated with the mortals that ruled our lives. I began to attend Elizabeth's public appearances whenever they were nearby. The inquisitive mind of a writer took hold of me and I began to talk to others about her. I gained audiences with officials, mostly bureaucrats however, with little more of use to tell me than the man sitting next to me in a pub. I read what others had written. I learned much with my inquiries, enough to contemplate writing a book.

Louella's death made me think anew about my writing. I had never written anything serious, anything with a purpose other than to bring laughs among the patrons of low places such as Rosalie's pub, or the occasional legitimate theater. I would not do that any more. I wanted to write something that I could dedicate with pride to my dearest daughter Louella.

Sherri noticed my preoccupation, the pile of notes that grew higher with each day. "Have you now fallen in love with the queen? Or do you intend to write a play for her to act in?" She alluded to the long-lived rumors that Elizabeth had on occasion acted in Shakespeare's plays.

I hesitated to admit my infatuation. "I may write her biography."

She laughed. "A formidable, and probably dangerous task."

As I learned more about Elizabeth, I began to compare her with other great rulers of the past, such as Khufu, Solomon, Pericles, Marcus Aurelius, Basil II, St. Louis, and Lorenzo de Medici. They all had much in common, despite the enormous differences in their circumstances, the eras in which they lived and made their mark on history. I grew fascinated with, and spent much time in contemplation of what made these rulers great. They were not the character traits that make for a good friend, a pleasant companion, a secure mate.

They were all shrewdly confident, though moments of self-doubt must surely hit every human from time to time. They accepted the need to make enemies, with cruel decisions that often cost lives or that brought injustice, for the sake of the nation or empire or city-state. They stubbornly held to a course of action, though the impediments seemed insurmountable. They took risks that lesser rulers would back away from. They accepted the inevitability of mistakes, and never labored over them. Overriding everything else, they trusted and took pride in their subjects, the deciding characteristic, I concluded, of a great ruler.

Then one day, without planning to, I began to write about Elizabeth. A strange thing happened when I picked up my pen and dipped it into ink. I *became* Elizabeth. She began to write her own story, *through me.* When I reread my first sentence, the words, their form, stunned me: *I feel I must say something about my damnable family, just to clear my name.* I kept on in this vein, letting the queen speak, writing for five hours without a break. Then I collapsed, feeling used up, and at peace. I slept for ten hours. I awoke to see Sherri reading my pages, her eyes glittering.

3

I feel I must say something about my damnable family, just to clear my name, although I suppose the stubborn English will always think of me as the *daughter of adultery.* No one thinks of my own feelings about this, that just before my third birthday, my father had my mother beheaded in the grounds of the Tower of London because I was not the male successor he prayed for, and probably ultimately went to Hell for! Yet, I believe, with all my heart, that Anne Boleyn, my mother, was the only woman that Henry VIII ever loved—truly loved. His first wife, the insufferably moody Catherine of Aragon, he never loved, and could barely endure. She was the intended bride of his elder brother Arthur before he died, strictly a diplomatic wedding. But my mother was different. I was not the child of adultery, but the child of love, and I am proud to say it.

But much more than this one female progeny resulted from Henry and Anne's love, although some so-called scholars have, after the fact, claimed that it was all inevitable anyway. Hogwash! Nothing is inevitable, and the tiniest most apparently insignificant event, such as my father catching sight of Anne Boleyn dancing, has led to momentous, world-shaking events.

I remember my father as other people do not, when he was young and vigorous, before excessive weight and gout took its toll. He was an athlete, a skilled hunter, quite handsome, a musician and scholar of the first rank, able to hold his own with Bishops and Chancellors and Cardinals. Everyone liked him, and the nation rejoiced when he took the throne, predicted to be the dawn of a Golden Age. Many would dispute it, tarrying over the conflict with the Church, the many wives, but I believe it was. It still endures, despite the awful intervening years when my half-sister Bloody Mary tried to lead us back into selfish clutches of the Pope.

When I first gained the power I always dreamed of having, some forty-two years ago, I quickly undid Mary's labors. The first years were hard for me, with the whole Catholic world believing that Mary Stuart, Queen of Scots, should rightfully be queen. I had all sorts of problems, with hostile religions dividing my subjects, the economy far from healthy, my army and navy neglected for five years, the unprotected coast inviting a Catholic invasion, French troops in Scotland making raids across the borders, the threat of assassination dogging my every step.

I did all right, in the end. England thrives, powerful enough to challenge any nation, with a navy second to none. I had only one policy at the start, only one choice: avoid war at almost any cost with every means at my disposal. I had to keep my enemies at each other's throats, prevent them from uniting against me, and I admit what people have said, that I threw myself into this diplomatic game by hinting, to whomever it pleased me, whenever it suited England's welfare, that my hand in marriage was perhaps, if everything worked out, available. But it never worked out as it could never, until England was strong enough to stand on her own resources—and that took thirty years.

When I was not hinting at marriage to the French or Spanish to keep them from uniting, I was encouraging and supporting revolts to keep them distracted, such as the Huguenot revolt in France, the Netherlands revolt against Spain, and the Protestant revolt against Mary Queen of Scots which sent her fleeing across the border into my protective hands.

With all this, I managed to gain thirty years of peace for England, one of the longest stretches in recent history. We took advantage of the grace period, lavishing all the resources I could muster on rebuilding the navy and encouraging (without publicly seeming to) would-be pirates like Hawkins and Drake to work under an English flag, and bring back as much of the Spanish New World gold as they could grab. They were mightily successful, I must say.

From Hawkins and Drake's successes I learned decades ago that sea power will always be essential for England's survival. Another man, a great friend of many years, helped me to promote this idea. People say that Sir Walter Raleigh once laid his coat in the mud to keep my feet and shoes clean, but it is only a tale—though he would have done it. This man, whom I love dearly, has done everything. He is an adventurer of the most daring kind, a skilled poet and orator, an intelligent philosopher and historian, and a gentleman. He makes me wish I was a man on one hand, and on the other, that I was free to marry. He did anger me once, forcing me to install him in the Tower for a time. He married one of my maids of honor without my permission.

His efforts to establish a colony in America, in a place he honored me by naming Virginia, unfortunately failed, a temporary setback. But his advice to take America away from Spain is good, a goal that my successors and I must pursue without fail. No one has ever preached the benefits of sea power more artfully when he said that *whoever commands the sea commands the trade, and whoever commands the trade of the world commands the riches of the world, and consequently the world itself.*

And then there was dear misguided cousin Mary, Queen of the Scots, mentally unfit to be a queen, who fell into my hands in 1568 when her Protestant subjects led by John Knox took matters into their own hands, tired of persecution. I would have kept her comfortably housed, out of the way, out of politics, if she had only acquiesced, but she kept working against me behind my back, fomenting plots to get back her royal crown, and with it England's.

When my agents proved her treachery beyond a doubt, I had no choice. I did what my father would have done. I could not afford to be any weaker, or let sentiment interfere, especially with Spain preparing an armada to invade our shores. I had Mary beheaded. I don't regret it. But I didn't enjoy it, and didn't do it out of spite, envy or revenge, as some of my enemies claim.

Damn them all!

4

Sherri looked up from my pages and saw me watching her. "What a strange way to write."

"It just happened. What do you think?"

She shrugged. "If it is published, the queen will probably have you thrown in the Tower."

"Nonsense! I have written nothing false. I have not in any way libeled her. If she took to write her autobiography, she might use those same words."

"You flatter yourself."

"It's always a mistake to let a wife read your work."

"Suit yourself. I'll be amazed if you can find a publisher willing to take the risk."

After I had time to calm down, and spent another afternoon shouldering my way through crowded pubs in search of Helen, I came to realize Sherri was right. The queen could easily judge these remarks as treasonous. She would likely misread and misinterpret what I considered praise. They have hanged authors for less. I returned home discouraged, and slightly drunk.

Sherri was waiting for me, the usual question in her eyes. "No luck" I said. "I'm beginning to think that she may still be in Portsmouth."

"I think they've returned to London. And if they've split up, where else would Helen go, especially in her condition?"

I couldn't answer that. We had gotten further disquieting news. Ludlow had heard from a friend of Hugh's that Helen had been pregnant before they dropped out of sight.

"We have to find her," Sherri said.

"I know. We will," I said, taking her in my arms.

Later, when we were sitting in front of the fire, I said, "I've decided to give up on the biography. You were right."

"You'd do better to write your own story, the saga of your crazy family. It might actually get published and make us some money."

With this off-hand remark, my life took another twisting turn. I didn't think about it at the time, but her words came back to me later. The more I thought of it, the more intriguing the idea became. It would not leave me alone. Thus, was born this book, recalling my crazy family as Sherri called us, with a certain degree of accuracy. I pushed aside Elizabeth's words, and began to write anew, beginning with the phrase, *I, Averill Bernard, a writer, son of Ransford Bernard, inscribe these words.* I started with my arrival in London at the age of seven, when my family migrated from Wales to escape a life of grueling poverty. I began to relive a lifetime, and seemed to sense Louella's approval from beyond the grave.

Unfortunately, something happened to make me relive the past far too literally. Genevieve, my former mistress, reentered my life. I had heard nothing of her for nearly two decades, since she married a Danish sailor and took our son, Gerlach, to Copenhagen. I had occasionally wondered about her, and what kind of a man Gerlach had grown into, but had no desire to reopen the affair that nearly ended my marriage.

A messenger brought me her note. By the time I finished reading it, my hands were shaking.

Dear Averill,

I am sorry to inflict myself on you again. I will understand if you tear up this note and read no further. For the sake of our son, I pray that you will not. I have returned to London. Gerlach is with me. My two daughters I have left in Copenhagen with their grandmother. My husband is dead—a disaster at sea. Two years ago now. I am all right. I am not asking for charity. I have come to London for a different reason. I want Gerlach to know his father, and I think you would want to know what a fine man he is turning out to be. I want nothing more. I expect nothing more. I will wait for a month to give you time to think about this. If I don't hear from you, Gerlach and I will return to Copenhagen, and you will never hear from us again. I have not yet told him anything about you.

With fond memories of our past love,

Genevieve.

She added the address of a house she was apparently renting that was remarkably only a mile or so from where I lived. I stuffed the note inside my shirt and headed for our neighborhood pub. Naturally, I said nothing of this to Sherri.

Though I tried to, I could not forget the letter's date, and I kept track of when one month would be up. I carried Genevieve's letter with me everywhere. I frequently reread it. Once I walked past her house. The days passed. I grew increasingly nervous as the deadline approached, but I could still not decide what to do.

5

Heathcliff moved back in with us after the funeral, so our house no longer seemed so empty. He and I still dealt with each other in a careful, subdued manner, artfully avoiding any mention of Twyla. I missed the wide-ranging talks we used to have, when a younger, more naive Heathcliff, curious about everything, would pepper me with difficult questions, sometimes leading us to chase off for facts on some obscure matter, that only we cared about. Now, we spoke politely, but inconsequentially.

Then one day I got up the courage to mention the forbidden subject. "Have you seen Twyla lately?"

We were alone in the house, late in the afternoon on a rainy day, Sherri away on some errand. We had been sitting silently by the fire. Heathcliff's face tightened. I thought it was anger, but he said, after a long pause, in a calm voice, "Why do you ask?"

"I haven't seen her since the funeral. I thought you might have. I'm curious about her. I wonder how she's getting along."

"I've seen her once or twice."

"No more trouble with your brother?" I laughed to make light of it.

He shook his head, but didn't smile. "We're friends again. We meet regularly in a cafe along the Thames to have a drink." He hesitated, as if trying to decide how much to tell me.

"You don't get tired of hearing about textiles?" I said, finding it painful to keep the conversation going.

"He complains about Twyla, her interference in his textile business. In my opinion, he is succeeding in no small part because of Twyla's business sense. I don't say this to Ludlow. He would love to buy her share, but can't raise the money."

I had gotten this far, so I decided to press on. "He no longer cares that you're seeing Twyla?"

"Why should he? He has lost all interest in her. She drives him mad, if you must know."

"And how are you getting along with her?"

Heathcliff stood up suddenly. I thought he was going to leave, that I'd pushed too far. He sat back down, shaking his head. He looked at me steadily, as if trying to read my intentions.

"Maybe I can help," I said, quietly.

"I don't think anyone can help. Twyla is too strong for me, I know that. She has a mind of her own, like no other woman I've ever met. But I can't live without her. And I won't give up. She sometimes laughs at me, sometimes yells at me to leave her alone, then changes her mind, and begs me to come see her again. I don't know what to think."

"I think you're making progress."

"I write her every day, even when I'm going to visit her, or meet her somewhere—letters, poems, little stories to intrigue her. I think I am winning her over, but I can't be sure."

I laughed, trying to ease his tense state, to make him see the humor of it all. "At least you're developing your writing skills."

Heathcliff had decided to become a writer. Though tempted, I had not tried to talk him out of it. I instead explained to him the extreme difficulties of such a career, painting as dismal a picture as I could. If he really had writing in his soul, it wouldn't matter. I told him that even if he did write something brilliant and popular, he might never profit from it. Too often, someone without talent would steal his words, and he would suddenly hear them spoken on stage, attributed to someone he'd never heard of.

I had, despite taking great care, several times been so victimized. A shameless opportunist could blatantly copy an author's literary labors and sell them in great quantities for a nice profit, without the slightest compensation to the author. But a solution was apparently close at hand, although I was skeptical that it would work. Reputable publishers, printers and booksellers had united in forming the Stationers Company. The plan was to allow authors to formally register their works with the Company, *copyrighting* they called it, to give authors the right to legally attack those who would attempt to steal their labors.

I took every opportunity I could to explain the business of writing to Heathcliff. It was a subject that took little prodding to get me started on, sometimes to Sherri's annoyance. She had heard my diatribes all too often. I told Heathcliff what he probably already knew—that writing had changed vastly during my lifetime. Audiences would not pay to see the old, tired classical formulas of drama. Authors ignored audiences' whims and demands at great peril. What audiences called for, above all, was action, a good belly laugh, and stories that reflected English life, not the life of some long dead Roman hero.

Some playwrights went to extremes to please their audiences, dabbling in paganism, the crudest obscenity and profanity. I had never gone this far to pander to audiences. I hoped Heathcliff would not either. Puritans vigorously protested such plays, which naturally made them instant successes. The Puritans also complained that women and even prostitutes found their way into audiences to stand shoulder to shoulder with the riffraff in the standing areas. The Puritans didn't care much either for the practice of lodging prostitutes handily next door to theaters. Perhaps their sorriest complaint was that producers intentionally staged plays on Sundays, to draw people away from church. It wasn't true. It was just a way to increase revenues.

Ironically, Rosalie, utterly abandoning her former life, became one of the Puritans who shouted the loudest. Her protests, joined by a few other extremists, often went far beyond words. She and her compatriots would sometimes bodily block the entrances to theaters, until dragged or carried away. She also argued for censorship and licensing, but, fortunately found few in Parliament who agreed. As long as Queen Elizabeth reigned, the theater would remain free of such encumbrances.

I took Hearthcliff to the Globe Theater, which had just opened across the Thames in Southwark. He forgot everything I said to discourage him from taking up his pen when he saw the performance of *Hamlet,* Shakespeare's latest work, staged in such a marvelous setting. It was the most modern theater in the world, seating two-thousand, with a wide open yard around the stage for an additional thousand to stand. The building was octagonal in shape, the galleries circling the stage. Shakespeare called the Globe *this wooden O.* Without him, it would never have been built.

William Shakespeare was without question London's most productive and popular playwright. I followed his career enviously, and made sure that Heathcliff understood that his success was a combination of good business sense and rare genius. Hugely successful, first as an actor, then with his theatrical company, he began to write his own plays—two a year on the average. Though not all masterpieces, they made money. I never missed one. People clambered to get tickets. He had really hit it big the last several years, with *Romeo and Juliet, The Merchant of Venice, Henry IV, Henry V,* and *As You Like It.*

After seeing *Hamlet,* Heathcliff and I went to a pub and talked about the play long into the night. Two days later we saw the play again. *Hamlet* astonished both of us with the depth of anguish and melancholy that Shakespeare managed to inflict on his hero. Years before, I had seen another author's version of the Danish tragedy, far inferior to Shakespeare's. Shakespeare was a master at taking old themes and turning them into popular drama. He was also bringing my son and I closer together.

In part it was Shakespeare's power over the English language that made him popular and unforgettable, though he played havoc with grammar, turning nouns into adjectives, adverbs into verbs, verbs into nouns, whatever made a good sound, and good sense. People walked the streets of London repeating his latest additions to the English language. His knowledge of geography was lamentably limited, as was his knowledge of the classics and history, but his audiences did not care, and most did not know. Why worry about a lake in the wrong country when the tragic hero lamented *what fools these mortals be*, or a diplomat urged that *brevity is the soul of wit*. My favorites were, *the Devil can quote Scripture to his purpose*, and *uneasy lies the head that wears a crown*, and most poignant of all, *the course of true love never did run smooth*. That phrase I understood completely. So did Heathcliff.

Coincidentally, the day after I had that talk with Heathcliff, Twyla sent me an oddly formal note saying she wished to meet me somewhere private, mentioning a pub I frequented near where she lived. When the messenger first handed me the note I thought it must be from Genevieve. Only twelve days remained. I was growing increasingly distracted by indecision. Now Twyla wanted to see me in private. It was with great trepidation that I went to the pub she mentioned, at the appointed time.

She was there waiting, a glass of ale in her hand. I saw her before she saw me. I stopped and looked at her, tempted to bolt. She had matured into a fine woman, an Elizabethan woman, a formidable challenge to any man. She wore her hair swept back, emulating the queen. Her face was less severe than it had been when younger. She looked more relaxed, but no less alert and intelligent. I remembered how much I had once enjoyed her as an intellectual challenge when I had tutored her.

"Thank you for coming, Averill," she said, extending her hand.

I wasn't sure whether to shake it or kiss it, so I just squeezed it for a moment, bringing a mischievous smile to her face. I had gotten a pint of beer before going to her table. It was already half gone.

"You look wonderful, Twyla," I said.

"So do you. Heathcliff has told me of your new project. I want to read it. I want to see what you say about me—about us."

"I'm not sure I'll let you read that part."

"You'd better be truthful, or I'll tell everyone what really happened."

We fell silent. We hadn't seen each other since the funeral, and should have had much to talk about. Questions about her and Heathcliff were on my mind, but I had resolved not to say anything. Finally she blurted out, while staring down into her near empty glass, "I don't know what to do about Heathcliff."

I gave a start, not expecting such a blunt opening. "Are his attentions so bothersome?"

"Sometimes."

I laughed. "He won't give up, you know. Even though you've told him that you'll never marry him—or anyone else."

She hesitated. "I haven't exactly said that to him."

Again, she had surprised me. "I don't understand. After all these years, you give him reason to hope? And now you complain because he won't leave you alone?"

Twyla looked at me at last, and I thought I saw a tear form at the corner of one eye. "I don't want him to leave me alone. I like his company. We have wonderful conversations, like you and I used to have."

"Has he asked you to marry him?"

Twyla laughed. "A hundred times. In every poem. Every letter. Even in his delightfully funny stories."

"What a terrible dilemma. Someone you love to have around—at least most of the time—wants to marry you, and is devoted to you, and will treat you like a queen. Do I have to tell you the obvious solution? Give up, this obstinacy. You're lost, I can see, as plainly as the dregs in the bottom of that glass."

Twyla touched my hand and drew away. "How can I marry your son, when it is you I love?"

"Twyla, don't say that. It isn't true."

"It is true."

"You're deceiving yourself."

She shook her head. "I am not. But perhaps I love Heathcliff enough. If not the father, then the son. Didn't Shakespeare write that?"

"Probably. He's written almost every other clever phrase on people's lips."

We talked a while longer, consuming two more pints, but I could not solve her problem for her. I finally left her, feeling hopeful, and again walked by the house where Genevieve and Gerlach were staying, this time pausing for several minutes, before moving on.

6

Five days left. I was frantic. Sherri knew something was wrong. I had not been able to tell her. A hundred times I made up my mind. As many times I changed it.

"What's wrong, Averill?" Sherri said, not for the first time. "You're like a caged bear. You're driving me mad. Go out. Look for Helen. Do something!"

I dutifully went out, though it was windy and raining. I had long before given up hope of finding Helen by the pitiful strategy of walking blindly through the streets of London, stopping at every pub I came to, but I kept on anyway. I wasn't surprised when I again found myself outside Genevieve's house.

I was numb, cold, miserably dejected. Without conscious thought, I took a step towards the familiar door, and just kept going. I didn't think. To think, would only bring more indecision. I just acted, bringing my fist up to knock on the door. When no one answered immediately, I turned away, swore under my breath, turned back and knocked with more authority.

A tall youth with long golden hair opened the door. I knew instantly who he was. I saw no recognition of me in his eyes. "Can I help you?" he said, with a strong accent that brought a smile to my lips, reminding me of Genevieve.

"Is your mother at home?"

"Yes. Is she expecting you?"

"I don't know—what she expects."

This seemed to make him suspicious. In the near month that Gerlach had resided in London, he must have had many run-ins with the more nefarious side of the populace.

"Who are you?"

"Tell her, an old friend."

He shrugged and shut the door in my face. I was tempted to run. My heart was beating wildly, my stomach twisting, and despite the cold, I felt sweat running down my sides. Then the door suddenly opened, putting me out of misery. We stared at each other for a long time, studying the features we had known so intimately, years before, attempting to recognize, seeing the familiar and the changed. Gerlach stood at Genevieve's elbow, a half head taller than her, staring wonderingly at us two, beginning to realize who I was.

"I got your note," I stupidly said.

"You took your time," she said, and a thrill went through me to hear her voice. Except for her voice, she had changed. I'm not sure, in a crowd, not expecting to meet her, that I would have recognized her. She was still beautiful, in her Nordic way, but there were deep lines in her face, and her hair was short.

"I wasn't sure whether I should come. It's been so long, and some things are better left buried." I glanced at Gerlach. She noticed and stepped aside.

"Gerlach, this is your father."

She wrote that she had said nothing about me, yet he looked neither surprised nor particularly pleased. How could he feel otherwise? I was a stranger, who didn't speak his language, an old man in his eyes.

"Hello, Gerlach."

I tentatively extended my hand, ashamed that it shook slightly. He took it with a firm grip, nodding, not saying anything. The last time I had seen him he was not yet three years old, but I found it easier to recognize him than I did his mother.

"Come inside, Averill, now that you're here, and let our son get to know his father."

I looked at Gerlach for confirmation. "Do you want that, Gerlach? I would understand—"

"You don't look anything like what I imagined," he said, stepping back out of the way.

I entered, Genevieve remaining behind to close the door. I followed Gerlach into a small sitting room, feeling the wonderful warmth of the fire, realizing suddenly how wet and cold I was.

Genevieve took my wet coat and hung it by the fire. "I'll get you something warm to drink," she said, leaving Gerlach and me alone. I stood by the fire trying to get warm. Gerlach remained standing, watching me curiously.

"Your mother has told you nothing about me?"

"Only the circumstances of my birth." Then he added in a rush, "I don't blame you. I don't feel anything for you, one way or the other."

"I didn't want her to leave. She chose to. But it was probably for the best. I was married."

"I know."

"You have two half-brothers, and a half-sister." Taking a deep breath, I added, pained to say the words, "You had another half-sister, but she died, recently."

"I have two sisters back home."

We fell silent. I didn't know what else to say, what to ask. Genevieve returned with a steaming mug of hot rum. My hand touched hers as I clumsily took the mug, and our eyes met briefly. They had not changed. Their greenish-blue color could still leave me breathless.

"I'm sorry about your husband," I said, and Genevieve turned quickly away.

"He was my *real* father," Gerlach said, with a hint of defiance.

"I know. That's as it should be. I'm sorry you lost him."

This seemed to make him feel better, putting everything in its proper place. He sat down, more relaxed. I took a long drink of the rum, sighing.

"This is a life saver," I said. "It's miserable out today."

"And yet, this is the day you chose to come," Genevieve said, sitting near Gerlach and placing her hand on his.

"I didn't exactly choose. I just stopped thinking about it and came."

She went to sit beside Gerlach, touching his arm. "Averill is a writer. He has a family—"

"He's told me."

"Some of the things you read when I was teaching you English, were his. You should be proud to be his son." She turned to me. "Gerlach wants to be a sailor, like his father."

The words started to come easier for all of us. I remained with them for more than an hour. I felt as if I was reliving a lifetime.

When I was about to leave, Gerlach left Genevieve and me alone, sensing that we needed the privacy. "Must you go back to Copenhagen so soon?"

"What would be the use of staying longer?"

I shrugged, uncertain, yet somehow not wanting her to disappear again. "I guess I just hate to say good-bye."

We were standing on the covered porch of her house. The rain had ceased. Genevieve reached back and closed the door behind her. "You didn't have to let me go before."

"You had found someone else."

She shook her head. "No, I hadn't. I only said that, to make it easier. I met my husband in Denmark two years later. And they were a difficult two years, raising Gerlach on my own."

"I offered you money."

"You didn't offer me yourself."

"How could I?"

"I don't know. I guess you didn't love me enough."

The romantics, who write the dribble too often seen on London stages, say it is impossible to love two women at one time. I once knew that wasn't true. As I stood beside Genevieve on her porch, water dripping off the roof, I realized that it still wasn't true. I said, barely getting the words out, "I've never stopped loving you. That's why it was difficult for me to come and see you."

Genevieve shook her head. "Poor Averill, a man with a heart too large for one woman." She laughed, quickly leaned towards me and kissed me on the lips. "I suppose that, in truth, I have never stopped loving you either."

"How long will you remain in London?"

"I don't know."

She reached back and opened the door. I turned and walked away. The rain had begun to fall hard again, but I didn't notice.

7

Rosalie found Helen for us. Rosalie had been delivering food to an east end slum inhabited mostly by immigrants from France, Huegonots fleeing Catholic repression. In a tiny basement room, flooded whenever it rained, she came across a young pregnant woman who spoke English far too well to be a foreigner. Rosalie didn't recognize Helen, though Helen did recognize her.

"She reacted strangely when she saw me at the door to her room, which was no better than a basement dungeon," Rosalie told us later. "She jumped back and covered her hand with her mouth, staring at me with eyes blazing. She looked like she wanted to say something, but kept quiet."

Rosalie offered her food, which Helen silently accepted. Seeing how far pregnant the young woman was, Rosalie was reluctant to leave it at that. "She looked at least seven months pregnant, but it was hard to tell because she was so undernourished, her cheeks sunken, eyes too large. And, of course she was filthy."

Sherri reacted badly to that, but Rosalie explained. "You can't expect more from these people, considering the conditions under which they live, and how they must earn enough money to stave off starvation."

"Why didn't she come home?" Sherri said, anguish in her voice. "Why won't she come home now? I don't understand."

Rosalie had eventually discovered who the pregnant woman was. Helen didn't say, but Rosalie refused to leave until she learned more about her. While wandering around the tiny room, Rosalie came across a miniature painting in a small, gilded frame, about the only thing of value in the room. When Rosalie stooped down to get a closer look, Helen grabbed it away.

"Don't touch that!" she said, pressing the picture to her chest, and backing away.

She was too late. "I had gotten enough of a look," Rosalie told us. "I started to cry. The painting was of Louella, in her nun's habit. And it had a black ribbon tied to the frame."

Helen had learned of her sister's death when she went to the convent after returning to London. "Louella was the only person she was willing to accept help from," Rosalie explained. "I think you know why. I argued with her for half the morning, refusing to leave that dismal place where she lives, but it was no use. She is as stubborn as everyone else in the family."

"Show me where she's living," Sherri said. "I'll go there at once. I'll drag her home, if I have to."

Rosalie shook her head. "I think it's better if Uncle Averill goes. Helen thinks that Hugh left her because of him. I couldn't convince her otherwise." She turned to me. "You'll have to make her believe the truth about Hugh."

Sherri looked stunned. "He'll never be able to."

"I had to promise not to tell either of you, to keep her from running away again," Rosalie said. "I told her I'd come back regularly with food, if she remained there. I don't know whether she believed me or not. She had the look of a half-wild savage, capable of anything."

There was nothing I could do to dissuade Sherri from coming along, and it was just as well that she did, for I could not have dealt with what we found. We could hear the screams a block away. The door to her cell-like room stood ajar. Sherri pushed me aside and rushed in ahead of me, for which I would be eternally grateful. Just inside she abruptly stopped, muttering "Oh my God!" She turned and pushed me back outside, saying, "Go find a physician, and hire a coach. Hurry!"

Sherri had not blocked my entrance soon enough to prevent me from getting a quick glimpse of what lay inside. Off to the side of the dimly lit room, Helen lay on a low cot, naked below the waist, a bloody lump lying between her spread legs, the bedding drenched in blood.

"What's wrong with her?" I said, idiotically.

"She's had her baby. Now go! And hurry."

I was frantic. It took me nearly an hour to find a physician and transport him back to Helen's basement. The screaming had ceased. Sherri looked at me furiously when we entered.

"I got here as fast as I could," I said. "There are no reputable doctors in this part of London."

Sherri held the baby in her arms, wrapped in the shawl that she had worn that morning. She said to the doctor, when he approached, "The baby is fine. See to the mother, please."

A blanket covered Helen. She lay absolutely still. I feared she was dead. The doctor pulled back the covers and I looked away. "She has lost a great deal of blood, and the bleeding continues," I heard him say, like a death sentence.

There wasn't much he could do, which was typical of the medical profession. They could only cure what you could cure yourself, and could only make worse what you had no power over.

We brought Helen home and watched helplessly for the next three days as her life seemed to slowly slip away. The bleeding stopped, but she seemed to gain no strength, eating little, sometimes unable to keep down what she did take in. One of us was at her side all the time.

I didn't care or need to know what had happened with her and Hugh, but she insisted on telling me. It took a long time, several days, to get it all out. She didn't have the energy to tell her tragic tale all at once. After she finished, for the first time in my life, I felt hate strongly enough to contemplate murder.

"It was wonderful at first. We were married by a priest in a small village south of London. It was so exciting to travel through the countryside as husband and wife. Hugh was gallant and fun, at first."

"Everything went wrong in Portsmouth. I hate that city. It is evil. It does things to people. Hugh changed. I must have not . . . satisfied him enough. I must have done something wrong."

"He went drinking every night. He came home drunk, angry. He gambled and lost, almost always. And then I discovered that I was pregnant. This seemed to anger him more. It was horrible."

"Did he ever . . . hit you?" I asked, barely able to say the words.

Helen nodded.

"Often?" I said.

She nodded again, fighting back tears. I gritted my teeth to keep from saying anything that might silence her.

"It was inevitable that he would have trouble with the navy. I tried to tell him, but he wouldn't listen to me. When they discharged him, he came home and cried on my shoulder. He said he was sorry. He said he would make it up to me. He made all sorts of promises, and for the first time in weeks I felt happy."

"Later that evening he went to his neighborhood pub. He never came home. I haven't seen him since."

"Why didn't you tell us?" I asked. She only shook her head. She would say nothing about how she had managed to reach London on her own, or what she had gone through until Rosalie found her.

Once she had told me all of this, she began to slowly recover, as if she had cleansed herself of her marriage's poisons. Her baby was healthy from the start, a daughter, a granddaughter for Sherri and me, a cousin for Alexander. Helen asked us if it was all right if she named her Louella. It was.

8

During the many weeks it took for Helen to recover I barely thought of Genevieve and Gerlach. When Helen grew well enough to take care of her daughter, and laughter returned to our house, I found time to wonder and worry whether Genevieve and Gerlach had returned to Copenhagen. It had been months since I had seen her. There was no reason for her to stay, except for me, and I hadn't even bothered to send her a message.

I went anyway to the place where they had lived before. A stranger answered the door, evidently the landlady. When I inquired about the Danish woman and her son, she said, "They don't live here any more. They left."

I thanked her and turned to leave, feeling a sense of relief, mixed with regret. The woman called after me. "Don't you want to know where they went?"

I turned slowly, feeling as if I was putting my hand back into a fire, having just pulled it free. "Where?"

"Just around the corner. Then two blocks, the third house on the right."

This time Genevieve answered the door. "You found me," she said, a hesitant smile on her lips.

"I was sure you had gone home. Why did you move here?"

"Do you want to come in, or have you learned what you want to know?"

I entered her small house, with a feeling of trepidation. "Where's

Gerlach?"

"He's not here. He has shipped out with a trading vessel heading for the East Indies. That's why I moved to this smaller place."

"You're alone?"

"So it seems. But now you're here."

"Why did you wait? Were you so sure I'd come back?"

Genevieve shrugged. "I had to wait for a different reason. I wanted to stay until Gerlach's ship sailed. I hope that doesn't hurt your feelings."

I told her about Helen. She told me more about her life in Copenhagen, about her two daughters, whom she terribly missed. We talked like old companions, casual friends reunited, but nothing more. Finally, I got up to leave.

"I wish I'd gotten a chance to talk to Gerlach again."

"You may still. When he returns to London in a year or so, he'll probably come to see you. I urged him to."

"You'll be leaving soon?"

"In another week or so."

"I'll miss you. In a way, I still love you."

"Yes, me too. A different kind of love now, isn't it?"

I nodded. But I didn't really think it was different. Only, with age, the passion had diminished. The insatiable need to resolve love's demands had subsided sufficiently to be controllable.

Genevieve came to me and opened her arms. I hesitated for a moment. Then I put my arms around her waist and pulled her to me. We kissed, with a controlled passion, giving our bodily craving a moment of freedom to briefly relive what we had experienced before. Then we reluctantly pulled apart.

"It would be so easy to fall back into the old pattern," I said.

"I don't think so. We've changed."

We parted with promises to write that we knew neither of us would keep.

A year and a half later when Gerlach's ship arrived back in London, he did come to see me. One afternoon he showed up at the door, unannounced, unexpected. Sherri had answered the insistent knock to find the young sailor standing there with hat in hand. Amazingly, she knew instantly who it was, though I had never told her about Genevieve's return.

She came back into the sitting room where I had a desk, and was busy writing what I thought would be the last chapter of this book.

She came up behind me and placed her hands on my shoulders, leaning over to see what I was working on.

"You have a visitor," she said. "A young man. I think he's your son."

I slowly got to my feet, still holding my pen in hand. I looked at Sherri, and saw humor in her eyes, tinged with a curiosity that would demand a later explanation.

That day was momentous in other ways. For the first time, Gerlach met his half brothers and sister. We sent for Ludlow, and for good measure had my sister Filberta and Twyla come by for a feast and something of a family reunion. Then the surprise of the evening came when Heathcliff stood up, and, after waiting to get everyone's attention, made an announcement in his usual slow and measured way.

"You all know that I have pursued Twyla for some time now." We laughed, but my heart began to race, anticipating what he was about to say. "I even did battle with my dear brother over her once, but he has since then quit the field." The laughter now was for Ludlow, who looked sheepish. "And I have asked Twyla to marry me, perhaps a hundred times. Well, apparently I have finally worn her out, for just a quarter hour ago, when I chanced upon her in the hallway, carrying a tray of dishes, I asked her again."

We all waited. Heathcliff looked toward Twyla, who had slumped back in her chair, a mischievous look on her face. She sat up and said, looking straight at me, "I said yes, of course."

Late in the evening, more accurately, early the next morning, while we lay side be side in bed, I told Sherri about Genevieve's return, leaving out nothing. She listened in silence until I had finished. Then she turned on her side toward me, nestled in close, and kissed me hungrily, signaling that we would surely miss more sleep that night.

"In a strange way, I'm happy that your love is the kind that endures, even if a portion of it is directed at others. I like the part I have," she whispered.

She began to stroke my chest, and I ran my hand down her back beneath the light shift she wore, to take a firm grip on her wonderfully preserved posterior. She slowly swung her leg over me, pulling the shift up above her waist, as we progressed into the familiar preliminaries.

"Do you remember when I first saw you walking across the square in front of St. Paul's?" I said, a little breathlessly.

"How could I possibly forget the leering way you looked at me, while pretending to study and write in your exercise book."

"You know what I said to Jasper? I said, see that girl? I'm going to marry her. He laughed at me, pointing out that you wore the habit of a novitiate. I told him, it doesn't matter. Love will conquer all."

Sherri slipped her hand down past my belly to check my state of readiness. "You were a hopeless romantic then," she managed to say. "You always have been. Now, shut up and let's get on with this so we can get some sleep."

I think, alas, it is time I ceased writing. The family reunion just described took place only a few days ago. I've caught up with time. If I keep on with this habit, my family saga will degrade into a dreary diary. And I'm too old to wait for the next crisis to erupt, with another family member at my doorstep asking for my help.

Yet, I should not complain of such attention, as I often have, for it has come to define my life. Without my family, with all of its strange quirks and penchant for disaster, what would I be? A tiresome, lonely old man, scribling imaginary adventures in my journal.

Thanks to my mad family, I have no need to imagine.

Afterward

I, Heathcliff Bernard, a writer, son of Averill Bernard, inscribe these words. Five years have passed since Twyla amazed me by saying "yes" in a back hall in my parents' old house. Much has happened. Queen Elizabeth is dead. James is king of England *and* Scotland, united at last. Twyla and I are married, and we have one son. I have had three plays produced, and though they do not draw crowds like a Shakespeare play, they put food on the table.

My cousin Brock, growing rich with his portraits, is spawning children as fast as his father had, five already. His mother Olympia, widowed four years ago when uncle Kendrik failed to wake up one morning, seems destined to live to be a hundred. Jasper and Nelwina continue to bicker, his career in business and politics—highly inter-twined occupations—in constant conflict with hers. He has made a fortune with the East India Company, and is a member of Parliament. Nelwina no longer dances. Instead she campaigns for women's rights, a novel concept that turns my uncle's hair gray. Their son Sebastian is a successful doctor, on call to London's aristocracy. Yetta is finally be-trothed, her fiancé a dancer like her. They are on the road all the time with a dance company.

My crazy Aunt Filberta has remarried at the advanced age of forty-five to a radical politician, a young man not much older than her daughter, my cousin Isabel. Isabel's husband is a conservative businessman, and mother and daughter have their hands full keeping peace in that branch of the family.

My brother Ludlow I fear, will never marry, or I should say he has married his business. He is rid of my wife's advice, as Aunt Filberta bought Twyla's share in the business—a great relief to everyone concerned. Filberta's only interest in textiles is with respect to what they eventually become—the expensive and latest fashions she adorns herself with.

Helen won a divorce from Hugh. A year later we heard that someone had murdered Hugh over a gambling debt. Helen has not remarried, and seems content to live with her mother. They both dote on little Louella, now six years old, looking remarkably like her namesake, whose tragic death we all still mourn. Louella's son, Alexander, also lives with my sister and mother, since Filberta remarried. He is a quiet boy, highly studious. Twyla thinks he is headed for the priesthood.

Rosalie braved scorn, persecution, and suffering for years in her Puritan causes, spending her days in London's slums seeing to the poor, or in the byways of Westminster, pleading for reforms. When King James began to imprison Puritans who refused to give in to conformity, she emigrated to America. She has settled in Virginia, and seems happy.

Every year or so we get a visit from Gerlach, my father's bastard son, my half-brother, when he returns from a long voyage. He recently made First Mate, and I suspect will one day captain his own ship. I will never forget the day when my mother called Helen and I into the sitting room to meet our half-brother. I remember looking at Helen to verify that I had heard right. She stared back at me wide-eyed, her hand over her mouth. I looked at father. His face had paled and he seemed to waver in his chair. It was true. Only then did I look at Gerlach, and instantly took a liking to him.

It was far easier to accept Gerlach as our half-brother than to accept our father's dalliance with Gerlach's mother, although it was certainly not uncommon in London for a man of high morals to sire a bastard. Nor is it now. However, I will never fall victim to such temptation, if for no other reason than that Twyla will kill me if I do. She made that abundantly clear the moment after she shocked me by accepting my proposal, that fateful day. That warning she didn't repeat to the others later when I made my excited announcement.

"I *will* marry you Heathcliff," she said, making my heart skip a beat. "But if you dare carry on as your father has, rest assured that I will simply put an end to you." I always knew, and accepted that if I married Twyla, it would be on her terms.

My father lived long enough to see the first of my children, a son, born. We named him Averill. My father died doing what he loved most—writing. My mother found him one morning, slumped over his writing desk, his pen still clenched in his hand. My mother sent for the family, everyone except Olympia who had trouble getting about, to bravely announce my father's passing.

"There's nothing to grieve," she said, and gave us her familiar smile. "Averill will live forever in his writing, and in your hearts."

She may not have cried, but the rest of us did.

The End.

A Personal Selection

The Scribe's Family is set in ten eras and ten civilizations, each unique in its own way, each providing a rich panoply of resources in which to set a tale, each well-deserving the title "Golden Age." These ten are however only a small sampling from the surprisingly long honor role of Golden Ages, that I had to work with.

I began my search for *The Scribe's* ten Golden Ages with a list of well over one-hundred eras, the earliest being the town of Jericho around the year 6000 BC, the latest being Los Angeles in 1955. As carefully selected as this initial list was, it no doubt left out eras that other historians would include, and included eras that some might question. From the start, this has been a personal selection.

To eliminate the questionable, I trimmed this initial list down to a "top fifty" Golden Ages (in the process dropping Jericho and Los Angeles), and stored them away as a stockpile of interesting settings for future works of fiction. The ten Golden Ages selected for *The Scribe's Family* (eleven actually with Tyre and Jerusalem combined) were never intended as a "top ten" selection. They were chosen in part because they fit in with the scribe's story as it unfolded, and because they were well-distributed over nearly five millennia.

The next planned novel in this series, *The Healer's Family*, will make use of an entirely different set of ten Golden Ages. Again, their selection will depend in large part on how the healer's story unfolds.

For the historically curious reader, here is my personal selection for the Top Fifty Golden Ages:

The Top Fifty Golden Ages

Uruk, Sumer 3000 BC
Memphis, Egypt 2580 BC
Agade, Akkad 2300 BC
Mohejo-Daro, India 2200 BC
Ur, Sumer 2050 BC
Babylon, Babylonia 1760 BC
Anyang, China 1680 BC
Knossos, Crete 1500 BC
Hattusas, Anatolia 1350 BC
Thebes, Egypt 1250 BC
Tyre, Phoenicia 925 BC
Jerusalem, Israel 925 BC
Nineveh, Assyria 640 BC
Babylon, Babylonia 565 BC
Susa, Persia 500 BC
Athens, Greece 445 BC
Alexandria, Egypt 280 BC
Pataliputra, India 235 BC
Moroe, Kush 200 BC
Rome, Italy 155 BC
Chang'an, China 120 BC
Jerusalem, Israel 30 BC
Rome, Italy AD 175
Persepolis, Persia AD 370
Teotihuacan, Mexico AD 400
Constantinople, Byzantium AD 550

Tikal, Yucatan AD 700
Chang,an, China AD 750
Baghdad, Arabia AD 810
Heian, Japan AD 880
Cordoba, Spain AD 950
London, England AD 970
Cairo, Egypt AD 990
Constantinople, Byzantium AD 1015
Kaiteng, China AD 1080
Mesa Grande, America AD 1150
Paris, France AD 1252
Venice, Italy AD 1300
Timbuktu, Sudan AD 1340
Zimbabwe, South Africa AD 1400
Copenhagen, Denmark AD 1410
Granada, Spain AD 1450
Tenochtitlan, Mexico AD 1480
Florence, Italy AD 1490
Vienna, Austria AD 1495
Cuzco, Peru AD 1500
Rome, Italy AD 1515
Istanbul, Turkey AD 1555
London, England AD 1600
Paris, France AD 1680

Readers interested in exploring any of these Golden Ages as an ancient traveler might view them, can turn to my WEB site at **www.GoldenGreat.com**. The site has a feedback page where you can make your opinions known, and choose your own favorite age.
Enjoy!

The Names

As the reader has noted, the names of the characters in *The Scribe's Family* change with each Golden Age, but in such a way as to presumably make recognition readily apparent. As much as possible, the names reflect the locale and era, with some compromise necessary to ensure recognition and ease of pronunciation.

Names of people and places are always a problem in historical novels for the simple reason that the citizens of the era referred to almost everything with different names than that of modern usage. The ancient Egyptians, for example, did not refer to their nation as Egypt. They called their land Kemet, which means "The Black" and refers to the unusually dark color of the fertile soil deposited along the Nile during annual floods, in stark comparison to the desert sand.

For the curious, here is a complete listing of names for all the major players in *The Scribe's Family*:

The Scribe
Abdullah, Abubakar, Abderus, Avraham, Abderus, Absyrtus, Avenelle, Aberto, Averill

Father
Rashad, Rashidi, Rasmus

Mother
Makarim, Mukarramma, Megara, Mahala, Malala, Malache

Eldest Brother
Kadar, Khaldun, Kadmus, kadar, Kasen, Kalman, Kajetan, Kendrik

Eldest Brother's Wife
Omorose, Omphale, Oma, Omphale, Ophelia, Olympia

Eldest Brother's Eldest Son
Butrus, Boreas, Burel, Bruno, Brock
Eldest Brother's Second Son
Benedetto, Bellerophon, Brigliadoro, Bertrando, Bentley
Eldest Brother's Eldest Daughter
Resanna, Resi Annys, Rosemarie, Rosalie
Middle Brother
Jamal, Jumoke, Jason, Jacob, Janus, Janus, Jasper, Joannes, Jasper
Middle Brother's Wife
Nefertiti, Nephele, Nedivah, Nebulia, Ninette, Natala, Nelwina
Middle Brother's Son
Seraphim, Sebastiano, Sebastianus, Sacripant, Sebastian
Middle Brother's Daughter
Zeta, Zezili, Yetta
Sister
Fadilah, Femi, Filia, Fadilah, Felita, Filicia, Filomena, Filberta
Sister's Husband
Chafulumisa, Charybdis, Chanoch, Charybdis, Chryses
Sister's Daughter
Isadore, Imogene, Iva, Isabella, Isabel
Wife
Sarah, Sharifa, Sirena, Shifra, Serina, Silana, Serena, Sherri
Eldest Daughter
Leila, Layla, Lelia, Laila, Lealia, Liliana, Louella
Eldest Daughter's Son
Alexandre, Alessandro, Alexander
Eldest Son
Lufti, Lateef, Lethe, Lufti, Lartius, Lothair, Luigi, Ludlow
Second Son
Hephaestus, Hezekiah, Hephaestus, Herminius, Hamilton, Heathcliff
Second Daughter
Helen, Helene, Heloise
Mistress
Germaine, Genevieve
Son by Mistress
Gelasius, Giuliano, Gelasius, Geoffrey, Gerlach
Student's Sister
Tanya, Tilly, Tullia, Twyla